Forever Mine

Theresa Hupp

Copyright

Dedication

This book is dedicated to my two children, who have added incredible richness to my life. I know they'll recognize my sternness in Cordelia, but I hope they recognize my love in her as well.

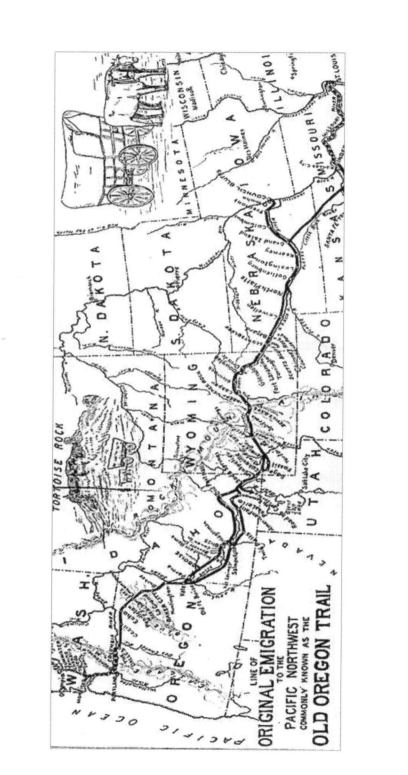

LINE OF
ORIGINAL EMIGRATION
TO THE
PACIFIC NORTHWEST
COMMONLY KNOWN AS THE
OLD OREGON TRAIL

Pershing and Abercrombie Family Members

The Pershings:

Franklin Pershing, wagon captain, Army sergeant from St. Charles, Missouri

Cordelia Pershing, his wife

Their family:

- Zeke, age 20
- Joel, age 17
- Esther, age 15
- Rachel, age 12
- Jonathan and David, twins, age 10
- Ruth, age 8
- Noah, age 4

The Abercrombies:

Samuel Abercrombie, farmer from Tennessee

Harriet Abercrombie, his wife

Their family:

- Douglass, age 31
  - Louisa, Douglass's wife
  - Annabelle and Rose, daughters of Douglass and Louisa
- Daniel, age 19

Chapter 1:   Independence

Thursday, 1 April 1847. Still seeking a few families for my wagon company. We should be ready soon. Franklin Pershing, Captain

"If Independence is this dirty, what'll the trail be like?" Fifteen-year-old Esther Pershing sighed as she scrubbed another garment in the washtub.

"Worse, I expect," her mother said. "But it ain't your place to question your father's choices. We're going to Oregon, and that's that."

Esther squeezed the suds out of Pa's shirt. Her family was camped in a muddy field outside the frontier town of Independence, all the way across Missouri from their farm near St. Charles. They no longer had an iron stove for heating water like they'd had in their cozy farmhouse kitchen, but Ma insisted on doing laundry even without the conveniences of home. "How can we get all the washing done with just two buckets to tote water and the pump so far away?" Esther asked.

"With a lot of hard work, girl. Like everything else in life." Cordelia Pershing hefted herself up from the tub, sighed, and wiped the back of her hand across her forehead.

"Where are Zeke and Joel when we need 'em?" Why did laundry have to be her chore, Esther thought, just because she was the oldest girl? Her older brothers never had to help, not beyond carrying some buckets and firewood.

"Your pa has Zeke and Joel with him, buying the last of the oxen. Find

7

the twins to help you carry the next buckets."

Esther took the two buckets and searched for her ten-year-old twin brothers. She found them playing marbles under a wagon. "Come on. Help me tote the water. Ma said."

Jonathan and David groaned, but followed their older sister.

Everything about this journey made Esther want to cry. They'd left St. Charles in late February, with as many of their belongings crammed into two wagons as would fit. Pa had it in his mind to lead a company of emigrants to Oregon, so he'd brought them all to Independence, a jumping off point for wagon trains. He'd been collecting emigrants to accompany him for the two weeks they'd been here, and now the wagon company was almost large enough to start out. Soon they'd be heading to Oregon, whether Esther liked it or not.

She'd been happy in St. Charles. The Army had stationed Pa at the arsenal in St. Louis for the last several years of his duty, and the family farm outside St. Charles was close enough for him to come home often.

Esther had been friendly with lots of girls in St. Charles. She'd known her best friend, Amy Boone, since they'd learned to read from the same primer almost ten years ago.

The night before the Pershing family left their home, Amy had brought Esther a lace handkerchief embroidered with an entwined A and E. "This is so you'll remember me," Amy said through her tears as she handed it to Esther. "My pa said to give you something small, so you could take it with you in your wagon."

"I'll treasure it always," Esther said, hugging her friend as she shed her own tears. "I couldn't forget you."

Amy and the other girls at school weren't the only folks Esther would miss. She'd had a secret beau, a boy who'd carried her schoolbooks and kissed her a few times behind the barn. Ma said she was too young for such goings-on, but some girls her age were talking about marriage. Esther wanted to find a handsome young man—if not the beau in St. Charles, who was no taller than she was, then someone else she could fancy even more. But what kind of man could she find in Oregon?

Now, as Esther let her brothers race ahead of her with the buckets, she imagined her ideal suitor. A tall figure strode across the path ahead of her. The man carried a bushel bag of corn on his shoulder as easily as she held the handkerchief from Amy. My, he was fine, she thought.

She turned her head to watch him as she walked. Tall, with light brown hair brushing his collar. But his face was hidden by a wide-brimmed hat—he might be ugly or old, no matter how broad his shoulders. She sighed, and hurried after the twins to the pump.

Once Esther and the twins left camp, Cordelia squatted on her haunches to rest. She tired so easily these days. It came with carrying a child. She should know—this was her eighth pregnancy. But she hadn't had this much discomfort with the earlier babes—not this soon, not even with the twins. And she still had four months to go.

She needed Esther's assistance. Franklin and the older boys had all they could do managing the wagons and oxen. Even in camp they spent their days buying provisions and caring for the animals. Cordelia had only Esther to help feed, clothe, and tend their large family. Rachel was some help, but the household chores fell mainly on Cordelia and Esther.

Why had Franklin decided to make this trek? And why now? It was just like a man to follow his notions, not considering what it meant to his family. She'd raised the young'uns mostly on her own while he served in the Army. Then he mustered out, and what did he decide to do? Because of his long expedition to Oregon Territory with Captain John Frémont, he uprooted the whole family and set out to farm in the Willamette Valley of Oregon.

Cordelia sighed. Where was that girl? How long did it take to bring two buckets of water? Esther knew how to work hard, but sometimes was as flighty as they came. Back home, the girl preferred spending time with friends rather than doing chores with her mother. Part of Cordelia wanted to let her oldest daughter be a child a while longer, but part of her knew Esther had to grow up soon. The girl needed to learn how to manage a home and children, so she'd be ready when she married.

Not like Cordelia, who hadn't known a thing before she and Franklin were married. She'd had to set up a house alone, while her husband traveled far from home with the Army. She wanted to prepare Esther for an easier life than she'd had. But how could life be easy in the West?

In the late afternoon, Franklin Pershing traipsed through the muddy field to his two covered wagons parked just outside Independence. Cordelia cooked over a campfire with Esther beside her. They'd been busy—laundry hung on ropes between the wagons. Some of the younger children knelt drawing in the dirt with sticks, and Zeke sat on a chair whittling with his penknife.

Franklin had a fine family, a wife and children he was proud of. Oregon would be a good place to build them a home. A home together, after all his years of wandering. He was ready to settle, but wanted more space around him than they'd had at the farm in St. Charles.

As he approached his wagons, Franklin wondered how Cordelia felt about the journey ahead. Zeke and Joel, their eldest children at twenty and seventeen, seemed glad for the opportunity, just as Franklin was. The younger children were cheerful enough, except for Esther, who was outspokenly against the trip. But Cordelia? She'd been tight-lipped since he'd announced they were leaving, which usually meant she was unhappy.

Too late to change his mind now. Not that he wanted to. He still wanted the freedom and space of the West.

"I signed on the last members of our company today," he told Cordelia when he reached their camp. "A young man and his bride. Married here in Independence just a few days ago, from the sound of it. But they'll be ready by mid-month. We'll head out then."

"That's fine, Franklin," his wife said.

"What else do we need afore we leave?" Zeke asked, looking up from his whittling.

"Check the oxen's and horses' hooves. And buy the last of our provisions." Franklin struck a match and lit his pipe. "Should be about it." He puffed to get the pipe going.

"Is there any money for cloth?" Esther asked. "I'd like a new dress."

"Ain't no point in new clothes on the trail," Franklin said, squinting at his daughter. She was a pretty lass, blond curls and blue eyes, but sometimes didn't show a lick of sense. Not like Zeke and Joel. Those boys could be counted on. "They'll just get dirty and ripped."

"But, Pa—"

"Your pa spoke, Esther," Cordelia said, more sharply than Franklin thought she needed to. The girl could be silly, but was still a good child.

"We can only take necessities, Esther," he said. "Nothing extra. We'll see what furbelows we can find for you in Oregon." He winked at her to soften his words.

"Go round up the boys—Joel has the twins off somewhere with him," Cordelia said to Esther. "Supper's ready." When Esther left the campsite, Cordelia turned to Franklin. "Don't you go easy on that girl. She's old enough to understand the value of a penny."

"Ain't a sin for her to like pretty things, Cordelia. She'll see plenty of work as we travel. Toil enough for everyone. She needs something to look forward to, and a new dress is a cheap enough dream for a girl to have."

Chapter 2: Final Preparations

Friday, 9 April 1847. Preparations almost complete. We leave next week. Franklin Pershing, Captain

The last days in camp dragged for Esther. Every blessed thing Ma told her to do kept her near the wagons. Dirty as it was, at least Independence offered shops for browsing. Their campsite offered only chores—cooking and scrubbing and watching the young'uns.

"We're leaving here with all our clothes clean," Ma said when Esther complained about doing laundry again. "Heaven only knows when we'll get another chance for washing."

"But, Ma, the boys will get their shirts and pants dirty the first day out. Ain't no way to keep 'em clean. And how many loaves of bread can we bake? They'll go stale afore we eat 'em all."

"You'll be plenty glad of baked bread first nights on the trail," Ma told her. "We'll be plumb tired, and you won't want to bake then. Not even biscuits." She stood up, a hand bracing her back, and looked around. "Where are the raisins?"

Esther's youngest brother Noah sat on a rock, one four-year-old fist full of the dried fruit, while his other hand put one raisin after another into his mouth.

"Boy," Ma said sternly, arms akimbo. "Those were for the bread. Did I say you could eat 'em?"

Tears welled in the child's eyes.

Esther hid a smile—it was hard to stay mad at Noah. Even as pesky as he could be, she wanted to hug him every time he cried. Eight-year-old Ruth annoyed Esther to no end with her whining, but Noah was still a cuddly baby. Someday she'd have a little one just like him, she hoped.

Ma sighed. "Well, Esther, I was planning to send you into town for any fresh fruit and vegetables you can find," she said. "You might as well go now and buy raisins, too. I'll put 'em in biscuits instead of the bread. Take Noah with you, get him out of my hair. And Rachel—she can help you carry the food back."

Esther took Noah's hand and called twelve-year-old Rachel out of the wagon, where she'd been patching together quilt squares. "Your quilt's coming along nicely, Rachel, but leave it for now. Ma says we're to go shopping in town."

Ma gave Esther two dollars, which she stuffed in her pocket. She and Rachel took Noah's hands between them for the walk along a muddy path from the campground into Independence. The roads in town were no better than the trail from camp. No cobblestones, just more mud. Esther wouldn't miss Independence, that's for sure.

When they got to the main street, the boardwalk was crowded with settlers passing through or preparing to leave for the West. They all bustled and jostled as if in a hurry to get somewhere.

"It'd be faster to walk in the road," Rachel said. "Fewer people."

Esther shook her head. "We'll stay on the boardwalk. I want to look in the store windows." She paused in front of one millinery store. "Look at that bonnet. Don't you wish you could have something so fetching?"

"It wouldn't keep much sun off," Rachel replied. "Brim's too narrow. Let's get our food bought. I want to get back to my sewing."

Esther moved on to the next storefront, where a bolt of blue calico sat in the window—bright blue with little yellow flowers. Oh, she wanted a dress out of a pretty pattern like that cloth. Ma only bought solid colors or dull plaids. Nothing cheerful or lovely. Sometimes Esther could find a little lace to sew around her collar, or a ribbon to hide the mark made when her skirt was lengthened, but otherwise all her clothes were drab. At least she was the eldest girl and didn't have to wear hand-me-downs, except for a blouse or two from Ma. Poor Rachel got most of her clothes from Esther.

As Esther stared in the window, she noticed a reflection behind her. A man in a wide-brimmed hat walked along the boardwalk, balancing a

13

saddle on one shoulder. He reminded her of the man who'd carried the bushel bag across her path in camp several days earlier. She turned.

It was him. And this time she could see his face. He wasn't just tall and broad-shouldered, he also had a pleasant appearance—big brown eyes beneath light brown hair that curled on his forehead. He was as handsome as his frame had promised when she first saw him. Esther cocked her head and gave him her best smile.

The young man smiled back and tipped his hat with his free hand. "Hello. Haven't I seen you in camp?"

Esther flashed her dimples. "I believe so. I'm Esther Pershing. My pa is Captain Franklin Pershing. He's leading a company to Oregon."

He nodded with a friendly grin. "Daniel Abercrombie—Samuel Abercrombie's son. Our wagons are in your father's company."

"We haven't met everyone yet. Pa said we'd get acquainted soon enough." Esther turned to introduce Rachel and Noah, but they'd walked on ahead. She said to Daniel, "What do you think of Independence?"

"Busy place. Bigger'n our home in Tennessee, that's for sure."

"We're from St. Charles, near St. Louis. Lots more folks in St. Louis than here. And Independence is dirtier than home, too."

"We'll probably see a lot more dirt afore we get to Oregon." Daniel set his saddle on the boardwalk, as if he planned to talk awhile.

"Is your family ready to leave?" Esther asked.

"I reckon so. I had my saddle restitched, and that's the last thing we needed in town."

"My ma sent me to buy vegetables." Esther saw Rachel waving at her from the grocer's farther down the street. "I'd best catch up with my little sister and brother."

"I'll be seeing you, Miss Esther." Daniel tipped his hat again, and leaned over to pick up his saddle.

After Esther and the other two left for town, Cordelia finished shaping the loaves and set the dough in the wagon to rise. Then she remembered she'd meant to tell Esther to buy more thread. Rachel had used up more white thread on her quilt than Cordelia had planned. They'd surely need to patch clothes along the way.

She sighed. There was no help for it—she'd have to walk to town herself. She started out after the children.

When Cordelia reached the main street, she spied Esther alone with a tall young man. Where were Rachel and Noah? There was a reason she hadn't sent Esther by herself—the girl would chat up any stranger, particularly a handsome young man.

This one looked familiar. He must be with one of the families in their wagon train. Cordelia had been so busy cooking and cleaning she hadn't met many of the wives in the company yet, let alone the menfolk. He reached down and picked up a saddle from the boardwalk beside him.

"Esther," she called.

Esther turned toward her, but not before Cordelia saw the girl give a dimpled smile to the young man.

Cordelia hurried to her daughter. "And who is this?" she asked.

The young man nodded and touched his hat. "Daniel Abercrombie, ma'am. Samuel Abercrombie's son. I seen you in camp with your husband, but Pa ain't introduced us yet."

"Nice to meet you, Mr. Abercrombie." Cordelia frowned at her daughter. "Where are Rachel and Noah? Haven't you been to the store yet?"

"Sorry, Ma. I got to looking in the windows. Ain't this calico pretty?" Esther pointed at a bolt of fancy flower-sprigged cloth in the store window.

"Your pa said you ain't getting any new dresses now," Cordelia said. "Let's get the shopping done." She nodded at Daniel Abercrombie. "We'll be seeing you. Now come along, Esther."

She scolded Esther as they walked to the grocer's. "Ain't I told you often enough not to talk to strange men?"

"Ma." Esther made the word three syllables. "He's with our company. We're going to be living with him for months to come."

"You will *not* be living with any young men. We'll come to know them, for sure, but that don't mean you let him be familiar with you."

Esther sighed as they entered the grocer's.

Rachel pulled Cordelia toward the display of produce. "Ain't much here, Ma. Just last year's apples. Too early for any new fruit, the man says. But I did find raisins."

Cordelia murmured to Esther, "Now why can't you be more like your sister? She found out what's what whilst you were flirting with young

Abercrombie."

"I would've got to the shopping, Ma. I was only being courteous to a man in Pa's company."

They bagged some apples and potatoes, and while she paid for the produce, Cordelia thought how difficult Esther was at fifteen.

Of course, at fifteen, she'd been the same—only had eyes for the boys. And look where it got her. Married at eighteen. Cordelia now recognized she hadn't been mature enough to wed, though she'd had the right number of birthdays. It took more than age for a girl to be ready to manage a home and children. Then she'd been alone throughout most of her marriage while Franklin went off with the Army. And carrying a child a good part of those years—every time Franklin came home he left another babe in her womb.

She wanted a better life for Esther. She wanted Esther to have a husband who stayed with her, who provided a stable home. And she wanted the girl to be ready for housework and child-rearing—as a mother, Cordelia was responsible for teaching the girl not to spend her time flirting and sighing after pretty goods in store windows.

Franklin Pershing made the rounds of the families in his company. He wondered how they would work together on the trail in the months ahead. Competent and congenial companions would make the journey pleasant. Men who argued and fought could cause injury and even death to other folks. Each man would have to pull his own weight and aid the others as well. There was only so much a captain could do.

He'd never commanded a company before. As sergeant in the Army, he'd had some accountability for men of lower rank, but the officers could overrule him, and sometimes did. On the expedition with Frémont, Franklin had led the cannon detail—moving the small artillery piece along the trail. He'd learned how to get men and animals to push and pull the piece through all types of terrain—rugged mountains and raging rivers— but that was a far cry from getting twenty-odd wagons and a hundred or more people to stay together for two thousand miles.

He reached Samuel Abercrombie's campsite. The large bearded man from Tennessee was an obstinate cuss, free with his opinion on everything. But he seemed knowledgeable about farming, and his wagons were as well-equipped as Franklin's. Plus, he had two strong sons who would be good laborers on the trail.

"You ready, Abercrombie?" Franklin asked, holding out his hand.

Abercrombie raised an eyebrow, but took the hand. "Was ready two weeks ago. Shoulda started out then."

"Others in the company weren't so prepared," Franklin said.

"Heard you got a doctor signed on," Abercrombie said, scratching his beard.

Franklin nodded. "Man named Abraham Tuller and his wife. And just signed up a young lawyer and his wife. McDougall, by name."

Abercrombie snorted. "Ain't no need for a lawyer. They just cause trouble."

"He knows about Frémont's maps. Seems eager to see the West."

Abercrombie spat a stream of tobacco on the ground. "And the others?"

"Farmers from all over. A Negro blacksmith—he's a carpenter and farrier also. Good man."

"Asking for trouble to bring them kind along."

"His skills'll be helpful. It's him and his wife and two little boys—a family man won't cause any ruckus." Franklin looked at Abercrombie's two wagons, both loaded to the top of the beds. "Your teams going to be able to pull that weight?" he asked.

"Bought the best damn oxen in town. Eight for each wagon."

"Should be enough," Franklin said. "But anything you can leave behind, you should sell now."

"Been through that already with the missus," Abercrombie said. "We're keeping what we got."

Franklin shrugged. "May have to dump it later."

"How you gonna divvy up the wagons?" Abercrombie asked. "I'll lead a platoon, but I don't want no Negroes in mine. No lawyers neither."

Franklin had considered assigning platoon sergeants before they left Independence, but at Abercrombie's remark, he changed his mind. Something in the blowhard's manner made him want to resist whatever the man said. He wasn't sure he wanted Abercrombie as a platoon leader. "We'll set out for a week or so, then I'll decide. See who knows what they're doing out on the trail."

Abercrombie sniffed, then spat again.

"But I'll keep your offer in mind, Abercrombie." And Franklin moved on to the next campsite.

Daniel Abercrombie reached his family's campsite after his trip to town. He dropped his saddle on the ground beside a wagon wheel. His father Samuel sat on a log nearby cleaning his rifle, and his mother stirred a pot over their campfire. "All stitched up," he told Pa, gesturing at the saddle. "Good as new."

"Shoulda done it yourself," his father said. "Saved the two bits."

Daniel shrugged. Sometimes it was easier to be quiet when Pa was cantankerous. Let him spout off. "I met Captain Pershing's wife and daughter today," he said. "Seem like a nice family."

"I ain't sure 'bout Pershing," Samuel said. "He ain't forming platoons yet. Says he'll set 'em up later."

Daniel didn't reply. He didn't know whether platoons were necessary at this point. His pa had been in the Tennessee militia back home and knew more than Daniel did. "Well," he said, grinning, "Pershing has a purty daughter. Esther."

"Wipe that smile off your face, boy," Samuel said. "Best stay away from the Pershings till we know what sort they be. And you don't need to be mooning over no girl, not till we're in Oregon and you got your land claim filed and crops in the ground."

"Now, Samuel," Ma said. She was really Daniel's stepmother, but his mother died when he was born, and Harriet Abercrombie was the only mother he'd ever known. "Let Daniel be. He'll need to make some young friends on this journey."

"He ain't got no call to be spooning till he's settled on his own farm," Samuel argued.

"What's for supper?" Daniel asked, if only to change the subject. As Ma replied, he smiled, thinking of Esther Pershing's pretty dimples. No doubt about it, she'd make the scenery along the trail more pleasant.

Chapter 3:   Setting Out

Tuesday, 13 April 1847. We leave tomorrow. Twenty wagons under my charge. F. Pershing, Captain

Franklin Pershing awoke before dawn on Wednesday—the day they were scheduled to leave Independence. The prior evening, he'd told each man in the company to have their families ready an hour after sunup. Now, by the light of a lantern, he roused his sons Zeke and Joel. "You boys get our two wagons ready. Hitch the teams. Have your ma and all the young'uns packed up as soon as breakfast is done. We need to set the example."

Then Franklin strode around the camp, checking to see which men were awake. Some had been drinking the night before and seemed the worse for it in the early morning damp. Franklin had joined them for a round at a tavern in Independence, but he'd left without doing himself any damage. He knew better. Getting drunk in town wasn't likely to cause harm. Getting drunk on the trail often led to slovenly rigs and bad decisions.

When he returned to his own campsite, Cordelia had eggs and steak ready to eat, along with biscuits. "Thank you, dear," he said, giving her a quick hug. She was a good wife, never complaining and doing her part to make his path smooth. As good as any Army cook or quartermaster.

"Esther," Cordelia said, "hurry up with your breakfast, then wash the dishes. Rachel, get Noah's and Ruthie's hands cleaned and hair combed. We want to head out of town looking fit." She turned toward the twins.

"Jonathan and David, you mind your manners and slick yourselves up."

"Our wagons will lead the company today," Franklin told his eldest son Zeke. At twenty, the boy was taller than Franklin, though not as broad in shoulders or girth. "You and Joel each ride your horse alongside a wagon. Your ma and the others will walk till they get tired. I expect Noah'll be riding afore midday."

Zeke nodded. Then he and Joel headed off to saddle their horses.

"Cordelia, you take care," Franklin said to his wife. "If you tire, climb in a wagon. No shame in it while you're carrying."

Cordelia turned away without comment. She did what he expected, but she didn't seem happy about it. Sometimes Franklin wondered what she really thought of him and of this journey.

"Need to make the rounds again," Franklin said. "When I get back, it'll be time to leave."

As he walked around the campground for the last time, he noted which men struggled to hitch their oxen or mules and which had their teams already in place. Some women had their cooking well in hand, but the smell of charred meat rose from other campfires. Samuel Abercrombie's oxen stood quietly in their yokes. And the Negro named Tanner—his mules looked ready to pull. A farmer named Purcell and a storekeeper named Bramwell were among those whose wagons already seemed disheveled and shabby.

Where was McDougall? Franklin wondered. He'd missed the young lawyer and his bride on the earlier walk-around. Then he remembered the couple had stayed at a boardinghouse in Independence. They were meeting the company at the outskirts of town. He had no idea whether they were among the capable travelers or the greenhorns. McDougall might have book smarts, but that didn't mean he had useful know-how for the trail.

When his pocket watch read 7:45 sharp, Franklin raised his hand and signaled his sons to head the wagons toward the trail. He rode his horse through the camp and pointed at each man in turn to lead his team into line. Some managed easily, and others had to yell at their teams or crack their whips near the animals' heads to get them to move.

Samuel Abercrombie smoothly maneuvered his wagons into place. The beefy Tennessean rode a large gelding beside his two wagons, with one son walking by the lead pair of each team. Was the older one Douglass and the younger Daniel, or the other way around? Franklin could barely remember all the men's names, let alone their family members. That would change in the days and weeks ahead.

McDougall waited at the crossroads from town. Franklin signaled to Zeke and Joel to lead the Pershing wagons ahead, then stopped the next wagon holding Doc Tuller and his wife. He motioned McDougall to cut in ahead of the Tullers. He wanted to keep an eye on the young attorney.

Within minutes after they left Independence, Samuel Abercrombie trotted up to Franklin. "What the hell you mean putting my wagons near the rear? I planned to set the pace."

"I got my boys leading today, Abercrombie," Franklin said. "I need to see who can manage their teams and who can't. Some got their loads so cattywampus, they'll have their wheels split or their wagons flipped at the first hill."

"That's why they belong in back with the cattle. Why'd you let folks with herds into this company anyway? They'll just slow us down."

"Tell you what, Abercrombie." Franklin had seen officers use this tactic in the Army and wondered if it would work for him. "You ride up and down the company, same as me, and let me know who you think's got problems. I'll set 'em straight."

"You shoulda organized the platoons in Independence. I'd have my men's rigs done right in no time." Abercrombie rode off after taking the last word. Franklin watched the curmudgeon inspect each wagon he passed, with an occasional shout to the driver.

Franklin rode over to his boys at the head of the line. "How are our oxen doing?" he asked.

"Fine," Joel said. "Leastways our second wagon's doing fine. Don't know about Zeke's." He grinned.

"Lead team's keeping a steady pace." Zeke took his hat off and wiped his forehead. "We put all our best oxen on it. Think tomorrow we'll mix 'em up, see which pairs like working together."

"Any problems with the wagons behind you?" Franklin directed this question to Joel.

Joel shook his head. "Couple behind us is doing fine. That man—what's his name? McDougall?—knows how to drive a team, though he started out

21

slow enough this morning. Got a fancy stallion he's riding alongside his wagon."

As the McDougalls passed him, Franklin tipped his hat to the young woman on the wagon bench. McDougall's black stallion pranced skittishly beside the wagon. He hoped the animal wouldn't cause a problem with the mares. Good thing it was the only stallion in the company.

Next came the old doctor and his wife driving behind the McDougalls. The couple both sat on the wagon bench, but their team seemed to pull the weight fine. Franklin hadn't wanted older folk in the company, but the chance to have a medical man along made him change his mind. Never could tell when a doctor might be needed.

When the wagons pulled out of the campground, Cordelia called her younger children to walk with her. She ticked off the names in her head as they came into view—Esther, Rachel, Jonathan, David, Ruth, and Noah— they were all there. Zeke and Joel rode with the wagons and their father. How would she keep track of all eight children along the trail? It had been hard enough on the farm.

Once they were beyond sight of town, Cordelia and her young'uns walked ahead of the wagons to avoid the mud and manure the teams churned up. Other women and children joined them.

One woman, Harriet Abercrombie, seemed pleasant enough, if quiet. Franklin had said the woman's husband Samuel was a blowhard, but his wife spoke agreeably to everyone. A younger woman walked with Harriet—Louisa Abercrombie, the wife of the older Abercrombie son. And Louisa's two daughters accompanied their mother.

Another woman, Amanda Purcell, was brassy, but able. She had three children in tow, including a little boy about Noah's age. Noah and the youngest Purcell lad raced back and forth amidst the women and older children. They'd be tuckered out long before the noon halt. And the doctor's wife, an older woman named Elizabeth Tuller, was just what one would expect of a doctor's wife—outspoken, but with well-founded opinions.

There'd be pleasant times with these women along, Cordelia thought. She wondered if any of them—well, not the doctor's wife, who was too old—were also with child, or if she was the only one who'd give birth on the trail. Then she saw a young woman, a Mrs. Dempsey, who was further along than she was. It was good to know she wasn't alone in her plight.

My, there were so many people. So many names to learn. Soon they'd know each other's stories. But for now, they spoke as strangers might, asking children's names and ages, speaking of homes they left behind.

Cordelia hadn't wanted to leave her farm near St. Charles. The land had been her father's wedding gift to her, and her brothers had farmed it for her along with their own land. Franklin, meanwhile, came and went as he pleased. He'd been raised on another farm nearby, but joined the Army at a young age. Home on leave one Christmas, he'd impressed seventeen-year-old Cordelia in his dashing uniform, and they'd been married in June 1826, when she turned eighteen. Then he left on a military campaign a few months later, with Zeke already swelling her belly. He'd still been gone when Zeke was born in April 1827.

Cordelia sighed. At least this time, Franklin would be with her when she gave birth. But she wouldn't be laboring in a soft bed at home. She'd be in a tent on the ground or in the wagon. She sighed again.

"Ma," Esther said, interrupting Cordelia's musings. "May Rachel and I walk back along the wagons a ways?"

"Why?"

"I want to see if there are any other girls our ages. I've met the Abercrombie girls, but they're too little. They're younger than Rachel."

"Who'll watch Noah?"

"Get the twins to keep him. He'll like that. Besides, he's about ready for a nap, I expect. Please, Ma?" Esther could whine as much as little Noah when she wanted something.

"All right, but not for long. Be back soon, or I'll send the twins after you."

Esther and Rachel headed back along the side of the road, lifting their skirts above the wet grass. "I was so bored, listening to Ma talk with the other married ladies," Esther said. "All about what they'd packed and what they left behind. They don't care 'bout the friends we left behind."

"We'll meet new friends in Oregon," Rachel said.

"I doubt I'll find anyone as nice as Amy. I ain't seen any girls my age—our ages—in our company. I should have told Pa to watch especially for families with girls. 'Twouldn't have hurt him a bit."

"Well, you like the young Abercrombie boy. The one you met in town."

"Daniel? He ain't a boy. He's a man. Looks old enough to file his own land claim in Oregon." Esther started dreaming about living in a cabin with a husband handsome as Daniel Abercrombie. Doing for herself in her own home. Managing her own affairs, not just helping Ma.

"Ma won't let you keep company with Daniel Abercrombie. Besides, his pa probably has chores for him to do." Rachel's words were practical, but Esther knew she could find a way to get to know Daniel. It was a long trip to Oregon, and she would need some fun as they traveled.

"I'm sure he's good with wagons and teams," Esther said. "But he's got both a brother and a father. Three men and two wagons—he'll have some spare time. I'll make sure he spends part of it with me." She tossed her curls over her shoulder.

"There's a young woman on the wagon over yonder," Rachel said, nodding her head. "She looks about your age."

"I think she's married." But Esther walked over to the woman Rachel indicated. "Hello," she said. "I'm Esther Pershing, Captain Pershing's daughter. This is my sister Rachel."

"Hello." The woman's timid smile made her look very young. "I'm Jenny. Jenny Calhoun. Or, Jenny Mc-McDougall now," she stammered.

"You're Mr. McDougall's wife, ain't you?" Esther asked. "Pa said he was a lawyer from Boston."

"Yes."

She seemed a shy thing, which made Esther feel older. "Would you like to walk with us, Mrs. McDougall?"

"Call me 'Jenny,'" the girl said. She wasn't more than a girl—she looked smaller than Esther, though it was hard to tell because she sat on the high wagon bench. Esther wondered how Jenny and the handsome young lawyer had met and married.

"Well, would you?" Esther asked.

Jenny looked around. "Mac isn't here. I'll stay with the wagon. Maybe after the noon meal."

Cordelia was exhausted by midday, when Franklin stopped the wagons at a large clearing near a trickle of a creek. She sighed and stretched her back, then called Esther to help prepare the noon meal. "We need to be quick about it," she told her daughter. "Pa wants us ready to leave again in an hour."

"May I invite the McDougalls to join us?" Esther asked, nodding at a young woman nearby. "She and her husband don't have no one else."

Cordelia glanced at the girl standing at the next wagon over, who was removing food from an oilskin bag. "Mrs. McDougall," she called. "Would you and your husband like to join us?"

The young woman nodded. "Just a minute, ma'am. I'll bring some biscuits and cheese."

When Mrs. McDougall walked over, Cordelia was struck by how young she was to be married. "How has your first morning gone?" she asked.

"My bones are rattling," the girl said with a timid smile. "Please call me 'Jenny.'"

"I'm Cordelia Pershing. Have you met my daughter Rachel?" Rachel nodded her head at Jenny.

"Yes, ma'am," Jenny said, smiling at Rachel. "Though I didn't catch her name."

Cordelia introduced Jonathan, David, Ruth, and Noah also. "I'm sure you won't remember us all. It'll take some time."

"Yes, ma'am. Would the children like some biscuits? They're buttermilk. Our landlady made them. But there's more than Mac and I can eat in several days. She gave me cheese as well."

The twins stared longingly at the biscuits, and Cordelia nodded toward them. "One apiece, boys," she said. "No more till your pa gets here and your elders get served their share."

Soon Franklin, Zeke, and Joel appeared, Mr. McDougall with them. After introductions, the men were ready to eat. Jenny's biscuits and cheese were consumed quickly, along with a cold stew Cordelia had saved from the night before.

"Would you care to walk with us?" Esther asked Jenny while the women washed dishes.

"Maybe tomorrow," Jenny said. "It's all so strange, and I'm tired. I think I'll sit in our wagon awhile."

Cordelia scrutinized Jenny more closely. The girl had the look of a woman with child. But Franklin had said the McDougalls were just married in Independence—was the girl a wanton? In any event, Jenny would bear watching, if Esther wanted her as a friend. Esther didn't need any more wayward ideas in her head than were already there.

Chapter 4:   First Night in Camp

Wednesday, 14 April 1847. Traveled to Cave Springs for our first night out. Only about eight miles. Most drivers can't yet manage their teams. F. Pershing, Captain

Samuel Abercrombie fumed the entire first day on the trail. He'd offered to set the pace for the wagons, but Pershing paid him no mind. As a result, the company only made eight miles all day, or so Pershing had said. Most of the men were greenhorns—some couldn't keep their oxen or mules in line, others had to stop to rebalance their wagon loads. They wouldn't make it to Oregon by winter at this rate. Samuel had never traveled west of Tennessee before, but he knew the importance of beating the mountain snows.

"It's only one day," Harriet said, when he complained to his family at supper.

His younger son Daniel sopped up gravy with a slice of bread. "Captain Pershing said most companies only make it here to Cave Springs from Independence the first day," he said before he took a bite.

"Some captain he is," Samuel said, tossing a scrap of beef toward his hound Bruiser. The dog grabbed the meat in midair.

"Well, Pa," older son Douglass said, "won't hurt to take it slow to start."

"Can't mollycoddle these folks. Or we might could run out of supplies in the mountains."

"You ain't never been to Oregon, Pa," Daniel said. "Captain Pershing has."

"Captain this, captain that." Samuel snorted, then frowned at the begging Bruiser. "Pershing ain't no captain. Hear tell he was just a sergeant in the Army. Yet he thinks he can lead a whole company to Oregon."

"Even so, he's the only one of us who's been there," Daniel said.

"No sass from you, boy. Pershing's only traveled under someone else's direction." Samuel took a swallow of ginger beer. The last bottle brought from Tennessee. "I want us safe to Oregon afore the snows hit. There's big mountains twixt here and there, and we need to get through afore the first frost. Ain't sure Pershing's got the mettle to lead."

"Give him a chance," Harriet urged. "He wants his family safe as much as you want yours. All those children of his, he won't see them hurt."

Samuel sniffed. "Just saying, I ain't sure he's the man what can do it. Takes a man with backbone to herd a bunch of farmers. They's stubborn cusses."

Douglass grinned. "Like you, Pa?"

"Like me. Don't you forget who's boss in this family." Samuel stood. "I'm turning in. Y'all should, too. Early start in the morning. Daniel, get your ma some water for the dishes."

Harriet followed him into the tent that held their blankets, along with Daniel's bedroll. Douglass and his wife and two daughters would sleep in another tent. "Samuel, go easy on the boys," she said. "They're working hard."

Samuel snorted as he shrugged out of his shirt. "We all got to work hard to make this trek. Douglass is too soft, and Daniel is too young to be much good. My job to toughen 'em up. Make 'em men."

Harriet smiled. "Douglass is thirty-one years old. He's man enough to father two children."

"Girls." Samuel sat on the ground and held out his feet.

Harriet bent and pulled off one boot, then the other. "They're lovely girls."

"And Daniel already has his eye on that young Pershing gal. All blond curls and dimples."

"Esther Pershing is very pretty. Her mother seems to be a good woman. I'm sure Esther is a fine girl."

28

"Don't want Daniel distracted along the trail." Samuel may not have been to Oregon, but he'd heard tales from fur trappers. It was no country for weaklings. Nor for boys in the throes of puppy love. "Keep him away from the Pershing lass." He wrapped his blanket around himself and turned toward the tent wall.

"I have to do the washing up," Harriet said and left the tent.

After she and Ma washed the supper dishes, Esther lugged the wooden bucket to dump outside the circle of wagons. She spied Daniel Abercrombie walking toward the creek carrying a pail. "Ma," she called, "do we need any more water for morning?"

"I suppose it couldn't hurt to fill the drinking pail," her mother said. "Is Zeke or Joel around?"

"I'll do it." Esther brought the wash bucket back into camp and leaned it against the wagon, then took the smaller water pail and hurried out toward where she'd seen Daniel.

"You come right back," Ma said. "It's dark now."

"Only folks around are in our company," Esther said. "They won't hurt me."

"We don't know that."

Esther shook her head. Ma was so wary about what she let her daughters do. What could happen in the hundred feet between the wagons and the creek? She reached the muddy ditch and called out to Daniel, "Could you give me a hand down the bank, please?"

He took her outstretched hand. First time they'd touched. His palm was calloused, but not as rough as Pa's. Even in the dim light of the new moon, she could see his smile.

"Ma thought we should have a full bucket for morning," she said, when she was standing right beside him. "So I come to get it."

"Let me, Miss Esther," he said, taking the bucket.

"Why, thank you. How very kind of you." She smiled as brightly as she could.

"I'll tote it up the bank for you." He strode up the side of the ditch in two steps, carrying both his bucket and hers, barely sloshing a drop. He put them both down, then reached a hand out to help her climb to level ground.

Esther took the hand he offered, again feeling his strength, and stumbled on her last step up the bank. "Oh!" she said, staggering against him. His chest was firmer than his hand. "I'm so clumsy."

"It's a steep bank. And muddy. You should get your brothers to haul your water."

She shook her head. "They're busy with the oxen. I don't mind. Ain't you helping with your teams?"

"Ma needed water, too. Pa had us tend the animals afore supper. He says we should care for them afore ourselves. Otherwise, we won't get to Oregon."

"Your pa seems like a strong man," Esther said. "And he has two fine sons as well."

"Thank you, Miss Esther."

"I'm the only full-grown girl in our family, so I do everything for Ma, though she treats me like a child often enough." Esther sighed.

"My pa still don't think I'm grown, it don't seem. But I'm old enough to file for land in Oregon."

"I'm fifteen," Esther said, smiling at Daniel. "Some of my friends back home were marrying. Did you leave a sweetheart at home?"

"No, Miss Esther." He cocked his head at her and raised an eyebrow. "I ain't been bit by that bug yet."

After Harriet left Samuel in their tent, she went to wash the supper dishes. Douglass's wife Louisa had started the chore, but hadn't done much yet. "Daniel just brought the water," Louisa said.

They washed and dried the dishes and pots, then Harriet returned to the tent where Samuel snored. She took off her dress and petticoats and found her nightgown. Glancing at Samuel, she wished she could sleep as easily as he did, but she worried about her family every night. Particularly since Samuel decided they should go to Oregon.

She hated it when he was hard on Douglass and Daniel. Samuel denied he was too harsh, or told her he needed to shape his sons into men. He'd always been strict, ever since the boys were children.

Harriet had still been a child herself when her older sister Abigail married Samuel. Douglass was born the next year, and Harriet served as his doting aunt from the day of his birth, even though she wasn't yet into her teens.

For years, Douglass was an only child. There'd been miscarriages, lost children for whom Abigail and Harriet had grieved together. Samuel became more and more gruff as time passed. Harriet didn't know whether grief or anger made him so difficult, and she didn't know whether his emotions were directed at Abigail or himself. She only knew the marriage grew less and less satisfactory to both Samuel and her sister.

Then, when Harriet was twenty, and Douglass eleven, Abigail became pregnant again. Abigail was ill through most of the pregnancy, and Harriet left their parents' home to help her sister, planning to stay only until the child came.

Baby Daniel was born healthy, but Abigail died within hours of his birth. After his wife's death, Samuel quit talking almost entirely and paid the new baby no mind. If not for Harriet, Daniel would have died, she was sure. She'd always felt Daniel was her child, more so than Samuel's. And Douglass was a dear boy also.

Six months after Abigail died, Samuel announced to her, "We should marry. The boys need a real mother."

She already was their mother, she thought. "And do you need a wife?" she asked.

"Someone needs to take care of us."

"I've been doing that, Samuel. Since afore Abigail died." Harriet didn't expect love from him, but she did expect some acknowledgment of her worth. "Why should we wed?"

"It ain't proper, you living here when we ain't. I have a care for your reputation." And that was as close to affection as she ever got from Samuel.

They'd muddled along now for nineteen years. No children of their own, though Samuel took frequent advantage of her presence in his bed. Her infertility was her cross to bear, along with Samuel's insensitivity. Still, she had Daniel and Douglass—they were her sons, as much as they had been Abigail's. And she had Douglass's wife and daughters. She had family enough, though she'd never given birth.

Harriet lay down on the blanket next to Samuel and nestled her back against his for warmth. She hadn't wanted to leave Tennessee—their farm life had suited her fine. But Samuel wanted more. More land. More wealth.

More power among men. He wasn't a bad man. He just wanted more—more than she could give him. She swallowed her tears, as she had done so often.

Chapter 5:   Split in the Trails

Thursday, 15 April 1847. Made 13 miles to Elm Grove on our second day. Hope to reach the Wakarusa River by tomorrow night. FP

On their third morning of travel, Esther walked along the trail ahead of the wagons with other women and children. Pa rode horseback farther ahead, until he came whooping and hollering back to the company. "Split in the trails," he bellowed. "South to Santa Fe. But we're all Oregon bound!"

Esther wanted to hide in the wet grasses she walked through. Or throw herself into one of the muddy creeks, except they weren't deep enough to drown her. She loved her pa mightily, but he embarrassed her with his enthusiastic shouting. She'd found nothing joyful to cheer about on this trek thus far. It was one long day of walking after another. Or jostling about in the wagon, which was worse.

"We're deep into Indian Territory now!" Pa yelled.

Indian Territory. Esther glanced around furtively, half expecting tribesmen to ride over the horizon and shoot an arrow into Pa. But the small rolling hills continued, nothing but blank sky above. Only an occasional tree broke the monotony.

The walkers reached the cause of Pa's excitement—a small wooden sign with two arrows, one pointing south to Santa Fe, the other north to Oregon. They passed the sign and continued to plod north until the noon halt.

When they were underway again, Ma walked beside Esther. "What do you know about young Mrs. McDougall?" Ma asked. "And put on your sunbonnet. Spring sun'll burn you afore you know it."

Esther pulled up the calico bonnet hanging down her back and tied the strings. Now she couldn't see anything except what was straight ahead of her. "Not much. She has a handsome husband, though he looks rather stern."

"Seems mighty young to be married."

"I think she's about my age. Shall I ask her?" Esther would rather walk with Jenny McDougall than Ma.

"Find out about her upbringing afore you get too friendly," Ma said. "Just because folks is in our company don't mean we need to be more'n courteous. We'll all need each other's help in the months ahead, so there ain't no call to snub anyone. But keep your distance till you know if she's suitable. Just like you would at home."

From the other side of Ma, Rachel asked. "Why wouldn't Mrs. McDougall be suitable?"

"Well, now, we don't know, do we?" Ma said. "That's my point."

Esther had had enough of Ma's caution. "I'm going to ask her to walk with me."

Esther marched ahead to where Jenny walked with Mrs. Tuller, the doctor's wife. She seemed like a gossipy woman, but Pa said having a doctor along was a good thing. "Morning," Esther said when she caught up with the two.

"Morning, Esther," Mrs. Tuller said, pausing a moment. "Why don't you two young girls walk on? I need to catch my breath. I'll wait for your mother and chat with her a spell."

Esther and Jenny strode on in silence. "That worked out well," Esther said when Mrs. Tuller was no longer in earshot. "I wanted to talk with you, not another old lady like Ma."

Jenny smiled.

"How old are you, anyway?" Esther asked, linking arms with Jenny. "My ma is awful curious, but she won't ask."

"Fourteen."

Esther stopped, pulling on Jenny's arm. "Fourteen? Why, I'm fifteen. You're younger'n me, and you're married?"

Jenny nodded.

"How ever did you get married so young? And to such a fine man as Mr. McDougall."

"It—it just happened." Jenny glanced around, appearing unwilling to say more.

The girl didn't seem to want to talk about her husband, and Esther wondered why. "Don't worry, I won't pry," Esther said. "I'm just surprised. I want to get married, but Ma says I'm too young yet. And here you are, wed at fourteen."

"Do you have a beau?" Jenny asked. "Someone you left back home?"

Esther shook her head. The boy she'd kissed behind the barn seemed so young, now that she'd met Daniel Abercrombie. And if Jenny could catch a man like Mr. McDougall, surely Esther could find a handsome fellow also. "No one who suited me. I want a good provider. Someone who can give me a nice home. Though only the Lord knows if there are men like that in Oregon." She saw Daniel Abercrombie on horseback off to the side. "Still, I wouldn't mind being courted a bit. Not if the man looked like that one." She nodded toward Daniel. "Or your husband."

"What do you know about Oregon?" Jenny asked, not even glancing at Daniel.

"Pa says the land is rich, good for farming. Though I can't say he knows a lot about farming. He was in the Army till a year ago. Ma kept our farm going, with her brothers' help. But Pa says he wants more space. More land." Esther sighed. "So the whole family had to leave St. Charles, sell most of our belongings, and cram the rest into our wagons." She was still mad at Pa for dragging them away from home and friends. He was the only one excited about the trek, except for maybe Zeke and Joel. "How 'bout you? Why are you going to Oregon?"

Jenny shrugged. "That's where Mac is headed."

"Ain't that the truth?" Esther said. "Women don't have any choice but to follow men. I'm following my father, and you're following your husband. Maybe marriage ain't any better'n being a schoolgirl." She tugged on Jenny's arm and said in a low voice. "Or is it?" Esther would dearly like to know more about being married.

Jenny blushed, but said nothing.

"I been kissed a couple times by a boy back home," Esther said, "but that's all." She sighed. "The kisses were nice enough, but I want a real man for a husband. Not a sweaty boy."

The girls walked along in silence. They came to a hill and started trudging up it.

Halfway to the top, Jenny stopped, gasping. "I need to rest a moment."

"You're as bad as Ma," Esther said. "She gets so tired walking. But she's expecting." Esther stopped and looked at Jenny. "Are you also?"

Jenny nodded, cheeks flaming again.

Esther stood by Jenny until Ma and Mrs. Tuller reached them. Mrs. Tuller, glad for a rest, stayed with Jenny, while Esther walked on with her mother again.

Franklin was elated to reach their first milestone—a sign indicating the split in the trails to Santa Fe and Oregon. Their first few days had been slow, but the small wooden marker showed they were leaving civilization and starting the trek across the prairie. Still, once they passed the fork in the dirt road, nothing in the terrain changed. Low hills and small creeks continued, one after the other.

He rotated riding alongside his family's two wagons with Zeke and Joel. The one not guiding a wagon rode ahead. There wasn't much need for a scout now, but in the weeks to come the route would become less defined. Then they would need men to reconnoiter, and Franklin intended to rely primarily on Zeke and Joel as his scouts. He wasn't sure yet which other men he could trust.

Samuel Abercrombie seemed to be angling for a leadership role, but Franklin didn't think the Tennessean was someone others would choose to follow. He'd already shown his cantankerous nature. Maybe one of the Abercrombie sons would prove to be capable, but Franklin doubted Samuel would allow his boys to outrank him.

McDougall? The lawyer had shown himself to be a quick learner.

Some of the farmers seemed like good men—Hewitt and Jackson—maybe they would step up as platoon leaders.

Time would tell.

Trotting ahead of the wagons, Franklin passed a group of women and children walking. His wife Cordelia and their daughters talked with young Jenny McDougall. He didn't see his ten-year-old twins, but they were probably skylarking somewhere. Those boys never walked when they could run.

By the end of the day, the caravan reached the Wakarusa River. It was too late to begin the crossing. Franklin waved his hat to signal the halt while he rode along the wagons. "We'll camp here for the night. Cross in the morning."

When the wagons had circled, he pulled the men together. "Pack everything up tight in the morning. Don't sit nothing water can damage on your wagon floors. Pile it carefully on boxes. This is our first test. Someone's bound to lose a barrel or something. Don't let it be you."

"I'll go first," Samuel Abercrombie said. "My oxen are strong. We won't have any trouble."

Franklin shrugged. "It ain't about how strong your teams are. It's how well your load is balanced. Current can catch a wagon and tip it, quicker'n the blink of an eye."

Abercrombie spat a stream of tobacco juice. "My load's fine."

Franklin swallowed his retort. The man would find out soon enough his overconfidence could lead to trouble. Franklin had learned that lesson in the Army—it was the easy tasks that often killed a man, not the heat of battle.

As Franklin sat smoking his pipe near the campfire after supper that evening, Cordelia lowered herself onto a crate beside him. She sighed.

"Tired?" he asked.

"Mmm. And worried. About Esther." Cordelia sighed again. "What kind of friends is she going to make in this wagon company?"

"Why is that a worry?"

Cordelia's voice was little more than a whisper. "This girl, Jenny McDougall. She's with child, Esther tells me. But you said she just married a couple of weeks ago."

"She wouldn't be the first young woman forced into marriage by a baby."

"But what kind of example is she for Esther? Our daughter's already silly enough about the boys she meets."

"Our Esther's a smart girl, Cordelia. Seems to me she wants the finer things in life. She won't settle for the first young man who smiles at her."

"You barely been around her growing up, Franklin. I'm with her every day." Now Cordelia's tone was louder and sharper. "Her head gets turned pretty easily. I seen her making eyes at the young Abercrombie boy."

"Daniel seems like a good lad. Not much more'n a boy. I doubt his parents want him marrying anyone soon."

"You know how young men are. They'll dally with a girl, whether they're looking to marry or not. Then both young folks find themselves forced into a marriage they don't want."

Franklin reached an arm around his wife. "'Tweren't like that with us."

She slapped him gently. "Not for your lack of trying. Be serious. I'm worried about Esther. Can you talk to her? She don't listen to me. She's at the stage when a daughter don't like her mother."

Franklin frowned. "How's a father supposed to talk to a girl about staying out of trouble?"

"Please, Franklin."

He took a long draw on his pipe, then blew out the smoke. Daughters were a lot harder to raise than sons. He just pointed Zeke and Joel at what needed doing, and somehow they figured it out. "I'll try."

"Take her to the river to get our water. Then you'll have a chance to talk with her. I sent her last night, and she came back escorted by young Abercrombie."

Franklin stood and tapped the tobacco from his pipe onto a stone by the fire. "Where is she now?"

"In the wagon, I think."

"Esther," he called. "Come help me fill the water buckets."

"Pa," she whined. "I was about to get ready for bed."

"We'll need water in the morning, and I'll be too busy then. Come now."

She climbed down the wagon wheel, presenting her backside to him. When had she grown so mature? She was taller than Cordelia, and rounded like a woman, though slimmer than her mother was. Esther looked just like the young Cordelia had, though that had been twenty years ago now. "Here's a pail," he said, handing it to his daughter. "I've got two more."

They walked to the banks of the Wakarusa. "Your ma says you were keeping company with Daniel Abercrombie last night."

"Pa—"

"I ain't going to tell you not to, girl. But watch your manners. We don't know the folks in this company well. And we're stuck with 'em for six months or more. It'll hurt me as captain if there's a falling out between any of the families, particularly if my own family is part of the spat."

"I ain't going to fall out with anyone."

"Just remember how you were raised, daughter. You be a credit to your ma and me, like you always been. If you do that, I ain't worried about you."

"Yes, Pa." He saw her smile in the dim light.

"Whether it's Jenny McDougall or Daniel Abercrombie, or anyone else you're talking to in the company, you just keep in mind you're a Pershing. You're the daughter of the wagon captain, and what you do reflects on me and your ma."

She didn't smile this time. "Yes, Pa." He guessed what he'd said had struck home.

Chapter 6:   Crossing the Wakarusa

*Friday, 16 April 1847. We cross the Wakarusa tomorrow.
Spring run-off is strong. FP, Cap^n*

A hard rain fell during the night. When Franklin Pershing checked the Wakarusa in the morning, the river had risen almost to the top of its banks. He stared into the swollen muddy current and considered the options for getting the wagons across. Their first big river crossing—he didn't want anyone drowned or maimed. Death and injury were possible even for experienced travelers, and most of his men and their teams were untested.

As captain, he had to minimize the chance of calamity. They could look for a shallower place to cross upstream or downstream, but the rains made finding a workable ford unlikely. They could wait until the river receded, but he'd have unhappy emigrants at the delay.

"We'll have to float the wagons," he finally announced.

"Most of 'em are too heavy," Samuel Abercrombie said. "They'll sink."

Franklin nodded. "Have to lighten 'em. Ferry about half the weight across each trip."

"It'll take twice as long," Abercrombie complained.

"Ain't no help for it," Franklin said. "Otherwise we wait for the water to go down."

"What about continuing on this side a ways longer till the water goes down?" Abercrombie asked.

Franklin shrugged. "We need to reach the Platte. It's north of here.

Sooner we get there, the easier we'll have it. So start unloading. We'll see how it goes. Might even need to float less than half a wagon-load at a time."

Many of the men grumbled, but they followed his direction. The adults and older children started unloading the wagons.

It took all day to remove half the goods from the wagons, haul one or two vehicles across at a time, unload the belongings ferried on the first trip, send the emptied wagons back for the remainder, then repeat the process with the other half of the goods. And then came the chore of repacking the wagons on the far side of the Wakarusa. Franklin kept the best drivers moving wagons and assigned other men, along with the women and children, to unpack and repack.

After shouting orders all day, he could barely speak by evening. But though the company was tired and filthy, no one had lost any provisions. He looked around the company, satisfied despite his fatigue.

"Good job, men," he croaked. "We'll stay here the night."

"Stay?" Abercrombie bellowed. "We ain't gone nowhere."

Franklin sighed. Would the man complain about every order all the way to Oregon? "We're too tuckered out to move now. We're wet and we need to dry our belongings."

"Got to move faster," Abercrombie said. "If we want to reach Oregon afore winter."

Franklin shook his head. "Some days we'll make good time, some days we won't."

"This ain't the way to travel. We need to push," Abercrombie grumbled.

"We'll move on tomorrow," Franklin said, "even though it's the Sabbath."

"We're traveling on the Lord's day?" said another man. "'Tain't proper."

Men started arguing both sides of the issue—whether to move on or keep the Sabbath. Finally, Franklin held up his hand for silence. "I'm captain. We'll stay here tonight. Set out in the morning after a short prayer." And he stalked off toward his wagon.

Fuming after his argument with Pershing, Samuel Abercrombie stalked into his campsite. "Damned captain can't lead worth piss," he told Harriet. "Mollycoddling the company. His wife is expecting—he most likely don't want her to work too hard."

"Samuel!" she said. "You have no call to talk about Mrs. Pershing that way."

"I ain't said nothing bad about her. Just her dad-blamed husband. He's a fool to hold us back during good spring weather. We oughta be well out on the prairie by now." Samuel feared getting stuck in the mountains with his family. Others in the company might not be able to travel so fast, but his family was well-provisioned and fit enough to travel at a fair pace. "You'll remember this come October when we're still on the trail. In the worst of it, most likely."

"Sit down and eat," Harriet said. "Louisa, call Douglass and your girls. And where's Daniel?"

Louisa left off stirring the beans over the fire and went to collect the rest of the family. After the younger woman was gone, Harriet turned to Samuel again. "You can complain to me all you want," she said. "But don't get our sons riled up against the captain. Don't let them get a reputation as troublemakers."

Samuel snorted. "I suppose it's all right with you if *I'm* a troublemaker. You're only worried about the boys."

"I've given up trying to reason with you," she said. "You never listen."

"Just keep me fed and my bed warm, and I'll be content." He grinned at her, not wanting to fight with his wife. She was a good sort.

Daniel Abercrombie ate his supper quickly. His father was in a foul mood, and Daniel didn't want to spend any more time in his presence than necessary. Pa had shouted at Daniel and Douglass all day while they unloaded and reloaded the wagons. Pa didn't trust either son to drive the wagons across the swollen river, so he did the driving himself. Daniel and Douglass hefted and hauled the family's boxes and barrels out of the wagons. Ma and Louisa helped some, but the two young men bore the brunt of the grueling day.

And Pa wanted to move on! He'd argued with Captain Pershing before supper. The women had already had campfires started and soup pots on, and Pa wanted to keep going.

There was no pleasing his father. Daniel had given up trying a long time ago. He just kept his head down when Pa got in a mood.

"Need any water, Ma?" he asked after supper. "I'll bring you some."

"Thank you, Daniel." She smiled and nodded toward the wagons. "Buckets are on their hooks waiting for you."

"Don't you go lollygagging with the Pershing girl." Pa spoke through his last mouthful of beans. "I'm of a mind we should have as little to do with the Pershings as possible. I ain't sure the man is fit to lead this company."

"Samuel—" Ma began.

"Don't 'Samuel' me, Harriet," Pa said. "Pershing needs to prove his mettle soon, or I'll find another company to take us to Oregon. We'll run into others along the way."

Daniel retrieved the buckets and headed toward the river. He looked, but Esther was not replenishing her family's water supply tonight. The current had receded some during the day, but the banks were a muddy mess from the wagons rolling back and forth and all the hooves and feet tramping the shore. He headed upstream to avoid the worst of it. He clung to branches as he slid down the slope, filled his buckets, then took them back to the campsite.

"Think I'll check on our oxen," he told his mother when he set the buckets beside her supper dishes. "Be back soon."

After he made sure the sixteen Abercrombie oxen were all grazing peacefully, he wandered around the campsite until he happened upon the Pershing wagons. He nodded at Mrs. Pershing, "Evening, ma'am. Your provisions come through the crossing all right? You need anything stashed away again?"

"Thank you, Daniel." She smiled at him. "We did fine, and everything's stowed where it should be."

Esther climbed out of one of her family's wagons. "Fancy a walk?" Daniel asked her.

She turned to Mrs. Pershing. "May I, Ma?"

"Take a couple of the young'uns with you," Mrs. Pershing said. "Noah and Ruthie might enjoy a look at the river."

"I saw some tadpoles when I was getting water for my ma," Daniel said. "The children might could catch a few, if they bring a bucket."

"Don't let 'em fall in. Nor get any muddier than they already are." Mrs. Pershing called her youngest children over. "You two stay near Esther, you hear?"

"Yes, Ma," Ruth said, but she and Noah scampered ahead toward the river, arguing over who would carry the pail.

Daniel offered his arm to Esther, and they followed the children. "Did the crossing tire you out, with all the loading and unloading?" he asked.

Esther smiled up at him, dimples on both cheeks. "No, of course not. Zeke and Joel did the driving and most of the heavy lifting, though I repacked our food to save Ma. She's having a bit of trouble moving around these days." Then Esther blushed and was silent.

Daniel knew Mrs. Pershing was expecting another child, but talk of it apparently embarrassed Esther. He changed the subject. "Mighty fine evening after the rain last night," he said.

"Very pleasant," she said.

They reached the river and Daniel clambered down the slippery bank to catch tadpoles. He held the bucket still under the surface, then scooped up the critters that darted inside. The children squealed and exclaimed as they watched tadpoles flit about in the dirty water. Ruth dared Noah to stick his hand in the pail. The boy did, and tossed a tadpole into Ruth's hair, causing her to shriek.

After a while, Daniel threw the tadpoles back in river and escorted the three Pershings back to their campsite. "Have a good night, Miss Esther," he said, tipping his hat, first at Mrs. Pershing, and then at Esther.

Esther lay awake long after she crawled into the tent with her parents and younger sisters. As the others slept, Pa and Ma both snoring, she relived every moment she'd spent with Daniel Abercrombie—from their first meeting in Independence to the last two evenings on the trail.

He surely was a fine specimen of a man, not like his brash and surly father. His brown hair curled over his collar, making her want to run her fingers through it. His smile came slow, but when he grinned his straight white teeth beamed against his tan face. She wondered if his beard was heavy enough for him to shave every day. She itched to feel his cheeks to see. But she'd never be so brazen as to touch his face. Not yet.

Finally, Esther slept. When she awoke, the camp was already stirring, and the morning light filtered through the open tent flap.

"Esther," Ma called. "Get dressed and come help me with breakfast. Pa wants to set out early."

After the Pershings ate a quick breakfast of bacon and cornbread, Pa led the company in a blessing for their journey, then they recited the Lord's Prayer. The first Sunday of their trek, but no Sabbath rest after all the toting and loading of the day before. Esther wondered if the whole trip would be so wearying. The short worship service ended with the song "Amazing Grace." Jenny McDougall's lovely soprano soared above the rest of the travelers' voices.

After the emigrants hitched their teams and got underway, Esther searched for Jenny. She wanted a confidante along the trail, someone to replace her friend Amy and the other girls she'd left behind in St. Charles. Jenny was the most likely young woman in the company, other than Esther's sister Rachel. "Will you walk with me this morning?" she asked, and Jenny agreed.

At Ma's urging, the two young women took some of the younger Pershings with them when they strode forward to walk ahead of the wagons. "I walked with Daniel Abercrombie last night," Esther whispered, taking Jenny's arm. "Ain't he handsome?" She hoped Jenny would talk to her about married life, about what it was like to be young and in love with a fine-looking husband. Esther had never seen Ma and Pa in love—Ma was worn out with babies before Esther could remember her any other way.

"He's the younger son of Samuel Abercrombie, isn't he?" Jenny wrinkled her nose as she mentioned the older Abercrombie. "His father is so loud."

"Yes, Mr. Abercrombie's been a thorn in Pa's side already," Esther said. "But Daniel is perfect." She sighed. "I am determined to have a romance on our journey. And Daniel's the only young man in our company I like."

"Be careful," Jenny said. "You don't know him yet. And if his papa causes problems for yours, there could be trouble. There'll be more young men in Oregon, won't there?"

"But I want a beau now," Esther said with a skip to emphasize the last word. "Otherwise, this trip will be such a trial. Walking out with Daniel will keep it interesting." Ma wouldn't let any romance get out of hand, and

Esther would have to spend time with women-folk also. Daniel would just be a pleasant diversion. As would Jenny, Esther decided, ignoring her mother's caution about the young woman. "And I hope you'll be my friend also, Jenny. Won't you?"

"I'm sure we'll have lots of time to get to know each other over the next six months." Jenny smiled. "Tell me about your friends back in Missouri."

Esther happily answered Jenny's questions all morning. Yes, Esther decided, spending time with Daniel and Jenny would make the long, tiresome journey much more pleasant.

Chapter 7:   The Kaw Ferry

Saturday, 17 April 1847. Crossed the Wakarusa without problem. Next we face the Kaw. FP, Cap^n

All day Sunday, the wagon company traveled across the prairie beyond the Wakarusa. The scenery continued unchanged Monday morning. Cordelia tried walking and she tried riding in the wagon, but she couldn't seem to catch her breath. She was six months along—this child wouldn't come until late July, she calculated—but she felt as awkward as she had when her other babes were just a month shy of birthing. Was it the journey or were her thirty-nine years making this pregnancy more difficult? She sighed. Only time would tell.

She wasn't the slim young girl she'd been when she caught Franklin's eye. Eight pregnancies did that to a woman. She'd kept the weight she gained while carrying Noah, and now she suffered for it.

Monday morning Cordelia started out sitting on one of the wagon benches. "Noah," she called to her youngest an hour into the day as he scurried past to catch up to the twins. "You climb up here with me." He'd turned four just before they left St. Charles, and he got cranky when he wore out.

"But, Ma," Noah complained, "I ain't tired. And the wagon squeals and bumps so much."

"You'll come see me when you get tired?"

"Yes, Ma." And the boy ran off.

Cordelia breathed in deeply. She might as well enjoy the quiet. Though Noah was right—the wheels squeaked as they turned, and the boards creaked with every stone the wagon encountered. She plumped up the pillow she sat on, but it made little improvement.

Worries about her children intruded into the peace of the moment as much as the wagon's noise. Zeke and Joel seemed to be handling the journey fine—they spent their days with Franklin and looked more and more like full-grown men every day. She wanted to cuddle them close, but knew they'd have none of her hugging. They barely allowed her to put a hand on their shoulders when she served them a dinner plate.

Her first two daughters—Esther and Rachel—were dreamers, though the girls dreamed of different things. At least Rachel was practical—she kept her head in books and sewing. But Esther's head was full of romance, wanting beaux and parties and fancy dresses. Just like Cordelia had in her younger years.

Esther caused Cordelia no end of consternation. Someday soon, her oldest daughter would want to settle down with a young man. Cordelia hoped the girl would cast off her frivolous notions before then, or she'd be in for a hard awakening. Cordelia could only teach her so much—the rest Esther would have to find out on her own. And, as Cordelia had discovered for herself after marriage, the finding out could be hard on a girl with a passionate heart.

Then there were the young'uns—Jonathan, David, Ruth, and little Noah. The twin boys were running wild on this journey. Just ten, and almost as tall as Cordelia already. No one paid them any mind, because Franklin had to manage the wagon company and Cordelia had all she could do to cook and clean for the family.

She would have to get Esther to help out more. The girl was capable, if flighty. And staying busy might keep Esther's mind off Daniel Abercrombie. Cordelia liked the young man well enough, though his father was a trial. But Esther had no call to get serious about any boy while they traveled to Oregon. Time enough for that once they were settled.

After the noon meal on Monday, Harriet Abercrombie sought out Cordelia Pershing. It wouldn't hurt to get to know the captain's wife better.

Samuel showed every sign of battling Captain Pershing along the trek—maybe Harriet could smooth the waters through Cordelia. It wouldn't be the first time she'd had to mollify recipients of Samuel's blustering.

"Morning, Mrs. Pershing," she called when she reached the Pershing wagons. "Would you like to walk a spell?"

"I'm plumb tuckered out today," Cordelia said. "But you're welcome to ride with me." She gestured at the bench beside her, then shouted to her son Joel to stop the wagon so Harriet could climb up.

"Thank you," Harriet said when she was seated, then nodded to Joel to move the oxen along. "My daughter-in-law Louisa ain't well today, and I was feeling sociable. Needed a woman to talk to."

Cordelia smiled. "Very kind of you to join me. I haven't been able to catch my breath all day. I fear how I'll manage in the mountains. And my children all want to walk, even the baby."

Harriet laughed. "I doubt your little boy would like you calling him a baby."

"True enough. Now he's four years old, he thinks he can keep up with the rest of 'em. But I predict he'll be ready for a rest soon."

"How many do you have? Eight?"

Cordelia nodded. "From Ezekiel down to little Noah. And a ninth babe on the way."

Harriet shook her head silently.

"And you?" Cordelia asked.

Harriet hated this part of getting to know someone, when she had to explain that the two boys—men now—weren't hers. "Just the two. Douglass and Daniel. My stepsons. I haven't been blessed with children of my own. Though I raised Daniel from birth, and Douglass was twelve when I married Samuel."

Cordelia was quiet for a moment, then asked, "And you have granddaughters?"

"Yes. Douglass and Louisa have two girls—Annabelle and Rose. Quite a change to have young ladies instead of the boys."

With a chuckle, Cordelia replied, "I don't know which are harder, sons or daughters. I never understood Zeke and Joel as boys. Loud and obstreperous, and now my twins—Jonathan and David—are as bad as the older ones were. Esther is like me as a girl, though Rachel is more settled. I know what Esther is thinking afore she says a word, and it's usually

49

something fanciful."

Harriet didn't know how to respond. Her stepsons had never been at all like her, but she'd loved them anyway. "We're off to a fine start to our journey, don't you think?"

"Tolerably well, I suppose. Though Franklin has had trouble getting the men to work together."

Cordelia didn't expand on her statement, but Harriet knew Samuel was one of those who argued with Captain Pershing. "I'm sure the men will sort themselves out," she said. "Meanwhile, we women have enough to do, keeping our families fed."

"Ain't that the truth. My Esther and your Daniel seem to have struck up a friendship already."

"Daniel's a fine boy." Harriet wondered how the Pershings felt about their daughter following Daniel like a puppy. It wasn't Daniel's doing—at least Harriet didn't think so.

"Esther's at the age when a young girl's head can be turned by any boy who smiles at her. We've raised her right, but she's a mite flighty at times."

Harriet's back stiffened. "Daniel's been raised right, too. I done the raising myself. He ain't likely to take advantage of a girl."

Cordelia turned to her with a small smile. "Well, then. We understand each other. Ain't no call for our young'uns to be courting while we trek to Oregon."

"No, there ain't." Harriet agreed with Cordelia about their children, but it hadn't been such a good idea to sit with her after all. The captain's wife could make a point as clearly as Samuel, and Harriet didn't like Cordelia's lectures any better than Samuel's.

By late Monday the emigrants reached the Kaw River crossing. It was the first time since Independence Esther had seen crowds of travelers not in their company. She tried to sneak peeks at what was going on near the riverbank while she and Ma prepared supper.

A French Canadian and some Indians operated a ferry across the Kaw. Pa and other men from their company had gone to talk with the ferry owner. Now Pa stalked back toward the wagons shaking his head.

"Dad-blamed fools in this company can't agree on a blessed thing!" Pa said fuming as he threw his hat on the ground and sat on a stool.

"Franklin, don't swear," Ma said.

"That ain't swearing. If you want to hear swearing—" Pa took up his pipe and puffed to light it.

"Franklin! That's enough." Ma stood up from the campfire, hands on her hips. "The children."

"What's the matter, Pa?" Esther asked.

"Ferry costs one dollar per wagon, and half the men don't want to pay. They'd rather risk their belongings crossing on their own."

"We did all right on the Wakarusa," Esther said.

"Kaw is twice as wide and twice as deep. Much harder to cross."

"What will we do?" Ma asked.

"We'll take the ferry." Pa seemed certain. "I ain't going to let Samuel Abercrombie run this company."

"Is he one of the men who don't want to pay?" Esther asked. It seemed Pa and Daniel's father were at odds every day over something.

"Yes." Pa blew out smoke from his pipe. "I can't convince the families with cattle to pay for their beasts. They're swimming the animals across. But the wagons will all take the ferry."

"It'll save unloading and reloading," Ma said, with a sigh. "The Wakarusa plumb wore me out."

After supper Esther and Rachel walked down to the shore. The current swirled in the deepening shadows of dusk, barely visible, but Esther could hear the water lapping against the bank.

"Are you scared?" Rachel asked.

"Why should I be?" Esther said. "Pa knows what he's doing."

Daniel Abercrombie approached the girls. "Howdy, Miss Esther, Miss Rachel." He tipped his hat, and Rachel giggled.

"What do you think about the ferry?" Esther asked him.

"Pa says it's expensive. And waiting our turn will be slower than crossing on our own." Then he shrugged. "But I don't mind letting the Indians do the work of hauling us to the other side. It was a hard, cold slog crossing the Wakarusa. I was soaked to my skin by the end of that day."

Esther imagined Daniel's shirt and pants plastered to his skin. She wished she'd seen him then. She'd seen Zeke and Joel in wet clothes after the wagon crossing on the Wakarusa, but looking at brothers wasn't the same thing.

Franklin stood outside the wagon circle, smoking his pipe and reflecting on the journey thus far. Most of the men were proving to be able companions. A few were lazy and others not as well equipped for the trail as they should be, but Samuel Abercrombie had the only truly obnoxious personality.

Zeke joined him, interrupting Franklin's reverie. "Ma says you should go after Esther and Rachel," his son said. "She says Daniel Abercrombie followed them."

"If Esther and Rachel are together, they'll be fine." Franklin puffed on his pipe. He wanted a whiskey to calm his mind, but he wouldn't drink on the trail without a good reason. The pipe would have to do.

"What's eating at you, Pa?"

"Abercrombie. The old cuss can't say a civil word to anyone."

"He argued against the ferry, didn't he?"

Franklin nodded. "It's safer, though it do cost money. Some men ain't got much cash. But Abercrombie ain't one of those. He just argues to be ornery."

"His sons don't seem so bad."

"Nor his wife, according to your ma." Franklin sighed and puffed again. "It's going to be a long trip to Oregon."

Zeke snickered.

"But I'm glad to have you by my side." Franklin clapped a hand on his oldest son's back. "You and Joel. You make your father proud."

Zeke smiled, his teeth flashing white in the dusk. "Thanks, Pa. I'll go see about Esther and Rachel. Round 'em up for Ma."

Samuel Abercrombie awoke before dawn the next morning. He prodded Harriet to have breakfast ready early. "I want to be near the front of the line for the ferry," he told her. "Not first, because I want to see how the damn thing works. I don't trust the Indians to get us across safely."

Then he shouted for Daniel and Douglass. "Where are those boys?" When they crawled out of their beds, he ordered them to get the wagons ready.

"Yes, Pa," Douglass said. "I'll tell Louisa."

Daniel sat and ate his breakfast.

As soon as Samuel ate, he left Douglass and Daniel to drive the wagons, then went to find Franklin Pershing. He refused to call the man "Captain" even in his thoughts. Pershing had let the men jaw on and on the prior afternoon, debating whether to take the ferry. Samuel wasn't in favor of the ferry—a dollar a wagon was a waste, as far as he was concerned—but the damn fool Pershing should have made the call, not let them all palaver. A misuse of time as well as money, and they had no time to spare on this journey.

"Are the wagons all ready, Pershing?" he asked when he saw the man at the riverbank. "Mine are."

"Thought you didn't like the idea of the ferry."

"I don't. But the call's been made. So let's have at it."

"You want to go first?"

Samuel shook his head. "Not till I see how the Indians manage."

"Then I'll take mine first. And McDougall seems willing. You be ready after McDougall?"

"All right." Samuel strode away to tell his boys where to line up.

When he returned to the bank of the Kaw, the Pershing wagons were across, and McDougall's wagon was being pulled onto the ferry. The craft was no more than two dugout canoes with logs nailed on top. It could hold only one wagon at a time, which the Indians hauled onto the ferry with ropes. With stout poles, the natives pulled the loaded ferry from shore to shore, following a thick rope strung across the river.

Samuel pointed at Daniel and told him to lead the oxen to the bank, then unyoke the team. His sons herded the family's oxen and horses across the river. Samuel, Harriet, Louisa, and the girls rode the ferry with the wagons. The first Abercrombie wagon crossed and the second followed, both without incident.

On the far bank, Samuel and his sons rehitched the oxen and pulled their wagons to a field beyond the ferry to wait for the rest of the company. Samuel went back to the shore to watch the river crossing.

Oxen, cattle, and mules milled about in the muddy water. Men on horseback herded the beasts across, as Douglass and Daniel had done. A calf and a mule didn't make it, pushed under the water by larger animals. A barrel or two rolled out of wagons when they tilted, and another family watched a huge horsehair chair float downstream until it became waterlogged and sank. Why in tarnation had anyone brought such a thing in the first place?

The chaos continued until late afternoon, when the last wagon in the Pershing company completed the crossing. "We ain't waiting here, are we?" Samuel asked Pershing.

Pershing shook his head. "Ferry owner wants to get another company across afore dark. Those wagons'll need this space. We're moving on."

"Thank heaven for small favors," Samuel muttered as he walked off.

"Abercrombie," Pershing called after him. "I met another wagon captain today. He and I agreed to reorganize our companies. We're going to divide the wagons by speed. That should make you happy."

Happy? Samuel wouldn't be happy until they were safe in Oregon.

Chapter 8:   Company Governance

Tuesday, 20 April 1847. Ferried across the Kaw. Met Captain Jim Dawson. Agreed to reorganize our companies before heading for the Platte. FP

On Wednesday the emigrants traveled along the north bank of the Kaw. Daniel rode his mare beside the oxen pulling the first Abercrombie wagon. Douglass managed the wagon behind him. A cold rain fell, and Daniel hunched under his oilskin coat and hat, trying to stay warm.

"You done good yesterday, son," his father said as he brought his gelding to walk by Daniel's mount. His father's words were approving, but the tone was grudging. Still, Pa didn't have to say anything, so Daniel relished the compliment. "'Twere a hard crossing, though I expect we'll see harder."

"Thank you, Pa."

"Pershing says we're divvying up our company with another. I aim to talk to him about how he's planning to do that. We need to be in the fastest group. I'll take us off on our own, if I must. Might talk to a few other men about going with us. You up for that?"

"Whatever you say, Pa." Daniel didn't want to anger his father, but it didn't sound like a good idea for a small group of families to head into the wilderness without a guide. "Who'll lead us if we leave Captain Pershing?"

"I can get us to Oregon, boy."

"Do you have a map?"

His father snorted. "Don't need no map. Hear tell you just follow the rivers. The Platte, the Sweetwater, then find the Snake to the Columbia. Leads straight there."

"Pa—"

"I'll stick with Pershing as long as he keeps moving. But if he cossets the slow folks, we'll go on ahead. Surely other men will want to move quickly as well."

"What's Douglass say?" Though he asked the question, Daniel had little hope his older brother could talk any sense into Pa. Maybe Ma could. Sometimes Pa heeded what she said.

"He'll do what I tell him."

Daniel sighed. "I'm sure we all will, Pa, but I hope we stick with Captain Pershing."

His father rode off, and Daniel assumed he was going to browbeat other men in the company into agreeing with him. From behind him under the wagon cover, his mother said, "I hope we stay with this company also. Daniel, you have to get your father to listen to you."

Daniel had forgotten she was riding in the wagon. He walked his horse closer and leaned toward her. "How, Ma? He don't listen to anyone. Except you."

His mother laughed harshly. "Me? I'm the last one he pays any attention to. You and Douglass are his sons. I'm just his wife."

"He don't think I'm grown enough. Nor Douglass, even though he's married and a father." Daniel sighed. Maybe he should have stayed behind in Tennessee. He would have had to work as a farmhand for someone else, although without his father around, he could have been his own man. But Pa wouldn't have stood for one of his sons abandoning him.

Once they were in Oregon, Daniel would file his own claim—he wanted to work his own land. Then he could marry and support a family. A vision of Esther Pershing flashed through his head. The thought of her dimples and curves made him warm, despite the cold and damp.

Franklin Pershing rode ahead of the wagons and the walkers. The route was an easy trail along the Kaw, and he didn't need to scout. But he needed some quiet thinking time, so he'd told his son Zeke to stay with the wagons and keep them in order.

At the Kaw crossing he'd met another company leader, a man named Jim Dawson. Dawson proposed reorganizing both groups based on speed of travel. "Half my folks want to travel hell-bent to Oregon, and the other half got herds they're trying to nurse along." Dawson gestured at the Pershing company's wagons and cattle stretched from bank to bank at the Kaw ferry. "Looks like you got the same. I can't keep everyone happy."

Franklin chuckled. "You hit the nail on the head. I got one family with older folk, and some with calving cows. And I got a man who thinks we should travel twelve hours every day, no rest even on the Sabbath."

"If folks agree to divvying up the wagons twixt the two of us, which group do you want?"

Franklin shrugged. "Don't matter much. I'd like to travel fast, if I can. But my wife might like a slower pace. You have a preference?"

"I've got a herd myself," Dawson said. "I'll take the slower group. Otherwise, I'd have to send my sons and our herd with you. I'd rather keep our family together."

Franklin nodded. "Fine by me. My Cordelia would raise a fit if I suggested splitting up our family. I won't put you in that position."

The two of them had agreed, and now Franklin had to decide how to raise the matter with his company. He'd mentioned it to a couple of men, including the lawyer McDougall, and they'd seemed amenable. If he could get the more reasonable men comfortable with the idea, maybe they'd help with the rest. He'd leave Samuel Abercrombie out of it.

The Army had been a hell of a lot easier—he'd just followed orders. He might be captain of this wagon company in name, but farmers were mule-headed cusses, used to doing as they pleased, and Abercrombie was the worst. Democracy wasn't an easy thing to manage.

In late morning Samuel Abercrombie cantered up beside Franklin. "Hear tell you want to split the company up," the man said without a "hello" or "howdy."

"I plan to ask the men what they want. What's your feeling on the notion?" Might as well sound the fellow out. Let him blow off steam.

"As long as there's a group that'll make good time, I'm for leaving the laggards behind."

"That's the plan." Franklin tilted his hat back so he could see Abercrombie's face. "You think there's enough men to make a faster

57

company?"

"Don't matter how many there is. I won't let my family be held back by a bunch of pregnant cows and ladies. Safer if we move ahead fast as we can. Provided we got enough men to fight any Indians we encounter."

"Most of the tribes are peaceable. Frémont's group didn't have any problem with 'em in forty-two." Franklin nodded. "But if you want to split the company for speed, you be sure to back the idea when we talk tonight."

"Ain't no need for talk. You're captain. You say what we're gonna do, tell us to pick one group or the other."

By the end of the day Thursday, Samuel had talked with over half the men in the company. Most agreed with the plan to combine their company with another and reorganize. He knew which men wanted speed as he did, and which had to nurse along their old folks and cattle.

He continued his parleys Friday morning. He found McDougall, riding his fancy black stallion ahead of the wagons. "What you gonna do when we split up?" he asked the young Bostonian.

"Wait and see how the groups divide, I suppose."

Just the kind of wishy-washy answer Samuel expected from a lawyer. "What you think of Pershing?"

"He knows the trail. That's my primary concern."

Samuel let fly a stream of tobacco juice off to the side away from McDougall. "Military man or not, I wonder if Pershing can fight the Indians. I been in the Tennessee militia. They're nasty savages."

McDougall shrugged. "I'm hoping we won't have any fighting."

There'd be fighting, Samuel was sure of it. He wondered if McDougall was as soft as Pershing.

At the noon halt, the Abercrombie and Pershing wagons happened to be parked side by side. Samuel sauntered over to Pershing and asked, "When do we meet this Dawson company?"

"Not sure," Pershing said. "We're halting tonight at the Potawatomie reservation. We'll wait for them there. They—"

"Wait!" Samuel bellowed. "I been telling you we need to move fast. Now you want another delay?"

Pershing's youngest child, standing behind his father, started to cry.

"Shhh," Mrs. Pershing said. "Can't you men take your arguments elsewhere? Noah's dead tired, and you got him scared now."

"God Almighty! He'll be worse'n scared if he gets his tail froze in the mountains," Samuel said.

"Mister Abercrombie." Mrs. Pershing enunciated each syllable of his name slowly. "I'll thank you to watch your language around my children."

Samuel knew he shouldn't cuss around the boy, though his sons had been raised tougher than Pershing's whelp. But he was livid at Pershing's deliberate pace. "Mistress Pershing," he replied, imitating her speech, "if your husband would lead this company the way he ought, I wouldn't have lost my temper. My apologies." He tipped his hat and walked off.

Back at the campfire where Harriet and Louisa cooked the noon meal, he threw his hat on the ground. "Damnation," he muttered.

Louisa looked up, her eyes wide. "Father Abercrombie—"

"Just let him be, Louisa," Harriet said.

"What is it, Pa?" Daniel asked.

They were all coming at him, wanting to talk. Samuel blew his top again. "We'll never get to Oregon at this rate. That damn—dad-blasted fool Pershing is gonna wait on the Dawson company tonight."

"Won't we go faster once we reorganize the companies?"

He didn't want Daniel to be so reasonable. "Well, it all depends on how long afore we get to that point, don't it?"

"Pa—"

"Don't argue with me, boy. All I want is to get our claims staked afore winter. Is that too much to ask?"

The Abercrombies ate the noon meal in silence. Harriet thought even her granddaughters were watching for another explosion from Samuel. She'd heard the exchange between Samuel and Cordelia Pershing at the Pershing campsite. He would alienate everyone before they reached the first mountain range. When the companies reorganized, she hoped Samuel would decide to join whichever group Captain Pershing was not leading.

The rest of their family departed the campfire as soon as they'd eaten, leaving Harriet alone with her husband. "Samuel," she began, not quite knowing what she would say.

"Don't you start in, too," he said. "I'm only doing what's best for us."

"I know you mean well."

"It's a long and dangerous journey, Harriet. If we don't stay strong—all of us—we'll never make it. Every day brings peril. River crossings worse'n what we seen so far. Mountains with snow on 'em even in summer. Deserts drier'n Egypt. I've heard men talk about this trail, even if I ain't seen it for myself."

She sighed. "Then why are we going?" Samuel had careened between jubilation and whip-cracking ever since he decided they would leave Tennessee.

"There's a chance for us to better ourselves in Oregon. For the boys to each get their own land. Six hundred and forty acres apiece. That's more'n we had in Tennessee for all of us. Good land. And all free. If we can just get ourselves there. Alive." She saw him swallow hard.

He'd always feared death. Ever since Abigail had passed. Even when a dog or horse fell ill on the farm, he went into a tizzy—first trying frantically to save the animal, then stalking off when it died as if to show he didn't care.

"You know we'll all do our best. Douglass and Daniel, Louisa, the girls—"

"It ain't us I'm worried about. We're strong. But we can't do it on our own. We need 'em all pulling their weight. And I don't trust 'em yet. Not Pershing, and not the rest of the lot."

Franklin mulled over his conversation with Abercrombie all afternoon. "You've got to do something about that man," Cordelia had said when Abercrombie left their camp after scaring Noah. "I won't tolerate rudeness to our children."

"I know, Cordelia. I'm hoping he'll join Dawson, but I doubt he will. Dawson's agreed to take the slower group, and Abercrombie'll never go along with that."

Franklin rode at the back of the company when they started up after the noon halt. He watched behind him, hoping to see Dawson's company to their rear. He didn't want to wait for the other group any more than Abercrombie did, but he'd made a commitment to Dawson.

He thought he saw dust behind them in the distance. With luck, the dust was from Dawson's wagons, and the other company would catch up.

The Pershing company arrived at the Potawatomie reservation in midafternoon, and Franklin called the halt. As he'd hoped, the Dawson group straggled in around sunset and set up camp nearby. The late-arriving wagons didn't look as fit as most of the ones in the Pershing company. It took them a good hour to sort themselves into a circle, corral their teams, and round up the hundred or so head of cattle trailing their wagons.

Franklin walked over to find Dawson, and the two captains arranged to meet with the men in both companies as soon as the Dawson party ate supper.

At the appointed time, Franklin took a bottle of whiskey from a stash he kept under a false bottom in one of his wagons, called his sons Zeke and Joel to accompany him, and strode to a hollow between the two emigrant camps.

When the men had all gathered, he passed his bottle around, and described his plan for travel. "I aim to run a family wagon train," he said. "I'll do what I can to keep the Sabbath, but I won't let that slow us down. We'll go at my pace and stop when I say." He glared at Abercrombie as he said, "Anyone can't follow orders shouldn't ride with me."

Then Dawson spoke. "My men are moving cattle. We're likely to travel slower. But we got months afore winter. Anyone wants to follow me, be glad to have you. By the same token, any in my company wants to go with Pershing, no hard feelings."

The men discussed setting watches and scouts, organizing platoons, and rotating wagons so no one had the worst of the dust in the rear every day.

"We want about twenty wagons in each company," Dawson said. "To defend ourselves in case of trouble."

"I'm taking the faster group," Franklin said. "Dawson'll take those with herds or who need to travel slower. The two of us are walking out toward the prairie. Line up behind the captain you choose. If the split ain't close to even, Dawson and me will sort it out." He turned on his heel and marched away.

For a moment he wondered if anyone would follow him. McDougall was the first man behind him, then Abercrombie, and the doctor as well. In the end, most of his original company remained with him. The two families with cattle herds and another family with elderly parents went with

Dawson, but five families from the Dawson company came after Franklin. He ended up with twenty-two wagons.

Franklin and Dawson assessed their new groups. "I don't see no need to swap anyone, do you?" Dawson said.

Franklin shook his head. "The numbers are close enough to even. Let's go name our platoons." Then he beckoned the men in his company to one side of the hollow, and Dawson and his men moved to the other side.

"Next step is deciding platoon sergeants," Franklin told his group. "I want five. Any volunteers?"

As Franklin expected, Abercrombie immediately stepped forward. "Me."

To Franklin's surprise, old Doc Tuller nominated McDougall. "McDougall's a lawyer. He can keep order."

"Who from the Dawson group?" Franklin asked. He wanted to play fair with the Dawson folks, but he didn't know any of them.

A mustached man waved his hand. "Josiah Baker. Been second to Dawson since we left Westport."

Franklin nodded. Now he had three sergeants. Abercrombie would be a thorn in his side, McDougall was young and untested, and Baker was unknown. He would name the other two—men he'd had his eye on. "How 'bout Mercer and Hewitt?" He pointed at the two farmers. "You five sergeants divvy up the remaining wagons. McDougall, put my family in your group." That way, Zeke and Joel could keep the lawyer in line if he did something foolish.

He instructed, "Sergeants, set some rules. McDougall, write 'em down. We'll go over 'em tomorrow." He sighed and walked back toward camp, glad to have the company reorganization behind him.

Chapter 9:   Walking and Talking

Friday, 23 April 1847. Twenty-two wagons in my company after splitting with Dawson. Good men with me, I hope. FP

On Saturday morning, the day after the companies reorganized, Esther walked ahead of the wagons through the high prairie grasses. Though still April, the sun beat down as warm as late spring. Birds perched on the highest stems and warbled—meadowlarks, she guessed. A soft breeze blew, just enough to brush her curls against her cheeks. She pushed her sunbonnet off her head.

Jenny McDougall joined her, and Esther grinned at her new friend and asked, "Ain't it a fine day?"

"It's a pleasure to be walking, so long as we stay out of the wagon dust," Jenny said, smiling. Jenny wore her bright blue sunbonnet firmly tied under her chin.

Esther spied Daniel Abercrombie striding ahead of them. She glanced around, but didn't see her mother. "Let's go talk to Daniel." She lifted her skirt and sprinted toward him as she spoke.

"Hello, Daniel," she said, catching his arm and tossing her hair out of her eyes. She waved back at Jenny. "Jenny and I thought we'd walk a spell with you."

A slow smile turned up the corners of his lips. "A pleasure to see you, Miss Esther." He nodded at Jenny when she reached them. "And you, Miz McDougall."

Esther almost groaned when she saw Ma approaching, and she quickly dropped Daniel's arm. Her three younger brothers fought and frolicked near Ma.

Daniel greeted her mother politely, then said, "I was about to ask Esther and Jenny to climb the hill over yonder." He gestured at a mound to the north.

"I need a word with Jenny," Ma said. Esther frowned, wondering what that was about. "But you can walk with Esther, if you take the young'uns."

"Ma—" Esther began. She'd rather have Jenny with her than her siblings, who would pepper Daniel with questions and shout so much she couldn't talk to him.

"Go on, now," Ma said. "The twins need to let off steam."

Esther sighed with an apologetic shrug toward Daniel. "Jonathan, David, which of you can get to the top of the hill fastest?" And the boys took off, with Noah trailing them.

Daniel chuckled. "You know how to manage 'em, don't you, Miss Esther?"

She glanced back over her shoulder. Her mother was in earnest conversation with Jenny. Esther took Daniel's arm again and leaned into him as she strode up the hill. "I've had lots of practice managing those boys," she said, smiling up at the handsome man beside her. "Younger brothers are a trial."

"Well, I'm one myself," Daniel said, covering her hand with his. "I'm glad we're going to continue in the same company."

"Me, too. I did fear your pa would decide to go with Captain Dawson."

"Your father and mine don't see eye to eye on a lot of things. But with Captain Pershing leading the faster group, that's all it took for Pa to decide to stay in this company."

"I won!" David shouted from ahead. His twin was on his heel.

"Good boy, Davey," Esther shouted back.

"How can you tell which of those boys is which?" Daniel asked.

"I been raising 'em for ten years. David is more athletic. Jonathan a little quieter. Though when the two of 'em are together—which is almost always—they egg each other on. They're both usually in trouble, and they bring Ruthie and Noah into it also."

By this time, Noah had reached his older brothers, and all three boys flopped on the ground at the top of the hill. Esther slowed her pace, and

Daniel matched his steps to hers.

"It's so empty," she said when they reached the boys. She turned to gaze over the vast prairie. The grass below her seemed to billow and churn as much as the clouds above. "But ain't it beautiful?"

"Not as beautiful as you, Miss Esther."

Esther felt a blush rising on her cheeks, and she didn't try to hide it. She nodded her thanks at the compliment, with a quick showing of her dimples. "Just call me 'Esther.' We'll know each other well by the time we get to Oregon."

"I hope so, Miss Est—" Daniel stopped and smiled down at her. "Esther."

Cordelia had been waiting for an opportunity to talk with Jenny McDougall about her marriage and pregnancy. She didn't relish the task, but it was part of being a mother. She had to protect her children—especially Esther, who was so impressionable.

As soon as her young sons had started up the hill with Esther and Daniel Abercrombie, she turned to Jenny and said, "Captain tells me you and Mr. McDougall were married in Independence."

The girl blushed and nodded.

"And I hear tell you're in the family way. Both the doctor's wife and Esther told me so."

Jenny nodded again.

"When you expecting?"

"September, ma'am."

It was true, then. The girl had been pregnant before her marriage. "Captain Pershing ain't aware of your condition, most likely. Or he might have had a thing or two to say to Mr. McDougall about you folks joining this company."

Jenny had the sense to remain silent, Cordelia was glad to see. "I'm worried about my children," she continued slowly. "I don't want 'em seeing or hearing anything indecent. You and Esther are friendly. She's silly enough already. You keep quiet on when you was married. I'll make sure Captain Pershing don't spread it about."

"Yes, ma'am."

Well, Cordelia thought, the girl seemed to understand. "Don't give me any cause to regret being charitable," she said. "I'm just protecting my family."

Jenny nodded, then asked Cordelia about her children. The difficult part of their conversation over, Cordelia was happy to oblige, and listed all her offspring and their ages from Zeke down to Noah.

When Jenny glanced at her stomach, Cordelia laughed. "Yes, girl, I've another babe coming in July." And though she probably shouldn't let on there was discontent between her and Franklin, Cordelia said, "The captain's only been home for one of my confinements. I told him last year he wasn't leaving me no more. So now we're all going to Oregon." She sighed. "Who knows what'll become of us?"

That afternoon black clouds writhed over the plains. Esther knew what thunderstorms in Missouri were like, and they could only be worse on the prairie—nothing to break the wind.

Pa called an early halt in a small valley. The men quickly circled the wagons and herded the horses inside just as it started to hail.

Ma shooed all the children under the wagon cover. Zeke and Joel went off with the men, but the rest of them clambered into one of the wagons and huddled together. Esther put an arm around Noah, who whimpered at the claps of thunder. Rachel did the same with Ruth. Though Jonathan and David tried to look unbothered, Esther saw them blinking wildly whenever lightning flashed.

It was a tight squeeze inside the wagon, and the air quickly grew hot and smelly with them all pressed close. Esther considered taking a couple of the young'uns to the other wagon, but large heavy hail hit the canvas above them. Plus, Ma was praying the Lord's Prayer over and over like she was scared, too, and Esther decided to stay put.

She tried to put the storm out of her mind and remember Daniel's smile when he said she was beautiful. Her own lips curved upward at the recollection.

"Esther's got a beau," Jonathan piped up. "He said she were purty."

"Jonathan!" she said. "You shouldn't listen to other people's conversations."

But it was too late. Ma scowled at her. "Esther, I told you to stay away from that young man."

"You let me walk to the top of the hill with him," Esther said. "I can't help what he said to me. He was perfectly nice."

"Oh, Daniel!" David pretended to swoon. "My, you're so strong, Daniel."

"I said nothing of the sort," Esther retorted.

"Children," Ma said. "Don't argue. I'll talk with you later, Esther."

Esther sighed. Rachel sent her a sympathetic glance. But even Rachel couldn't understand how she felt. No one could. Esther was sure she was falling in love with Daniel. That must be why she wanted to spend every minute with him, to touch his arm and hand when she was close. It must be why she thought about him every night until she fell asleep. She sighed again, dreading Ma's threatened conversation.

They stayed in the wagon until the hail quit. Rain continued, but Ma ordered everyone but Ruth and Noah out of the wagon. She sent Jonathan and David out to gather wood—"Dry as you can find it"—and told Esther and Rachel to start supper.

Ma arched her back and grimaced as if in pain when she stood on the soaked ground next to the wagon.

"You all right, Ma?" Esther asked.

"My bones are getting old, child. The wet don't help."

Esther swallowed. She needed to help her mother. That was her duty as the oldest daughter. But she wished she could go find Daniel.

After the thunderstorm, Samuel Abercrombie took his sons Douglass and Daniel out to check on the teams. "Our animals look fine," he said. "But some poor fool lost his horse. I seen a gray mare racing across the prairie during the storm."

"Should we help in the search, Pa?" Douglass asked.

Samuel spat and hitched up his suspenders. "Ain't our problem. Unless Pershing orders it, ain't no call to get wetter'n we are. Lost horse ain't even from our platoon." Samuel relished his role as sergeant, commanding his two wagons and those of three other families.

Pershing didn't ask for extra men for the search party, but he did order double guards. "Animals are restless," he told the sergeants. "I want four men riding circuit all night. Two-hour shifts. Set the schedule for your platoons."

Samuel grumbled, but recognized Pershing was right.

Then Pershing continued, "We're taking a day of rest tomorrow. It's the Sabbath, and we didn't stop last week."

"We halted early today, and you're planning to lay by tomorrow?" Samuel argued.

"The women want to dry out clothing and bedding. And the search party probably won't be back till late."

"You're planning our days around women now?" Samuel sneered. He never worried about Harriet or Louisa or the children. If they got tired or poorly, they could ride in the wagons. It'd be a bigger problem if an ox had a bad hoof—if the teams couldn't keep moving the whole family would perish.

But Samuel passed the word among his platoon, then went to his own campsite to eat. A cold supper.

"Ain't much wood, and none dry enough to burn," Harriet told him. "I sent Louisa and the girls out to look. All I can fix is biscuits and cold meat."

"Dad blame it," Samuel muttered. "I'm wet and hungry, and all we got is cold food?"

"If you can start a fire, Samuel, have at it," Harriet said. "And since we're staying here tomorrow, I'll cook all day."

"A man can't even find any comfort in camp after a long day," he grumbled as he went to help Douglass and Daniel put up the tents.

Chapter 10: A Day of Rest

Sunday, 25 April 1847. Hailed yesterday. Today we must chase a runaway mare while the company takes a Sabbath rest. FP

Sunday morning dawned bright, the prior day's storm long blown away. Cordelia pulled herself out of her blanket when the first rays of sun lightened the tent wall. Franklin was already gone.

"Time to get up, children," she said, kneeling to dress under the low-slung canvas.

Esther and Rachel stirred and sat, but Ruth and Noah grumbled and snuggled into their bedrolls.

"Right now." Her voice sounded sharper than she meant it to be.

"Ain't we laying by?" Esther asked.

"Yes, but we need to dry out our provisions and clothes," Cordelia said. "See what's spoiled. If any food is still damp, we'll have to cook it or throw it out." She was dressed now, except for her shoes. She picked them up from the corner near the opening, then stuck her feet outside the tent to don and lace her muddy boots.

As she moved to crawl out of the tent, a sharp pain lanced through her middle, taking her breath away. "Uh," she couldn't help groaning.

"Ma?" Esther said. "You all right?"

"Just a stomach cramp. I'm fine. You come along now." Cordelia breathed deeply. The pain didn't return, and she stood.

Franklin had kindled the fire and brewed coffee, leaving a half-full pot near the flames. No sign of any other cooking. Cordelia got out the skillet and started frying bacon. In a while, she would fry flapjacks in the bacon grease. "Esther," she called, "come mix up the flapjack batter." Her oldest daughter emerged from the tent, dressed but hair uncombed. "But make yourself decent first."

Esther disappeared behind the wagon for several minutes, then returned with a bright face and braided hair. "Where's the flour, Ma?"

"In the wagon where it always is. Hurry up—bacon's done."

By this time, the rest of the children were milling about, ready to eat. She sent the twins to fill up a water bucket, then plated the first of the flapjacks for Ruth and Noah. The children ate as quickly as she could cook. Just as the younger ones finished, Zeke and Joel appeared.

"Anything left, Ma?" Joel asked, hugging her.

"Pa's gone with some of the men to chase down that runaway mare," Zeke said. "He told us to see to any wagon repairs the company needs."

Cordelia fed her older sons, then set Esther and Rachel to doing dishes. "Quickly now," she said. "Doc Tuller said he'd lead a prayer service shortly."

When others gathered, the doctor managed a brief prayer, then the company sang a few hymns. Young Jenny McDougall had a lovely voice. The girl would be a fitting companion for Esther, if it weren't for the baby she'd started before she married the lawyer.

After the Sabbath service, Cordelia took her brood back to their campsite. The older girls and the twins took everything out of the wagons, while Ruth and Noah played underneath. They spread out wet clothes and blankets and towels.

"Only one bag of flour damaged," Esther said. "Everything in the barrels stayed dry."

"Thank heaven." Cordelia sighed. "We'll have to bake bread today— use it up. You start on the dough, Esther." Then she turned to Rachel. "You go see what provisions other folks need to cook. We'll plan a company meal for noon, and again for supper. Use up what'll go bad otherwise." As captain's wife, she felt a responsibility to keep the women organized.

"Yes, Ma," Rachel said, and headed off.

"Boys," Cordelia said to the twins. "Go find all the dry sticks you can."

Rachel reported other women were baking bread also, either wheat or corn, and one family had a bag of beans that had soaked through. "Bean soup and bread," Cordelia said. "That ain't bad. With a little salt pork, we'll eat fine."

Across the way, Jenny McDougall struggled to repair a rip in her wagon cover. Cordelia started to send Rachel over to help, but saw Elizabeth Tuller, the doctor's wife, was already assisting Jenny.

While the bread dough rose, Cordelia told Esther to wash her hands and invite over any women who needed to mend. Cordelia's sack of torn clothes was full already, just two weeks out from Independence.

Elizabeth Tuller and three other women soon joined Cordelia and Esther, all of them with bags of mending or quilting pieces. Amanda Purcell was a farmer's wife with three children. The heavily pregnant Marybelle Dempsey and Harriet Abercrombie were the other two who took part in the sewing bee.

"How near your time are you?" Cordelia asked Marybelle Dempsey.

"Baby could come any day, but probably another week or two." The young woman clicked her tongue. "I told my husband we should emigrate next year, but he insisted we go now. Said there'd likely be another child next year anyway."

"Well, he could be right," Cordelia said. "But it's hard on us womenfolk being with child and walking or riding all day."

"Not that we had it easy back home," Amanda Purcell said. "Cooking and cleaning and laundry. I was on my feet morning till night while I was carrying. I'm thankful I'm not with child on this journey, but I never have had it easy in life."

Cordelia kept her opinion to herself, but Mrs. Purcell seemed a bold sort. She'd bet the woman henpecked her poor husband daily voicing her complaints.

Because Franklin had been away so much, Cordelia had learned to manage without him. She'd spent most of her marriage alone with the children. She could handle whatever crises the young'uns had, but she'd never learned to argue with Franklin when he was home. If she'd argued this time, maybe she could have convinced him to wait a year, to wait until after this babe came.

"You have a fine family, Mrs. Abercrombie," Cordelia said. "Douglass and Daniel are strong young men, and Douglass's wife and children must be a comfort also."

Harriet nodded. "They are. The boys are my stepsons, but I consider them my own."

"Then you have no children yourself?" Mrs. Dempsey asked, holding her own belly as if to show it off.

"No." Harriet sighed, then turned to the doctor's wife. "And you, Mrs. Tuller, did you leave your children behind in the States?"

Mrs. Tuller pursed her lips as she shrugged. "In a manner of speaking. Doc and I had three boys. Two died of fever as children. Then our oldest was killed last year when a horse fell on him. Nothing left for us at home. Doc wanted to go where he could do folks some good, so we're headed to Oregon."

"I'm so sorry for your loss," Cordelia murmured. She realized how fortunate she was. Eight healthy children, not a one lost to illness or injury. They made her frantic with worry at times, but she had nothing to grieve.

Esther worked on her embroidery—for her trousseau, Ma said. Ma had insisted she bring a set of pillowcases to make on the journey. "No telling when you'll find good linen in Oregon," Ma told her when they'd packed up back in St. Charles. But Esther hated embroidery, and she grew bored listening to the old women talk. All about sick children and laundry.

She sighed. "Ma," she interjected when Mrs. Purcell paused in describing the layout of her farm back in the States. Esther didn't care how far the woman's chicken coop was from the barn. "May I go see if Jenny McDougall wants to walk on the prairie? We could look for birds' nests." That seemed like a good enough reason to escape the camp.

Ma nodded. "See if Rachel or Ruthie want to go also."

Esther crammed the pillowcases in her sewing bag and stood before Ma could change her mind. Rachel and Ruth were in the wagon, and Ruth was asleep, so Rachel said she'd stay with their younger sister.

Esther found Jenny in her wagon pulling on the cover. "Don't you have that mended yet?" Esther asked.

"Just about," Jenny said. "I don't know how well it'll hold in the next storm."

"Would you like to walk a while?"

"You were sewing with your mama?" Jenny asked. "Are they still mending?"

"Yes, but I can't stand their prattle."

With a wry look, Jenny said, "Prattling with married womenfolk is what's ahead for us, isn't it? I need to start making clothes for my baby."

Was Jenny right? Esther wondered. Her new friend had only been married a short time. Surely romance didn't turn to drudgery and boredom so quickly. "You have months yet. Come with me now."

Jenny smiled. "All right. Just for a bit."

"I told Ma I'd look for birds' nests. Maybe find some eggs. But mostly I just want out of camp."

As they walked, Daniel Abercrombie strode away from his family's campsite and joined them. "Afternoon, ladies," he said touching his hat brim.

Esther took his arm and leaned against him. This was even better than she expected. They walked and talked, Esther asking Daniel all about his life in Tennessee.

After a while, Jenny said she was tired. "I think I'll go back and start supper."

"We're eating together," Esther said. "Ma said so."

"I still need to fix something to share," Jenny said.

"Ma wouldn't like me staying out with Daniel," Esther said. "We'll all have to go back."

"I'll sit with you near your wagon, Esther," Daniel said. "In sight of your ma and mine. I'm enjoying our talk too much to let it end now."

Yes, indeed, the afternoon had turned out better than Esther had expected.

"Another day wasted," Harriet Abercrombie heard her husband say.

She sighed. Samuel had grumbled all day, though he'd found plenty to do—wrapping a splintered oxen yoke, mending and resealing a wagon cover where hail had torn a gash, and even playing cat's cradle with his granddaughters. He was more likely to coddle his beasts than his family, so she liked seeing him talk to the girls. "It's important to remember the Sabbath," she said. "And even the oxen deserve a day of rest."

"Maybe so. But we can't take too many such days."

"Help me put this barrel back in the wagon," she said. "The cornmeal in it is dry. I scooped out the damp this morning and made cornbread."

He lifted the barrel effortlessly. The man was strong in body, no matter how petulant his spirit. He might be over fifty now, but he was more muscled than either of his sons.

"Cordelia Pershing has organized a potluck supper," Harriet said. "Would you find the honey in the wagon, please?"

"Why would I know where the honey is?" Samuel said with a snort. "Have one of the girls look. Where's Daniel?"

"He was near the Pershing wagons a few minutes ago," Harriet said. "Talking to young Esther."

"Thought I told you to keep him away from her."

"How am I supposed to do that? He's a full-grown man now. Can't he choose his own companions?"

"It ain't the lass I disapprove of, it's her father. Pershing ain't the captain we need."

Samuel said the same thing every day. It was wearisome. "Give the man some respect, Samuel," Harriet said. "No matter what you think in private. Or he'll never get the respect of other men, the ones who look up to you."

Samuel spat a stream of tobacco juice into the campfire. "I'm gonna find Daniel."

Poor Daniel, Harriet thought. She hoped he would stand up to his father. If not over Esther, then over something. Samuel needed to learn to let the boy go his own way, and he wouldn't unless Daniel demanded it.

After their combined supper, the travelers relaxed with music. Daniel sat by the large fire in the middle of camp listening to fiddles and singers. He wished there'd been dancing. Someone suggested it, but another woman said, "Not on the Sabbath!" It wasn't his place to argue with his elders, and none of the older folk seemed inclined to dispute her pronouncement either.

He watched Esther Pershing sway in time to the music. He'd like the opportunity to hold her in his arms, and dancing was the only good excuse to do so. Other than helping her up and down riverbanks. She was a comely girl, and nicer than anyone he'd known in Tennessee.

Before supper Pa had found him talking with Esther and called him away curtly. "Come, boy. I need your help."

He'd tipped his hat to Esther and followed his father back to their wagons.

"Thought I told you to keep away from her," Pa said, taking out his tobacco pouch.

"She and Miz McDougall came to talk with me. I enjoy their company."

"Miz McDougall is married. Best stay clear of her, too. You ain't got no need to be stepping out with any female while we're traveling. We gotta mind the road ahead of us. This is a dangerous trek we're on."

"Yes, Pa. You've told us that often enough. But I don't see the harm in spending time with Esther on our rest day."

"There'll come a day, boy, when I'll have to raise more hell with her pa than I have thus far." Samuel bit off a plug of tobacco. "I ain't satisfied with how he's leading this company. And I won't let his weakness kill me and mine."

"Esther don't have anything to do with her pa—"

"What choice will she have, if he and I split? And what choice will you have? You'll be with me."

"Pa, there ain't nothing serious between Esther'n me." Daniel liked the lass, maybe more than any other girl he'd met, but he'd only known her a few weeks. "I want to listen to the fiddling."

But watching Esther from across the campfire, he realized he'd like to become better acquainted with her. No matter what Pa said, Daniel would find more opportunities to spend time with Esther. He went to sit beside her as the fiddles started playing "Old Dan Tucker," and they clapped together in time with the music.

Chapter 11:   More Prairie and Rivers

Sunday, 25 April 1847. Found the mare. Now headed for the rivers in Indian Territory. FP

Esther tramped across the prairie with other women and children after they broke camp Monday morning. At least the weather remained dry. She'd seen Daniel Abercrombie staring at her across the campfire the evening before, and she'd wished he would come talk to her. Then he had, causing Esther to worry her mother would have a fit of hysterics over them sitting together. Now she looked for Daniel, hoping she could walk with him—or even better, that he would take her riding behind him on his mare. But he was nowhere in sight.

"Esther." Ma interrupted her reverie. "Walk with the twins off a ways and work with 'em on their multiplication tables. The boys are deliberately giving the wrong answers and confusing poor Ruthie something terrible."

"Ma," Esther whined, and the twins whined with her.

"Jonathan, you said six times seven was fifty-four. That ain't right, and you know it."

"'Twere just a mistake, Ma," the boy said. "You surprised me by asking."

"Well, you need to know them figures well enough a surprise don't matter." Ma shook a finger at her sons. "Now go on with Esther."

Esther spent the morning listening to the twins recite the times tables, while Rachel walked with Ruth and worked on sums. Only Noah got to roam freely, and he and another little boy, Henry Purcell, threw clumps of grass at each other.

"Five times six is thirty," David called.

"Six times six is thirty-six," Jonathan said next.

Then from David, "Seven times six is forty-two. See, Esther, we know it."

And on and on they plodded, the boys' recitations keeping time with their steps.

Esther didn't see Daniel all morning, though she craned her neck searching for him. She would have dropped her sunbonnet for a better look, but the twins would surely tell Ma.

Cordelia fretted about her children more and more each day they traveled. They were turning into rapscallions, especially the twins. Even Esther and Rachel had lost some of the sense of propriety Cordelia had drilled into them since they were toddlers. Only Zeke and Joel were maturing properly on this journey. But then, she saw so little of her two young men—her eldest boys spent their days with Franklin.

Cordelia couldn't bear any more nonsense from her offspring after the twins started teasing Ruth about her sums. Cordelia's feet were so sore she could hardly concentrate on correcting and comforting Ruth, let alone chastising the boys. After she put Esther in charge of the twins and ordered Rachel to mind Ruth, she only had to keep an eye on Noah, who raced about the prairie with his new friend.

Harriet Abercrombie and Elizabeth Tuller joined her midmorning. They were both pleasant women, and Cordelia let them do most of the talking. She needed to save her strength to cope with her aches and pains.

The doctor's wife asked her, "Are you feeling all right, Mrs. Pershing? You're wheezing today."

"This babe plumb tuckers me out," Cordelia admitted. "Must be my age. Having a child at thirty-nine is a lot harder than when I was younger."

"You should rest a spell," Harriet Abercrombie said. "We have months ahead of us. You want to be healthy when your time comes."

Cordelia gave a genteel snort. "Rest. How's a woman supposed to let up when cooking is twice as hard on a campfire as at home, and cleaning is nigh impossible?"

"Ain't that the truth," Elizabeth said.

"And with Franklin being captain, I feel our family needs to set an example. But I just don't feel up to it sometimes."

"Don't do more'n your health can bear," the doctor's wife said.

Maybe she shouldn't have mentioned being an example for the company, Cordelia worried. Harriet Abercrombie had simply pursed her lips when Cordelia spoke. There was already animosity between their husbands. Would Harriet pass her comment along to Mr. Abercrombie? After the scene Mr. Abercrombie had caused with Noah, Cordelia didn't trust any of that family, no matter how amiable Harriet and Daniel seemed.

The wagons reached the Red Vermillion River late on Monday. Franklin Pershing gathered the platoon sergeants, and they went to find Louis Vieux, an old French trapper who now ran a ford across the stream. The Frenchman explained how they would brake the wagons with ropes to get them down the steep banks of the river.

The next morning Franklin ordered the company's wagons lined up. Samuel Abercrombie, of course, wasn't happy with the arrangement. This time he demanded his platoon be first in line.

"Can't have my wagons wallowing in the muck behind others," the man bellowed at Franklin and Vieux and anyone else who would listen. "I don't want my oxen drinking others' filth."

"We'll all take our turns at being first and being last," Franklin said.

Vieux stood there, hands on hips, watching the argument with a bemused grin. "*Moi*, I do as you say," he said. "But a delay will cost you more money. I pay my Indian workers by the hour."

That shut Abercrombie up. Franklin would have to remember the man was as parsimonious as he was belligerent. Franklin shouted at Hewitt's platoon to start across.

He put Abercrombie's group in the middle, deciding not to push the matter by saving the Tennessean's platoon for last. That honor Franklin gave to McDougall—the lawyer didn't seem to object. McDougall simply turned his wagon over to the Indians and pulled his wife up behind him on his horse to ride across the stream.

Daniel sat on his mare in silence watching the argument between his father and Captain Pershing on the bank of the Red Vermillion. He wondered what made Pa so cantankerous. Only rarely would Pa let a matter rest without a fight. When he wanted to avoid conflict, Daniel often considered how his father would handle a situation, then did the opposite.

Pa said this journey was dangerous—the weather and land were a match for any man. Why, then, didn't Pa save his strength for the battles ahead, instead of feuding with his fellow men? And especially the captain. Captain Pershing seemed to be doing the best he could, and he was Esther's father.

"Ho!" the owner of the ford shouted. "Get them wagons into place." He pointed at the Abercrombie wagons, and Daniel moved away.

The Indian laborers forded his family's wagons, hauling on ropes to brake them as they rolled down the near bank, then pulling on the same ropes to drag them up the far side. Daniel rode behind the second wagon, watching to be sure nothing was lost. When the wagons were out of the way, he kneed his horse to heave up the bank. The mare staggered at the top and blew out a noisy objection to the climb.

"Make sure everything's dry, son," Samuel called, and Daniel waved in response.

He rode over to the wagons and found Ma and Louisa already checking their provisions. "Looks like it's all fine," his mother said.

"I'll go see how the rest of our platoon is faring." Daniel tied his horse to the wagon, and tramped off to talk to other families. He wondered if the Pershings had crossed yet, then saw Mrs. Pershing standing with hands on hips beside a wagon. Esther crouched inside the wagon, peering out.

"A blanket got wet," Esther said. "But that's it."

"Hand it to me," Daniel said, stretching his hand toward her. "I'll help you spread it over the wagon cover to dry."

Esther smiled and passed him the blanket. "Throw it over the top, and I'll catch it."

When they had finished, Daniel asked, "Anything else I can do?"

"No, thank you, Daniel," Mrs. Pershing said. "We're much obliged."

"Would you like to watch the rest of the wagons, Esther? The last few are still crossing."

She climbed out of the wagon and took his hand.

Franklin Pershing felt proud of the way the crossing of the Red Vermillion had gone. The company had now crossed three large rivers. They'd handled the Wakarusa on their own. Then with the aid of enterprising landowners, they'd ferried the Kaw and forded the Red Vermillion. The only snag had been Samuel Abercrombie's repeated complaints. But there was a man like that in every crowd.

On the morning after the Red Vermillion crossing, Franklin called the company to order, and the line of wagons snaked out onto the prairie. It was nearing the end of April now. The sun was warm, and the grasses in full bloom. A good day to be a farmer, Franklin's father would have said.

Franklin had hated the farm he grew up on, enlisting in the Army as soon as he could. His absence might not have been fair to Cordelia and the children, but he'd relished the constant movement of Army life. That's why he wanted to emigrate to Oregon—another adventure. Though he wanted his family with him this time.

Not only the explorer John Frémont, but also the renowned scout Kit Carson had assured Franklin the land in Oregon was fertile, ready for the plow. If Franklin had to farm, he'd rather farm in the West. A new beginning with his wife and children. And more excitement than in already settled land.

They were moving farther into the wilderness now, soon to traverse a stretch of dry prairie to the Platte River and buffalo country. It would be Indian country as well.

He'd traveled this route with Frémont's exploration to Oregon, and Franklin was confident he could find the Platte. He had Frémont's maps— carefully drawn by the cartographer Charles Preuss. He'd spent many evenings with Frémont and Preuss talking about the geography. Preuss boasted anyone with an eye could follow the landmarks drawn depicted on his maps.

Franklin's company was off to a strong start. He'd get them to Oregon safely, he was sure. There would be more challenges, bigger challenges, ahead—many more rivers, many mountain ranges. But he could manage.

Samuel Abercrombie rode his large gelding alongside his wagons Wednesday afternoon. The company was beginning to work together, no thanks to Pershing. Samuel had his platoon well in hand, as did the other sergeants—even the lawyer McDougall. If each platoon did well, they'd make it, no matter how Pershing mucked things up.

Samuel wasn't satisfied with the pace, even without the cattle herds slowing them down. Tomorrow would be the last day of April, and they hadn't even reached the Platte River. From the tales he'd heard, they should still beat the mountain snows in the West, but a man couldn't depend on winter to hold off for his convenience. He'd learned that from his decades of farming.

His first wife Abigail had died on a cold November day, the morning after birthing Daniel. Over nineteen years ago. How did the years pass so quickly? He'd been lucky Harriet was willing to have him and the boys, when she could have found a young beau. He didn't love Harriet the way he'd loved Abigail—maybe a man only loved like that once. Still, Harriet had turned into a comforting sort of woman, working hard during the day and warming his bed at night. A man could do far worse.

He'd have to ask young Daniel whether he thought the Pershing lass would be as good a wife as his stepmother. Or perhaps his son wasn't thinking about marriage to the girl, just a bit of canoodling. Though spooning with a girl could get a man in a heap of trouble.

When they stopped for the night on the banks of the Big Vermillion, Samuel took Douglass and Daniel down to the river to scout the crossing. Pershing and his sons were downstream a few yards, McDougall and his wife with them.

"What you think, Pershing?" Samuel shouted as he approached the Pershing men. "Current's purty fast."

Pershing nodded. "But it's fordable. We seen how Vieux's men did it. We can handle this one on our own."

"We ain't got much choice," Samuel spat a stream of tobacco juice.

"It's wider'n the last river, ain't it, Pa?" Douglass asked. "Louisa and the girls were scared of that one. And this looks more fearsome."

"They'd better get used to it, son. We've a lot more rivers ahead."

Chapter 12:   The Big Vermillion

Wednesday, 28 April 1847. Another river crossing tomorrow.
Big Vermillion. FP

Thursday morning began cool and cloudy. Franklin Pershing paced the shore of the Big Vermillion. The river was about seventy yards wide, though it didn't appear too deep. He'd sent Joel across on horseback, and the mount didn't have to swim. Fast current, as Abercrombie had pointed out the night before, but manageable.

"Women and children in the wagons!" Franklin shouted. "Along with any man that ain't got a horse to ride. Let's move across quickly."

"You all right?" he asked his wife Cordelia. "Joel's in the other wagon with the twins and Noah. Zeke'll drive you and the girls across."

Zeke said, "I told McDougall I'd ride with his wife. She's afraid of the water."

"I'll drive," Cordelia said, tight-lipped. Franklin could never tell how she felt when she didn't say much, but now she didn't sound happy. He'd have to stay close to her wagon, in case of a problem.

Franklin lined up the rest of the company and stationed men on horseback in the river, telling them to keep steady in the current. He made each man responsible for keeping an eye on a few wagons and attending to any problems those folks had. He'd watch his own two wagons, the Purcell wagon, and another.

He yelled at the lead oxen on the wagon Cordelia drove while she snapped the whip to get them pulling. The team headed into the current. He frowned as he observed her wagon roll across the river, hoping she could manage. She was doing fine. Joel drove the next wagon, the Purcells following him.

As the Purcell wagon started into the current, Franklin turned his mount and walked the horse toward the far bank, upstream of the wagons.

"My baby!" Amanda Purcell screamed.

Franklin pivoted. Peering between the Purcell wagon and the one behind it, he saw a small body float downstream. With the wagons between him and the child, he couldn't do a thing.

Charles Purcell dove from his wagon bench into the water, went under, then came up churning his arms. Zeke had also plunged off the McDougall wagon and swum downstream. McDougall splashed after Zeke on horseback.

Women shrieked. He recognized Cordelia's voice yelling, "Zeke!"

Franklin halted the company's progression across the river and threaded his horse downstream between two wagons. When he could view the scene clearly, Franklin saw McDougall on horseback walking his stallion out of the water, a small body slumped over his shoulder. Zeke, coughing vigorously, staggered out of the current behind McDougall.

By this time, the Purcell wagon and several others had reached the far bank. Amanda Purcell jumped off her wagon bench and grabbed the child from McDougall, sinking to the ground. She sobbed over the tot—her youngest boy Henry—and was still crooning to the lad when Franklin reached her.

Doc Tuller rushed over and took the child. After Doc pounded on his back, Henry puked up water, then wailed, causing his mother to weep even more loudly.

Franklin's voice shook as he questioned Zeke. "Is the boy all right?"

Gulping for air and shivering, Zeke gestured at Doc.

"He's fine," Doc said. "Scared, most likely. But he's crying loud enough his lungs must be clear."

"Thank you," Mrs. Purcell said, clasping the doctor's hand. Then she froze. "Charles?" she screamed. "Where's Charles?"

Franklin's stomach dropped. He'd seen Charles Purcell dive into the water, and now he was nowhere to be seen.

"He went under," Zeke said, seeming finally to have caught his breath.

"I couldn't get to him."

Amanda Purcell's screams turned to moans.

Cordelia approached and took charge. She sent the sobbing little Purcell boy with Mrs. Tuller to dry off. "Go on, Franklin," Cordelia said. "Set up a search party. I'll find the other Purcell children." Then she left, while Jenny McDougall stayed with Mrs. Purcell.

Dazed, Franklin turned his horse back to the river. Several wagons hadn't yet crossed, and others stood stalled in the current. "Zeke and Joel," he said, "get them wagons moving." He turned to McDougall, "Ride downstream. Take a few men with you. See if you can find Purcell."

McDougall was gone before Franklin finished speaking.

Distraught, Franklin wondered what to do. Should he look for the lost man or see to the rest of the company? He sat on his horse, staring first downstream at the search party, then at the wagons still crossing.

Finally, he took his horse downstream. McDougall rode toward him. "They found him, captain." The lawyer's voice was somber. "Dead."

Cordelia had never seen Franklin speechless. He'd always seemed in control, no matter what the situation. He'd been charming as a dashing young soldier, confident when home from skirmishes and expeditions, even persuasive in mustering men to join this trek to Oregon. Never at a loss for words.

She hadn't had much use for Amanda Purcell thus far, finding the woman brassy and uncouth. But Cordelia felt for her now—widowed less than a month into their journey. In addition to the little boy who'd fallen into the river, Amanda had another son about eight and a daughter of eleven. All three children now wept in their mother's arms, while she keened softly.

"Come now," Cordelia said. "Let's get you fed. You'll feel better with something warm in your bellies." Her words distracted the young'uns, but not their mother.

Cordelia turned to Esther, who stood nearby. "Build a fire, and get some stew cooking," she told her daughter. Esther looked as stunned as Franklin did. Well, the girl needed to learn life had its share of tragedy. It wasn't all smiles and dimples. Come to think of it, her children hadn't seen much of death other than farm animals—Cordelia's father still lived in St. Charles, and her mother and Franklin's parents had died before she'd married him, so the young'uns hadn't faced the loss of grandparents.

"I've brought some bread," Harriet Abercrombie said from behind Cordelia. "And coffee." Now there was a woman who'd known sorrow—she'd lost her sister, she'd told Cordelia. Harriet would understand the importance of hot food and a good night's sleep.

With supper preparations underway, Cordelia looked for her brood to count noses. Zeke and Joel must be off with the men, but the other children—all but Esther—sat somberly beneath the wagons. Even the twins seemed bewildered.

"Esther, is the stew hot yet?" Cordelia turned back to the campfire. The pot stood suspended over the fire, but her daughter was nowhere to be seen.

Esther's tears threatened to choke her. She didn't want to cry, but she couldn't watch Mrs. Purcell or her children any longer. To think—they'd never see their pa again! She couldn't imagine how horrid that must be.

Esther had watched from the bank as Mr. Purcell dove into the water. She'd seen him surface once and go under, then she'd lost track of him while she worried about his young son, the little boy who played with Noah. Zeke and Mac McDougall had rescued Henry, and she'd forgotten all about Mr. Purcell while Doc Tuller pumped water out of the child's lungs.

Then she'd learned Mr. Purcell had died. Maybe she'd watched him take his last breath before he went under. Had he drowned? Hit his head? Been trapped in a tree root? All sorts of macabre possibilities raced through her mind. But it didn't really matter, because he was dead. He'd never hug his children again. She wished Pa were there to hug her.

Ma was so calm. Ma did what she did every night—got Esther cooking the meal, had the twins setting up tents for the night, put Rachel in charge of the young'uns. Everyone had chores, and Ma saw to it the tasks all got done. Didn't she realize a man had died?

When Esther couldn't get enough air through her tightened throat, she abandoned the stew pot and ran from the campsite into the brush near the river upstream of the wagons. She didn't care if her shoes got muddy, if her skirt caught on branches. Her breath wheezed in and out—she needed to be alone.

She burrowed into the weeds on the riverbank, found a log to sit on, and sobbed. For poor Mr. Purcell. For his wife and children. For herself—bereft of her friends and home in St. Charles. She cried as she hadn't cried in years, not since her puppy had been stepped on by a cow.

Daniel Abercrombie watched Esther run out of camp and wondered where she was headed. It wasn't smart for a young woman to go off alone on the prairie. He started after her.

"Daniel, where do you think you're going?" his father shouted. "There's work to be done, setting up camp. Your ma took bread over to the Purcells. Least you could do is pitch our tents."

"Yes, Pa."

Louisa was busy cooking, and he didn't know where Douglass was, so he got his nieces Annabelle and Rose to hold the tent poles while he pounded in the pegs. "Roll out the bedding, girls," he said, as he put away the hammer and peered beyond the camp to see if Esther had returned.

Not seeing her, he walked off. Pa yelled something after him, but since he didn't hear the words, he ignored them.

"Esther?" he called. And then again, "Esther, where are you?"

Only a few trees and bushes near the river offered a place to hide, so he headed there. Not far upstream from camp, he heard a woman sobbing—Esther.

"What's wrong?" he asked when he reached her.

"M-m-mister P-p-purcell is dead," she wailed.

"Yes," Daniel said, squatting beside her. "It's a terrible tragedy."

Esther cried all the louder. He'd never had to deal with a woman's tears before, only Annabelle and Rose when they scraped a knee. Esther's pain went deeper, he could tell, though he didn't know why she was so concerned about a man she barely knew. "Why does his death bother you so much?" he asked.

"I don't want my pa to die," she sobbed. "Nor my ma. Nor anyone. And all my friends are back in Missouri. I don't have anyone of my own to love."

Daniel knelt and took the girl in his arms. He didn't know if he was hugging her for her sake or his. Nor did he know if it would do any good. It felt nice to have her soft curves nestled against his chest, though he wondered if she even knew who held her as she wept into his shoulder.

After several minutes, she stilled and sniffled. "I'm sorry," she said, turning her tear-streaked face up to his and wiping her eyes.

He reached in his pocket and pulled out a handkerchief. "Here."

She took it and blew her nose. "I'm sorry," she said again, with a faint smile this time. She pulled away from him, though he kept his hand on her arm. "I'm surely a bother. I don't know what got into me."

"His death is a loss for all of us. We been lucky till now."

"Pa's taking it hard. Ma just keeps cooking."

"That's what my ma does when a neighbor dies. She takes food to them for weeks." Daniel took Esther's hand and rubbed her fingers. "I guess sometimes women are stronger than men. Women are the ones who keep families together."

"Then you must think me awful weak," Esther said, threading her fingers between his. "I ran away instead of helping Ma."

"There's no shame in running when you can't bear it." Daniel didn't know if that was true or not, but he hoped so. He'd run away from his father often enough.

"I guess we should go back, now I'm cried out."

Daniel stood and pulled Esther to her feet. Leaning over, he touched his lips to hers. She tasted sweet and salty. "Hope you feel better now."

"Oh!" she said, and put her fingers to her lips. "It wasn't supposed to be like that."

"Like what?"

"The first time you kissed me."

Daniel grinned. "Then you been thinking of me kissing you?"

Esther ducked her chin. "My face is all red and blotchy, I'm sure."

"I hadn't noticed." And he hadn't—the approaching dusk made it too dark. "Shall we try again?" He pulled her closer and repeated the kiss. She kissed him back, more sweet than salty this time.

Then he took her hand and walked her back to camp.

Samuel saw his son Daniel head out of camp. The boy was probably seeking out Esther Pershing, which was total foolishness, but Samuel was too tired to care. He'd watched that idiot Charles Purcell dive into the river after his child. Didn't look like the man could even swim, the way he thrashed about in the water. The tyke was alive, no thanks to Purcell, who'd ended up drowned. Samuel shuddered.

How would the child—and the rest of the Purcells—get to Oregon without their father? The entire family would likely perish before the wagons were past the Platte.

All due to Franklin Pershing's stupidity. The man hadn't stationed enough men downstream of the wagons. Only Zeke Pershing and Mac McDougall had been in place to go after the child and father. The company "captain" was as big an idiot as Purcell.

Samuel spat his chaw of tobacco into the campfire and stood. "I'm gonna talk to Pershing," he said to Harriet.

"Be careful, Samuel. Captain Pershing has a lot of worries at the moment."

Samuel snorted. His wife had no call to tell him to be careful. A man had to speak his mind when his family was in danger. And Pershing would put them all in danger if Samuel didn't set him straight. But Harriet was partly right—he should remain calm when he talked with Pershing.

He found Pershing by the riverbank and stood by the man in silence for a moment. Then he said, "Hard day."

Pershing grunted. "I thought we'd lose a few folks along the way, but not on an easy crossing like this."

"Guess it weren't so easy." No crossing ever went perfectly—Pershing shouldn't have let his guard down.

"We'll have to bury Purcell tomorrow."

It was Samuel's turn to grunt.

"Your wife was a big help to Cordelia today, as was the doctor's wife. Those three took charge of the widow and orphans." Pershing sighed, almost a sob. A man didn't cry over someone else's loss. "Poor Amanda. And her children. Whole company will have to step in to help 'em now."

"You needed more guards downstream," Samuel said. "Men in place to stop fools like Purcell."

"Fools?" Pershing turned to Samuel, fists clenched. "You think Purcell was a fool? What would you do if it'd been your child in the water? Though after the way you treated my boy Noah, maybe I know your answer."

Samuel shrugged. "Until he faces trouble, no man knows what he'll do. Alls a man can do is stay away from trouble. You let this happen."

Pershing swallowed hard. The man might be anguished over Purcell's death, but Samuel didn't care. What he cared about was keeping his family safe. He continued, "Don't let it happen again."

"Well, you be sure to tell me if you think I'm doing something wrong." Pershing's low voice was bitter.

Samuel couldn't let it go. "Reckon I will."

Harriet kept an eye on Samuel when he reached the shore of the Big Vermillion. He and Captain Pershing stood side by side talking. She blew a strand of hair out of her mouth, then brushed her damp cheeks. She'd been hiding tears since she left Amanda Purcell with Cordelia Pershing.

While there was work to do, she could smother her feelings, so she'd cooked supper, made bread dough to rise by morning, then washed dishes. But with the chores done, her emotions rose, and she gave way to heaving sobs. Poor Amanda! Poor children! How would they get to Oregon without a man?

Of course, men were the ones who set their families on the path west. No woman would leave home for a two-thousand-mile trek to the unknown. And now one woman and her offspring were at the mercy of the rest of the company.

Samuel had complained to her about Captain Pershing. She wondered what he was telling the captain now. The captain had grieved as much as any of them when Charles Purcell's body was carried to shore. But Samuel couldn't accept death as an accident. It was an enemy, and someone had to be responsible when the enemy won.

By the time Samuel returned to camp, she'd conquered her tears. She huddled in the tent, shivering in her blankets.

"I told Pershing he needed more men watching downstream," Samuel said after he crawled into the tent. "Purcell's death was his doing. He ain't fit to lead us to a picnic, let alone to Oregon. I want to take over as captain."

Harriet gasped. "You can't do that, Samuel. These families came because of Captain Pershing. Charles Purcell's death is a tragedy, nothing more. Pershing has been to Oregon, and you can't even read a map."

"I know how to keep men from foolishness."

"We need to work together, all of us. You yourself said so." Harriet wondered if Samuel was listening to anything she said. "I know you're upset—"

"Damn straight I'm upset. Next time it could be Annabelle or Rose in the water. Did you ever think of that?"

"You wouldn't let our granddaughters drown. Nor would Douglass or Daniel. Now stop talking and go to sleep. It'll be better in the morning." But would it? she wondered. In the morning they'd bury Charles Purcell on this Godforsaken prairie.

Chapter 13:   Esther Sets Her Cap

Thursday, 29 April 1847. Charles Purcell drowned in the Big Vermillion. FP

If not for Daniel's kiss beside the river, Esther would have been as melancholy as the rest of the company the next morning. After the travelers laid Charles Purcell in a shallow grave and covered it with stones, Pa began reading, "The Lord is my shepherd . . . ."

Esther's mind wandered from the familiar words to the feel of Daniel's lips on hers. Refreshing as green pastures. But not still waters—no, Daniel was deep, she decided. More grown up than the boy back home who'd kissed her. Daniel was a man, a man a girl could rely on. He made her cup runneth over. At the thought of Daniel's rod and staff, she stifled a small giggle—she wasn't supposed to imagine such things, particularly during a funeral service.

Pa finished the psalm and started a prayer. Esther listened, and her throat closed when Pa spoke of Mr. Purcell giving his life for his child. Would she give her life for anyone? For her parents? Her brothers and sisters? For Daniel? Who would give their life for her?

She felt alone, so alone. She hated the feeling and feared it. She wanted so much to have someone who was hers.

The wagons rolled away from the campsite beside the Big Vermillion, the scene of Mr. Purcell's drowning. Ma walked beside Esther and asked. "What amused you so during the burial?"

"I wasn't amused," Esther said. Ma's reminder of what she'd thought about Daniel made her blush, but her face was serious now. "The Purcell children have lost their pa. It's so sad." She swallowed hard, tears not far away. "What if it had been Pa?" What if she did lose one of her parents—then where would she be? Even more alone and with more responsibilities than Ma gave her now.

"Don't even think such a thing." Ma said sharply, then sighed. "Keep an eye on the Purcell young'uns, would you? Those wee mites. Their ma ain't strong enough to cope, I don't think. She seemed so bold afore yesterday, but it was all I could do to get her dressed to bury her husband."

More children to mind—it wasn't fair of Ma to ask. "Ain't it enough I watch our own brood? Now you want me to take on three more?"

"We all have to pitch in, girl. Each man and woman, young and old. Your pa's seeing to their wagon. It's a good thing we have Zeke and Joel to mind ours. You can watch those children."

"Pa's the wagon captain. How can he tend the Purcell wagon, too?"

"That's his way of helping."

As they walked, Ma droned on about supplies and cooking. Esther's mind wandered back to Daniel's kiss. He'd comforted her as she cried over Mr. Purcell's death. She wanted Daniel's strength now. She wanted it always.

And then she knew, her feet stumbling at her realization. She was in love with Daniel and wanted to marry him. He was the man who could give her the home and family she yearned for.

How could she make it happen? She needed to make him fall in love with her. She needed him to want her as much as she wanted him.

But cranky Mr. Abercrombie would fight her attempts, as would her parents. Their fathers were at odds, and Ma still thought of Esther as a child.

That afternoon Esther walked with Ma again. "I don't know what's gotten into you," Ma said, after heaving in a deep breath. "You been mooning all day, ever since the funeral this morning. I'm going to sit in the wagon for a spell. You and Rachel watch out for our young'uns and the Purcells. Their girl can help. She's almost as old as Rachel."

Esther and Rachel sent the younger children racing ahead, while they walked through the tall grasses. "I feel so sorry for the Purcells," Rachel said. "The older two have been crying all morning. It's good to see them playing now. And little Henry don't know what's happening. He asked me three times where his pa is."

"Mmm," Esther said, craning her neck to look for Daniel's horse among the men riding by the wagons. She didn't see him.

"Who you looking for? Daniel Abercrombie?"

"Maybe."

"Don't let Ma catch you."

"I'm going to marry him." Esther didn't have her friend Amy to talk to, so Rachel would have to do.

Her sister stopped. "How can you say that?"

"I just know. He kissed me."

Rachel gasped. "You ain't known him but a month."

"I was crying by the river last night, and he came to comfort me. I'm sure he'll be in love with me soon. I mean to do everything I can to encourage him."

"But Pa and Mr. Abercrombie—"

"I ain't marrying Mr. Abercrombie. I'm marrying Daniel." Now Esther could see him. He was riding horseback behind her, next to his family's wagons.

Rachel sniffed. "Ma and Pa won't put up with your foolishness."

"They won't know unless you tell 'em." Esther grabbed her sister's arm. "Don't you say anything. In fact, I need your help." She nodded toward Daniel. "I need you to watch the young'uns while I talk to Daniel." She knelt. "I've got a rock in my shoe."

Rachel halted.

"Go on," Esther whispered. "Stay with the children."

Rachel shook her head and walked on, glancing back at Esther a time or two.

"Something wrong, Miss Esther?" Daniel asked from his saddle when he caught up with her.

"Just a rock." She stood. "Can you help me take off my shoe?"

He dismounted. "Lean on my shoulder, and I'll pull it off."

She smiled and did as he said.

He shook out the shoe. "I didn't see nothing, but maybe this'll feel better." He put the shoe back on her foot. "Would you like to ride?"

"Oh, I couldn't—"

"Of course, you can." He lifted her into his saddle. "I'll walk along, and we'll rest your foot."

"Thank you. And thank you again for rescuing me last night by the river."

"We were all distressed, Miss Esther. I'm glad I could help."

"You been calling me 'Esther.' I like that better. We'll be fine friends by the time we get to Oregon."

When the emigrants stopped Friday evening, Daniel busied himself about his family's campsite. He went with his nieces Annabelle and Rose to gather buffalo chips to fuel the fire. It had taken several days for his nieces to get over their squeamishness, but now they filled their sacks with chips as fast as they were able, selecting the driest ones they could find.

While Daniel worked, he mulled over his time with Esther earlier in the day. She'd seemed forward, quite a change from the grieving girl she'd been the night before. Maybe he shouldn't have kissed her, but he'd wanted to console her, and she'd seemed to need his comfort. Today she acted like the fast young ladies he'd known in Tennessee—the ones his mother warned him to stay away from.

Which girl was the real Esther?

He put up tents and toted water, then ate in silence while his father talked endlessly over supper.

Pa had gone hunting with some of the other men. "Shoulda taken you with me, Daniel," Pa said. "Shot some antelope late in the day. Got to get away from the wagons to have any chance of finding game. Maybe I'll try again tomorrow."

"We can only use so much fresh meat afore it spoils, Samuel," Ma said. "What you brought back today will last us awhile."

"There's others what can use the meat. The widow Purcell, for one. And Pershing ain't gone hunting—he's got a big brood."

"Good of you to help 'em, Pa," Daniel said, pulling out of his reverie about Esther. He thought about going with his father—he didn't relish sticking around camp for Esther to waylay again. He could use a day with men folk, though hunting was not a pastime he enjoyed.

That evening after supper Cordelia pulled Rachel off to the side of the wagons and asked, "What was Esther doing with Daniel Abercrombie this afternoon?" Cordelia had watched Esther make eyes at Daniel since the noon halt. It wasn't fitting, particularly when the company had held a funeral that morning.

Rachel shrugged. "Just walking, Ma. And he gave her a ride."

"That girl's been as moonstruck as can be all day."

"Yes'm." Rachel stared at the ground.

"You sure she ain't said nothing to you?"

"No, Ma."

Cordelia frowned at her second daughter until Rachel looked up. Guilty. Cordelia had been a mother for twenty years now—she knew guilt when she saw it. "Tell me."

"Esther says she's sweet on Daniel. But you knew that."

Cordelia sighed. Another trial for her to deal with. "All right. Go get Ruthie and Noah cleaned up for bed. I'll talk to Esther."

Rachel scampered away.

"Esther," Cordelia called.

"Yes, Ma." Esther climbed out of one of the wagons.

"Rachel says you told her you're sweet on Daniel Abercrombie. I thought I told you . . . ." Cordelia's voice trailed off when she saw Esther's mouth turn mulish. "Now don't you blame your sister. Would you have her lie to me?"

Esther shook her head, but her expression didn't change.

"You're too young to be serious about any boy. And Daniel's father is causing Pa all kinds of grief. You best stay away from him."

"But, Ma—"

"No 'buts' about it. I don't want to see you and Daniel alone again."

Saturday morning Samuel Abercrombie listened to Franklin Pershing outline their route. The man was going to make them rest on the Sabbath the next day.

Samuel opened his mouth to object, but Pershing interrupted, "Abercrombie, some families are running out of meat. You think you could lead another hunting party today? Take a few men away from the wagons looking for game? I seen signs of antelope, and buffalo can't be too far away. There's fresh buffalo chips along the trail. If you don't find game, you can hunt again tomorrow—range farther from the wagons while we stop."

For once, Pershing's idea made sense. Samuel was an excellent shot with a rifle. He could take a couple of men, scout ahead while hunting, and get a sense of what the territory would bring next. He spat on the ground and nodded. "Too late to find any morning game. I'll go after the noon halt. Leave my boys to tend my wagons. Who's with me?"

Hewitt and Jackson raised their hands.

The emigrants reached the Big Blue River at midday. Pershing said the crossing was at Alcove Springs, a few miles upriver. "You take your hunting party out, Abercrombie. Meet us this evening at the springs."

After the noon meal, Abercrombie mounted his gelding and beckoned to the other two men. They rode away from the wagons, and as he glanced back, he saw Daniel climbing a hill with Esther Pershing. He snorted. He'd have a word with the boy tonight.

The three men cantered a mile or two beyond the wagons. The prairie undulated in all directions, grasses waving in the winds. Near a small creek they flushed a band of antelope, and Samuel shot one before the other men had pulled their rifles out of their scabbards.

"Why didn't you wait?" Jackson said. "If we'd all shot we could've got two or three of 'em. Now the rest are gone."

"If I'd waited, I would've lost my shot." Samuel had no patience with a man who couldn't act without speechifying first. "Next time, just shoot."

They stopped and dressed the carcass, and Samuel slung it behind his saddle. They rode on for another hour, but didn't see more game.

"Good thing we can go out again tomorrow," Hewitt said when they stopped to drink. "Sun's getting low. Better turn back."

"We'll ride along the creek," Samuel said. "Maybe see another herd."

They turned southeast but saw no more game. Shortly before dusk they found the wagons circled at Alcove Springs on the Big Blue River. At least that's what Pershing called the waterway—Samuel didn't know one western river from the next.

He curried and watered his horse and tethered the mount. Then he went to his wagons and ate the supper Harriet had saved for him. "Where's Daniel?" he asked.

"I don't know. He left after we ate. Douglass is around—you need him?"

"No. I want Daniel. I seen him with the Pershing girl again."

"Don't bother him, Samuel. Daniel's a responsible boy. You don't have to worry about him."

Samuel snorted. "Maybe it ain't him I worry about. Maybe it's her."

"I talked to Cordelia Pershing already. They aren't any more interested in Esther and Daniel taking up with each other than we are."

"Why not? Daniel'd be a catch for any girl."

By Saturday morning, Cordelia had another worry besides Esther— Zeke. She'd seen her oldest child staring after Jenny McDougall, seeming as infatuated with the young woman as Esther was with Daniel. Zeke had been tending Jenny's wagon when Charles Purcell drowned. Jenny was afraid of the water, he'd said later. Afraid of water—how silly, Cordelia thought with a snort. But then, water had killed a man.

Jenny was married, with a baby on the way. The doctor's wife had commented on Zeke assisting her. Cordelia suspected other women were gossiping about Zeke and Jenny also.

Cordelia would have to put a stop to Zeke's attentions immediately, though she wasn't sure how to talk to her son. He was full grown now. Still, she'd sent Franklin to talk with Esther, so it was only fair she figure out what to say to Zeke.

After the noon halt, she told Zeke she'd ride awhile in the wagon, if he'd ride with her.

Zeke shrugged. "Land's flat enough. Won't be a burden on the oxen." He vaulted onto the bench beside her.

They sat in silence while the sun beat down, and Cordelia tried to decide what to say. Finally, she said, "Folks is talking about you and Jenny McDougall."

"Talking?"

"They say you spend too much time with her."

"Ma—"

"Now listen, son—"

"I'm only trying to help her out. I've helped Miz Purcell also. Miz Jenny—"

"Shouldn't you call her Mrs. McDougall?"

"She told me to call her 'Jenny.' Mac is busy with his platoon, which leaves Miz Jenny by herself. And she's in a family way, like you, and—"

"I know all about her, son. Which is why I'm telling you that folks is talking."

Zeke didn't respond. Cordelia stared off at the blank horizon. This was surely barren country. No trees, not even shrubs. Nothing but grass, and the blank sky above.

"Ma?"

"Hmm," she said.

"How'd you know Pa was the one for you?"

Now why was Zeke asking that—surely he wasn't seriously brooding over Jenny McDougall? "Well, he was a charmer," she said. "Turned my head, all right. Don't you be acting that way toward any young women you know." Then she squinted at him. "Particularly not married ones."

"I wouldn't." Her son sounded truly offended. "I just wanted to know about you and Pa."

Cordelia sighed. "Like I said, he was a charmer. Told me I was pretty. Asked me to dance. Smiled at me so wickedly, wearing his handsome uniform. Words smooth as butter. So be careful who *you* charm, or you'll end up married to her."

Zeke reached around and gave her a quick sideways hug. "Thanks, Ma. I need to check our other wagon." He jumped off the bench, leaving Cordelia alone with her thoughts.

She remembered what young men were like. She didn't want Zeke flirting with girls any more than she wanted boys flirting with Esther. Or Esther flirting back, she thought in fairness.

Chapter 14: Advice

Sunday, 2 May 1847. Alcove Springs. Laying by on the Little Blue. FP

Samuel didn't see Daniel until Sunday morning. He rousted his son out of bed. "Time's a wasting. Hunting party leaves at first light. You're with me today."

A minute later Daniel crawled out of the tent, fully dressed.

"You was with the Pershing girl again yesterday. Thought I told you not to take up with her."

"She took up with me, Pa."

"Well, a smart man knows how to let a girl down easy. I expect you to do as I say. She ain't the one for you. We're stuck with her family, least ways till I can find another company going to Oregon. But I don't want you any friendlier than you need to be."

"Yes, Pa."

As Samuel packed his saddlebags with food and ammunition for the day ahead, he noticed Cordelia Pershing carrying a bucket toward the spring. If Daniel was telling the truth about Esther, a word with the girl's mother might stop the lass from harassing Daniel. He didn't trust that Harriet had been firm enough. "Can I help you, Miz Pershing?" he called, and went to take the bucket from her.

"Thank you, Mr. Abercrombie," she said, nodding.

"I seen Esther talking to Daniel yesterday. Harriet told me you and she talked 'bout keeping them two children apart."

"I've spoken to Esther, Mr. Abercrombie."

"Just so we're clear. I've talked to Daniel as well. I don't want any scandals betwixt our families."

"Certainly not, Mr. Abercrombie." She spoke in a huff. "Esther is—"

"Daniel said Esther was flirting with him, Miz Pershing. That's how rumors—"

"Mister Abercrombie." He'd noticed before she enunciated her words precisely when she was riled. "A young man of Daniel's age—he's nineteen, ain't he?—can surely handle a fifteen-year-old girl's crush. My daughter is a good girl, and her pa and I are watching her. You can be sure we have no intention of letting her fall prey to any young man."

"Now, look here, Miz Pershing—"

"I think we should each keep our own house in order. Whether we're in town or on the prairie." She thrust out her hand. "My bucket, please. I can get my own water."

Samuel grinned and handed her the bucket. A feisty woman. "My pleasure, ma'am. I'm glad we understand each other." He tipped his hat and turned back to the wagons.

He was still smiling when he reached his campfire. "Spoke with Miz Pershing," he told Harriet. "'Bout Daniel and her daughter. I don't think we'll have any trouble. She won't let Esther out of her sight, after what I told her. But best keep an eye on Daniel, in case Esther gets away from her ma."

"What did you say to her, Samuel?" Harriet looked up from stirring a pot, eyebrows furrowed.

"Just let her know we wouldn't tolerate no nonsense from her silly daughter. She agreed. I like that woman."

Harriet shook her head in silence.

Samuel mounted his horse and led the hunters out of camp as the sun broke over the horizon.

Franklin Pershing joined the Sunday hunt, but was content to let Samuel Abercrombie lead the way. Franklin planned to scout as he rode, though the route was easy—follow the Blue until the Frémont map said to cut north to the Platte.

The hunters were a good group of men, most of whom he'd begun to trust. Mac McDougall was a solid presence, a hard man to ruffle. Hewitt was another good platoon sergeant. Jackson was impetuous, but not a bad sort. And, of course, his sons Zeke and Joel were proving themselves invaluable as his aides. Abercrombie couldn't do much harm with this lot.

They crossed the Blue, to the side where Franklin expected there'd be more buffalo, but stayed close to the river. Daniel Abercrombie spotted fresh buffalo dung, and in the next valley they found a herd, grazing placidly. The great beasts seemed to ignore the riders who had entered their domain.

"Must be a thousand," Hewitt said in awe.

"Let's go," Abercrombie said, about to kick his horse toward the herd.

Franklin had seen buffalo hunts on his earlier journey west. "Careful," he said, holding up his hand. "Buffalo are fast." He outlined a plan to box the beasts in a canyon to the south.

Abercrombie squinted at him. Franklin knew he hadn't improved his relationship with the man by taking over the hunt. But he couldn't let Abercrombie send the others into peril. Franklin directed some men to herd the buffalo. "You want to lead the shooters at the head of the valley?" he asked Abercrombie.

Samuel spat and nodded.

"Don't shoot more'n two or three. We can't carry any more meat back to camp."

Franklin's plan worked. Men whooped and galloped from behind the beasts on both sides of the valley. The buffalo bellowed and stampeded, but headed into the canyon as expected.

Abercrombie and his men shot, adding the noise of gunshots to the chaos. Five buffalo fell.

Franklin shook his head in disgust. A waste of good meat—the hunters couldn't handle five carcasses. Only the coyotes and birds would benefit. "Need to butcher 'em here," he said. "And we'll need a wagon to carry the meat back to camp."

Daniel volunteered to find their company and bring a wagon back to the hunters with extra men to help with the butchering.

It took the rest of the day to complete the task and return to camp, but that evening all the emigrants dined on fresh buffalo meat.

"I want two haunches and tongues," Abercrombie said as the families divided the meat. "I led the shooters."

"Your family can't eat that much afore the meat spoils," Franklin argued. They had plenty of meat now, but he wondered how families like Amanda Purcell's would have enough when they reached the mountains— particularly if Abercrombie took more than he could use.

Cordelia placed a hand on his arm and shook her head. "But no matter," Franklin said. He'd let Abercrombie win this skirmish.

Esther had a hard time getting away from her mother on Sunday while the men were hunting. First, Ma had her toting and fetching, then she needed Esther to watch the young'uns. After they fixed a noon meal, Esther asked if she could spend time with Jenny McDougall. "Jenny's sewing clothes for her baby," Esther said. "I'd like to help her."

Ma frowned, but nodded. "The children are looking for turtles with Tanner." The Negro man Tanner was handy with tools and a fishing pole, though he didn't join the other men shooting. "I can spare you for a while." Esther wasted no time in walking to Jenny's wagon.

Esther sat on a stump beside Jenny and sighed. "Ma don't let me out of her sight. She's afraid I'll do something silly. And Daniel's not even here."

"Your mama wants to keep you safe."

"How much trouble can I get in out here on the prairie?" Esther stabbed her needle into the little shirt she was stitching.

"You'd be surprised where you can get into trouble." Jenny's voice was soft, but Esther heard something serious in it.

"You'd never get in trouble. Ma thinks you're a steadying influence on me."

Jenny laughed. "I doubt she said that."

"How'd you know Mr. McDougall was the man for you?"

Jenny shrugged, serious again. "I don't know. He wanted me to come with him to Oregon. I didn't have a reason to say no."

Esther couldn't believe Jenny was so unsentimental about her courtship. "That's how you knew you were in love?"

"I didn't say I was in love. I said I didn't have a reason to turn him down."

"That's not very romantic." Esther breathed in deeply. "I'm in love with Daniel."

"You barely know him."

"He kissed me. After Mr. Purcell died. I was crying, and Daniel kissed me." Esther smiled at the memory, feeling Daniel's arms around her again.

"A kiss doesn't mean much."

Esther frowned at Jenny over her sewing. "It means he cares for me, don't you think?"

"I think you should take it slowly, Esther. Get to know Daniel and his family."

"You didn't. You married right away."

"Maybe I shouldn't have. Mac is a good man. I'm lucky. But maybe I shouldn't have left home." Jenny bit her lip and stared at her lap. Esther thought she saw tears on Jenny's lashes.

If Jenny regretted her marriage, maybe Ma was right. "Ma says I shouldn't be in such a hurry to marry."

Jenny looked up and smiled. "Your mama is a wise woman. You should listen to her, if not to me. It's a long way to Oregon. You don't have to spend all your time with Daniel now."

Monday morning Daniel helped his father and brother hitch the oxen to the wagons in preparation for the river crossing. A cold rain fell, making Daniel's fingers clumsy. Pershing was hurrying the wagons, because the water in the Big Blue was rising.

"It's passable," Pa said, "but I hope we're among the early wagons to cross. Current'll come up fast if the rain keeps at it." Daniel and his father maneuvered the Abercrombie wagons toward the head of the line.

But all the wagons crossed without mishap, though the mood of the company seemed as gray as the sky. No doubt, many of the emigrants remembered the last crossing, where Charles Purcell had died.

At Captain Pershing's request, Daniel scouted ahead of the wagons with Zeke Pershing. He liked the captain's oldest son, a young man about Daniel's age. But the thought crossed his mind that Captain Pershing might have sent them ahead to keep Daniel away from Esther. It wasn't his doing—she'd approached him the last time. Not that he had objected.

The prairie spread ahead of them, flat and treeless, and wet from the rain. Grasses taller than he'd ever seen brushed against his mare's belly. Herds of buffalo and antelope grazed in the distance, but Daniel had no desire to hunt. The killing the prior day had been enough. He liked riding the prairie, but the buffalo hunt was more overwhelming than anything he'd experienced before—far bigger in scale than butchering hogs back home. Five huge carcasses to skin, dress, and butcher. More meat than he'd ever seen at once in his lifetime.

He liked animals. He'd enjoyed rearing horses on his father's farm in Tennessee more than plowing the fields, though he could spend time alone with the horses while plowing. He'd been more involved in the training of Pa's dog Bruiser than Pa had.

He even liked raising chickens for Ma. One time when Daniel was about five, Douglass had chased him around the barnyard with a squawking hen to tease him, and Daniel had been scared witless. When Pa yelled at them both afterward, Daniel set his mind to collecting the eggs to get over his fear. And he came to like the pesky birds. Ma said he found more eggs than anyone.

There wasn't much to talk about as he and Zeke rode ahead of the wagons, so Daniel had plenty of time to think. His mind turned to Esther.

"Zeke?" he asked.

"Hmm."

"What's Esther like?"

Zeke looked at him sideways. "What do you mean?"

"Is she silly or sensible?"

Zeke shrugged. "Sometimes one. Sometimes the other. She's a girl."

"Your parents seem awful hard on her."

Zeke snorted. "When she's silly, they are. But Ma relies on her for help. Esther can do 'bout anything she puts her mind to. Back home, she did her best to keep up with me and Joel when Ma let her loose. She's a stubborn one. And hard-working."

"That ain't bad."

"No. She's a good girl at heart." Zeke turned to Daniel. "Why you asking?"

It was Daniel's turn to shrug. "No reason. She's purty, I guess."

"Purty enough. But don't go getting any ideas. She's my little sister."

"Don't worry. My pa's told me well enough to leave her alone. And I wouldn't hurt her for the world."

"See you don't." Zeke spurred his horse and rode ahead.

The next several days passed tediously. Daniel split his time between scouting with the Pershing men and tending his family's wagons. When he was with the wagons, he saw little of Esther. He wondered if she was avoiding him.

The emigrants ate buffalo at every meal—fried as steaks and boiled or roasted with potatoes or beans. They ate it hot and as cold leftovers. The men took slices of meat to eat with biscuits when they scouted, and they sopped up buffalo gravy with biscuits in camp. Buffalo meat was lean, less tasty than beef. But Pa wouldn't let Ma fix anything else until the buffalo was gone. "Meat won't keep. Salt pork will."

Not only did they eat the meat, they cooked with the beasts' waste for fuel. During the day children gathered chips as they walked, and in the evening they gathered more.

The emigrants saw only an occasional tree by a creek bed, nothing for hours on end between one gully and the next.

For three days after the Sabbath hunt, they traveled through grassland. On Wednesday evening Pa came back from a meeting with Captain Pershing and the other platoon leaders. "We're finally crossing to the Platte tomorrow," Pa told the rest of the family. "Twenty-five miles without water, Pershing says. There oughta be a better way, but that's what we're doing."

"Can we make twenty-five miles in one day?" Douglass asked.

Pa shrugged. "We're gonna. Fill up every barrel we got with water. Every pot and glass. Harriet, you see to it."

Daniel spent the evening lugging water for his mother.

Chapter 15:   Long Day to the Platte

*Wednesday, 5 May 1847. Tomorrow we cross to the Platte.
Twenty-five miles. Hope to hit the river at Grand Island. FP*

Franklin was up before dawn to get his company ready to move. They needed to travel twenty-five miles, and they would have no water until they found the Platte River. At least, that was his estimate of the distance, based on the Frémont map. When he and Dawson had talked about reorganizing their companies, they'd discussed the route to the Platte. Dawson had told Franklin where he planned to cross. But Dawson had never been to Oregon, so knew even less than Franklin.

When he called the wagons into line, most were ready, and he sent those families out, Samuel Abercrombie leading the way. He told Abercrombie to make good time, but not to get too far ahead of the others. "We need to stay together," he said.

"If folks can't stay with me, they'll have to catch up," Abercrombie said. "I aim to be to the Platte afore dark."

"We need to help each other along, Abercrombie," Franklin said. "I'm putting you in front because I know you'll keep a good pace. But you're one of the sergeants. You have a responsibility to work with everyone."

Abercrombie muttered something under his breath, but through the day Franklin saw him riding up and down the wagons to make sure the line didn't get too strung out.

Franklin stayed in the rear, watching for stragglers. He rode horseback, he drove oxen, he spelled Amanda Purcell in leading her team while she walked awhile with her children.

Despite his obligations as captain, he kept an eye on Cordelia. He'd never spent much time with her when she was pregnant. He'd planted the babes when he was home on leave, then returned to the Armory in St. Louis or left on another expedition. But from the little he remembered, he didn't think she'd been so tired in the past before a confinement. Travel was hard on everyone, he reflected, but maybe hardest on women who were in a family way.

Where would they be when she delivered? Probably in the mountains. She wouldn't have an easy time of it, but at least there'd be other women in the company to help her.

"Yaw!" In late afternoon, Franklin heard a shout from ahead. It was Zeke riding back from searching for the Platte. "River's 'bout an hour from here. Wide as an ocean."

"You ain't never seen the ocean," Joel said to Zeke.

"Well, it's a lot of water. Wider'n the Mississippi," Zeke said. "Wider'n any river I've ever seen."

Franklin told Zeke to mind the wagons and rode ahead to see for himself. Soon he saw it—the broadest river they would encounter on their journey, though others would be more treacherous. An island lay in the middle of the river. Grand Island. They'd arrived just where he'd hoped to hit the Platte.

Harriet didn't take time to brew coffee before the travelers began the long trek to the Platte. At the first sign of dawn, she handed out cold meat and hardtack to her family. Her granddaughters complained at being awakened so early, and Harriet told them to sleep in the wagon until the sun was up.

"But, Grandma, the wagon is so noisy," Rose, the younger girl, whined.

"Your choice, child. Sleep or walk," Harriet said.

She and Louisa trudged beside the wagons. Samuel rode at the head of the company, then back along the caravan. Daniel scouted with Zeke Pershing, and Douglass minded the oxen. Their wagons led through the day, and Samuel made sure they traveled as fast as the teams could pull at a steady pace.

When they started, the light was so dim Harriet could barely see the ground. She stumbled on the uneven grassland. If other emigrants had passed this way, they hadn't yet beaten down the prairie. It was rough and untamed.

Hour after hour they walked, heading due north toward the Platte. Once the sun rose, Harriet could see for miles from the high plateau on which they trod. Captain Pershing called a halt every two hours, but only for five minutes. Harriet had just enough time to relieve herself and sip a little water.

Another wagon train could be seen to the east, also heading north. Captain Pershing had called the Platte "the great river road"—a fanciful name, if Harriet had ever heard one. There were no roads in this vast wilderness, merely open space that sapped the spirit.

They stopped for a midday meal, but ate only cold food. "No fires," Pershing said. "No time to rest. We need to make the Platte afore nightfall."

Finally, near dusk, Harriet heard a cry from the scouts, "River ahead!" But she saw nothing for another half hour. As twilight approached, she walked over a low ridge and in the fading light made out a broad river, wider even than the Mississippi their family had crossed when they left Tennessee. The river valley was miles wide, the shoreline so flat it appeared to be part of the water.

They had reached the Platte.

Samuel gazed out over the Platte River. A milestone reached, and he'd led the wagons to it. They'd had scouts, of course, his son Daniel among them. And Zeke Pershing as well. He was glad to see Daniel assuming a scout's role, and Pershing letting him. Daniel was no good as a hunter, but the boy had potential as a farmer and horse trainer. If the lad could scout, he'd be worth something on this trek.

Douglass, on the other hand, couldn't do much more than drive a wagon and shoot a rifle. And beget daughters.

Samuel had been glad to set the pace today. For once, Pershing let him do as he pleased, so Samuel pushed his teams to their limits. He'd had to hold back at times, because others had fewer oxen than the eight yoked to each of his wagons. And some folks had stuffed their wagons to the cover with too much weight.

Twenty-five miles. If they could do twenty-five miles every day, they'd be in Oregon by mid-August. Time enough to clear land and plant winter wheat.

But he was getting ahead of himself. Pershing would never keep this brisk pace. To tell the truth, Samuel wasn't sure he or his teams could keep up the grueling speed for two months. His backside was sore from riding all day.

He turned around, looking for Daniel. He should tell the boy he'd done good.

"Abercrombie," Pershing said as Samuel reached the camp. "Tell your platoon we're laying by tomorrow. Resting up."

"Laying by?" Samuel shouted. He might be tired, but if they rested after every hard day, it'd be winter before they settled. No time to clear the fields. "Now see here, Pershing—"

"We got to the Platte, and you brung us here. But if we're going to make it all the way, we have to pace ourselves."

"There's pacing and then there's poking along. And you're as pokey as they come, Pershing." Samuel stormed off toward his wagons.

Harriet fixed supper, bread, and a quick buffalo soup warmed over the fire. She wanted something hot in her stomach before bed, though she was so exhausted she could hardly stand to tend the pot.

Samuel came clumping through the campsite and sat on a flour barrel he pulled out of the wagon. "Damn that Pershing. He's laying by again tomorrow."

"We're all tired, Samuel."

"I ain't. And our teams ain't. Damn fool is holding us up. Most likely to cosset his wife. She looked peaked today."

"She's having a child in a few months. Carrying that extra weight."

"She has some extra weight of her own, too. There's other wagon companies passing us by. We'll be eating their dust all the way to Oregon. And their teams'll get the best grass."

"One day of rest won't matter." Harriet ladled a bowl of soup for Samuel.

Samuel took the bowl. "Ain't we got anything heartier?"

"No, Samuel, we don't," Harriet snapped. She ached from the top of her head to her toes. "We're down to the tougher cuts of buffalo. I'm too tired to cook. I walked for fourteen hours today, while you rode horseback."

"I been busy, too. Put together another hunting party for tomorrow, since we're stuck in place. Bring you home some better meat to fry tomorrow." Samuel slurped his soup. When he finished, he put the bowl down. "Think I'll turn in. Want to get an early start in the morning."

Harriet sank to her knees to wash the dishes. Daniel squatted beside her. "I'll do it, Ma. You're tired."

She smiled at him. "Ain't you hunting with your pa tomorrow? You should get some sleep."

Daniel shook his head. "I'll stay near camp. Douglass can go. I had my fill of shooting buffalo last Sunday."

"You don't like the butchering, do you?"

Daniel shrugged. "I know it's necessary. But, no, I don't like it. And you know I can't shoot as well as Pa and Douglass."

"I wish your pa would go easier on you. You're a good boy."

Daniel's mouth twisted wryly. "He should go easier on all of us. You, too."

"He said he talked to you about Esther Pershing."

"Don't worry, Ma. I won't do nothing wrong."

"I know, Daniel. Just take it slow with that girl. Or any girl. You have your whole life ahead. Be careful who you choose to spend it with." But then, Harriet had lived in the same house as Samuel for months before marrying him, and what good had knowledge of his character done her?

Daniel grunted.

"Spend your time with Mr. McDougall. And Zeke Pershing. They're good men. Men you can look up to." She didn't say it, but she knew they were both thinking "unlike your pa." "Just watch out for the captain—he's a good man, too, but your pa don't like him."

"Why don't he like Captain Pershing, Ma?"

Harriet sighed. She'd wondered that herself. "Maybe because he's never liked a man put over him. As a farmer, he was his own man."

"But Pa was in the militia in Tennessee."

"Those drills only lasted a few weeks. And he knew he had the farm to come home to."

"Sure makes it hard to get to know Esther, when Pa can't stand Captain Pershing."

"If you and Esther are meant to be together, it'll happen. Once we're in Oregon, her pa will just be another farmer, no different than yours."

Daniel lay in the tent with his parents, Pa snoring loudly. He should probably do as Ma said—take it slow with Esther. The girl seemed to want him as her beau, which was more than he wanted at the moment. He just thought she was pretty, someone nice to spend time with. He'd enjoyed kissing her, but he didn't want her hanging on his arm all day.

He liked the other young men Ma mentioned—Mac McDougall and Zeke Pershing. Mac was educated and wealthy, to listen to him talk. Daniel could learn a lot from a man with book learning and polish. And Zeke was the captain's son. Both Daniel's parents wanted him to keep away from the captain, but Zeke was experienced at handling the teams and a good scout. If Daniel spent time scouting, he could stay out of Pa's way. And Esther's, too.

She was a pretty thing, with her blond hair and blue eyes. And dimples when she smiled.

He turned over and drifted off to sleep, still thinking about Esther.

Chapter 16:   Dance With the Soldiers

Saturday, 8 May 1847. Found soldiers surveying a new Army fort. FP

The morning after their twenty-five-mile trek across the plains, Cordelia awoke body-sore and mind-weary. She was glad Franklin had decided to lay by, though many of the men objected, Samuel Abercrombie and his platoon in particular. What was it about that man that made everyone want to argue? He was a contentious sort, to be sure. Though as parents the Pershings and Abercrombies had a common interest, Cordelia decided—keeping Esther and Daniel apart.

She stretched, every muscle aching. She'd ridden in the wagon for much of the day, but the jostling hadn't been any easier than walking. And she worried about the effect of her exertions on the babe she carried. Could a child be shaken loose from the womb? Even in her eighth pregnancy, she didn't know everything about birthing.

Cordelia's mouth watered at the scent of frying meat. She'd been too tired to eat last night and crawled into bed as soon as Zeke and Joel set the tent up. Now she was ravenous. That was one thing about babies she did know—she had to eat for two, then worry about the weight later.

Esther poked her head into the tent. "Ma?" her daughter asked. "You hungry? I made you a plate of antelope steak and flapjacks. Mr. Abercrombie gave us the meat."

Cordelia sat up. "Mr. Abercrombie? Why'd he do that?"

Esther shrugged. "Don't know. Come eat. I saved the tenderest part for you."

Cordelia dressed and hurried out of the tent. The day was bright, with a soft May breeze. As she ate, her mind eased along with her hunger pangs.

"Where's your pa?" she asked Esther. The girl was the only child around the family's wagons. "And the young'uns?"

"Pa's down by the river. Twins went with him. Rachel took Ruthie and Noah to hunt for bird's eggs. Zeke and Joel are hunting with Mr. Abercrombie. Just you and me here for now."

"Your pa didn't go hunting?"

Esther shook her head. "He wanted to check out the Platte. Says it's full of quicksand."

Cordelia looked up from her plate. "And he has the twins with him? They'll get stuck in it for sure."

"It's all right, Ma. He'll watch 'em."

"He don't know how fast those boys can move."

When Cordelia finished eating, she and Esther washed dishes. "Think I'll do laundry today while we're resting," she told her daughter.

"That ain't resting." Esther sighed. "I'll tote the water, Ma. You stay here." She headed toward the river with two buckets.

Cordelia relished the quiet as she sat in the sun, which now shone from high above the horizon.

Franklin returned with the twins and Esther. Franklin and Jonathan carried one full bucket between them, and Esther and David had the other pail. "I'll bring you more water, Cordelia," Franklin said. "You and Esther get the washboard out. Boys," he said to the twins, "you're with me."

While she and Esther washed, Franklin and the twins toted bucket after bucket of muddy water. When it came time for rinsing, they had to let the sediment settle to the bottom of the pail, then pour the cleaner water slowly over the wet clothes, hoping not to add more dirt than they'd scrubbed out.

As soon as the clothes were hung on lines tied between the wagons, it was time to prepare the noon meal. Rachel and the younger children had brought back dried buffalo chips and a few small eggs. "Enough for a cake, do you think?" Cordelia asked Esther.

"Oh, Ma!" little Noah piped up. "A real cake? Like you made for my birthday?"

Laughing, Cordelia began mixing cake batter, while Esther and Rachel put salt pork and beans in a Dutch oven to boil. "I wish we had greens," Cordelia said.

"Maybe Mrs. Tuller or Hatty Tanner can help you find some," Franklin suggested. "Lots of plants growing along the river. Hatty seems right smart about such things."

It was worth asking, Cordelia decided. Negroes back home had gleaned wild foods Cordelia would never fix for her family. Here on the prairie, none of them could buy what they wanted in the store, and she'd dearly like some greens.

After they ate, she went to find Hatty, and Hatty took Cordelia and other women down to the riverbank to point out what was edible. That evening, they had boiled greens along with fresh antelope meat Zeke and Joel had shot.

They'd made it to the Platte, Franklin mused, as he sat in camp after supper. He didn't like the looks of the river, but it would guide their journey for the next several weeks. He wouldn't have to worry about following maps and recollecting what Frémont and Preuss had told him. Zeke and Daniel had done a good job of scouting, leading them straight to Grand Island. Franklin hadn't been worried about finding the Platte—head north, and they'd make it. But hitting the river at Grand Island meant they'd made it across the waterless plain in the shortest distance possible.

Despite the ease of following the Platte, he aimed to spend the next few days ahead of the wagons, looking for campsites. The maps marked a variety of waypoints, but he didn't want to blindly trust their accuracy— he'd rather see firsthand that the travelers would have adequate drinking water and grazing each night.

The next morning Franklin called the company to line up their wagons and ordered Samuel Abercrombie to lead them along the Platte. "I'm taking McDougall and Zeke ahead to find tonight's camp," he told Abercrombie. "You want your sons with you or with me?"

"Take Daniel as scout. I'll keep Douglass."

The four men set out on horseback ahead of the wagons. McDougall and Zeke rode first, Franklin and Daniel behind them. A warm wind blew from the southwest toward the Platte. Buffalo grazed in the hills to the south. Franklin nodded at the herd, then said to Daniel, "Your pa'd have half of 'em shot by now." Then he realized he probably shouldn't have maligned the young man's father.

Daniel shrugged. "Pa's always been one for shooting. Likes to hunt. Me, I can't shoot straight. Rarely get any game at all."

They rode until midday, when they encountered a group of Army surveyors. Franklin trotted ahead of the other scouts to talk to the man in charge, a Lieutenant Montgomery he'd met during his career. He saluted the officer, forgetting he was no longer in uniform.

"What's the Army doing here, Lieutenant?" he asked.

"Surveying land for a fort," Montgomery said. "Washington thinks Fort Kearny needs to be farther west to protect emigrants from Indians."

"But it ain't been many years since the Army built the current fort. Generals wanted it on the west bank of the Missouri, I thought," Franklin said.

"Don't matter. If Washington wants a new site, I'll find 'em one. You're leading wagons to Oregon? You seen any Indians?"

"Only those working at the river crossings," Franklin said. "I been watching, but ain't seen any tribesmen yet."

"Well, keep an eye out. They ride the hill crests, watching the pioneers. As long as they have river access and can hunt their buffalo, they usually just want to trade. But we've had a few horses stolen."

The other scouts arrived, and Franklin made the introductions. They agreed McDougall would stay to mark off a campsite near the Army tents, and the other three men would return to the wagons.

On the trip east toward the company, Franklin let Zeke and Daniel ride ahead. He kept the younger men in sight. He'd ask Zeke later what his opinion was of Daniel. Not that Franklin had any intention of letting young Abercrombie court Esther along the trail. Still, the young man seemed a quiet, reliable sort. Unlike his ornery father.

They found the wagons, then led the company west to the campsite McDougall had staked. Another emigrant company was also camped nearby.

Samuel Abercrombie groused about how the other company had passed them during the noon halt. "They're traveling faster'n we are. If you hadn't left me in charge and taken my son Daniel, I might well have asked if I could join up with them," he told Franklin.

Franklin pushed his hat back on his forehead and wiped his brow. He wished the Abercrombies had switched companies. "I'll keep that in mind. If you don't want me to use Daniel as scout again, I'll find someone else."

Abercrombie spat. "Lad needs experience. But he's a good tracker. Keep him scouting."

"You could talk to the other captain tonight." Franklin kept his voice mild. "About joining them."

"Might just do that."

"I'm planning to take a Sabbath rest tomorrow," Franklin said, hoping that might be the push Abercrombie needed to make the move.

"God damn it, we laid by yesterday." Abercrombie threw his hat on the ground. "You just want to jaw with Montgomery."

Pershing squinted. "Do what you think's best for your family. The rest of us are staying."

Daniel had enjoyed scouting with Captain Pershing, Zeke, and Mac McDougall. It was a relief to be away from his father for the day, and the fine weather made it a pleasure to ride. The vast valley of the Platte appealed to him. Buffalo herds with their craggy heads and shaggy bodies grazed majestically, while hawks soared overhead until they swooped to take their prey. As long as he wasn't supposed to be shooting them, Daniel loved watching the animals.

They set up camp near the soldiers, and word passed that after supper there would be a gathering of the soldiers and the two emigrant companies.

Pa said he wanted to talk to the other captain about joining his company to move faster.

"Do you think it's wise to change, Samuel?" Ma asked. "We don't know anything about those people."

"If they'll get to Oregon quicker, don't matter who they are. We'll be spending less time with them."

"Captain Pershing knows the route," Daniel said. "Shouldn't we stay with him?"

"You just want to make eyes at his daughter," Pa said. "I'm gonna see the other captain."

"What do you think he'll decide to do, Ma?" Daniel asked, after his father left.

She sighed. "He's probably right. It probably don't matter much who we travel with. But I like Cordelia Pershing and Elizabeth Tuller. I'd be sorry to leave them."

About the time Ma was ready to dish up supper, Pa returned, muttering under his breath. "Damn fool wants a hundred dollars for us to join up. He's a thief, not a captain."

"Some captains are making a living hiring their services, Pa. You know that," Douglass said, taking a plate. "We're lucky all Pershing wanted was a commitment to stand guard and pitch in with our labor."

"Has the other captain been to Oregon?" Daniel asked.

"Says he has. But he don't have a map." Pa shoveled in food from the plate Ma handed him. "Don't know what to believe. Guess we'll stick with Pershing awhile longer."

After they ate, the Abercrombies moved to the large bonfire between the camps. The men passed bottles of whiskey, and fiddlers played. They started with hymns, such as "Rock of Ages," but soon switched to songs like "Coming Through the Rye," then to "Durang's Hornpipe" when someone shouted for a dance tune.

There weren't enough women to partner all the soldiers and emigrant men in both companies. The younger women were in particular demand. Daniel watched Esther dance first with a bearded man from the other company and then with a grizzled sergeant. She wrinkled her nose at Daniel as they passed by, then sent a quick glance his way, raising her eyebrows. Her smile was more of a grimace.

When that song wound down, Daniel rose, wanting to claim her before some other old man took her away. He was at her side the moment the music stopped.

"May I have the next dance, Miss Pershing?" he asked, bowing and offering her his hand.

"Thank you, Mr. Abercrombie," Esther said, dropping the sergeant's hand and taking Daniel's. As he spun her away on the field, she smiled. "I've never been so happy to see anyone. That old man stank."

Daniel pulled her a bit closer. "Happy to be of service. But I hope the sergeant's strong scent isn't the only reason you're glad to see me."

Esther laughed. "Of course not, silly. I'd be happy to dance with you any day." She relaxed in his arms as they turned about the field. Her feet moved with his in time to the music, following like they'd danced together forever.

The music ended too soon, and another soldier stepped up to claim Esther, a young man this time. Daniel's arm tightened around her, and he had to force himself to release his protective hold. He bowed again, then went to sit by Mac McDougall.

Daniel watched Esther and the young soldier cavort across the dance area. "Esther sure is purty, ain't she?" he said to Mac.

"Lots of pretty girls," Mac said with a shrug.

But Esther was the only unmarried pretty girl Daniel noticed. He grimaced. "Why's she spending time with the soldiers? I'd dance with her all night."

"Tell her, not me," Mac said, getting up. "Think I'll turn in."

Daniel tormented himself watching Esther dance with one soldier after another, then claimed another dance himself. But Ma had always said he shouldn't dance with a girl more than twice, or he'd give her ideas. He wasn't sure he wanted to give Esther ideas. But he was darn sure he didn't want her dancing with the soldiers.

Chapter 17: Thinking of Marriage

Sunday, May 9, 1847. Laying by. Going hunting. FP

Esther frittered away most of the Sabbath morning after the prayer service. Many of the men—including her father, older brothers, and Daniel Abercrombie—went hunting. Her mother sat in camp sewing with Jenny McDougall and the doctor's wife. Jenny needed to make baby clothes, and Ma said she had mending to do. Ma took Ruth and Noah with her to Jenny's wagon, and the twins were wandering the prairie looking for buffalo chips. That left Rachel and Esther by themselves at the Pershing wagons. Rachel tended the stew for the noon meal.

Esther turned her face toward the bright sun and let it warm her skin. She should put on a sunbonnet to avoid freckling, but the heat made her too lazy to move. She exhaled a deep breath.

"Stop sighing," Rachel said. "You sound like a sick mare."

"There ain't nothing to do." Esther didn't want to sew. She had no cloth for new clothes, and the only fine work she had was a piece of embroidery. She hated needlework and had been working on the same pillowcase for months.

"Go help Ma with the mending."

Surely she could find something better to do, Esther thought. She and her friend Amy could chatter for hours, but she and Rachel didn't have as much in common. Without Jenny or Daniel available, Esther had no one she wanted to talk to. "Guess I'll take my embroidery over to the McDougall wagon." She fetched it and walked across camp.

The women sewed and talked about babies and diapers—boring topics, in Esther's mind. She wanted to think about romance, not the practicalities the married women discussed. She sat beside Jenny and glanced at the baby shirt Jenny had cut out of a piece of muslin. "Ain't that big for a newborn?" she asked.

"Mrs. Tuller told me to make it big," Jenny said. "So it'll last longer."

"Babies grow so quickly," Ma said, then frowned. "I'll need to find some shirts and diapers for my own. Guess I'll have to cut down what Noah's outgrown. That's all the cloth I got."

When Esther sighed, her mother looked at her. "You sound tired of living. Must be because young Daniel's out hunting."

"Ma!" Esther felt her cheeks redden. She didn't want Mrs. Tuller knowing her business.

"You do right to blush, girl. You spend too much time with that fellow." Ma pursed her lips after she spoke.

"I only danced with him twice last night," Esther muttered.

"Daniel seems like a nice young man," Mrs. Tuller said in a mild tone.

"Maybe," Ma said, sniffing. "Too soon to tell."

"You don't want me to have any fun," Esther complained. "I enjoy talking to Daniel. You don't want me to have any friends."

"You have Jenny," her mother said. "And there's plenty of fine women to talk to."

"But I want a beau." She saw Mrs. Tuller's lips twitch at her words. "Jenny's younger'n I am, and she's married. My friends back home were marrying. I want my own home in Oregon. My own babies." She wasn't sure where those words came from—hadn't she just been thinking about romance, not babies? But a little baby all her own would be sweet. And a husband coming home to her every night—that's what she really wanted.

"Careful, child," Ma said. "You don't know what you're saying. A house and babes are work. You like everything light and easy. I know how you try to get out of your chores."

"I do everything you tell me to, Ma—"

"But would you do it without me asking? When you're in charge of your own home, it's all up to you."

After the noon meal, Cordelia sat resting by the smoldering coals. The twins were by the river with other boys. She hoped they had the sense to avoid the quicksand—Franklin said he'd told them to watch where they stepped. Esther was with Jenny, and Rachel cared for Ruth and Noah.

She tried to nap, but all she could think of was Esther's foolishness. The girl was head-over-heels about Daniel Abercrombie, despite everything she and Franklin had said.

Cordelia would have to see that Esther spent more time with Jenny McDougall. Despite being pregnant before her marriage vows, Jenny was hard-working and level-headed, though she didn't seem to know a thing about caring for a baby. Esther could do worse than use her new friend as a model—she certainly shouldn't be mooning over Daniel.

Cordelia had other worries as well. Mrs. Dempsey would give birth any day now. How would the emigrants handle her confinement? Would Franklin stop the whole company? Would most of the wagons go on without the Dempseys, leaving them to catch up? Cordelia was prepared to help if need be, but she didn't want to be separated from her husband and children. Maybe Doc and Elizabeth Tuller would assist in the childbirth.

And Amanda Purcell remained almost incapacitated since her husband died. Cordelia and the other women still prepared meals for the Purcells. Cordelia would have been glad to provide for the stricken family had they been settled on farms, but out here in the wilderness, food supplies were less certain. She didn't want her family lacking to keep the Purcells fed.

Of course, the woman had a right to grieve. If it had been Franklin— Cordelia couldn't even finish the thought. She could not even consider crossing the foreign wilderness without him.

Though there was more risk of *her* dying than Franklin.

There, she'd articulated her biggest fear. That she would die in childbirth in this empty land, leaving her husband and eight children behind—or nine, if the babe survived. That she would be buried on the plain. Alone. Forever.

She shouldn't be so morbid. But she—like every woman she knew— feared dying in childbirth. It happened all too often.

"Ma?" Zeke's voice invaded her maudlin musings. "We shot eight buffalo. Rest of the men are field dressing the carcasses now. We'll haul the meat back in the Army wagon. Pa sent me to tell you to organize the women to divide and pack the meat when it gets here."

"So much for keeping the Sabbath," Cordelia said, sighing.

She rose and asked Clarence and Hatty Tanner and the older boys to build up the fires, then she rounded up women from the company. They set pots of water to boiling to cook the tougher cuts of meat and sharpened knives and saws to cut haunches into roasts. When the Army wagon pulled into camp, emigrants and soldiers worked together until late in the night carving the carcasses and distributing the meat.

By the time they finished, Cordelia was so tired she could barely undress. She crept into her blanket and felt Franklin's arms embrace her. Finally, she could relax.

Rain pounded the tent when Franklin awoke Monday morning. Today they would pull away from Grand Island and roll upstream along the Platte. The progress the company had made thus far pleased him, though the death of Charles Purcell caused waves of remorse whenever he thought of it. Samuel Abercrombie believed Franklin could have prevented the death. In his soul Franklin agreed.

He dragged himself away from Cordelia's warmth, dressed, and thrust his face out into the rain. Behind him, Cordelia stirred and murmured to Esther and Rachel to wake up.

Franklin went to check on the animals. McDougall stood by one of his oxen. "This one's lame," Mac said. "Favoring his left hind hoof."

The beast snorted when Franklin touched its hoof to examine it. "Best not yoke this pair today," he told Mac.

He continued his rounds, chatting with men throughout the company, and returned to his campsite. Cordelia had buffalo meat and johnny cakes frying.

After breakfast he ordered the men to pull the wagons into line. "You stay in the back, McDougall. You're short a team today."

"We ain't slowing down to favor his beast, are we?" Samuel Abercrombie groused. "If it ain't one thing causing you to poke along, it's another."

"I didn't say nothing 'bout slowing down." Franklin tried to keep his voice mild. "That's why I'm putting McDougall in the rear. If he can't keep up during the day, he'll have to catch up at nightfall."

Samuel grumbled and steered his wagon toward the front of the line.

Despite the rain, which fell steadily all day, the emigrants traveled eighteen miles along the river before supper time. Franklin smiled in satisfaction when he saw McDougall had stayed right behind the wagon ahead of his. The lawyer was no slouch. He'd come to the company with a level head and picked up plenty of trail knowledge along the way. And he could read a map better than Franklin.

As Franklin chewed more fried buffalo at supper, he wondered if Daniel Abercrombie's temperament might be more like McDougall's than Samuel's. If Daniel had half the common sense McDougall had, the lad might not be a bad husband for Esther.

Chapter 18: Women's Work

Monday, May 10, 1847. Traveled 20 miles along the Platte. FP

Rain still fell Tuesday morning. As soon as Cordelia pulled herself out of the tent, she checked the sack of buffalo chips under the wagon to be sure the twins hadn't left it out in the damp. After breakfast, she chose to begin the day riding rather than soak her skirt in the wet grass. She had only two skirts that fit now, swollen as she was by pregnancy. She hoped they would last another two months until the baby came.

It was hard to keep her family fed and clothed along the trail. They had meat from the hunting parties. Clarence and Hatty Tanner were resourceful about finding poke and other edible greens on the prairie and along the streams. Still, flour and cornmeal were running out faster than Cordelia had anticipated. The children ate a lot after walking for miles each day. Cooking for so many over an open fire was back-breaking work. Preparing meals and cleaning up afterward took most of the time Cordelia had in camp.

And she didn't know how they all managed to rip their clothes so often. Every day, it seemed, there was a new garment in her mending bag, and she'd only made a few shirts for the baby. She couldn't sew while bumping about in the wagon, which meant more work for evenings in camp when she was bone-weary.

"Ma," Esther said, "Daniel says he'll take me riding, if it's all right with you." Her daughter traipsed alongside the wagon. Cordelia didn't know where the girl had been since they started out that morning—probably talking with young Abercrombie, making plans to go riding now.

"Do you think that's wise?" Cordelia asked.

"It's so wet in the grass. Riding will save my skirt." Esther wore an oilskin cloak with a hood, but her skirt hung beneath it. She was soaked to the knees, her hem black with grime.

"I thought we talked about you staying away from that young man. And it's already too late for your skirt."

"But, Ma—"

"Where are Zeke and Joel? Can't you go with one of them? Or your pa?"

"Oh, Ma—"

"If all you want is to save your skirt from getting dirty, riding behind one of your brothers'll do fine."

Daniel Abercrombie rode over to the wagon and tipped his hat at Cordelia. "Morning, ma'am. Esther said she's getting wet. I'd be pleased to have her accompany me a spell."

The boy was so polite—unlike his father. His wide smile reminded Cordelia of Franklin when she'd first met him. She ought to forbid it, but found herself saying, "All right. But stay within sight of this wagon."

"Yes, ma'am." Daniel touched his hat brim again and gave her another grin. He removed his foot from the stirrup so Esther could use it as he pulled her up behind him. Then he reset his foot and kneed his horse into a fast walk. They rode off about twenty paces to the side of the wagon.

Cordelia kept her eye on them. Daniel pointed to something off in the distance. She tried to determine what he was showing Esther—perhaps the herd of antelope grazing ahead of the wagons near the Platte. Esther's laugh drifted across the prairie back to her mother.

Esther rode with Daniel an hour or more while the rain continued unabated. She felt warm, her torso protected by her heavy oilskin cloak and by the heat of Daniel's back against her breasts. Her skirt stayed wet, but it was out of the mud and grass.

At the noon halt, when she tried to remember what she and Daniel had talked about, she couldn't. She knew they'd laughed, and he'd pointed out antelope and a covey of quail that his pa's dog Bruiser flushed. The morning passed quickly, and she was sorry when Pa stopped the wagons for their midday meal.

Ma was in a bother, fussing over the food and barking orders at Esther and Rachel to hurry up.

"Why are you so cross, Ma?" Esther asked after the meal while they were scrubbing dishes. "It ain't because I was riding with Daniel, is it? I had a lovely time, and he was a perfect gentleman."

Ma snorted. "Not everything in life is about you, girl. Mrs. Dempsey's having contractions. Likely birth her babe today. I'm hoping she makes it to camp tonight afore she's too far into it."

"Shouldn't we stop here?"

"Could be hours yet. You know birthing takes time. And this is her first—could be all night."

"But ain't she uncomfortable?"

"Your pa suggested we halt, but Samuel Abercrombie won't have none of it." Ma sighed. "Threatened to go on."

"Well, we're following the Platte," Esther said. "We can't get lost."

"That's what Mr. Abercrombie said. But Pa said we'll all go on for now. Stop only if we have to. Doc and Mrs. Tuller'll look out for her."

Esther glanced up from wiping the skillet dry. She whispered the thought she'd had earlier—"I want my own baby. A little one to cuddle." She meant to say it only to herself, but Ma overheard.

"A baby! Esther Pershing, you have no need of a baby. You have a lot of growing up to do first."

"Ma—"

"If that's what riding with the Abercrombie boy makes you think of, you've had your last ride with him."

Ma's unfairness filled Esther's heart. Daniel was the best friend she'd had since leaving Amy in St. Charles. "My friends back home starting to marry. And here I am on this Godforsaken prairie—"

"Don't you blaspheme, young lady. You listen to me—"

"You don't care how I feel. All I want is someone of my own to love, like you and Pa have."

Ma's face fell. "Esther," she said softly, "it'll happen someday. There's no cause to rush. And not out here in the wilderness, where you're trapped with only folks in this company to consider."

"But, Ma, Daniel is nicer than any boy I've ever known. He'll have his own farm in Oregon. We can wed—"

"Wed? Has he said anything to you about marriage?"

"No."

"Well, you put a stop to it if he does. And no more horseback rides, that's for certain."

In midafternoon with the rain only slightly diminished, Harriet watched the Dempsey wagon pull out of line, followed by Doc Tuller's wagon. The birth was underway. Word had spread quickly among the women in the company over the noon hour that Mrs. Dempsey was in labor.

Harriet felt torn—wishing the baby about to come was hers, but glad she was not the one giving birth in the back of a cramped wagon in the wilderness. Motherhood was hard on a woman—hadn't it killed her sister Abigail?

When Samuel heard about Mrs. Dempsey's confinement, he fussed with Captain Pershing to keep going. Many of the women thought Samuel was heartless. But Harriet knew he was only trying to escape the sounds of a woman in pain, the sounds that preceded Abigail's death.

The Dempsey wagon kept up with the rest of them for a couple hours after the noon halt, occasional wails issuing from the woman inside. Just before their wagon and the Tullers' pulled away from the others, a loud scream sounded. Harriet said a small prayer, wondering how Doc and Mrs. Tuller could be of much help in the crowded confines of the Dempsey wagon.

The wagons rolled on until Captain Pershing stopped them for the evening in a small ravine near the Platte. The company set up camp and began supper preparations. Harriet glanced back along the trail, wondering whether the Dempseys and Tullers would catch up that night.

She sent Annabelle and Rose to collect buffalo chips, but all they found were damp patties, which she had them hang in a sack under the wagon to dry. "At least we have dry chips enough to cook tonight," she told them.

Another band of travelers camped in a ravine a quarter mile farther upstream on the Platte. Emigrants from that company wandered into the Pershing group's camp after supper, including two Roman Catholic priests from France.

Samuel refused to talk to the "papists," as he called them. "Don't need no bead-rattling idol worshipers," he said. "Keep our girls away from them."

Harriet didn't see what harm talking to the priests could do. A blessing for the woman in labor might even help. Still, to appease Samuel, she stayed away, praying for Mrs. Dempsey on her own. She saw Jenny McDougall talking to the priests, and even praying with them in French.

Not long after, the Dempsey and Tuller wagons pulled into camp. Elizabeth Tuller came to tell Harriet the Dempseys had a baby girl.

"I'll dish up some buffalo stew," Harriet told Mrs. Tuller. "I have enough for the Dempseys and you and your husband as well." She took the meal to the Dempsey wagon, where she saw the tiny infant cradled in her mother's arms. Mrs. Dempsey beamed.

Harriet swallowed her envy and said, "How blessed you are. Your daughter is beautiful."

Esther and her mother took a meat pie over to the Dempsey wagon, but found Harriet Abercrombie had already brought stew. "We'll leave the pie," Ma told Mrs. Dempsey. "You can eat it for breakfast. You won't want to be cooking in the morning."

"Thank you kindly, Mrs. Pershing," Mrs. Dempsey said. She all but preened over her status as a new mother.

Esther wondered again if she'd have a child someday. If Ma had anything to say about it, Esther wouldn't marry for another decade. Ma had forbidden her to spend time with Daniel, and Esther wouldn't meet any other eligible young men until she reached Oregon. She hadn't forgotten her plan to marry Daniel, but she wasn't making much progress toward the goal.

The Dempsey baby was a puny one. Esther remembered Ruth and Noah's births, eight and four years ago respectively. Both of those newborns had cried lustily, their little chests pumping and their cheeks reddening with the effort to make their needs known. Her babies would be Pershings, she was sure—healthy from the start. Daniel Abercrombie's family looked hale also—he'd make strong babies. Her body pulsed at the notion of creating a child with Daniel.

Jenny McDougall visited the Dempsey camp while Esther and her mother were there. "Let's go sit a spell," Esther whispered to Jenny when the older women began comparing labor pains. Daniel's stepmother, Harriet Abercrombie, walked away with pursed lips.

Esther steered her friend toward Jenny's wagon. "Your campfire will be quieter than ours. I don't know when Ma'll be back. She told me I can't ride with Daniel anymore. All because I mentioned marrying him."

"I've told you to get to know him better before you think about marriage." Jenny poured them each a cup of coffee.

"We talked so easily this morning. And it felt so comfortable and safe, riding behind him." Esther sipped the coffee. "I want a baby like Mrs. Dempsey and Ma. And you—aren't you glad you're pregnant?"

Jenny's coffee sloshed from her cup. "Gracious, I'm clumsy."

"Well, aren't you? You have a handsome husband and a baby on the way." Esther sighed. "I wish I were so lucky."

"I know I'll love my child," Jenny whispered into her mug, then she frowned at Esther. "But it isn't easy, you know. I've been sick, and I'm starting to get heavy—like your mama—and I don't want to give birth in a wagon like Mrs. Dempsey, though we'll likely still be traveling when my time comes. And I don't know who'll help me—" Her voice rose into hysteria.

Esther dropped to her knees beside Jenny. "Shhh, it'll be all right. My ma'll help you. And Mrs. Tuller. I've helped at Ma's births, too. Lots of women around. You'll be fine." Her dreams of romance didn't include the drudgery of being a wife and mother, only the love she hoped to find. Ma handled all the hard work in stride—the chores, the childrearing, the cooking and cleaning. But seeing Jenny overwhelmed by impending motherhood made Esther think. There was more to marriage than snuggling up to Daniel and seeing the sights on the prairie.

Chapter 19:   Indian Strike

Tuesday, 11 May 1847. Horse went missing in the night. Found it by noon. Rained all day. FP

Daniel's father rousted him out of bed while it was still dark Wednesday morning with the words, "We're hunting today. Saddle up." Daniel would much rather have had Esther ride with him again than shoot at buffalo or antelope, but he knew better than to argue when Pa gave him a direct order. Bleary-eyed, he dressed, ate the biscuits and gravy Ma had ready, then rode off behind his father.

At least the rain was past. They trotted south away from the river. As the sun rose over Daniel's left shoulder, the sky turned purple, then amber, before lightening to bright blue. A herd of antelope bounced out of a small ravine as the men came to its crest. Pa raised his rifle and dropped one.

"Why didn't you shoot?" he shouted at Daniel.

"Didn't think I had a good shot, and didn't want to spoil yours."

Pa led the hunting party into the ravine and back up the far side to where the dead animal lay. They dressed the carcass, and Pa slung it behind his saddle wrapped in oilcloth. "Let's see what else we can find. Maybe you can get a trophy for your girl," Pa said as he lashed the parcel tightly.

"Esther? She ain't my girl."

"You spent half the morning yesterday with her hanging on your waist, cuddled up behind you. 'Oh, Daniel, this,' and 'Oh, Daniel, that.' She gave a purty good impression of being your girl."

Daniel kept silent. He wasn't sure whether he wanted Esther as his girl—whether he was ready to call any girl "his"—but he didn't like his father taunting him about it.

By midmorning they headed back to the wagons without killing any more game. Their company had passed other parties of emigrants, which put Pa in a good mood when they rejoined their group at the noon camp. Pa gave the antelope meat to Ma and told her to cut a piece for the Pershings and another for the Purcells. "Keep the steaks for us, but the others might need stew meat. Let Daniel take it to them. He can't shoot worth a darn, but he can make nice to the neighbors."

They made good time that afternoon and camped for the night in a hollow near the Platte.

The next day brought more fine weather and another hunting party. Pa took Douglass with him, leaving Daniel to tend the wagons.

"Think we'll look for buffalo today," Pa announced as the hunters left camp. "I have a hankering for the tongue." His father spoke loudly enough that Daniel thought Captain Pershing must have heard.

Sure enough, the captain's jaw tightened, and he stared at the departing men. "Don't know why Abercrombie's always hunting," Captain Pershing said. "Buffalo will be around for weeks yet. Don't need more meat, and all the killing will rile the natives."

With his father gone, Daniel looked for Esther, hoping to walk or ride with her again. But she stayed close to her mother and siblings, and he couldn't get a word privately with her. He didn't want to brave Mrs. Pershing again, so he scouted with Mac McDougall and the captain.

Pa returned in the evening. Each man in the hunting party had bloody packages of meat tied to his saddle. "Shot five antelope," Pa said. "Fresh game again tonight. Come take what you want." His gesture invited everyone in the company to partake. Captain Pershing turned away, spitting on the ground, but most families took something.

"Don't look like five whole carcasses here," Doc Tuller said. "What'd you do with the rest of the meat?"

Pa shrugged. "Indians'll take our leavings. Unless wolves or coyotes get there first."

Daniel ate the fresh antelope willingly, but he hated the idea of so many animals dying when their company didn't need the food. Pa treated his own stock fine, but didn't care about the wild beasts on the plains. And he didn't care what others in their group thought of him either.

After listening to Samuel Abercrombie describe the hunt and the antelope meat they'd left behind, Franklin Pershing stalked off to his campfire in disgust. "Waste of good meat. Likely to stir up the Indians in these parts, too," he told Cordelia.

"Shhh, Franklin. You'll scare the children," Cordelia whispered. "Are there Indians nearby?"

Too riled up to stay still, he rummaged for his pipe and tobacco and lit the pipe. "Damn straight. Indians everywhere. They depend on the buffalo and antelope. Don't mind us white folk killing what we need, but they don't want good meat rotting on the ground. See it as taunting the spirits, or some such nonsense."

"Do you think the Indians will bother us?"

Franklin shrugged. He didn't want to upset his wife. "They don't usually. But they're not predictable. Best keep the young'uns close to the wagons tonight."

"You tell 'em," Cordelia said. "They mind you better'n they do me."

That evening Franklin talked to the platoon sergeants about posting double guards.

In the middle of the night, Franklin was awakened when a man yelled, "Indians!" followed by the sound of bloodcurdling whoops. The hair rose on his arms and neck—he'd heard similar howls during Army skirmishes with the tribes.

Franklin pulled on his pants, grabbed his rifle, and stuck his head outside the tent. Men, women, and children dashed about the camp in confusion, hollering and shrieking. "Get in your wagons or take cover, if you're not armed," he called, racing into the melee. "Men, what happened?"

"I seen Indians," a man named Lennox said. "I had the watch, and they come right through camp, leading some of our horses." He gestured at a gap in the wagon circle. "Wagons ain't chained. Damn savages come right through to the horses."

"God damn it," Franklin shouted. "I've told you fools every night to check the wagons. You said you were on guard?" he asked Lennox.

"I musta dozed off," the man said sheepishly.

As he questioned Lennox and others, Franklin deduced five horses had been stolen. "Saddle up!" he ordered. "We'll track 'em down."

"Jesus," Samuel Abercrombie said. "It's pitch black, and my horse was rode hard yesterday."

"That's your own damn fault. You should have stayed with the wagons," Franklin said. "You can be a part of the search party or not, your decision. But most likely the tribes got stirred up because you been wasting meat."

Franklin sent men east, west, and south. He didn't think the Indians would go north across the Platte at night. Franklin took command of the group headed south, and put Abercrombie in charge of the party headed east—the direction he judged the tribesmen least likely to go. He didn't want Abercrombie to cause any more trouble with the Indians than he already had.

Cordelia took her crying children back to the family's wagons. "Bed down in my tent. Esther'll watch over you," she said, though Esther was shaking as much as Ruth and Noah.

She was sure she wouldn't sleep until Franklin returned. He'd seemed to know what he was doing—his Army training had risen to the challenge. But she'd never seen him handle a skirmish, and she worried for his safety. Plus, Zeke and Joel were in the search party. She might lose three loved ones tonight.

Once her children were in bed, she walked around camp, comforting other women and children. Many had built up their fires. "I want to be able to see the thieving bastards when they come back," Mrs. Baker said—a woman not normally given to harsh language. She brandished an old musket, and Cordelia wondered if she even knew how to load it.

When Cordelia reached Jenny McDougall's wagon, she found the girl sobbing inside.

"What's wrong?" Cordelia asked.

"Mac's with the search party, and I'm scared."

Cordelia sighed. "You're all alone, poor thing. Come to our camp. You can sit with me, or bed down with Esther. I won't be sleeping."

Jenny clambered out of her wagon and pulled a shawl around her shoulders. "Thank you," she whispered, squeezing Cordelia's arm with one hand. Jenny's other hand cradled her belly, which now showed a small swell of pregnancy.

After leaving Jenny to crawl into the tent with Esther, Cordelia continued to encourage and comfort other women in camp. She noticed Harriet Abercrombie and Elizabeth Tuller doing the same.

"At a certain age a woman realizes comfort's all we got to give," Elizabeth said to the other two after they'd done their best to calm their fellow travelers. "That and a hot cup of coffee. I got some brewing. You want to sit a spell?"

The three women talked until dawn, then roused the rest of the camp to make breakfast. The men didn't return until midmorning.

Franklin was in the first group back. When he returned, Cordelia rushed over and clung to his arm, glad to have him close again. "Where are Zeke and Joel?" She wanted her boys with her as well as her husband.

"Sent 'em to bring back the other search parties. We found the horses."

"Where?" She still clutched his arm.

"In a small Pawnee camp south of here. Tribe'll bring 'em here in an hour."

"The Indians are coming here?" Cordelia's voice rose, and her free arm clasped her womb to cradle the unborn child—poor babe might not make it to birth, she thought.

"I traded with the tribe. They'll give us the horses for blankets and a knife." He grinned. "They already got my knife." Every inch a commander, he turned away from Cordelia and shouted at his men. "Each man that lost a horse needs to give a blanket." He pulled away and left her alone to wait for Zeke and Joel. And the Indians.

Samuel Abercrombie led his men into the wagon camp. A wild goose chase. They'd seen no sign of any Indians. He'd been about to turn back on his weary mount when Zeke Pershing rode up to say the Indians and stolen horses had been found.

"Where?" he asked, and Zeke explained.

"Your pa is trading to get them horses back?" Samuel shouted. "Why didn't you just shoot the savages?"

"There were only seven of us and a whole village of Pawnee," Zeke said.

"I'll have a word with your pa," Samuel fumed, irate at the notion of bargaining with Indians.

Just after his group returned, several braves rode into camp, herding the five horses the tribe had taken. Pershing gave the Pawnee chief five blankets, and added a small bag of tobacco, saying, "Keep away from our camp."

The Indians rode off silently.

Samuel snorted and spat. He glared at Pershing and said, "They'll come begging every night, if'n you treat 'em nice. Indians only understand buckshot."

"It's almost noon," Pershing said, turning to the rest of the company. "Let's eat, then head out."

All afternoon Samuel rehashed the wasted night and day. His gelding plodded along, stumbling on occasion. Poor horse must be exhausted after hunting for two days straight, then riding the prairie all night, and now another day on the trail. Pershing was no leader, if he couldn't keep his men from letting a bunch of Indians steal their horses.

"Why don't you walk a bit and let your horse rest, Pa?" Daniel said.

"This horse can go longer'n any other mount in the company," Samuel said. "He'll still be going when I'm dead. Despite what Pershing does. The damn fool paid too much to get those horses back."

"Just a blanket each, Pa—"

"And come winter, those families what had to give up blankets will be sorry."

Esther could tell the incident with the Pawnee had upset Pa. And Ma, too. Ma clung to Pa when she thought the children weren't watching, and she snapped at little Noah when he complained of hunger in midafternoon.

On the day after the confrontation with the Pawnee braves, Esther saw Indians riding the ridge to the south as the emigrant wagons rolled along the Platte. She pointed them out to Pa.

He nodded. "You keep close to the wagons today, daughter. Don't go riding or walking off too far. Stay near me. Don't rely on that young Abercrombie boy to protect you."

"I'm not, Pa—"

"Just do as I say, girl. I'm serious. I don't think the Pawnee'll bother us again, but I don't want some young brave thinking a white girl with pretty yellow hair would make him a good squaw."

Esther swallowed hard. She knew Pa was serious about her staying close, and she understood why. But she didn't like him trying to scare her either. She wasn't a child he could frighten into behaving. If she was old enough to have noticed the Indians, she was old enough to take care of herself.

Though it would be nice to have a man watching out for her. Not her father, but a man who cared just for her. A man like Daniel Abercrombie.

Daniel had stopped by their camp after supper last night while Esther scrubbed mud from the twins' shirts. "You all right?" he asked.

She smiled. "Fine. You must be tired after riding all night."

He nodded. "It was worth it to get the horses back."

"Yes. Pa seems to have handled it well."

Daniel shrugged. "My father says yours paid too much. But I say, all's well that ends well."

Esther wondered if Daniel really thought that or was just being nice. Did he think like his father did—that Pa wasn't a good captain? She loved her pa, but she didn't know how men reckoned, or what made one man respect another. She didn't understand this strange world on the prairie.

Still, if Daniel was going to be her husband someday, she'd have to figure out how to get him and Pa working together. Or would Daniel follow what his pa said all his life?

Chapter 20:   Talking of Marriage

Saturday, 15 May 1847. Pawnee continue to follow our wagons, but no more trouble yet. FP

Harriet Abercrombie felt eyes on her back all day Sunday as they trekked along the Platte, uneasy about the possible return of Indians. She'd anticipated another argument between Samuel and Captain Pershing over whether they would take a Sabbath rest or continue their journey. But either the men worked it out quietly or the captain didn't even suggest laying by.

The rain returned, and the dark skies added to her sense of unease. Something evil lurked in the atmosphere. She wasn't usually given to fancies, but she feared more death or disagreement would find them.

Daniel walked over to join her. "How you holding up, Ma?" he asked.

She smiled for his sake. "Fine, Daniel."

"Captain Pershing sure managed to get us out of the Indian skirmish easy enough. No blood shed, anyway."

"Yes, son, that's a good thing."

"Pa don't think so."

Harriet sighed. "No. But your pa don't often see the benefit to taking the peaceable way out of a problem."

"Thinks it makes him less of a man." Daniel snorted. "But a real man needs a kit of ways to deal with trouble. Not just belligerence."

Harriet took her son's arm, leaning on him a bit. "You're turning out to be a wise young man, Daniel."

"I just wish I had more ways to deal with Pa." Daniel hugged her arm close to him. "I don't like arguing with him. But he's plain wrong sometimes, and won't listen to reason. You should've heard him arguing with Captain Pershing about giving blankets to the Pawnee."

"I know you don't like fighting, son. And it's fine to avoid it when you can—like Captain Pershing did. But there will be times when you need to take a stand."

"Like about Esther," Daniel commented.

Harriet swallowed hard. Was Daniel serious about the girl? She hadn't thought so, but maybe she didn't know everything about her son. "What do you mean?" she asked.

"He tells me to stay away from her. But there's no harm in us larking about. Ain't many young folk in the company."

"I told you to stick with Zeke and Joel Pershing. And Mac McDougall."

"I meant girls, Ma. Esther's the only girl in the company I like."

"Are you serious about her?" She wanted to know, though she wasn't sure she'd like his answer.

"I don't know. But I'd like to figure that out myself. Without Pa interfering."

Harriet sighed in relief. "Just take your time, son. You have all the way to Oregon and beyond to find out."

The emigrants ate a quick noon meal of cold stew while rain continued to pour. When they got underway Esther begged her mother to let her ride with Jenny. "It's so crowded in our wagon, Ma," she said. "And Jenny's all alone. She was with Mrs. Tuller this morning, but now she's by herself." Esther had plans to make—plans that needed Jenny's assistance.

When her mother nodded, Esther ran to Jenny's wagon and called, "May I join you?"

Mac McDougall stopped the wagon long enough for Esther to climb in. She sat on the bench by Jenny and asked, "Will you walk with me and Daniel tomorrow?"

"If it's nice," her friend replied.

"I'll bring Rachel or Ruth, so you have someone to stay with you,"

Esther told Jenny. "I need to be alone with Daniel, so he'll declare."

"Declare what?"

"That he wants to marry me!" Esther wondered again if she was the only person in this wagon company with any romance in her soul. "How'd you get Mr. McDougall to ask you?"

Jenny shrugged. "It just happened."

Esther sighed, wondering how Jenny had made steely Mac McDougall decide on marriage. "Didn't you know he would?"

Jenny shook her head. "I was very surprised."

"Well, I'm going to make it happen," Esther said, clasping her hands to her breast. "Ma says the Lord helps those who help themselves."

"You've only known Daniel a month."

"He's handsome enough, ain't he?" Daniel wasn't as polished and educated as Jenny's husband, but Esther didn't covet her neighbor's spouse—she liked Daniel better.

"His father's a tyrant."

Esther shrugged. "I ain't marrying his father."

"What do your parents think?"

"I haven't asked 'em." Esther sighed. "Of course, Daniel will have to ask Pa. But Pa'll let me do what I want." She knew she could get around Pa, it was Ma she worried about. Still, Ma wanted her married at some point—why not to Daniel?

"Esther!" Ma's voice came sharply from beside the McDougall wagon. "Esther, I need you. Ruthie's feeling poorly. Will you sit with her in our wagon?"

Esther shrugged at Jenny and clambered to the ground. As she walked back to their wagon with Ma, Ma asked, "What will Daniel have to ask your father?"

"Nothing, Ma." She gulped, wondering how much Ma had heard.

"You're not serious about the Abercrombie boy, are you? I've told you—"

"I know, Ma." They reached the wagon where Ruth lay on a pallet. "What's wrong with her?" Esther asked, as Joel stopped the oxen to let Esther climb up.

"Something she ate, I think. She was puking."

"Wagon bumping about won't do her no good."

"Just sit with her and keep her quiet. There's a basin, if she pukes again." Ma put her hand on the wagon so Joel wouldn't start the teams moving yet. "Don't you think about wedding that boy. You're way too young."

"I thought you wanted me to settle down." Esther cuddled her little sister, who whimpered and moaned.

"Not yet. You need to grow up some more afore you have babes of your own. You're not ready to be a wife and mother."

Travel along the Platte remained uneventful through Sunday and Monday, for which Franklin gave thanks. They saw no more signs of Indians, though he was sure the tribes were still in the vicinity.

He turned his worries to crossing the south fork of the Platte. How would he know when they reached the ford? He had Frémont's maps, but finding the exact point to cross might be difficult. He knew they needed to pass the junction of the North Platte and South Platte branches before they would cross. Then, would he remember enough from the trip in forty-two to find the best location?

The rains had left them, and the weather turned warm. Franklin rode ahead of the wagons, map in his hand. Now mid-May, spring was well advanced. The hills to the south were verdant, grasses growing taller by the day and wildflowers adding bright colors to the green. The buffalo herds they passed grazed lazily, and a pair of finches chirped from small bushes near the river.

Franklin watched McDougall and his wife ride their black stallion through the hills, and he wondered who McDougall had watching his wagon. Franklin wished he could lark about with Cordelia the way the young couple did. But he had a wagon company to lead.

Samuel Abercrombie had taken another hunting party out, and Franklin heard gunshots from the south. No doubt Abercrombie would return that night boasting about his prowess with a rifle.

Franklin hoped Abercrombie was shooting buffalo, not Indians. The company had been damn lucky to get their horses back from the Pawnee without anyone getting hurt. He'd managed to let the Indians save face at little cost to the settlers, but would he be able to avoid similar skirmishes through the next several months? Oregon was still a long way off.

Returning to the wagons, Franklin saw Esther walking near the river with Daniel Abercrombie. Cordelia had cornered Franklin the night before, telling him Esther was too serious about the boy.

"I heard her tell Jenny McDougall Daniel would have to talk to you," Cordelia said. "He hasn't, has he?"

"Talked to me about what?" Franklin asked.

"About marrying her."

"Marrying! The boy hardly knows her."

"I think she's a lot more serious about Daniel than she's telling us, Franklin. You have to put a stop to her nonsense."

"I talked to her already." He remembered the conversation he'd had with Esther on the banks of the Wakarusa. Maybe she hadn't understood him then, though he thought she had. Maybe another chat was in order.

He snorted. It was easier to make sense of Samuel Abercrombie than his own daughter.

By nightfall they reached the junction of the north and south forks of the Platte. Franklin examined the river, but it looked too broad to cross. He debated whether to travel another day on the south fork. Abercrombie argued for staying south of the river because he thought the hunting was better. The Tennessean had shot more buffalo that day, taking tongues and organs for his family and letting the rest of the company butcher the remains. The hunters left more meat in the field than they took.

As Franklin paced the shore of the muddy river, Esther joined him. "Ma says you want to talk to me," she said.

Franklin grunted. Just like Cordelia to push him to act. He had more important things on his mind than an infatuated girl. Staring into the water, he said, "Your ma thinks you're getting too serious about young Daniel Abercrombie."

"Pa, I ain't—"

"I worry about your ma." Maybe guilt would keep Esther in line. "She's got the babe coming and all our family to care for. She ain't as young as she used to be. She needs you to be a help, not a bother."

"But, Pa, I already work as hard as Ma does."

"I know you do, daughter. You're a good girl." He put an arm around

Esther's shoulders. She was taller than Cordelia. Full grown, and a lovely young woman. Dimples like Cordelia's. "Just make sure she don't have cause to fret about you. We all have enough concerns without a couple of young'uns thinking they're in love. Besides"—he gave her shoulders a squeeze—"you can do a lot better'n Samuel Abercrombie's son."

Esther was silent.

"Then I won't be hearing anything from young Daniel about the two of you wanting to wed, will I?"

"No, Pa," she whispered.

Tuesday morning dawned bright and warm. Daniel rode his horse along the Platte near the wagons. According to Captain Pershing, they would reach the river crossing today. For the moment, he was alone, and he relished the solitude. Pa and Douglass were tending the wagons. Pa was upset about a raw sore on one ox's neck from the yoke. Though Pa's ranting wouldn't help the beast to heal. Daniel's horse liniment was more likely to do the trick.

Daniel remembered Ma's caution two days earlier to move slowly with Esther. Hell, he wasn't the one trying to push a romance—Esther was. Esther was a pretty girl, and he liked her, but he didn't want to rush into marriage. He'd kissed her one time and taken her for a horseback ride on the prairie. That didn't mean he had to wed her, did it?

Still, if he were married, he'd be his own man. Have his own house on his own land. And Esther in his bed every night. He could think of a worse future—such as living with Pa while they built their farms in Oregon. Doing Pa's bidding every day. And every evening, too.

Was he ready to rile his parents by marrying Esther? Was Esther really angling to get hitched, or was she playing some girlish game?

The Platte didn't offer any answers to his questions as he stared into its muddy waters.

"Daniel!" Esther called from behind him. He turned. She hurried toward him with Jenny McDougall and some of the younger Pershings following her.

He dismounted and waited for them to catch up. "What is it?" he asked.

She smiled. "Just wanted to walk with you a spell." She took his arm.

He smiled back at her, and they walked on, Jenny behind them with Esther's siblings. He decided he could take his time considering his questions about Esther—move slowly with her, as Ma had suggested. For the moment, he would simply enjoy the pretty girl's presence beside him, her hand on his arm, his mare's reins grasped in his other hand.

Shortly after the noon meal, the emigrants encountered another wagon company in the process of fording the Platte. Captain Pershing had scouted ahead with two of the platoon leaders, Mac McDougall and Josiah Baker. The three men now talked with others in their company.

"We watched them other wagons cross. They didn't have any trouble," Captain Pershing said. "We been across on horseback. Never reached the horses' bellies. We'll ford here."

"Any quicksand?" Daniel's father asked the captain. "You been telling us there's quicksand in the Platte."

"As long as we keep moving, we'll be all right. But if we stop, the wagons and teams could get stuck."

"River's still mighty broad here," another man said.

Captain Pershing nodded. "We'll post men in the river to hurry the wagons along. Make sure no one stalls in the water."

"Best make sure you got men downstream as well as up," Pa said. "So no one drowns like Purcell did."

"We'll set out in the morning. First light," the captain said.

Chapter 21:   Crossing the South Platte

Tuesday, 18 May 1847. Reached the South Platte ford. Tomorrow we cross. FP

Esther fretted about her talk with Pa. He'd been so serious about her not marrying Daniel, even though she enjoyed spending time with Daniel and yearned to be wed.

For now, she concentrated on the wagon Pa had told her to drive across the Platte. Pa insisted Zeke and Joel stay in the river with him and other men to guide the company across, so Ma and Esther had to manage the Pershing family's wagons. Esther sat on one bench, the twins and Ruthie behind her under the cover. Ma dealt with the other wagon and had Rachel and Noah with her.

Daniel Abercrombie was also with the men in the river. Esther watched for him every day, wanting to always know where he was.

When it was Esther's turn, she tapped the whip on the lead ox and yelled, "Go!" The placid beast snorted, then moved ahead into the water. She looked back—Ma's wagon followed.

It was a long way across the broad Platte, but the water didn't quite reach as high as the wagon bed. Still, the twins and Ruth shrieked when they reached the deepest part. "Stop it," Esther ordered.

"They're going to push me out!" Ruth wailed.

"Boys, don't tease her."

The twins chortled, and Ruth whimpered.

After about half an hour of lumbering across the wide river, the oxen climbed out the north side, shaking their huge heads and quickening their pace. Ma's wagon remained right behind Esther's.

"You doing all right?" Esther shouted at her mother.

Her mother steered the other wagon beside Esther and nodded. Ma was wheezing, but she smiled. Esther went first as the Pershing wagons pulled away from the river to a small rise and into a line with the other wagons that had finished crossing.

Esther climbed down and told her mother, "I'm going back to watch the wagons behind us. Jonathan and David, you mind this wagon." The twins took her place on the bench.

When Esther returned to the bank of the Platte, she noticed a commotion in the middle of the river. One of the last wagons to cross had stopped, apparently stuck. Four others halted behind it. Men thronged around the stalled wagon. She couldn't make out whose wagon caused the problem, only that it was pulled by mules. The next wagon behind veered around the mired wagon, until the oxen hauling it bellowed and a woman screamed.

Her brother Zeke—at least she thought it was Zeke—jumped off his horse and onto the bench of the wagon that had turned out of line, while another man pulled on the lead team. The wagon with Zeke now driving made its way slowly toward the shore where Esther stood. Then she could see it was the McDougall wagon, with Jenny cowering on the bench beside Zeke. Daniel waded out of the river, herding two of the McDougall oxen that were no longer yoked to the wagon.

"Are you all right?" Esther asked, hurrying over to Jenny after casting a smile at Daniel. She wondered if he would have rescued her if she'd been in trouble like Jenny had been. Though she hadn't needed rescuing, Esther realized smugly—she'd handled her wagon as well as Zeke or Joel could have.

"Sinkhole," Zeke said. "Quicksand. Tanners' wagon got caught, too." He nodded back at the wagon and mules just now pulling out of the river. "McDougall's lead pair plunged into it."

Mac McDougall helped Jenny down from the wagon, and Zeke pointed to a strip of nearby grass where she could sit. Esther followed Jenny, passing by her mother's wagon.

"Esther," her sister Rachel called. "Ma's poorly."

145

Esther stopped. "Ma? What is it?"

"Just a stitch in my side," Ma said, but she was holding her stomach.

"It ain't the baby, is it?" Esther asked, fear rising to her throat. It was far too soon.

Ma shook her head. "Don't think so. Just the excitement." But her color didn't look good.

Esther forgot Jenny and climbed up beside her mother. "You get in back, Ma, and rest. I'll mind this wagon. Rachel, you help the twins with the other one."

Cordelia gratefully crawled into the back of the wagon, where Noah sat on a pallet. He moved over and made room for her. She put an arm around her youngest boy and tried to breathe deeply. But her chest caught when she got half a lungful of air. Was the baby pushing up too hard? She still had two months to go. The child would be pushing a lot harder before she was done.

"You comfortable, Ma?" Esther said from the wagon bench. "We need to move on now."

"I'll be fine," Cordelia said, closing her eyes when the wagon slowly swayed. Esther might be flighty, but when it counted, the girl could be trusted.

"I'll tell Pa," Jonathan said from outside the wagon.

"Don't you trouble your pa," Cordelia said. Franklin had plenty to worry about without her.

After a few minutes, the wagon stopped. "We're waiting on the Tanners, Ma." Esther said. "They got mired in the river and had to unload. Now they're loading back up. The McDougalls got stuck, too, but they're all right."

Something always seemed to go wrong on a river crossing, Franklin reflected, as he inspected Tanner's wagon—a cracked wheel spoke was the worst of the damage, along with some spilled food. It was late afternoon. Franklin had ordered all the wagons moved along the north bank of the

Platte, away from the crossing.

"That ain't too bad," Samuel Abercrombie said, standing beside Franklin. "He's a carpenter. He can fix it." The Negro was a good handyman, capable of mending almost anything made of wood or iron.

"How long will it take?" Mac McDougall asked.

"Day or so, I 'spect," Tanner said.

"We'll lay by tomorrow then," Franklin decided.

"Lay by? The rest of the wagons are fit. He can catch up," Abercrombie said, spitting a stream of tobacco juice.

"You can hunt again tomorrow. Don't that keep you happy?" Franklin knew he sounded churlish, but he'd had about all he could take of Abercrombie. The man told Franklin to issue orders like a captain should, then he argued with everything Franklin said. "I said we're laying by, and we will."

He sought out his own wagons and found Esther and Rachel making supper. "Where's your ma?" he asked.

"Sleeping in the wagon," Esther said.

"She all right?"

Esther shrugged, and Rachel looked unhappy. "She got tired. Says it hurts to breathe," Esther said.

"The baby?"

Esther shook her head. "She says not."

Franklin climbed up the rear wheel and stuck his head in the wagon. "Cordelia? What's wrong?"

"I'm fine, Franklin." She sounded tired.

"You rest. The girls can manage supper. And we're laying by tomorrow. Got to fix the Tanners' wagon."

He went to the campfire, but his daughters had meal preparations well in hand. "I'm going to make my rounds with the platoon leaders. I'll be back to eat," he told Rachel.

"Yes, Pa."

Twilight had fallen by the time he returned to his family's wagons, hungry for supper. The men he'd talked to had wanted to chaw over the river crossing and whether to lay by on the day ahead. Some were upset at Abercrombie's continued belligerence, and others thought there was no need to wait for the Negro carpenter and his family. Franklin declared time and time again the company needed to stick together—he didn't want them

147

leaving anyone behind to fend for themselves.

"We left the Dempsey and Tuller wagons," one man told him. "For a woman in childbirth. That ain't no different than a broken wheel."

"That was two wagons, not one. And I probably shouldn't have left them," Franklin said.

"Bet you'll halt the whole company when your wife's time comes," another man said.

"Yes, I will. And you'll damn well halt with me." Franklin thought again of Cordelia's seeming fragility. He wished he knew whether she'd been like this with her earlier pregnancies.

The next morning a cold rain soaked everything in camp. Cordelia seemed heartier, and Franklin decided to scout the route to the north fork of the Platte, where they would cross the water again. "I'm taking Zeke with me," he told Cordelia.

"Best you talk to him about Jenny McDougall," she said. "Elizabeth Tuller says folks are gossiping again. This time about how he helped her out yesterday."

Franklin snorted. "Weren't nothing to it. Woman panicked, and Zeke stepped in. He done the right thing."

"We don't need any talk about our children in the company."

"First Esther, now Zeke. They ain't done nothing wrong." Franklin had enough on his mind without worrying about his offspring. If Cordelia felt better, she could handle them. She always had in the past.

Samuel Abercrombie stomped back to his campfire after talking with Franklin Pershing and other men at Tanner's wagon. "Now that damn fool Pershing is laying by for the Negro carpenter. Got a broken wheel, but the man can fix it quick as a wink. Probably just being lazy, wanting a day to sleep."

"Samuel," Harriet's voice was quiet in warning, but he ignored it.

"There ain't no call to make white folks wait on a colored man."

"The Tanners are as good as you or me in the eyes of God."

She stood rigidly, as straight-backed as any soldier at attention. Harriet came from a long line of abolitionists, and her older sister Abigail had regaled him with the rights of Africans throughout his first marriage. But he was of the opinion if God wanted different peoples to live together, God should have made them all look alike. "Now, Harriet—" he began.

"No, you listen, Samuel. I've let you talk about Captain Pershing throughout this journey, because the man can stand up for himself. But when you pick on the downtrodden in this world, you shame yourself. And you shame me." She turned away from him. "Your supper's in the Dutch oven. I'm going to bed." She crawled into the tent.

Daniel sat by the fire, holding his empty plate. No sign of Douglass and his family. "Where's everyone else?" Samuel asked.

"Gone to bed," Daniel said. "Eat your supper, Pa, and I'll wash the dishes."

The lad was a mama's boy. Doing women's work. "I'm going hunting tomorrow, since we're stuck here. You're coming with me."

"Why don't you take Douglass, Pa?"

Samuel ate his tepid stew, chomping every bite vigorously. His younger son hated shooting, but that was because he was no good at it. "You need to work on your aim, boy."

Daniel shrugged. "All right."

The argument won, Samuel continued eating. Didn't anyone understand the importance of speed on this journey? Pershing let every mother's son slow the pace for a splinter. And to let a Negro tell them what to do was just plain sinful. Harriet was wrong to talk back to her husband, and in the presence of his son no less. A man surely deserved better respect than he'd been given today. "You hold with that nonsense?" he asked Daniel.

"What nonsense, Pa?"

"About Tanner."

Daniel was silent a moment, then said, "Tanner's a good man, Pa. He's shared his fishing catches and the rabbits he's snared with all of us. I'm glad he's with this company."

Samuel snorted and finished his meal.

After he washed his father's supper dishes, Daniel walked out of camp. He needed to be by himself. It worried him when Pa argued with Ma. Pa was so forceful, and Ma was a little woman.

Sometimes it hurt that he'd missed knowing his real mother. As a boy, he'd liked listening to Douglass tell stories about their mother Abigail. But in his heart he knew Harriet was as good a mother as a boy could want. She wasn't always easy, and she had her own opinions. But he was certain she loved him as much as if she'd birthed him.

Slavery was a confusing topic. Men were either meant to be owned by others or they were not. But what he'd learned in school didn't resolve the question. The Declaration of Independence said all men were created equal, though it was written by slaveholders. The Bible talked about both slaves and free folks. How could good men write one thing and do another? Why wasn't God's word clear?

"Daniel," Esther called to him from behind.

He stopped and turned. "You shouldn't be out here alone," he said, waiting for her to catch up.

She hurried over and took his arm. "I'm not alone," she said, smiling. "You're here." Her teeth gleamed white in the moonlight.

He sighed, and they walked awhile in silence.

"Why are you out walking?" she asked.

"Ma and Pa were arguing over slavery. I wanted to think about where I stand."

"We only have Tanner here. He and his family are free. And Oregon's free territory." Esther made it sound like there was no problem to worry about.

"Pa don't think we should be stopping for Tanner."

"Well, of course, we should. Just look at all he's done for the company. There don't seem to be nothing he can't do."

Thursday morning Harriet Abercrombie sipped her coffee quietly after Samuel and Daniel left to hunt. The men departed early, and she had all day ahead of her in camp. She wanted to wash clothes and maybe cook a meat pie or two to ease the chores tomorrow, but she hadn't slept well after the argument with Samuel.

She'd promised to love, honor, and obey Samuel, but sometimes he was wrong. He knew of her abolitionist beliefs, yet he continued to speak of Negroes as inferior. She had tried to raise the boys to adhere to her point of view, and Daniel seemed to agree with her. Douglass appeared to follow his father's attitude, in this as in so many other things.

She wanted Daniel to be his own man, to get out from under his father's thumb. How could she help the boy be independent? Particularly now, when they were forced to live together day and night for months.

Maybe she should encourage him to spend more time with others who were more open-minded than Samuel, like the Pershings and the McDougalls. Captain and Cordelia Pershing were a fine couple. Mr. McDougall was a well-educated man from Boston, a Northerner—surely he would agree with her. And his wife Jenny was a sweet young woman, even if she did hail from a part of Missouri known for its slave-owning sympathizers.

She wondered what Esther Pershing's position on slavery was. Perhaps she should find out in case Daniel grew serious about the girl.

Chapter 22:   Hunting Parties

Thursday, 20 May 1847. Laying by today, repairing a wagon damaged in the crossing. FP

Daniel awoke Thursday morning when his father called, "Time's a wasting, son. Saddle up."

"Shhh," Harriet said. "The rest of the camp is still sleeping."

"If we want to beat the coyotes, we'll leave here quick. What can you give us to eat while we ride?"

"I'll pack you each some food." Harriet sighed and left the tent.

Daniel pulled on his trousers and shirt while still in his bedroll, then followed her. He nodded gratefully when she handed him a cup of coffee, which he gulped, then took the filled saddlebags she gave him. "One for you and one for your father," she said.

He found Pa saddling their horses. Daniel handed his father one bag, tied the other on his own mare, and mounted. The mare wasn't a pretty animal, but he'd trained her from the time she was a filly, and she did what he asked without complaint. Then he followed his father's large gelding out of camp. Other men came with them—Amos Jackson, Josiah Baker, and Zeke Pershing.

As dawn broke, sunlight streaked across the sky through wispy clouds on the horizon. The clouds would lift by midmorning, and the day would turn warm. A lark sang in high spirits that matched Daniel's. He didn't like hunting, but he was glad to be out on the open land away from the wagons' dust. There was a beauty to the vast prairie that the rolling hills of Tennessee couldn't match. He wondered how Oregon would compare.

A herd of antelope bounded out of a ravine. Pa raised his rifle and shot. "Damn!" he swore when he missed.

They rode on, but didn't see any more game. They stopped at midday to eat, and Pa announced, "Need to flush the antelope out of the ravines. They'll have holed up there for the heat of the day. Who wants to seek 'em out?"

"I will," Daniel said. His aim wasn't good, and his father would be happier being the one to do the shooting.

At the next watershed on the plateau, Daniel steered his mare into the gully. Three small deer leapt away from him into the open. Rifles cracked, and two of them fell.

"That's my boy," Pa shouted, as the other men whooped.

Daniel couldn't help but take some pride in his father's praise, even though he didn't enjoy the hunt.

They dismounted and gutted the carcasses, all the while arguing about which man had shot which beast. Then they slung the dressed deer behind Baker's and Zeke's saddles and rode on.

At the next ravine, they repeated the maneuver, but without success. In midafternoon at another gully, they tried again. This time Daniel scared a small herd of antelope. At the firing of rifles, more animals fell.

"That's enough, ain't it, Pa?" Daniel asked after they had dressed the antelope. "We got enough for the whole camp now."

His father assented, and the hunting party returned to camp. Pa acted like a big man, doling out meat to each family. "We'll hunt again tomorrow," he said. "Keep fresh venison in every pot. You coming, Daniel?"

"Why don't you take Douglass tomorrow?" Daniel said. "I'll mind the wagons."

Once the company was underway Friday morning, Esther and Jenny walked off to the side of the wagons, searching for eggs in the sparse grass on the high plateau. The sky was as bright and warm as yesterday. Esther wouldn't mind the trip to Oregon half as much if every day were so lovely.

"Wouldn't a fried egg taste wonderful," Esther said, her mouth watering at the thought. "We've had so few since we left Missouri. I'm hoping we find enough for my whole family."

They chatted about food and the warm weather and sunbonnets and marriage. "I'm going to marry Daniel and settle in Oregon near Ma and Pa," Esther told Jenny.

"Life doesn't always work out like you plan," Jenny replied. Then she fell silent, seemingly lost in her own reverie. Esther wondered what Jenny had to be so pensive about—she was young, married to a handsome man, and carrying his child. Jenny had the life Esther hoped to have some day.

Daniel walked alongside one of the Abercrombie wagons, and Esther ran toward him, wanting a more cheerful companion. She took his arm, and they strolled beside the lead team hauling his wagon. His mother and sister-in-law walked behind them near the second Abercrombie wagon.

"Your pa go hunting again?" she asked.

Daniel nodded. "Took Douglass today. I had my fill yesterday."

"Don't you like to hunt? Zeke and Joel relish anything out of doors." She was curious to know everything she could about Daniel.

He shrugged. "I don't shoot well. And I don't like to kill things. I'd rather raise animals than shoot them."

"But what about butchering hogs and cattle?"

"Some killing is necessary." Daniel sighed. "But when it ain't, I'd rather not."

"Well, we need meat along the trail." Esther held his arm close to her side. "Otherwise, we'd starve out here on the prairie."

"I'll let other men have the pleasure of provisioning the company." Daniel smiled down at her. "I'd rather walk with you than shoot a deer."

"Daniel," his mother said from behind him. "I'd like to speak with Esther, too." She joined them, and took Esther's other arm. "Come along, girl. I have a question for you."

Esther raised an eyebrow at Daniel, and he shrugged to indicate he didn't know what his mother wanted. Esther walked off with Mrs. Abercrombie. "Yes, ma'am?"

"Your father was kind to wait for the Tanners to fix their wagon yesterday."

"Yes, of course." What did Mrs. Abercrombie's comment have to do with anything?

"Are your parents abolitionists?"

Esther shrugged. "I've never talked to them about slavery."

"I was raised in an abolitionist family, though we lived in Tennessee. My husband, however, is a Southerner through and through."

"What does Daniel think?" Esther asked. She didn't much care about the rest of the Abercrombies.

"I would hope I have had some influence on him over the years."

"I'm sure you have, ma'am. Daniel speaks of you with great respect and affection."

Mrs. Abercrombie smiled. "Well, child, you are quite the diplomat."

"Daniel says he don't like to hunt."

"No, he never has. He likes animals. And I think his eyesight is poor."

That would explain his reluctance to shoot, Esther realized. Though he seemed to see her all right, even when she was a fair distance from him. But then, she hoped he had more motivation to look for her than for antelope to shoot.

The Friday hunting party was made up of the same men as on Thursday, except Douglass substituted for Daniel. In truth, Douglass was a better shot than Daniel, but Samuel was still irritated at his younger son's refusal to go again. He'd hoped this journey to Oregon would make a man out of the boy.

Josiah Baker agreed to flush the prey out of the ravines on this occasion, as Daniel had the day before. They only found birds. Samuel knew there were larger animals hiding in the hollows along the creeks, but the men saw nothing.

Samuel grew frustrated as the day went on. By midafternoon, he had about decided to return to the trail to find the wagons, when Baker yelled, "Hie!" and headed into a gully.

Out bounded a group of antelope, bouncing ahead of them. As Samuel raised his rifle to shoot, another gun sounded, then a man screamed.

Amos Jackson fell from his horse, writhing in pain and moaning. His horse bolted, but stopped a short distance away.

Samuel jumped off his gelding, shouting at Baker to get Jackson's horse. Then he knelt by Jackson, who held his gut and continued groaning.

"What happened?" Samuel asked.

"Dropped my rifle. 'Twas cocked and went off," Jackson said through clenched teeth. Blood began oozing from his mouth.

"Gut shot?" Samuel asked. He pried Jackson's hands away from his belly, fearing what he would find. As he'd guessed, a large wound bled from Jackson's stomach. When he ripped the man's shirt open, he saw loopy intestines covered with blood. Bad.

Jackson's moans turned to keening and he shivered in shock. "Hurts," he whimpered.

Samuel couldn't stand watching the man in pain. He'd seen the damage a gut shot caused, on a patrol once with the Tennessee militia. Such injuries were typically fatal. Out here on the prairie without any way to cleanse the wound or keep Jackson still, he was a dead man for sure.

The other men had all dismounted nearby. Baker held the horses, while Douglass and Zeke joined Samuel beside Jackson.

Samuel stood and pulled the two younger men aside. "We oughta just shoot him and be done with it," he said. "He'll be in dreadful pain till he bleeds out or turns septic."

"We can't do that!" Zeke said.

Even Douglass shook his head at his father.

"We'll wait it out," Zeke said. "Should one of us go find Doc Tuller?"

"Ain't nothing Doc can do," Samuel said, spitting. "Build us a fire if we ain't going nowhere. I'll get water. Give me your canteens."

Samuel grabbed the canteens and rushed to the ravine where Baker had rustled up the antelope. He had to get away from the sight of Jackson's blood oozing from the wound. Samuel scrubbed his hands and arms in the trickle of water in the gully to wash off the injured man's blood. After drying his hands on his shirt, he filled the canteens with water. He stood, steeling himself to return to the other men.

They waited all evening while Jackson's cries grew weaker. He passed out around dusk, and as the first stars twinkled in the sky he breathed his last.

"That's it," Samuel said, standing. "Let's go find the wagons."

"It's too dark," Zeke said. He stood, took an oilskin off his horse, and covered Jackson's corpse. "We'll head back at first light."

Samuel argued, but the other men agreed. He had no choice but to camp by a dead body on the open prairie all night.

Cordelia arose on Saturday morning and began cooking breakfast. She'd been glad of the chance to lay by on Thursday while Tanner fixed his broken wheel, but walking on Friday had tuckered her out again. She didn't think she'd be truly rested until they reached Oregon—or she was buried, whichever came first.

Thoughts of dying came more frequently the farther they moved from Missouri. Charles Purcell's death had brought her fears to mind, and now she couldn't escape them. More folk would die before they set foot in Oregon, she was sure. And she worried she might be one of them.

Yesterday's hunting party led by Samuel Abercrombie had not returned. Her son Zeke was with that group, and she fretted over what might be keeping them away. What dangers had they encountered?

A woman's wail sounded from the far side of the camp. "My baby!" the woman screamed.

Cordelia placed her frying pan beside the fire, called Rachel to tend it, and bustled across camp. She couldn't ignore a woman crying about her child.

She found Hatty Tanner, the Negress, sobbing, "My baby's dead, my Homer." Hatty knelt on the ground with her younger son on her lap. She keened as she rocked the small body in her arms, holding the boy more tightly than any lad no longer in diapers would tolerate. Homer's eyes were shut as if he slept, but no breath moved his little chest. The child had been about Noah's age, and a picture flashed through Cordelia's mind of the two young'uns running and playing alongside the wagons.

Doc and Elizabeth Tuller were there also. Doc took the boy from Hatty and examined the body briefly. "Gone. Nothing I can do," he said. He returned the still form to Hatty's arms, then left.

Tanner knelt beside Hatty and embraced his wife. She beat on his chest. "You done this, Clarence! I tole you we shouldn't go west. Our baby's dead."

While Jenny McDougall held a whimpering Otis Tanner, the older son, Cordelia made breakfast for the grieving parents. It was all she could offer as comfort.

When the food was ready, she had to spoon-feed Hatty to get the woman to eat. Tanner sat stoically with a plate. He ate, but Cordelia could tell he didn't taste a bite.

She'd been right, Cordelia thought, more folks would die. She hated that their second loss had been a child.

While Tanner and Mac McDougall dug a grave, the hunting party galloped toward camp, a body slung across one horse's saddle in place of a rider.

Franklin Pershing ran toward the returning riders, stopping at the edge of camp as Samuel Abercrombie dismounted in front of him.

"Damn fool shot hisself!" Abercrombie shouted. "Jackson's dead."

Amos Jackson? Franklin's heart thumped in his chest. Jackson had been a clumsy weakling, but he was a good man. "What happened?" he asked, as Jackson's wife ran toward the body and threw her arms around her dead husband. The Jackson children were right behind her, the oldest, a lad about fourteen, gripping his mother's shoulders.

"As I said, he shot hisself," Abercrombie repeated. "We didn't even find any buffalo."

Franklin sent an inquiring look to Zeke, who simply nodded.

"Better dig another grave," Doc Tuller said.

While a few men went to dig a hole in the parched land beside the grave already prepared for Homer Tanner, Cordelia and other women bustled to the Jackson wagon to console another grieving family. Franklin watched haplessly, hands at his sides.

Zeke dismounted, then led his horse to the wagons. "Come on, Pa. I need to brush him down. I'll tell you about it."

At the wagons, Zeke curried his horse. As he worked, he said, "It's like Abercrombie said. We'd flushed some large game and were about to shoot. Jackson dropped his rifle, it went off. Got him in the gut. Took much of the night for him to die. We started back here at first light."

"Damn." Franklin swallowed. "Then it wasn't Abercrombie's doing?" He wanted to blame the obstinate son of a bitch, but it sounded like the accident was just carelessness.

Zeke shook his head. "Can't fault Abercrombie. Jackson did himself in—dropped his cocked rifle. Lucky none of the rest of us was hurt."

"We lost Homer Tanner in the night, too." Franklin couldn't help thinking this journey was doomed.

Zeke stared at him. "One of the Negro children?"

Franklin nodded. "Doc thinks it was fever. Others in camp sickening, too. And we got Windlass Hill just ahead of us."

"What's that?" Zeke asked, putting his brushes away.

"Steepest hill twixt here and Oregon. Or so they say." Franklin sighed, slapped his hat on his head, and said, "Need to get these poor souls buried, then head out."

It was almost noon by the time the somber emigrants parted camp, leaving two of their company behind. Franklin was as glum as anyone.

Daniel rode ahead of the wagons as they traveled away from the graves of little Homer Tanner and Amos Jackson. More death. Pa had been strangely silent since his return to camp. He'd decided his horse was too winded to ride, so he and Douglass walked with the wagons, leaving Daniel to ride off on his own.

He'd asked Ma why Pa seemed so melancholy. "He's afraid of sickness and death," she said. "You seen him after Mr. Purcell died. This is the same. It all reminds him of your mother's death."

Pa? Afraid? His father had never been afraid of anything. Though Daniel remembered Pa always tried to avoid funerals and wouldn't visit his sick aunt before she died. Maybe Ma was right.

Then why did Pa love to hunt so much? Always killing more animals than they needed for food. Daniel shook his head. It was a contradiction he couldn't answer. For his own part, he would continue to avoid killing when possible, but take it in stride when it was unavoidable.

He saw Esther walking alongside her family's wagons and trotted over.

"Want a ride?" he asked.

She smiled wistfully. "I can't. Ma's feeling poorly. I should stay close to her today."

"She in the wagon?" Daniel gestured at the wagon next to Esther. He wondered if Esther's mother was getting a fever like the Tanner boy.

Esther nodded.

"Tell her I hope she feels better soon." He tipped his hat and rode away.

Chapter 23:   Windlass Hill

Saturday, 22 May 1847. Lost a man and a child today. One to gunshot, the other to fever. Reached Windlass Hill. FP

That evening Franklin Pershing stood at the top of Windlass Hill, staring down the three-hundred-foot drop. And they called this a hill? It was almost a cliff. The ruts of earlier wagons fell from the plateau they'd been crossing between the branches of the Platte into a ravine. That ravine was where Frémont's map showed Ash Hollow to be—a good resting place. But it would be the devil to get there.

This was the first long, steep grade they'd faced. Franklin would rather ford a raging river than descend this hill. They'd have to lock the wagon wheels and lower the wagons with ropes and chains, he decided.

"We're going down that?" Samuel Abercrombie bellowed into his ear from behind. "Why'd you bring us this way?"

"We got down it with Frémont in forty-two," Pershing said. "Including our cannon." He turned to the platoon leaders standing around him. "We'll start in the morning. Empty your wagons tonight."

Abercrombie snorted, but said no more.

Working until full dark had fallen, the emigrants took everything out of their wagons, piling their possessions to be carried down the steep hill the next day.

"Good thing the weather's nice," Cordelia commented, as she rose from hefting a bag of cornmeal and braced her back with a hand. Esther stood beside her mother, still holding a sack she'd removed from the wagon.

"You fit enough to be lifting?" Franklin asked Cordelia. "Get Zeke and Joel to help you and Esther."

"They're helping the Purcells and Jacksons," Cordelia said. "Those women don't have a man to lift and tote for 'em."

At this reminder he'd lost two good men from the company in little over a month, Franklin pursed his lips. He took the remaining whiskey bottles from the hidden bottom of one wagon and stowed them in a trunk of clothes. Then he left his campsite to see which other families might need his assistance.

He came upon Doc Tuller lifting a rocking chair out of his wagon. "Elizabeth won't let me get rid of this," Doc said, shaking his head with a grin. The doctor's wife stood nearby, arms crossed, watching her husband ease the chair to the ground.

Franklin smiled—first bit of humor he'd heard since Homer Tanner's death the morning before. Then he turned serious. "Any more folks with fever, Doc?"

The doctor shrugged. "Not that I've heard. Ain't much I can do if we get more."

Daniel listened to his father mutter about the foolishness of taking wagons down a straight drop. Daniel had been encouraged when Captain Pershing said Frémont's party had lowered a cannon down this hill, and he told his father so.

"He weren't talking 'bout no garrison gun," Pa said, spitting his tobacco juice. "Ain't nothing to a six-pounder like the Army hauls around. Our wagon's heavier 'n that."

Shortly after dawn on Sunday, Captain Pershing called the emigrants together for a short Sabbath service. The men shuffled, ready to get to work, but the captain prayed for the Lord's blessing on their endeavors and for the families of those they'd lost already.

"All right, folks," he ordered after the last "Amen." "Let's get to work. Line up the wagons. No crowding—take it slow."

"Slow," Pa muttered. "We been going too dang slow for over a month now."

161

Captain Pershing assigned Daniel to yoke the animals hauling each wagon into place and lead the wagons to the top of the hill. Pa, being one of the largest men in the company, worked on a team of men manning the ropes used to lower the wagons. The ropes were tied to the rear axle of the wagon descending the hill, and the wagon's wheels were locked to provide more drag. Just one pair of oxen led the wagon down, while from the top of the hill Pa and other large men pulled on the ropes with all their weight to control the descent.

One wagon at a time went down the hill. In between wagons, while Daniel led the next wagon into position, women and older children carried the company's possessions to the bottom of the hill, then trudged back up for another load. Once the wagons were moved away from the base of the cliff, more women and children repacked them.

Daniel kept an eye on Esther as she made trip after trip carrying belongings to the bottom. Her cheeks flamed from the grueling labor, he noticed when she stood beside him resting a moment before lifting another load.

He smiled at her. She smiled back wearily, pushing a strand of hair out of the corner of her mouth and tucking it into her sunbonnet.

The oxen snorted at the top of the hill as Daniel turned them over to the man guiding the wagon down. The animals pulled as the wagon teetered on the brink. Then when the wagon passed its tipping point, it pushed the oxen faster than they could move. At that point, Daniel shouted at the men on the ropes to pull harder to slow the wagon, until the oxen could walk it down the hill.

All day this went on, one wagon after another, each taking half an hour to put in place and descend.

Shortly after noon, when about half the twenty-two wagons were at the bottom, Daniel heard a cry, "She's coming down!"

Horace Mercer's wagon, in the middle of its descent, had broken loose of its ropes and was crashing down the lower half of the hill. Mercer had been leading the oxen yoked to his wagon. He yelled and dove out of the way, but one of the rear wheels rolled over him.

All activity stopped, and except for Mercer's cries and bellows from the two oxen struck by the careening wagon, there was silence.

Daniel sprinted down the hill toward Mercer. Doc Tuller was already there.

"Wheel went over my foot," Mercer said, gritting his teeth.

"Ankle's broke," Doc said. "I can splint it." He stood up and squinted toward the bottom of the hill. "Wagon's worse'n he is. Move him out of the way."

"At least the oxen ain't hurt. They can still pull," Daniel heard a man say.

Daniel and another man carried Mercer the rest of the way down and laid him on a blanket on the ground. Doc followed.

Captain Pershing sent Daniel back to his position and charged other men with moving the Mercer wagon out of the path. "Next wagon!" he shouted to those at the crest of the hill.

Later in the afternoon, another wagon broke loose, this one running over an ox and breaking its leg. The ox was shot, and the women butchered it for meat.

It wasn't until near dusk, when the last wagon had descended, that Daniel learned the extent of the damage to Mercer's wagon—the front board shattered, one oak wheel cracked, and the iron tire on that wheel separated from the wood.

"Got to leave it for now," Captain Pershing said. "We'll move on to Ash Hollow for the night. Stay there till we get Mercer's wagon fixed."

Harriet Abercrombie trudged wearily behind the wagons as they left Windlass Hill. Captain Pershing had assured them their camp was only a mile or two ahead, and she didn't have the strength to move ahead of the wagons out of their dust. She had toted bags of cornmeal and flour, stacks of bedding and clothes, tools, and everything but the heaviest furniture—why did people bring chests and bedsteads on a trek like this?—until she was so exhausted she could barely think.

Yet now that the monumental effort of descending Windlass Hill was behind them, Harriet thought of poor little Homer Tanner. Her husband had belittled the Negro family, but they grieved the loss of their child as much as any white parents would. She thought of Amos Jackson—his wife now widowed like Amanda Purcell, his oldest boy the man of the family at age fourteen.

She thought of her lost home. Her parents' and sister Abigail's graves left behind, as well as the house where she had raised Douglass and Daniel.

And she thought of the family members still with her—Samuel, as obstinate as ever, despite the difficulties of surviving in an alien land. Douglass, a meek soul, so solicitous of his wife and daughters. Daniel, a lad striving to become a man, to escape his father's tyranny. Louisa and her granddaughters. She couldn't bear to lose any of them. Yet there was no assurance they would all survive the journey to Oregon.

By the time she reached Ash Hollow, the sun had set and most of the wagons had been pulled into a circle. Harriet almost clapped her hands in joy at the sight of the lush green grass by a burbling spring. Tall, shady ash trees and cedar made a bower over the water. She took a moment to breathe in the cool air, then went to her wagon to cook supper.

Cordelia Pershing sagged to the ground at Ash Hollow, her breath coming in shallow pants. She never seemed to be able to get a good lungful of air these days.

She had tried carrying baskets and sacks of provisions down the steep slope, but on every trek back to the top of Windlass Hill, she wheezed harder than the time before. Finally, Esther told her, "You stay here, Ma. Repack the wagons. The twins and I'll carry what we can."

Cordelia nodded gratefully. Zeke and Joel, of course, were working with the men. She had only her younger children to help. She and Rachel did the bulk of the packing, then started a stew and biscuits for the noon dinner. Other women pitched in, and it became a communal meal, the women carrying bowls to the men to eat as they worked.

Not what the Lord meant by a day of rest, she was certain. But she kept that notion to herself, knowing Franklin didn't need any interference with his supervision of the wagons descending the hill.

When they finally reached Ash Hollow, she reflected on Psalm 23—green pastures and still waters. This was where the Lord meant them to restore their souls. They had been through the valley of the shadow of death, losing Homer Tanner and Amos Jackson, and she was ready for the table of plenty. But Horace Mercer had been injured and his wagon broken—would they ever find God's mercy?

As soon as Esther and the twins put up the tent, Cordelia crawled in and slept like the dead, deep and dreamlessly.

The next morning she awoke early to a cold rain, but felt refreshed. She began cooking breakfast and had ox steak and flapjacks frying by the time the rest of the family was up, the smell of the meat making her mouth water.

"Shouldn't you be in bed, Cordelia?" Franklin asked, taking the cup of coffee she handed him.

She snorted. "And who would fix your breakfast?"

He grinned. Then his face turned sober. "We have a few folks sick today. Fever."

She looked up, worried. "Like the Tanner boy?"

Franklin shrugged. "Don't know yet. Doc's making the rounds."

"Who is sick?"

"Mac McDougall for one. And another man. Plus a woman and child, I think."

Esther lay wrapped in a blanket while the pungent odors of frying meat and coffee seeped into the tent. She was hungry, but every muscle in her body hurt. She had worked harder yesterday than ever before in her life. And that was carrying things down a hill. She wondered if the mountains they'd have to climb farther on would be as steep to ascend as Windlass Hill had been to descend.

She hadn't wanted to tote all those boxes and bags, but there'd been no one else to do it. She was used to relying on Ma, doing whatever her mother told her to do. But Ma had looked poorly, and Esther had worried. She'd taken on the work, telling Ma to rest at the bottom of the cliff. Then she'd cooked supper once they got to Ash Hollow—Ma had been too tired.

This morning Esther wanted to be lazy. She'd earned it. She burrowed back into her bedroll.

"Esther," Ma called. "Time to get up. Breakfast is ready."

She groaned. "Ma, I'm tired."

"Now, Esther."

She sighed, rolled out from under her blanket, dressed, and crept out of the tent into cold rain.

Ma handed her a cup of coffee and a plate of food. "Eat up, then do the dishes. There's sick folks in camp, and I need to visit them."

Just like always, Esther thought. The daily chores never stopped. "You feeling better, Ma?"

"Well enough. I'm off to the McDougall wagon now."

"Is Jenny sick?" Esther looked up in alarm.

"It's her husband. Fever. Lots of fever going around. I'm leaving you in charge of the young'uns. Don't let them wander off. Don't want them catching anything."

Esther stretched her aching back, finished her breakfast, and started washing the dishes.

Chapter 24: Cholera in Camp

Monday, 24 May 1847. Laying by. Horace Mercer injured in the descent, and cholera appears to have stricken our company. FP

In heavy rain Monday afternoon, Samuel stood by the spring at Ash Hollow watering his horse. His dog Bruiser nosed through weeds along the bank. Samuel didn't care about the lush grass and trees, though his gelding drank deeply of the cool clear water and Bruiser wagged his tail.

Samuel felt antsy after sitting in camp all day, but there was no need to hunt. The meat from the ox that broke its leg would feed the company for a day or two.

On Windlass Hill, Pershing had let another man be hurt—Horace Mercer would be useless for weeks. Ankle now splinted, the man hobbled around on a crutch. And a strong ox had died on the descent as well.

All day reports of sickness spread through the camp. At least four folks in camp were ill, maybe more. The Negro boy who died on Saturday had only been the first. Another child died just before Samuel headed to the spring. Hearing of the fever and vomiting and diarrhea the stricken were experiencing made Samuel's skin crawl.

Cholera. The dread word was whispered in every conversation. Doc Tuller wouldn't say for sure that's what it was, but Samuel reckoned cholera was likely, what with all the mud and filthy water they'd traipsed through.

He couldn't let his family stay in a place harboring such pestilence. He hadn't been able to escape Abigail's fever after childbirth, but he'd be damned if he kept Harriet and the rest of his kin around folks who were sickening with a plague of any type.

The Abercrombies were leaving this accursed place—with Pershing or without him.

Samuel pulled his horse away from the water, took him back to the wagons, and tied him up. Then he sought out Pershing.

"We need to move on," he announced when he found Pershing wrapping wet rawhide around a split ax handle.

"What do you mean?" Pershing looked up with a raised eyebrow.

"Folks is sick. We can't stay here."

"Well, we can't move 'em. McDougall looks near death, and the others even worse." Pershing cut off the rawhide strip and knotted it.

"I'm moving my family out tomorrow," Samuel said. "The rest of you can come if you want."

Pershing stood and curled his fists. "See here, Abercrombie. It ain't safe for you to leave."

"It ain't safe to stay neither." Samuel's fists curled involuntarily to match Pershing's. He could best the man in a fight, if need be.

"You can't go off into the wilderness. You don't even have a map."

Samuel didn't care about a map. "Others'll go with me. My platoon."

"Have you talked to them?" Pershing sounded concerned. His brow furrowed, though his hands relaxed.

"I done you the courtesy of telling you first. I'm off to talk to them next." Samuel left, seeking out the other men he led.

To a man, they were ready to follow him. None of them liked the idea of holing up at Ash Hollow with cholera raging through camp. Once he'd gained his platoon's support, he went to all the wagons, and soon had over half the camp committed to leaving.

After supper he returned to Pershing. "We're packing up. You'll only have about a third of the wagons left."

"I'll call a meeting for the morning," Pershing replied. "We'll talk then."

"Talk." Samuel spat. "Talk all you want. I'm leaving."

After Abercrombie stated his intention to leave and take most of the company with him, Franklin did his own reconnoitering. Many of the men hemmed and hawed, but said they agreed with Abercrombie. They didn't want to wait days for the sick members of their party to die or improve. And they didn't want to stay in a camp where cholera might run rampant.

"Cholera spreads like the devil," Baker said. Baker was a level-headed man, Franklin thought. "I don't want my children catching it."

Franklin tried to convince him. "Doc says cleanliness can keep it away."

Baker snorted. "Cleanliness? How we going to keep our young'uns clean amidst the filth of the trail?" He shook his head. "We best move on."

Doc Tuller was one of the few who said the group shouldn't split up. "I'll stay with the sick, Pershing. And you should, too. We're in this together."

Franklin tossed and turned through the night, trying to decide what to do.

"What's wrong?" Cordelia whispered when she returned from using the latrine. The light from the almost-full moon silhouetted her form against the tent wall. She crept under her blanket slowly and none of the children in the tent stirred.

"The men want to split the company. Let the healthy move on while the sick recover."

"You can't do that, Franklin!" Cordelia said, fear evident even in her hushed tones. "The ailing families need our care."

"Some folks are leaving, no matter what I do. Don't I owe them an obligation as well as the sick? The others can follow."

Cordelia shook his shoulder. "Is that what you'll do when I have this babe? Go on ahead and let me follow when the birthing's over? You can't leave me."

"That's different." Franklin swallowed hard. "That's different—you're my wife."

"We're all yours to command through this journey."

"I'm still thinking on it."

But in the morning, he'd come to no resolution. The men met, restated their arguments, and all Franklin could do was persuade those who wanted to leave to remain for one more day.

Harriet waited for Samuel to return from the platoon leaders' meeting. Only the men had spoken at the company-wide assembly, but many of the women listened from the sidelines. As always, the women bore the brunt of tending the ailing folks. Doc Tuller made his rounds, but cleaning up vomit and worse was left to the women.

As well as cooking for the healthy in camp.

Harriet spelled one woman whose husband was near death and unable to keep down even water. Elizabeth Tuller helped young Jenny McDougall while her lawyer husband lay in a stupor. Cordelia Pershing spent part of Monday tending the sick, but later collapsed in fatigue. Harriet hoped the captain's wife wasn't harming herself or the child she carried with her exertions. The oldest Pershing daughter Esther took over when Cordelia could no longer manage.

Harriet stood by Esther while the men talked. She'd been appalled to learn Samuel instigated the crisis—he was the one urging that they move on. She left the meeting and returned to their tents.

Now, when he stormed back into their campsite and sat on a crate beside the fire, she asked, "Well?"

"Damn fool Pershing says we'll wait another day. But he'll go with us."

"Who's staying?"

"Sick families. Doc and his wife. Tanners. Mercer, with his broken ankle. And Zeke and Joel Pershing to help the ailing."

"The captain is splitting up his family?" Harriet's voice rose in surprise. "What does his wife think?"

Samuel shrugged. "Pershing decided. He wanted Daniel to stay behind, too. But I refused. Our family will stick together."

"Samuel, you mean you started this whole mess, and you won't do our neighbors the Christian courtesy of offering our son to assist them? But you'll let the captain split his family?"

"Do you want Daniel to stay behind?"

"No, but—"

"I'm getting this family to Oregon, come hell or high water. And we're likely to see both afore we get there. You be ready to head out tomorrow morning at first light, and we'll leave this pestilence behind us. I will not let my family take sick."

Esther rushed away from listening to the men as soon as her father said Zeke and Joel would stay behind. What was Pa thinking? How could he let her brothers remain while the rest of the family went ahead? She didn't know which group would have the harder task—those forging ahead with a smaller company or those waiting for the sick to heal or die. All she knew was she might never see her brothers again.

By the time she reached the Pershing family's wagons, she was sobbing. "Ma, Ma—" was all she could get out.

"Shhh, child, what is it?" Ma sat her down beside the wagon and dropped to her knees beside Esther.

"Pa says we're leaving."

Ma's mouth narrowed into a thin line, her eyes turning to slits. "We'll see about that—"

"And Zeke and Joel—he says they're staying."

Ma gasped. "My boys!" She hefted herself to her feet with a grunt. "Franklin! Franklin!" she called, and she hurried off.

Esther sat sobbing, until she felt a large hand rest gently on her shoulder.

"What's wrong, Esther?" Daniel's calm voice broke through her tears.

"We're leaving tomorrow. The company is splitting."

Daniel squatted beside her. "I heard."

"Are you staying?"

He shrugged. "Don't know. Captain wants me to. Pa says I should go with him."

"My pa says Zeke and Joel will remain here. Says the sick folks need help."

Daniel sighed. "Maybe I should stay."

"Wouldn't it be dangerous? Couldn't you get sick?"

"I suppose. But someone needs to wait here. The menfolk in the group that's staying are mostly sick or old or injured. I'll talk to Pa again. See what he thinks. But don't you worry, Esther. It'll all work out." He touched her cheek and left.

Esther wiped a hand across her eyes to dry them, then began packing the

171

wagon with things they wouldn't need before they left. As she finished, Ma returned, her lips still in a narrow line. "What'd Pa say?" Esther asked.

Ma shook her head and climbed into the wagon without a word. Esther heard her mother crying.

The twins and Ruth came running past the wagons. Rachel trailed behind them, holding Noah's hand. When the twins hollered in their play, Esther shouted, "Be quiet! Ma's not feeling well."

The young'uns all stopped.

"Rachel," Esther said with a sigh, "help me with the noon meal. The rest of you, go wash your hands."

After talking to Esther, Daniel returned to his family's wagons. His parents argued as he approached, and both turned to him when he entered their camp.

"You can't stay, Daniel," Pa said.

"I may be needed, Pa."

"Please don't," Ma said, grabbing his arm. "I can't bear to leave you behind."

"Don't we owe the wagon company our help?" Daniel asked.

"You're a good boy, Daniel," Ma said. "We shouldn't be splitting the company"—she flashed a glance at Pa—"But it's worse to split up families."

"But the Pershings—"

"He's the captain. He can decide what to do with his own kin." Pa stood and said, "I decide where mine go. You're coming with us." And Pa left camp.

Daniel sat, elbows on his knees and head in his hands.

"Don't worry." Ma put a hand on his shoulder. "They'll manage. Our family needs to stay together. You're all I have in this world."

That wasn't true, Daniel knew. She loved Douglass and her granddaughters. And she loved Pa. But Daniel also knew he was her favorite. He couldn't disappoint her. He couldn't leave her. "All right, Ma. I'll stay with you."

Chapter 25:   Splitting Up

Tuesday, 25 May 1847. Illness spreads in camp. Most of us will move on in the morning. With God's grace our company will reunite soon. FP

Wednesday morning after breakfast, Cordelia hugged her sons Zeke and Joel, clinging to each boy briefly, then climbed onto the wagon bench, her heart heavy. She had argued with Franklin late into the night. She begged. She prayed.

He refused to stay with the ailing folks, saying the company had decided. And he refused to let Zeke and Joel leave with the rest of the family. "I've got to do what I can for these people, Cordelia. I'm responsible."

"What about your own kin, Franklin? What about me? What if I never see my sons again?" Her voice broke as she said the last words, but she didn't care if she sounded weak. When it came to leaving her oldest two children behind, she *was* weak.

She considered staying with the boys, but the rest of her family needed her. She couldn't make Esther responsible for all the cooking and mending for Franklin and the young'uns.

She considered staying and keeping all the children with her, but she couldn't let Franklin go on alone. They'd been separated for so much of their marriage, and she needed his strength more than ever.

Yet leaving Zeke and Joel behind was the hardest thing she had done in her life. Harder than leaving the farm in St. Charles. At least then she'd been buoyed by the delight of having her family all together.

Franklin's decision was driving the two of them apart as well. They might be together in body, but in spirit, she left him. In spirit, she remained in Ash Hollow.

She sat on the wagon bench, staring straight ahead, her only movement to sway in response to the jostling of the wagon.

Franklin rode ahead of the wagons, scouting alone. Without Zeke and Joel, and without McDougall, he had no scouts he trusted. Daniel Abercrombie was a possible replacement—the young man had begun learning to watch the ground for trail blazes and the horizon for landmarks. Daniel was a good lad, though too much under his father's thumb for Franklin to be sure he was reliable. Still, traveling along the Platte would be an easy way to teach the youngster.

He'd hated asking his sons to remain behind, but it was the only way he could justify his decision to split the company. He was responsible for the entire group. Leaving Zeke and Joel was like cutting off his right arm. But he could count on them to lead the other wagons when it was time for those families to set out on the trail again.

He'd talked to his sons about catching up to the main group as quickly as possible. "I'll try to keep a slow pace to Scott's Bluff," he said. "You move out smartly as soon as folks can. We'll meet at Fort Laramie if not before. I won't go beyond the fort till I've seen you again."

"It's all right, Pa," Zeke said, clapping his father on the shoulder, one man to another. "We'll be fine. You take care of Ma. Make her rest."

Franklin had nodded, then given the signal for the wagons leaving Ash Hollow to head out. He'd stayed by his family's wagons for a while, trying to talk to Cordelia. But she wouldn't say a word to him. Finally, Esther said, "You scout ahead, Pa. I'll stay with Ma."

And so he had. It was a fine day, a beautiful morning for traveling. He'd be happy, if only the whole company were united and Cordelia would try to understand.

At noon he ate the quick meal Esther seemed to have thrown together without help from Cordelia. His wife still sat silently, not meeting his eye.

When they started up again, Franklin asked Daniel to scout with him.

Samuel objected, "My son stays with me."

Franklin glowered at the large farmer. "I need another scout trained. My boys are tending the sick because you instigated a rebellion. Daniel comes with me." He gestured to Daniel, who shrugged and followed Franklin.

"We'll travel along the North Fork of the Platte for a long distance," Franklin told Daniel, once they were mounted and riding ahead of the wagons. "Ain't much to watch for, other'n where to stop for water and where to camp. I'll show you how to match the trail to the map and find where Frémont camped. Should see Chimney Rock soon. That's our next landmark."

"How far is that?" Daniel asked.

"Three or four days. But the rock rises high above the plains. We'll see it soon."

Esther worked all day at one task or another. She drove the oxen as they pulled the wagons. She cooked the family's meals. She tended the children, though Rachel took on most of the minding of Ruth and Noah. Ma sat on the wagon bench without speaking from the time they left Ash Hollow until after the noon meal.

As she tended the oxen, she thought about her farewell with poor Jenny McDougall just before they left Ash Hollow. Her friend had sat with her sick husband in a tent reeking of foul body odors and sickness. Esther had never smelled death, but she suspected that's what it smelled like. Mac McDougall moaned weakly when a flash of light from the open tent flap fell across his pallid face. Sure she would retch if she talked for long, Esther quickly told Jenny she'd see her again and left.

She'd hugged Zeke and Joel, then she'd taken up her position by the lead team while Ma said good-bye to her two oldest children. Ma had sat like a stone ever since—not helping with the animals and barely paying attention to the children. Esther did all the work. She didn't even suggest her mother assist with the noon meal.

"That was a right tasty soup, Esther," Ma said, when they headed out again after eating. Pa was scouting, and the children wandering to the side of the wagons. Again, Esther walked near the oxen, while Ma sat on the bench.

Esther glanced up in surprise. She didn't think her mother had even tasted the oxtail broth. "Thank you."

"You're a good girl." Ma nodded at her.

Esther nodded back. She walked along in silence for another quarter hour or so.

Then Ma said, "Be careful whom you marry, child."

Esther stared at her mother, startled.

"A man does what he wants, no matter what his wife says." Esther heard bitterness in her mother's tone. "Find a man who'll listen to you. Maybe there's one out there somewhere who'll pay heed to a woman."

Would Daniel listen to her? Esther wondered. He seemed so kind. He'd comforted her twice now—after Charles Purcell died and again at Ash Hollow. His touch was gentle. "Yes, Ma."

They plodded along mutely the rest of the afternoon. The only break in the monotony came when Noah trudged over to the wagon wanting a rest. Ma took him into the back, and they napped together, leaving Esther alone with her thoughts again as she minded the oxen.

Daniel rode beside Captain Pershing in the heat of the late May afternoon. A breeze blew from the west. Coming from the highlands ahead, it cooled his face. He couldn't see the mountains yet, but the terrain along the North Fork of the Platte was rougher than what they'd seen in earlier days, with craggy cliffs to the south of them. Daniel wondered what Chimney Rock would look like—it stuck up above the horizon, Captain Pershing said.

The two men didn't talk much, though Captain Pershing pointed out a creek he said could make a good resting spot, if it weren't so early in the day. Daniel spent his time mulling over the arguments he'd heard before they left Ash Hollow. He didn't feel right about moving on with the main company while Zeke and Joel remained behind, and while Mac McDougall and others lay near death.

He knew his mother felt the same way he did. And Mrs. Pershing. And Esther. The women all wanted to keep the company together, to keep their families together. Ma came along because Pa insisted they leave Ash

176

Hollow. And then she insisted Daniel stay with them. His thoughts were in discord. Part of him knew his family should remain together, but another part felt an obligation to serve where he was needed most—and that felt like it was with the group still in Ash Hollow.

Poor Esther. Her brothers left behind, her mother unhealthy and distraught. Everyone in the wagon company could see Mrs. Pershing and the captain had had a falling out. Daniel knew how uncomfortable parents' arguments could be for their offspring—when Ma stood up to Pa sometimes, Daniel wanted to be far away.

He didn't know whether he should raise the matter with Captain Pershing. How could he ask how the captain's wife was holding up without sounding impertinent? How could he ask about Esther?

In late afternoon, but well before dusk, Captain Pershing pointed to a small, sandy creek running into the Platte. "We'll camp there," he said.

"Still early," Daniel said. He wouldn't mind stopping, but he knew how his father would react.

"No need to push it. We'll take it slow until the rest of our party catches up."

Daniel raised his eyebrows, but said nothing. Pa would complain bitterly if he believed the captain was deliberately keeping a leisurely pace. But Daniel wouldn't tell his father.

Sure enough, when Captain Pershing gave the signal to circle the wagons, Pa trotted his gelding over. "What you mean stopping so soon, Pershing?"

"Folks is tired, Abercrombie. We'll halt here."

"Your wife's the only one tired, Pershing. Maybe she should have stayed with the sick folks."

If Captain Pershing hadn't been on horseback, Daniel thought the man might have taken a swing at Pa. "We can make more time tomorrow, Pa," he said to break the tension. "Lots of water and grass here. It's a good campsite."

Pa spat on the ground.

"Want to go hunting?" Daniel asked him. "There's plenty of time afore dark."

Harriet stirred the stew in her Dutch oven, checking to be sure it wasn't burning on the bottom. Her granddaughters had gone out on the prairie to look for sticks from the scrubby trees or buffalo chips to burn. Louisa sat darning a stocking. The men had gone hunting. It was a pleasant evening, and she relished the quiet.

She hated leaving the sick and injured, but she also feared cholera. She'd argued with Samuel about going—suggesting instead they move their camp at Ash Hollow a short distance away from the stricken families.

He refused. "The mountain snows won't wait for us, Harriet. They won't care we been nice to some sick folks. It's my duty to my family to get us to Oregon quick as we can. Get our claims filed and build a house afore winter."

"You seem to know a tolerable amount about Oregon for a man who's never been there." She didn't usually argue with him so directly, but this journey was bringing out the worst in him—maybe in both of them. "Captain Pershing knows what he's doing."

"He agreed to abide by what the men wanted. Most of 'em are like me—hellbent for Oregon."

"What about what the women wanted?" she said under her breath.

Harriet watched children racing between the wagons. A couple of them looked like Pershings. Why weren't they under better control? She sighed and walked over to shoo them back to their wagon.

"Evening, Mrs. Abercrombie." Esther Pershing approached the children from the other direction. "Jonathan and Ruthie, go on back to our campsite. And be quiet. Ma's resting."

Harriet frowned at Esther, assessing. The girl looked frazzled. "Is your ma poorly?"

Esther sighed. "Yes'm. She ain't feeling well. I think she's mostly troubled over leaving Zeke and Joel. She's been quiet all day."

"May I speak with her?" Harriet moved to follow Esther back toward the Pershing wagons.

"Thank you, ma'am. Though I don't know what anyone can do to help."

Harriet found Cordelia sitting on a crate placed near one wagon, leaning back against the wheel for support. "It's a fine evening, ain't it?" Harriet said.

Cordelia glanced at her. "Mmm."

"I'm planning biscuits for supper," Harriet ventured. "Would your brood like some?"

"That would be right nice," Esther said. "I've got beans boiling with bacon, but biscuits would be tasty. Will you and your family share supper with us?"

Harriet nodded. "I have a stew going also. Don't know when the menfolk will be back. I'll set aside some food for them, and Louisa, the girls, and I will sup with you."

Esther nodded. "I forgot we don't need so much cooked without Zeke and Joel here to eat it. We got plenty to share."

Samuel returned from hunting happy. He and Douglass had each shot a deer, so the family would have venison for several days and enough meat to share with others. He might even give a haunch to the Pershings.

Daniel couldn't shoot worth a darn, but he worked hard enough at dressing the carcasses. Maybe Harriet was right—maybe the boy's eyes were bad.

"What's for supper, Harriet?" he asked. "Can you fix us venison steaks? I've a hankering for fresh meat."

Harriet got out the spider skillet, added a bit of lard, and cut steaks off the deer. "There's biscuits to go with the drippings. And stew."

"Don't you want any?" Samuel asked a few minutes later, when Harriet slid steaks onto just three plates.

Harriet shook her head. "We ate with the Pershings. Cordelia ain't well."

"What's wrong with her?" Samuel liked the woman, but she seemed to tire every day by midafternoon.

"She's worried about her sons."

Samuel heard an accusation in his wife's voice. "Now, Harriet, we agreed to move on. Couldn't wait for the folks with cholera to die."

Harriet picked up a bucket. "I need some water."

"I'll get it, Ma." Daniel stood up.

She shook her head. "You eat your supper. It's late." And she walked toward the creek with her bucket.

"Ma's upset, just like Miz Pershing," Daniel said.

"She'll get over it." Samuel sopped up pan drippings with a biscuit, then snorted. "Pershing's going slow enough, it's likely the others'll catch up with us. Those that don't die." He took a bite.

"Don't you care, Pa? Mac McDougall's a fine man, and he was near death's door."

"It's in the Lord's hands now," Samuel said. He didn't much cotton to what the Lord did—he took good folks young and left the mean ones behind. But there wasn't much he or anyone else could do about it. Except run away from pestilence and hope it didn't follow. That's what he aimed to do for as long as he could. "I'll have to keep pushing Pershing along. He's got you scouting. You tell me if he starts dawdling on purpose."

"I'm sure the captain wants to get to Oregon, too, Pa."

Samuel grimaced. "No telling what that fool wants."

Chapter 26:   Another Kiss

Wednesday, 26 May 1847. We continue along the North Platte, leaving eight wagons at Ash Hollow. FP

A warm sun shone Thursday morning. When Franklin gave the order to move out, the wagons headed along the Platte promptly. No delays caused by illness or death.

Cordelia was not well, Franklin acknowledged as he rode at the head of the wagons. His wife tried to hide her discomfort, and Esther handled as many chores as she could for her mother. He worried about his oldest daughter. She was young and healthy, but if she worked herself too hard caring for the family, she'd be susceptible to illness.

After the teams settled into their paces, Franklin rode along the fourteen wagons—all that were left of his company. Despite the pleasant late-May weather, many faces were glum. These families had all agreed to continue their journey, but Franklin knew leaving their fellow travelers behind grated on their consciences.

Except for Samuel Abercrombie. The man's arrogance had only grown since they'd left Ash Hollow. He'd won a battle, and he knew it. Now he sat his large gelding like king of the realm, practically sneering at Franklin as he rode past.

If Samuel had won, then Franklin had lost. He'd wanted the wagons to stay together, but to his chagrin he'd been outvoted. Would Captain Frémont have left a third of his men behind? Franklin didn't know how his

Army superiors had felt during their commands—he'd only seen the results of good leadership and bad. The weakness of his own leadership preyed on his mind. Should he have pressed harder to keep the company together? Could he have overcome Abercrombie's obstinacy?

Daniel Abercrombie rode over to Franklin. "Captain Pershing," the lad called, "may I take Esther riding with me? The buttes to the south are like nothing I've seen before. I'd like a closer look."

Franklin squinted at the young man. He was doing his part to fill in for Zeke and Joel. And it would vex old Samuel to let Daniel spend time with Esther—Daniel's father wanted to keep the young folks apart. So did Cordelia, but right now Franklin cared more about thwarting Samuel. And Esther could use a rest from minding the young'uns. He nodded. "If she's willing, it's fine by me. Tell her to have Rachel tend the children. But stay within sight of the wagons while you're riding."

Daniel grinned. "Thank you, sir." And he cantered off toward the Pershing wagons.

Soon Franklin saw them riding toward the buttes. Esther must have been willing. And Cordelia must not have objected to letting the girl go.

When Daniel asked if Esther could ride with him, Cordelia itched to say no. She wanted her daughter with her. But it was only her desire to keep Esther close, to not let loose of another child, that made her want to object. In truth, Daniel was a good young man, and Franklin spoke highly of him. Even if Samuel Abercrombie was a bombastic bully, his son was not.

Cordelia still felt poorly, though she decided it was mostly her nerves— she wouldn't feel well until she had her whole brood tucked under her wing again. But Cordelia's health was not a good reason to keep Esther nearby. The girl had worked like a slave since they left Ash Hollow, filling in where Cordelia could not, caring both for their family and for others in the wagon company.

Cordelia simply nodded when Esther turned to her with a beaming face after Daniel appeared. Daniel pulled Esther behind him on his mare and they trotted toward the rock formations in the distance.

"Not too far," Cordelia called after them, and Esther waved back in acknowledgment.

In the tent the previous night, after the children were asleep, Franklin had whispered to her not to be too harsh on Esther. He'd always had a soft spot for his oldest daughter, but Cordelia knew he was right. She had to trust the girl to act as they had raised her. In recent days, Esther had shown she was maturing out of her giddiness—one good result of this journey.

Cordelia watched Daniel's horse slow about halfway between the wagons and the rocks. Sand and wind had created spires and huge blocks out of the red sandstone. Franklin had pointed out Chimney Rock, still days ahead of them, he said, though now visible. The land looked alien to someone who came from fertile river bottom land in Missouri. Cordelia didn't think this land could grow anything more than a little grass in the ravines.

She wondered what Esther and Daniel talked about. The lad pointed at something beyond them, and she thought Esther nodded in response, but they were too far away to determine what they might be looking at.

Of course, she and Franklin hadn't needed anything to talk about when they were courting. Or rather, they could talk on any subject and find it fascinating. Or talk about nothing and be perfectly happy.

Such foolishness. Cordelia shook her head and turned to listen to Noah, who wanted her to walk with him. She sighed. Well, she'd ridden in the wagon for two days now—she should walk awhile. She signaled to the twins to stop the oxen so she could climb down.

Esther clung to Daniel's waist as they rode across the barren land. He pointed at Chimney Rock, and she nodded against his back. She knew what the spire was—Pa had shown the whole family the night before. It was still far ahead of them, but peeked over the surrounding land like a church steeple, almost orange in the glow of the morning sunshine.

"It's hundreds of feet high, your pa told me," Daniel said.

"Yes," she said smiling. Pa had told her the same thing, but she wouldn't let on. She liked the sound of Daniel's voice.

"Have your younger brothers and sisters seen it?" Daniel asked.

"Yes," she said, her smile widening.

Daniel half turned in the saddle and caught her eye. "You know all this already, don't you?"

She nodded, still beaming. She felt silly, but she was so happy.

"I'll be quiet, then."

"No need." She squeezed his waist slightly.

"I don't want to bore you."

"You're not."

"Then why are you laughing?" He turned back to the front.

"I'm just glad to be away from the wagons. To have quiet."

"So I shouldn't talk?" He sounded fretful.

"Your talking ain't bothering me. It's the children. And Ma. And doing for folks all day long." She pressed on his side again. "I like being with you. I don't mind what you say."

"What do you want to talk about?"

"Why don't you like to hunt?" she asked. She hadn't meant to blurt that out. Maybe he was sensitive about not seeming manly, but she'd been curious since her father reported Daniel was a good tracker, but a bad shot.

"I like watching the deer and buffalo. We slaughter cattle and hogs for food, but it's always seemed a shame to me to kill wild game."

"But your pa—"

"I ain't my pa." Daniel spoke in clipped tones.

"No, you ain't," Esther said. "You're much nicer."

At that, Daniel chuckled, then asked her about her life back in St. Charles. She talked for a long time, about their home and her friends, and how it felt to leave Amy behind, and he peppered her with questions. She asked him about Tennessee and Douglass and his nieces. Then she asked, "Do you remember anything about your real mother?"

"No," Daniel said with a sigh. "She died when I was born. Douglass remembers her, but I don't."

"Then Mrs. Abercrombie is the only mother you've ever known?"

"Yes. She's always felt like my true mother."

Esther was silent a moment. "Is she like your father?"

"Do you mean, is she as cantankerous as he is?" Daniel shook his head. "She supports him most of the time, but she argues with him, too. They fought over slavery a few nights ago. She's an abolitionist. A good woman."

"Mmm." Esther wondered—didn't a wife take on the attitudes of her husband? But then, Ma didn't always agree with Pa. Maybe a wife could have independent opinions and speak her own mind. Still, women couldn't control where they lived or how they were provided for. Husbands determined those things. A wife had to follow her husband—for richer or poorer, in good times and in bad, in sickness and in health. Taking a husband was not a thing to consider lightly.

No matter how much Esther wanted a man to love, a home of her own, and children, she realized she shouldn't rush into marriage. Whether Daniel was the man to provide her with what she wanted remained to be seen.

But it felt so lovely to ride across the open land pressed against his firm back. She wished she could stay with him all day.

Daniel brought Esther back to the wagons at the noon halt. He helped her off his mare. She thanked him bashfully and ran off toward her mother.

He tied his mount to his family's wagon, then lifted a crate out of the back and found the dinner plates. Ma was already frying johnny cakes.

"Did you have a nice ride?"

"Mmm," he said.

"Fine day."

He nodded.

"Lovely companion?" she asked with a slight smile.

Daniel looked up sharply. What was she getting at? "Yes, Ma. Do you approve of Esther now?"

"She's toiled like a grown woman in recent days. Caring for her ma and for the rest of her family. She's a good girl."

"Then you don't mind if I spend time with her?"

"Are you courting her?" She slid johnny cakes onto the plates he'd laid out.

"Maybe."

She stood straight and frowned at him. "Esther ain't a girl to trifle with, son. You either court her or you leave her alone."

"How do I know . . . ?"

"Know what? Whether you want to court her? Just treat her with respect. Like you treat me."

He could never think of Esther like he thought of Ma, and he shook his head. "I'll find the others."

There was no more talk of Esther through the noon meal, and when they set out again, Captain Pershing asked Daniel to accompany him scouting. As they rode ahead of the wagons, the captain pointed out buttes in the distance and they tried to compare those to the map the captain carried.

"Have a nice time with Esther this morning, son?"

Son? What did it mean for Captain Pershing to call him "son"? "Yes, sir. Beautiful day for a ride."

"She seemed to enjoy it also. Kept her dimples out all through our meal."

Daniel was silent. He spent most of the afternoon recalling the feel of Esther's breasts against his back—soft, even through his buckskin jacket.

They camped that evening where a small rivulet flowed into the North Platte. After supper, Daniel watched Esther across the camp. She wasn't smiling now, but seemed harried by chores and her siblings. He wanted to see the corners of her lips turn up when she laughed at him. He wanted to see her dimples.

After the sun set, Esther picked up a bucket and a lantern. She gestured toward the river and spoke to her father, but Daniel couldn't hear what they said. Captain Pershing nodded at one of the twins, who picked up another bucket. Esther and the boy then headed into the dusk.

Daniel got up to go after them. Esther shouldn't have to carry a full bucket back from the river in the dark, he thought.

He loped after Esther and her brother to the riverbank. "Good evening, Esther," he said, from behind them.

She swirled around and gasped. "Are you following us?"

Whichever twin it was turned and grinned. "Hey, there, Daniel."

"I seen a raccoon and her pups downstream," Daniel told him. "Why don't you go have a look?" He held out his hand for the lad's bucket, which the boy relinquished without a word and dashed off. Daniel took both buckets and filled them with water.

"Why'd you send him away?" Esther asked.

"So I could talk with you."

"Thank you for the ride this morning." He could barely see her face in the shadow, even with the glow of the lantern she held. She stood, waiting, as he climbed the riverbank to her side. "Well?" she asked.

"Well, what?"

"What'd you want to talk about?" Her hair glowed like moonlight, her curved figure silhouetted by the lantern.

He put down the buckets, then took her lantern and placed it on the ground. "Maybe I didn't really want to talk." He pulled her close and kissed her.

This wasn't like the first time he kissed her. Then he'd meant to comfort her after Charles Purcell had died. There was no comfort in this kiss, only heat. Her breasts, which had nestled against his back all morning, were now crushed against his chest, sending fire to his already heavy groin. Too many clothes, he thought, as he pulled her hips against his.

He explored her mouth, soft and wet and sweet. She clung to his shoulders, and when he tried to break away from her for sanity's sake, she pressed against him, right where it felt best. "Esther," he whispered.

"More." She tightened her embrace.

"Daniel, I ain't seen no raccoons." Her brother's voice came out of the darkness.

With a moan Esther pulled away, staring at Daniel, her lips parted as if ready for another kiss. "I'm here, Jonathan," she called. "Let's take the water back to the wagon."

Daniel's throat was tight when he swallowed, and his heart thumped. He watched silently as she and Jonathan lifted the buckets. She looked back at him once as she and her brother hurried toward camp.

He should have helped her with the water, as he'd meant to. In fact, he itched to follow her. But he needed to quiet himself, so he sat by the creek bank.

Kissing Esther had only made his doubts worse. Was he courting her? If not, what was he doing? His ma said to treat Esther with respect. Did he respect a girl who kissed like she did, throwing her whole body into it? But he wanted her to kiss him like that again. And more.

Chapter 27:   Sickness and Injury

Thursday, 27 May 1847. Made 14 miles today. Chimney Rock in sight. FP

Friday morning Samuel Abercrombie walked his gelding off to the side of the wagons. They'd made decent time the day before, and he was pleased. They'd left the pestilence behind in Ash Hollow, and the families still with them were willing to push the pace. They might make it to Oregon before winter after all.

Franklin Pershing trotted over to Samuel. "Another pleasant day," the man said.

Samuel nodded. "That it is. Should make good speed today."

"We have a family sickening." Pershing's tone seemed to accuse Samuel. Hell, Pershing was the captain. He was responsible if anything went wrong.

"So?"

"We may need to stop."

"Pershing!" Samuel exploded. "We split this company up to make good time. We been doing just that. Now you want to slow down again?"

"If we have more illness, we'll have to."

"They ain't got cholera, do they?"

Pershing grimaced. "How would I know? I ain't a doctor."

Samuel spat his tobacco juice.

"We left our only doctor back at Ash Hollow." Again, Pershing seemed to imply it was Samuel's fault.

"We got a couple of women what's as good as doctors. Ain't your wife been around sickness a lot? Harriet has, too."

"I want to keep Cordelia away from any illness, at least till we know what it is. In her condition . . . " Pershing's voice trailed off.

"But it's all right if my wife takes ill? Is that what you're saying? Just because she ain't breeding—"

"At the noon halt, I'd appreciate her taking a look." Now Pershing sounded apologetic. As well he should. Samuel didn't want sickness in his wagons. He'd lost one wife to fever already.

He snorted. "We'll see what's what at noon."

Franklin didn't know why Samuel Abercrombie had to argue all the time. The man couldn't hold a civil conversation about anything but the weather. And even that turned into an opportunity to push for faster travel.

Esther told him that morning a woman in camp and two of her children were feverish. He'd considered sending Cordelia to check on them, but Esther urged against it. "Let Ma be," she said. "I gave them some of our willow bark for tea. To take down the fever. That's what Ma would do."

Franklin shrugged and took his daughter's advice. She was growing up so fast. "You enjoyed your ride with Daniel yesterday?" he asked.

She looked startled, and there was something else in her eyes he couldn't read. Something furtive. "Yes, Pa."

"You let me know if you hear folks are getting worse." With that, Franklin left Esther in charge of the family's wagons while he rode ahead.

When they stopped for the noon meal, it was clear they had illness with them. The sick mother and children were unable to walk and sat in their wagon listlessly. A man in another family complained of fever also, though he still tended his team.

"We should stop, Franklin," Cordelia said as she handed him a plate of beans and cornbread. "Those poor children are sickening fast."

His next bite stuck in his gullet. "How do you know? I told you to stay away from them."

"I talked to their ma from outside the wagon. They're just little mites. And they ain't eating or drinking a thing."

He ate in silence, then stood. "I'll talk to the men." But he knew what they would say, particularly Abercrombie. He was right—the men insisted on moving on, at least for the rest of the day.

Cordelia rode in the lead Pershing wagon through the afternoon. Esther strode alongside the oxen, and the twins and Rachel minded the wagon behind them. Most of the emigrants were somber that afternoon, despite the spectacular land around them. With death hovering over the wagons, it was hard to exclaim over rocks, no matter how massive.

Off to the side, huge bluffs rose in the middle of the desert—formations Franklin called Courthouse Rock and the smaller Jailhouse Rock. But they didn't look like a courthouse or jailhouse to Cordelia. They looked like tombstones marking the graves of travelers felled as they attempted to reach the West.

She glanced at Esther. The girl had seemed troubled all day. Was it the specter of cholera and mortality? Or had something happened to her daughter—maybe something on the ride with Daniel yesterday? Though Esther seemed fine through the afternoon. Cordelia hadn't noticed her daughter's distress until bedtime last night.

"Esther," she called. "Come sit a spell."

"I'm fine, Ma."

"Then stop the wagon, so I can walk with you." When the oxen paused, Cordelia clambered down and trudged beside Esther.

"Shouldn't you be resting, Ma?"

"What's bothering you, child?" That direct approach had never worked with Zeke or Joel, but Esther generally responded to her mother.

This time, Esther merely shrugged.

"Did something happen with Daniel?"

"Oh, Ma!" Esther wailed.

"Did he hurt you?" Cordelia asked in a panic.

Esther shook her head, but Cordelia saw tears on her cheeks.

"What happened?" she said sharply.

"He kissed me," Esther whispered.

Cordelia sighed. "Is that all?" She assumed her daughter had been kissed back in Missouri.

"And I liked it!"

Cordelia bit off a chuckle. Well, well. Her daughter *was* growing up. Now what was a mother supposed to do with a daughter who liked to be kissed? "You need to keep him in his place, Esther. Young men don't always control themselves."

"But how do I control *me*, Ma?"

"You behave like I raised you," Cordelia said in the firm tone she had perfected during her years of mothering. "So you don't bring shame to your family. Remember that, young lady. Or I'll tie you to the wagon day and night."

Esther sniffed.

Cordelia spoke more gently, "I remember what it's like to be young, Esther. And Daniel has the makings of a good man. But if you don't want to find yourself married and carrying a child afore we reach Oregon, you'd best be careful. And not let yourself be alone with him or any other man."

"But I like him, Ma—"

"If you didn't like him, it wouldn't be so hard. I mean what I say, don't let him near when there's no one else around."

Esther made supper that evening, still feeling uneasy after her conversation with her mother. She was embarrassed to have even mentioned such a personal thing as Daniel's kiss. But she didn't know how to handle it. She'd never felt anything so wonderful or so frightening as his tongue stroking her mouth while his body pressed against hers. She'd never wanted the kiss to end.

When Jonathan interrupted them, she'd been angry and relieved and sad and glad, all at the same time. Then all night she'd lain awake, reliving the moments of Daniel's kiss, until her body throbbed from head to toe, until her private parts ached.

What would it be like to lie with a man? She knew what happened between a man and a woman—she'd grown up on a farm, seen her brothers naked, and now slept in a tent with her parents in a bedroll nearby. But what would it feel like? She couldn't ask Ma! Esther and Amy had speculated about such things back in St. Charles, but now she wished Jenny McDougall were around—she needed a young married woman she

191

could talk to.

While she fretted about Daniel, Esther also worried about her mother. Ma tired easily, but seemed healthier than she had the first day or so after they left Ash Hollow. Still, Esther didn't want Ma to get sick, so she tried to keep her mother away from the families with fever.

After the Pershings ate supper, Esther took a pot of soup to one family. She found Daniel's mother and another woman already tending them.

"Thank you, Esther," Mrs. Abercrombie said, taking the pot from her.

"How are they?" Esther asked.

"The mother is improved, but the children are still ailing. I got some willow tea in 'em. We'll try your soup now."

"Do you need me to stay?"

Mrs. Abercrombie shook her head. "We'll watch 'em. You tend to your own family. How's your ma?"

"Better. Missing Zeke and Joel is her primary worry."

"I'm sure your brothers are fine. You go on to bed."

"Come wake me, if you need me," Esther said, and went back toward her campsite.

"Esther," Daniel called as she passed.

She stopped and stared at him.

"Would you like to take a walk?"

She wanted to walk with him, but she mustn't. Not after what Ma said. Esther shook her head. "Not tonight. Ma needs me." And she swallowed hard as she walked away, the ache still low in her belly.

The next day, the last Saturday in May, the wagon company trekked along the North Platte again. Samuel was glad Pershing hadn't suggested laying by. None of the sick had died yet—the children still clung to life, and the adults had improved.

Samuel chafed at the plodding pace Pershing set today. The man was hedging his bets—not pushing the emigrants, but not stopping to rest. A slow pace was the worst possible course, in Samuel's opinion. Any movement wore on the animals, but dallying did little to get them to Oregon. He'd almost rather they laid by so he could hunt freely.

The whole company was out of sorts. Harriet was worn out nursing the sick. Without a doctor to bleed folks, there wasn't much she could do. And with Cordelia Pershing feeling puny, she couldn't be of much help to Harriet. Good thing her daughter Esther was around. That girl was turning out to be as strong as Harriet. Better than Louisa—Douglass's wife was a lazy thing, Samuel had always thought.

By supper time they reached Courthouse Rock and made camp along the river parallel to the colossal butte. Pershing stopped by the Abercrombie campfire and announced, "We're laying by tomorrow. For the Sabbath."

"Pershing—" Samuel started.

"I ain't asking, Abercrombie. I'm telling. Today's travel sickened folks again. I don't think those two children will make it till morning."

"Then what's the harm of moving on, once we get 'em in the ground?" Samuel knew his words were harsh and saw Harriet stand up from her cooking, hands on her hips.

"Others are ailing also," Pershing responded.

"You don't just mean your wife?"

Harriet opened her mouth as if to speak, but said nothing.

Pershing shook his head. "Another man in his prime is down with fever tonight. Maybe we're carrying cholera with us, though without Doc Tuller I can't be sure. I'm hoping Doc and the others catch up soon."

"Then you *have* been deliberately going slow?" Samuel snorted. "I reckoned you was."

A scream sounded from across the camp. Pershing turned and ran toward the sound. Samuel followed at an easy pace—no sense rushing until he knew what the problem was.

At Bramwell's wagon, Jacob Bramwell lay on the ground, blood spurting from his arm. Pershing and Bramwell's wife were tying a rag around the arm to stop the bleeding.

"What happened?" Samuel asked.

"Chopped his forearm with the hatchet," Mrs. Bramwell said. She was about thirty, several years younger than her husband. Their five children stood in shocked silence watching.

"Sarah," Cordelia Pershing said to the oldest Bramwell girl. "Get a bucket of water boiling."

"We need to cauterize it with fire," Pershing said, grimacing as he twisted the rag to tighten it. "Find a shovel or other metal tool."

"Use the damn hatchet," Samuel said. "It oughta be good for something after maiming him."

Once the commotion over Mr. Bramwell's injury calmed down, the Abercrombies ate their supper. Daniel was out of sorts and didn't relish Pa telling them all what a piss poor job of leading this company Captain Pershing was doing. "I've a mind to take over and move us on," Pa proclaimed.

"You don't know the route," Daniel mumbled, wishing he dared to say more to Pa.

"How hard can it be to follow a river? At least I'd keep us going, not stop at every sniffle and ache. And now he's committed to laying by, after that fool Bramwell cut himself."

"It's more than a cut, Samuel," Ma said. "The man will probably lose his hand."

Pa snorted. "Says the kindling he was cutting slipped. Damn carelessness, if you ask me."

While Pa continued to rant, Daniel remembered his afternoon. He'd asked Esther to walk with him, and she'd refused. He thought she was afraid of her mother for some reason, or maybe she was afraid *for* her mother. He asked his mother about Mrs. Pershing's health, but Ma didn't have much of an answer.

Now his father spouted off when he had no cause to. Daniel had spent enough time with Captain Pershing to know he was conscientious and fair. The captain might be more cautious than Pa, less prone to push ahead as fast as they could, but he was a good man. Yet Pa took every opportunity to beleaguer the man—which wasn't right.

And Mr. Bramwell's injury was certainly not the captain's fault.

Daniel couldn't do a damn thing about any of it—not about Esther, Pa, Mr. Bramwell, or the sick folks. He didn't swear much, even in his thoughts, but now he felt like cursing the world. He saddled his mare and rode out on the plains at a fast trot. He wanted to gallop, but that wouldn't be fair to the horse, not in the gathering dusk. Though he stayed away from camp until the first stars came out, the ride wasn't enough to dispel his fury, and he returned as hot and bothered as when he'd left.

On the Sabbath morning another family reported fever—now three stricken families out of the ten or so still with the company. And Mr. Bramwell was drunk on whiskey to keep him from moaning with pain. His hand had swollen, and according to Ma, it was likely to have to come off. Who would act as surgeon without a doctor around?

After Captain Pershing conducted a brief prayer service, Daniel sought out Esther. She had already reached the wagon of one of the ailing families.

"Would you like to escape for a bit? Take another ride?" he asked.

"Oh, Daniel," she sighed, reaching for a toddler who fussed and whined. "I can't. This poor mite is fevered, and I need to rub him down. His ma's too poorly to care for him."

"Where's your ma?"

Esther shook her head. "She's got our family to tend to. She and Rachel. Pa's with the men, and looking in on the Bramwells often. I'm the only one free to help those with fevers."

Daniel scratched his head. He couldn't pull her away from her duty. "I'll see if my ma or Louisa can help you." He found his mother and told her about the spreading illness.

"I'll go," she said. "Louisa's feeling poorly. I hope she ain't catching the fever. Your father and Douglass are going hunting. They don't want to waste the day. Will you go with them?"

Daniel shrugged. "I don't have a mind to."

"You're upset with your pa, ain't you?"

"He's so hell-bent—"

"Language, Daniel."

"—on making good time that he don't care about people. Esther's slaving away while her mother is pining, all because Pa wanted to move on. And folks need the doctor."

"Most of the men agreed with your father about moving on."

Daniel took a deep breath and frowned. "You didn't."

"No. But that don't make your father wrong."

"Think I'll see what the captain needs," Daniel said.

Harriet spent the day split between doing laundry and tending to the sick, including her daughter-in-law Louisa. Louisa wasn't as ill as most, and so Harriet walked throughout the camp, trying to determine who was fit and who was ailing. Esther Pershing was ahead of her, already caring for the feverish children, bathing one little toddler who'd gone into seizures earlier that morning.

Cordelia Pershing made the rounds of the wagons also, though the woman looked pinched in the mouth, as if in pain. Harriet stopped her as they both crossed the middle of the wagon circle. "You feeling all right, Cordelia?"

"Can't seem to catch my breath." The captain's wife smiled, but her eyes seemed strained. "I thank you for your concern."

"You best rest. Your girl Esther is doing the nursing of two women today."

Cordelia nodded. "It's good for her to be occupied."

"Daniel seems quite taken with her. Has your opinion of them courting changed from when we started the journey?" Harriet asked.

"Daniel is a fine lad. Franklin speaks highly of him. But—"

"But they are young," Harriet said, staring into the distance. "I wish we were settled. I wish they had more young folk around them, that they weren't thrown together. That we knew where we'll be living a year from now."

"The future is never settled," Cordelia said with a sigh. "Though you're right. If only they'd seen more of life afore being trapped in this wagon train together."

"Is that how you see it? We're trapped?"

"'Tweren't my choice to leave home."

Harriet smiled in sympathy. "Nor mine."

By evening when Samuel and Douglass returned, Harriet had supper waiting. Louisa's fever had worsened—it might be cholera after all.

While Samuel recounted their hunting successes, Daniel sat staring toward the Pershing campfire nearby. Harriet followed his gaze. Esther stood ladling food onto her family's plates, fatigue showing in her stooped shoulders and mussed curls.

Chapter 28: A Ride at Chimney Rock

Sunday, 30 May 1847. Bramwell cut his arm with a hatchet this a.m. More in our small group sicken. FP

The sun rose warm and bright Monday morning, the last day of May. Samuel smiled when he saw Harriet had already fried antelope steaks from his hunt yesterday. Steak and cornmeal mush—a hearty meal to start a man's day right.

"Louisa is still poorly," Harriet said in a low voice as she forked a steak onto his plate.

Samuel grunted. "We can't stay here."

"Pa, maybe—" Douglass began.

"I'm sorry, son. But no Abercrombie will be the cause of any delay." He ordered his family to pack the wagons as soon as breakfast was over. He was hitching his oxen in their yokes when Franklin Pershing walked over.

"Folks is still ailing, Abercrombie. And Bramwell is delirious. His arm is turning septic, I fear. I've a mind to lay by another day."

"The hell you do," Samuel said. "We're moving on."

"Even though your daughter-in-law is sick?"

Samuel gestured at the horizon. "We been in sight of Chimney Rock for days now, and we ain't getting any closer. I'm determined to reach it today."

"I'm captain of this company. You told me awhile back I should give the orders."

Samuel snorted. "That was afore I seen what a mollycoddler you was. You worry about the sick, but what about us that's fit? Don't we deserve to move along smartly? It's a fine day. Too fine to waste." He snapped the bolt on the last yoke into place. "I'm taking my platoon forward. The rest of you can follow or not."

Pershing cursed and turned on his heel.

As Samuel pulled his wagons out of the circle, Pershing shouted, "Pack up, we're leaving."

Once the wagons were underway, Franklin rode off to their side by himself. Abercrombie and his platoon were ahead of the others, but still within sight. Franklin didn't care if Indians picked off those lead wagons—it would serve the obnoxious Tennessean right.

Franklin realized he'd made a mistake splitting the company at Ash Hollow. Folks in the remaining group were sickening also, they had a man with a serious wound, and they had no doctor to help.

He wasn't sure if the fever striking his fellow emigrants was cholera or something else, though it had every sign of cholera—not only the fever, but the diarrhea and vomiting. Whether it had followed them or they'd found another source for the putrid illness, he couldn't guess. Doc Tuller might not even know, but at least the doctor could tell them how to treat the suffering.

Bramwell's arm needed to come off above the elbow. Franklin had seen such surgeries during Army skirmishes, but they'd all been done by Army doctors. He'd never cut off a man's limb, but if he didn't do it, who would? He wished Doc were here. He had half a mind to send Daniel Abercrombie back to find the others, but old Samuel would never tolerate splitting up his family—though he didn't seem to care that Franklin had left two of his sons behind.

Cordelia, Esther, Harriet Abercrombie, and a couple of other women had spent the Sabbath bathing the sick, trying to get them to drink, and cleaning up after their illness. He hated to move the ailing, but he wouldn't divide the company further. If Abercrombie moved on, then Franklin would have to follow with the rest of the wagons.

But he feared for them all, wondering who would sicken next. He hoped it wouldn't be Cordelia—her health was not good.

Cordelia sat on the wagon bench, her tired body swaying as the wheels jolted along. The twins and Rachel minded the teams—Esther had decided to ride with the poor little boy suffering from fever. Cordelia didn't think the toddler would survive until evening, and she hated for her daughter to see him die. Even worse, she feared Esther would catch his illness.

Though worried for Esther, she also continued to fret over her older sons' absence. Mr. Bramwell's accident reminded her men could be injured at any time, even while working at a simple chore like chopping wood.

Not a waking hour went by that she didn't pray for Zeke and Joel. It had been a week since they'd parted—the longest she'd gone without seeing her sons since they were born.

She knew they were men now, and she wouldn't have them with her forever. They'd take wives. As soon as they reached Oregon, Zeke would file his own land claim. Joel would probably stake a claim as soon as he reached eighteen. But they'd be close by. Joel talked of exploring the West, but she hoped in the end he would settle down near her. If he listened to his mother, he would. If she had the chance to tell him her opinions. She sighed, wondering when she would see her boys again.

"Ma!" David shouted. "Pa's calling the halt."

"All right," she said. "Turn the oxen like he showed you."

As soon as the wagons were stopped, Cordelia handed her skillet and provisions down to the twins. She climbed out of the wagon and made a fire to start cooking the noon meal. "Rachel, go find Esther. See how she's doing."

Rachel walked off, but soon returned sobbing. "The baby's dead!" she cried.

Cordelia straightened up from the fire. "And Esther?"

"She's washing the body."

Her heart sinking, Cordelia thrust the skillet toward Rachel. "Fry the bacon and get out the bread. I'm going to help Esther." She hurried toward the stricken wagon.

"Why didn't you send for me?" she asked when she found her oldest daughter. Cordelia enveloped Esther in a hug and felt the girl sag against her breast.

"Oh, Ma! His breathing just slowed to nothing. And then it weren't there at all."

"Where's his mother?" Cordelia asked, smoothing Esther's curls away from her damp face.

"In the wagon. She's sick, too."

"Does she know?"

Esther nodded. "I told her, but I don't know whether she understood."

Cordelia climbed in the wagon to see the grieving woman. Tears ran down the poor mother's face, but she was too weak to wipe them away. "My dear," Cordelia said, taking a corner of a blanket to dry the woman's cheeks. "I am so sorry." By then, Cordelia was crying also.

"What shall I do, Ma?" Esther asked from outside the wagon.

"Go find your pa. We'll have to bury the poor child afore we move on."

"No!" the tot's mother wailed. "I can't leave him here. Not in this Godforsaken country! Not where the wolves and savages can find him."

"Shhh," Cordelia soothed, rocking the woman in her arms.

"I can't bear it," the sobbing mother moaned.

"With God's grace, you can," Cordelia murmured. "You ain't got no other choice." She thought again of Zeke and Joel, and prayed to see them alive.

By the time they buried the dead toddler, it was midafternoon. When they got underway again, Ma refused to let Esther ride with the sick family any longer, insisting she would take Esther's place. When Pa motioned the wagons to continue their trek along the North Platte fork, Esther walked beside her family's wagons with her younger siblings, while Ma sat with the dead child's mother.

Esther could hardly breathe for the lump in her throat, which threatened to turn into sobs at any moment. She'd never experienced anything so dreadful as holding the little boy's fevered body while he died. She'd never watched anyone die before. A moan escaped her, and Rachel put an arm around her shoulder. "You did the best you could," Rachel said.

"Esther," Daniel called as he rode over. "Come with me."

She grabbed the hand he held out, clutching it as if his touch could rescue her from the horror of the day. He pulled her up behind him on his mare.

"Take me away, Daniel," she pleaded. "Take me far away." She buried her face in his warm, strong back.

He urged the mare into a canter south across the plains, out of earshot of the wagons, while she wept until the tears were gone.

Daniel didn't say a word while she cried, but he seemed to know when she finished, because he slowed the horse to a walk, pressed a handkerchief into her palm, and squeezed her fingers briefly. She dried her face, then laid her cheek against his back again. "Your shirt's all wet," she said. "I'm sorry."

"It's all right." He shrugged against her face.

"How did you know I needed to escape?"

"I been watching you." He took her hand, which was clasped at his waist. "I knew you felt awful after the child died on you this morning."

"Oh, Daniel," she sighed, "it was dreadful." And she described the whole experience.

When she finally quieted, he pointed toward their left. "Look."

Chimney Rock loomed just ahead of them to the south. Its conical sandstone base rose to a needle-like spire glowing in the afternoon sun. They'd seen it for days, but now it was so close, its majesty awed Esther—it was far more noble than a chimney. "It's like a church," she whispered. "A steeple. Or the finger of God."

Daniel nodded. "It reminds me of the church near our home in Tennessee. It's even grander, I know, but our bell tower was white and glowed in the sun, just like this pillar."

He turned his mare toward the tower, and they rode in silence as they approached its base. Esther knew her parents wouldn't want her to get too far from the wagons, and Ma had told her not to be alone with Daniel. She started to tell him to turn around. "We should—"

"Esther," Daniel interrupted in a rush, "I always reckoned I'd get married in that little church in Tennessee. That can't happen now. But I know who I want to marry. It's you. Will you marry me?"

Stunned, Esther sat silent. The morning had been so dreadful, and now Daniel offered her everything she'd ever desired.

"If you need to think about it—"

"No," she said. "No, I don't need to think. Yes, yes, I'll marry you," and she hugged his back.

His hand grasped hers and held it to him just above his waist. "You will?"

She nodded. "Yes. I decided to marry you after the dance with the soldiers, you know." She giggled, remembering how she'd vowed to make him fall in love with her.

"Well, why didn't you say so then! You could have saved me a lot of trouble."

Esther swatted his back. "Don't be ridiculous. A girl can't ask a man to marry her." Though it would certainly make the world an easier place to live, she thought.

"I want to stake my claim in Oregon," Daniel said. "Then build a house for us. We'll have a fine spread. It'll be a lot of work, but it'll be ours."

"Yes." That's what she dreamed of also—her own home, her own man to love. Daniel did love her, didn't he? He hadn't said. "Daniel . . . "

"What?"

"Do you . . . Do you love me?"

"Of course, I do. Well, at least, I think I do. I've never felt like this about any other girl. I wouldn't have asked you to marry me if I didn't, would I?"

"All right, then." She snuggled closer.

"Do you love me?" he asked.

She did! She thought she did. No, she knew she did. "Yes, you silly man. Or I wouldn't have set my cap for you."

"All right, then."

She peeked around his shoulder and saw a smile light his face. "We'd best get back," she said.

He turned the mare away from Chimney Rock. Esther leaned against his strength for the long slow ride back to the wagons.

As he steered his mare toward the wagons, Daniel felt dazed reflecting on the long day.

That morning as he'd listened to Captain Pershing conduct the burial service for the little boy, Daniel had been overcome by all the suffering that had hit their company. All able-bodied members of their company were present, but many in their party were sick, including Louisa, and Mr. Bramwell still lay in his wagon moaning in pain.

Daniel had seen Esther at the gravesite, her face so stricken it had stabbed his heart. More than fatigue, he'd seen despair on her face. He'd wondered whether to ask her to ride with him again—she'd refused his last invitation. But her anguished expression had convinced him to try again.

"Take me away, Daniel," she'd said, and he had, feeling like her knight in shining armor, like he would slay dragons for her.

She cried against his shoulder for a long time. When she told him about the child's last breath, he ached to spare her any such pain again.

Then Chimney Rock shone in the sunshine, like a beacon from God, and he'd blurted out his proposal. He hadn't planned it. He hadn't known he would ask her to marry him, not then, but once the words were out, it felt right. He wanted her. He wanted to protect her. He never wanted to lose her. And the only way to keep her was to marry her.

And then she said, "Yes."

The reality of what he'd done hit home. He would have a wife to provide for. He could no longer rely on his father for support, he would have to farm his own land. Staking his own claim had been his plan, but now it was essential. He described the house he would build for her, but all she seemed to worry about was whether he loved her.

Love? What was love? He wanted her, needed her, cared for her. Was that love? He hoped so.

Did she love him? Her kisses of a few days earlier made him think so.

How would they discover what love was? Was it any more than building a home and a family together?

"Daniel," Esther said as they reached the wagons. "Let's not tell anyone yet. Let's keep our plans to ourselves."

He felt both relieved and scared. Relieved not to have to talk to his parents . . . Or her parents. Scared she might be having second thoughts already. "Are you sure you want to marry me?" he asked, his voice quavering.

She nodded. "It ain't that. I just want to get used to the idea afore we tell anyone."

He smiled. "All right. It do take some getting used to, don't it?"

Chapter 29:   Toward Scott's Bluff

Monday, 31 May 1847. A child died this morning. Others remain ill. We move forward at Abercrombie's insistence. FP

Esther didn't think she would sleep at all Monday night. Her mind whirled as she remembered the poor dead child and Daniel's proposal. It had been both the worst day and the best day of her life. She yearned to have someone to talk to, but she couldn't tell Ma, her friend Amy was far away, and Jenny McDougall was with the wagons left behind.

Daniel hadn't kissed her again when he returned her to the wagons, though she'd hoped he would. But her family was nearby, and they'd agreed to keep their engagement secret for the time being. She must have been exhausted, because after no more than a few minutes of remembering her ride with Daniel, she slept deeply until first light.

A wail from across the camp awoke her. "What is it?" she asked her mother.

From the other side of the tent, Ma said, "The other baby's dead, most likely. Poor mite was suffering terribly last night."

Esther swallowed hard. She'd let Ma do all the nursing through the afternoon and evening. After losing one child, Esther had been too drained to help. "Were you over there all night?" she asked.

"Till midnight," Ma said. "Then Harriet Abercrombie took over. That woman is a blessing."

Pa stuck his head in the tent. "Time to be rising. We'll be burying another afore we leave this morning."

Their company had encountered such tragedy and tribulations, Esther mused, as she stood beside another small grave after breakfast. The settlers sang "Amazing Grace," though their voices were weak without Jenny McDougall's soprano leading them. Still, they sang all the verses, all the way through the last:

> *The earth shall soon dissolve like snow,*
> *The sun forbear to shine;*
> *But God, who called me here below,*
> *Will be forever mine.*

Forever mine—the words echoed in Esther's mind. This little girl and the lad they'd buried the day before would be forever God's.

And she would be forever Daniel's. The notion came to her in the whisper of a breeze touching her cheek. She hid a small smile behind her hand. It was blasphemous to compare human love with God's, but that's how she felt. She would be Daniel's, and he would be hers. Forever.

That idea buoyed her through the morning. It was now the first of June, and the sun shone warm and bright as she walked. She wouldn't think of dead children on a day like this. She'd think of her future, hers and Daniel's, which would be as warm and bright as this day.

"You all right, Esther?" Pa asked, when he rode past the wagons on his rounds.

"Yes, Pa."

"You've been a great help to everyone, daughter. I know you've had it hard."

"No harder than Ma," Esther said. "Or you. Can't be easy being captain when folks is dying."

Pa looked sad as he smiled down at her. "That's a right grown-up thought to have, Esther. I think this journey has shown you a thing or two."

"Yes, it has, Pa." She let her secret smile slip out into a grin. "It surely has."

Harriet was worn out Tuesday morning after spending half the night with another dying child. She'd relieved a bleary-eyed Cordelia Pershing, sending the captain's wife off to bed, and she hadn't had the heart to ask Esther to take over. The poor girl had had enough to deal with when the first child died in her arms. That was too much for a fifteen-year-old to handle.

Though Douglass had been only twelve when Abigail died, and he'd handled his mother's fever and death stoically.

After the little girl passed away shortly before daybreak, Harriet washed and dressed the body and wrapped it in a quilt for burial. As she worked, she heard Mr. Bramwell's moans from his family's wagon nearby. Something would have to be done for him, or he would die also.

When Harriet had done what she could for the dead child, she returned to her wagon to fix breakfast for her family. She fried meat, then stuck her head in the tent where Douglass and his family slept. "How's Louisa?" she asked.

"I'm improving, I think, Mother Abercrombie," her daughter-in-law whispered.

Harriet smiled. "I'm glad. Would you like some broth? Douglass, you and the girls come eat now."

"Yes, thank you," Louisa said. "How are the others in camp?"

"Another child gone." Harriet sighed.

Louisa gasped. "Oh, Mother Abercrombie, how terrible! But don't tell the girls." Annabelle and Rose were barely stirring beside their parents. "They're too young to see so many children die."

"They seen the little boy's funeral yesterday," Harriet said. "And there'll be another one today."

"Another burial?" Samuel said from behind her. "That'll slow us down."

"Yes, Samuel, it will," Harriet said, backing out of Douglass's tent and standing, hands on hips.

"We didn't make but thirteen miles yesterday," he grumbled. "What with burying the child at our noon halt. Won't make any better time today."

"Probably not."

"Need to leave the sick folks. And Bramwell. We've traveled so slow, Doc Tuller and the rest of 'em can't be too far behind."

"We're already down to fourteen wagons, Pa." Daniel filled his plate with a quick nod and smile of thanks at Harriet. "If we split any more, we won't have enough men for guards at night."

Samuel pointed his fork at Daniel. "No sass from you, young man. We'd be safe enough with me'n Douglass. And you can at least raise an alarm when on guard duty, though you ain't no shot. No savages would bother us twice."

"Please don't argue," Harriet said, sighing. "We'll attend the funeral this morning, and we'll act respectful. That poor family has lost both their children."

"As long as we move out smartly afterward," Samuel grumbled.

Captain Pershing did not let the emigrants dawdle after burying the child. The mother who'd lost both her children, still feverish herself, lay weeping in her wagon. Harriet rode in her own family's wagon, too tired to walk after the long futile night of nursing. She sat on the wagon bench watching the strange landscape as they rolled past sandstone bluffs and buttes. Some were gray, some were reddish-orange, none bore any vegetation taller than sedge grass. It was a lonely, empty land, stark to the point of desolation—a sad place to bury a child.

Franklin led a doleful group of pioneers Tuesday after the girl's burial. The deaths of the two children and Bramwell's suffering frightened and saddened everyone. Everyone except Samuel Abercrombie—the Tennessean still pushed for a faster pace, even after seeing what it had done to the ailing in their party.

Franklin deliberately held the oxen and mules to a slow walk and stopped frequently to water the teams in the river. They would continue to follow this branch of the North Platte for many more days—past Fort Laramie, which was at least a week's journey from where they were now, according to Frémont's map.

By midafternoon, they'd only made ten miles. Louisa Abercrombie was improved, but the woman who'd lost her children was worse, and Bramwell was still delirious. When they reached a point where the river ran smooth and calm, Franklin waved his hat to signal a halt and shouted, "We'll camp here."

Abercrombie rode over. "There's hours of daylight left," he called.

"Why we stopping?"

"I don't want to lose any more of our party," Franklin said. "We're halting."

"Ain't no call for it," Abercrombie said.

"If you go on," Franklin said, "your family will be alone." He wasn't sure he could hold all the others, but he reckoned he could keep most of them from following Abercrombie. The travelers were plumb tuckered out and dispirited.

To Franklin's surprise, Abercrombie didn't try to move on. Franklin suspected Samuel's wife Harriet had had a word with him—she'd spent half the night nursing the sick girl to no avail. And her son Daniel likely backed her up.

"Where do you think Zeke and Joel are?" Cordelia asked him as they ate supper.

The younger children all sat listening, so he made a good story of it. "I'm sure they're catching up. We ain't been traveling too fast. Once their sick folks healed"—he hesitated, but didn't voice the alternative—"they'll make good time."

Cordelia sighed. "I miss my boys."

Little Ruth's chin quivered, and Franklin said to his youngest daughter, "Let's you, me, and Noah go down to the river to look for frogs after supper."

The twins chimed in, "We wanna come," and so after supper he took all his young'uns, leaving Esther and Rachel to help their ma.

While Franklin and his children were catching frogs, a shout arose from the camp. He looked back and saw a rider galloping toward the wagons.

Joel! He'd caught up with them.

While Joel Pershing ate the meal his mother pulled together, several men in the company sat around the Pershing fire listening to him recount what had happened to the travelers at Ash Hollow. Samuel leaned against a wagon wheel chewing tobacco, while Pershing sat beside his son smoking his pipe and asking questions.

"We're about a day behind you," Joel said. "It's been stop and go, but we've made good time the last couple of days."

Samuel spat. He considered telling Pershing their party ought to have made good time, too, but he wanted to hear what Joel had to say.

"Anyone die, son?" Pershing asked Joel.

Joel nodded grimly. "We lost four." As he told his tale, Samuel had to admit the other group had had a rough time of it, with few able-bodied men and several sick and grieving families.

"Zeke worked harder'n I did," Joel said, when Pershing praised him. "I scouted, but Zeke kept folks together. He's a leader—like you, Pa."

Samuel snorted, though he remained silent.

"We lost two children," Cordelia Pershing said. "And still have sick folks."

"And a man who's likely to lose his arm," Pershing added. "Cut himself with a hatchet."

"Our group is mostly recovered," Joel said. "Though I thought we'd lose McDougall for a day or two. He's still feeling puny."

"We'll wait here for you," Pershing said.

"Now wait a minute—" Samuel began, taking a step forward.

"No, you wait a minute," Pershing turned on Samuel. "I made a mistake in splitting up the company, and now we have a chance to fix it. We'll lay by until the rest of our wagons catch up."

Cordelia turned an evil eye on Samuel, as if daring him to argue. "My boys have been gone long enough," she said.

Samuel knew enough not to fight with a mother hen. He nodded and went back to his wagons to tell Harriet.

That night in the tent Cordelia whispered, "Thank you," to her husband as she snuggled close to his warmth.

"What for?" Franklin asked.

"For getting Joel back. For him and Zeke being safe. For making Ruthie happy tonight—she's our worrier."

"I didn't have nothing to do with the boys. Zeke and Joel took care of themselves. And of the rest of their party also, it seems."

They were silent, and Cordelia thought Franklin had fallen asleep, until he said, "Bramwell's arm has to come off."

She stifled a gasp, not wanting to wake the children.

"I don't know how to do it." Franklin exhaled slowly. "But it has to be done. Tomorrow, while Joel is here. He can help."

"Oh, Franklin! He's only seventeen."

"He's a man, Cordelia. One I trust. He and Daniel Abercrombie are the most reliable men in our company at present."

"I'll help."

She felt him nod against her shoulder. "I'll need you, too," he said.

"But not Esther. It's not a fit sight for a girl."

He didn't respond, and presently she felt him relax. Cordelia lay awake a long time, torn between joy at seeing Joel again and knowledge of the gruesome task awaiting them the next day.

Chapter 30:   Arrival at Scott's Bluff

Tuesday, 1 June 1847. Joel found us. We will wait for the rest of our company to catch up. Must amputate Bramwell's arm. FP

A cold rain fell Wednesday morning. "Time to take Bramwell's arm off," Franklin announced as soon as he finished breakfast. His sleep had been fitful. He couldn't delay the amputation without risking Bramwell's life, though the surgery itself might kill the man.

"Can't it wait, Pa?" Joel asked. "Doc Tuller will be here in a couple days."

"Wish it could, son, but I've been holding off. He looks worse this morning. I've got to take the arm. And I need you to hold him."

Joel gulped and turned white.

"I'll do it, Pa," Esther said.

Cordelia shook her head at Franklin from behind Esther.

Franklin sighed. His daughter's face looked pale, but determined. "I need a strong man to hold Bramwell down," he told Esther. "You and your ma stand by with water and towels."

Franklin and Joel laid Bramwell across several crates. Standing next to the gangrenous arm, Franklin took the saw, then looked around. "Everyone back," he shouted at the gawkers. "Save Cordelia and Esther." Then he turned to Joel. "You got the whiskey?"

Joel nodded, now looking green.

"Take a swig yourself, then get enough down Bramwell's throat to render him insensible. Keep the bottle handy—we'll pour the rest on the wound once the arm comes off."

Joel did as Franklin said.

After Bramwell was in a stupor, Franklin tied a tourniquet around the arm and started cutting. Bramwell woke, bucking and screaming, despite the whiskey. "Hold him!" Franklin yelled at Joel. Joel leaned on the man's shoulders to keep him still, Franklin finished cutting, and Esther ran over with the towels. "Whiskey first," Franklin told her. She poured from the bottle, and Bramwell moaned incoherently when the alcohol touched the gaping wound, but he no longer thrashed.

"I'll sew him up," Cordelia said, pushing Esther out of the way.

By this time, Joel was retching off to the side. Daniel Abercrombie had appeared and had his arm around Esther, who sobbed into his shoulder.

Franklin picked up the whiskey bottle and carried it to his campsite, where he sat and drank, heedless of the rain.

Samuel Abercrombie stood over Franklin and handed him his hat. "Might need this to keep off the damp," Samuel said.

Franklin grunted.

"It needed doing, Pershing. You was man enough to do it." Abercrombie clapped Franklin on the shoulder, then turned away. "I'll get the wagons lined up."

Samuel stayed far away from the Bramwell wagon while Pershing performed the surgery, but he heard it all. He couldn't have stood to touch the man's skin with a saw himself.

Afterward, it was the least he could do to take over from the shaken Pershing for a while. He ordered the wagons packed up and into line. And the travelers headed out in miserable spirits, plodding along the riverbank.

Ahead of them, Scott's Bluff loomed hundreds of feet above the river— a tall gray cliff made of layers of sandstone and ash. The river went right through a gap in the cliff, and the trail wound along the bottomland. The bluff rose to several craggy peaks, but Samuel knew they wouldn't get anywhere near those. The wagons would stay below, close to the river.

Around noon they halted near the base of Scott's Bluff, and as they were finishing their meal, a thunderstorm struck, adding to the discomfort of the cold rain. "We'll stop here," Franklin Pershing announced. He seemed recovered from the ordeal of the morning.

"We had a short day yesterday, Pershing. Need to make up the time now," Samuel argued.

"Bramwell's barely alive. Other folks is still sick. Plus, I'm sending Joel back to the rest of the wagons tomorrow. No need to make his journey longer."

"He's young," Samuel said.

Pershing shook his head. "Wind's coming from the west, and the cliff provides some shelter. Be best for the animals if we stop awhile."

Samuel didn't think the bluff added much protection, but he had noticed his oxen lagging. Maybe another slow day wouldn't hurt. "Let's give it an hour. See what the weather's like then."

Pershing shrugged and left to talk to others.

Daniel heard the exchange between his father and Captain Pershing. Would Pa never stop arguing? They were all worn out—people as well as oxen. A short day wouldn't hurt them.

Daniel had watched the captain take Mr. Bramwell's arm off from a distance. He considered volunteering to take Joel's place—he'd seen cattle and horses get sewn up and had done some stitching himself a time or two. Joel looked like he'd never seen a man bleed.

And Esther! She bravely helped her father. Daniel wanted to rush her away from that wretched scene. After having a sick child die in her arms just a few days earlier, she shouldn't have to deal with more suffering. Yet a part of him was proud she was so stouthearted. She'd make a fine wife, able to cope with whatever life brought them. Now that he'd declared his intentions, he'd begun thinking about the life they would build together.

Pa continued to rant about laying by here at Scott's Bluff. Daniel grew weary of listening. "I'm going to marry Esther Pershing," he announced quietly. "I've asked her, and she's said yes."

Pa cut off his speechifying in mid-sentence. "You what?"

Ma gasped. "Oh, Daniel!"

"I'm going to marry Esther."

"You didn't ask me first."

Daniel stood. "No, Pa, I didn't. I'm man enough to know who I want to marry."

"Man enough? What land you got? What tools or house? You ain't got nothing but what's in my wagons." Pa's hands fisted, and beneath his beard his upper lip curled in a sneer.

"I'll have as much land as you in Oregon," Daniel said. "We'll wait to marry until I can provide for her, but I'm telling you, she will be my wife. So anything you say about her pa, you're saying about family."

"Family." Pa spat on the ground. "Family is who does for you. Pershing ain't done a thing for me."

"Samuel," Ma said. "Don't—"

"Don't what, Harriet?" Pa turned on Ma. "Don't tell my son what's what? He don't know a damn thing."

"Daniel knows what he wants, Samuel. And he knows what he has to do afore he can marry Esther."

Pa stared at Daniel. "We'll see what he knows." Pa spat his tobacco juice again, then strode away.

Harriet sighed as she watched Samuel leave, then turned to her son. "Well, Daniel, that's quite an announcement."

"Are you pleased, Ma?" he asked, heaving a sigh as he sat on a box near the fire.

She pushed his hair off his forehead. She would lose him someday to some woman—but why now, and why to Esther Pershing? "Esther is a nice girl."

"But you don't like me marrying her," he stated.

"I don't know," she said, wondering what to say so her boy wouldn't run off like Samuel had. "I want you to be happy. If you think Esther will make you happy, then I'm pleased."

"But?"

"You're young yet, Daniel. Esther is younger still. This journey has been hard on both of you." She paused. "Are you sure?"

Daniel nodded. "I think so."

She smiled—her son didn't sound too sure after all. "Who knows of your engagement?"

"Just me and Esther. We said we wouldn't tell anyone. But I couldn't stand Pa talking so harshly about Captain Pershing. He's Esther's father. And he's a good captain."

"Well," Harriet said. "You certainly stopped him. Will Esther tell her parents now?"

Daniel looked up, stricken. "I guess I better warn her what I said."

Harriet nodded. "I think that would be wise." She watched Daniel walk off toward the Pershing wagons. Would he talk to Esther alone, or would he blurt out the engagement to her parents without warning as he had to Samuel and her?

From inside the tent, Louisa moaned. Douglass's wife still felt poorly, and it would be better if she could rest. Regardless what Samuel said, Harriet was thankful they were laying by. She scrambled into the tent to tend her daughter-in-law.

After chatting for a few minutes, Harriet determined Louisa had been dozing and hadn't heard Daniel. Thank goodness, Douglass and his daughters were out gathering wood. Only she and Samuel had heard Daniel's news—it might still be contained until Samuel had a chance to get used to the idea.

Harriet smiled to herself. As she'd told Daniel, Esther was a nice girl, and would make him a fine wife. If only Daniel's betrothed were a little older and both young people more settled.

Chapter 31:   Waiting

Wednesday, 2 June 1847. Bramwell's arm is off. He lives. Camped at Scott's Bluff, where we await the rest of our party. FP

Franklin was up with Joel at first light on Thursday. The young man had stayed with them two nights and a day. His help had been invaluable, both with Bramwell's surgery and with traveling the short distance to Scott's Bluff the day before. They were down several able-bodied men, due to illness and injury.

"We'll wait here, son, until you bring the rest of the company," Franklin said, clapping Joel on the shoulder. "Thank you for your assistance."

"If you can keep Abercrombie from moving on," Joel said, flashing his easy grin.

Franklin shook his head. "Don't matter what he does. We'll be here when you and Zeke catch up. I ain't splitting us up again. If Abercrombie leaves, that's on him."

Joel kissed his mother, mounted his horse, and rode off.

"We've raised fine sons, Franklin." Cordelia wiped a tear from her eye as she watched Joel leave.

Franklin hugged her. "That we have."

Samuel Abercrombie squinted and mumbled something as Franklin passed on his way to see Bramwell, but the large Tennessean seemed subdued.

As he returned to his own wagon, relieved to learn Bramwell was no longer delirious, he called to Abercrombie, "You hunting today?"

Abercrombie looked up. "I might at that."

"How's your daughter-in-law?" Franklin asked.

Abercrombie shrugged, as if he hadn't given the woman a thought.

"And the rest of your family? No one else sickening?" Franklin would have made the same inquiries of any other family in the company, but he knew civility ate at Abercrombie.

The man merely grunted in response and spat tobacco juice toward his fire pit. He didn't even bother to look at Franklin.

"Joel says he should find the other wagons today. Hopes they'll catch up tomorrow." Franklin wondered if that would appease Abercrombie or set him off.

The latter. "They damn well better catch up. I ain't waiting here any longer." Abercrombie nodded at the high bluff behind them. "Sitting under that cliff gives me a creepy feeling."

Franklin glanced up. He couldn't disagree with Abercrombie. The high rock formation loomed above them, and the legend of the man named Scott who'd died here some years earlier came to mind. Was that what bothered Abercrombie, or was there something else?

Cordelia stood staring into the distance until she couldn't see Joel's horse any longer, then called Esther and Rachel to help with laundry. They needed to make good use of this day in camp, though they would soon reach Fort Laramie, and she hoped for a longer respite there.

She ordered the twins to haul water. She set Esther to scrubbing and Rachel to rinsing, while Cordelia herself took on the mending. As she sewed, she smiled—it had been so good to see Joel. Now she knew he and Zeke weren't but a day's ride away, she felt better.

Harriet Abercrombie wandered over. "May I join you?" she asked. "I've brought some mending also. Louisa ain't up to it yet."

"How is she?" Cordelia asked with concern.

"Improved, but weak. Don't know what she had. Symptoms weren't as bad as cholera, but it was some kind of fever and digestive upset." Harriet sighed. "I surely will be glad to have a doctor back with us."

Cordelia nodded. "Yes. And the rest of our company."

"You'll be especially pleased to have your sons with us, no doubt," Harriet said.

"Yes."

"We have our children for such a short time afore they're grown." Harriet seemed to emphasize her words beyond their obvious meaning.

Cordelia frowned, wondering what Harriet was trying to imply. "Yes."

"Your sons are young men. As is Daniel. And Esther is a grown woman also."

Over at the wash tub, Esther gasped. Cordelia turned to her. "Something wrong, dear?"

"Lye soap stung my hand, Ma."

Harriet raised an eyebrow toward Esther, then turned the conversation to the mending in her lap. "My granddaughters seem to rip a seam every day," she said. "You must have it worse with so many boys. I remember when Daniel was a child."

And so the morning passed.

Daniel left camp in late morning to hunt with his father. "Why not Douglass?" Daniel asked when Pa ordered him to go.

"Let him stay with his sick wife. And mind his girls. Give your mother a rest from them."

Daniel raised an eyebrow—his father wasn't usually solicitous of Louisa or Ma. But he gathered his rifle and ammunition and saddled his mare. Pa probably wanted to talk him out of marrying Esther. Daniel wouldn't let it happen.

"Hear tell there's goats in the hills nearby," Pa said when they were underway. "Mountain goats."

"We ain't in the mountains yet, are we?" Daniel asked.

"Close enough."

They rode mostly west along a creek skirting the base of Scott's Bluff. Neither man said much. Pa's hound Bruiser trotted beside them. A few scrubby trees lined the creek's bank. Otherwise, the land was mostly dry grass poking out of sand, with only an occasional pine struggling to reach the sky.

"How do you think we'll find game here?" Daniel asked. "Nowhere for the animals to hide in the heat of the day."

Pa shrugged. "Bruiser'll nose the beasts out, if they're there. If he does, don't shoot the dog, all right, son?"

If Pa thought he was such a bad shot, Daniel wondered, why'd he make him come along?

After a while, Pa cleared his throat. "You sure 'bout this Pershing girl?"

Daniel frowned at his father. "Yes, sir." Now wasn't the time to voice his doubts.

"When a man marries, it's for keeps," Pa said. "Till one of you dies."

"Yes, sir, I know."

"Don't matter if you get a hankering for another woman," Pa said. "You're bound."

Did Pa feel bound to Ma? How had Pa felt about his first wife, Daniel's mother? Daniel didn't know how to raise those topics.

"I been lucky," Pa continued, answering Daniel's unasked questions. "Had two good women. Your ma, and now Harriet. We ain't always seen eye to eye, but they're mighty fine women." He turned and glowered at Daniel. "You think Esther's of a par with Harriet?"

Daniel swallowed. "I hope so, sir. I seen her handle the same things Ma and Miz Pershing have on this journey."

Pa squinted toward the hills ahead of them and nodded. "I don't think much of her pa. Pershing can't decide which boot to put on first. And he's soft. But his daughter—she may be different. She's got a strong mother."

They rode again in silence. Then Pa looked at Daniel again. "She said anything to her folks?"

"You mean Esther? Has she told Captain and Miz Pershing?" Daniel shook his head. "Last night she seemed upset I'd told you."

"You speak to her pa soon." Pa spat and whistled at Bruiser. "What's that dog found now?" He kneed his gelding to trot after the hound.

Esther's stomach plummeted when Mrs. Abercrombie told Ma Daniel and Esther were grown. Was she going to tell Ma their secret—that Daniel and Esther were now promised to each other?

Esther had almost cried when Daniel told her last night he'd spoken to his parents. How could he do that? They'd agreed not to tell anyone yet.

Daniel explained he'd been trying to stop his folks from arguing. But it wasn't right for him to go against Esther's wishes. Not if he loved her. Now she had to worry one of the Abercrombies would let their engagement slip before Daniel had a chance to ask Pa properly. Before she had a chance to smooth the way—to find out how Ma and Pa felt about Daniel at this point in their journey and about Esther marrying.

She remembered Ma's words after they left Ash Hollow—that a woman had to do what her husband wanted. Was this just the first time Daniel would act against Esther's wishes? How many more times would there be in her future? She swallowed hard, and scrubbed the shirt in the tub even harder.

She was so tired of the dirt and the work. Back home in St. Charles, she'd worked. But she'd spent time with friends. Parties. Sing-alongs at church. Ma hadn't been so worn out, Pa hadn't been overwhelmed with keeping folks in line—or if he had, he'd been away and Esther hadn't seen it.

Along the trail, she'd seen sickness and injury and death. She shuddered remembering Mr. Bramwell's screams, the feeling of the dead child's body growing cold in her arms.

True, she had Daniel now. He comforted her, was a source of strength. But as the years went by, would he provide more comfort, or would he be another burden? She thought she understood her parents' relationship more than before this journey. Most likely, a marriage was made up of both comfort and burdens. It wasn't all kisses and cuddles.

Why hadn't anyone told her growing up would be so hard?

She would have to talk to Daniel soon, tell him to speak to her pa. If his parents knew of their engagement, it was only fair for her family to know as well.

Chapter 32:   Company Reunion

Friday, 4 June 1847. At Scott's Bluff. Waiting for the other wagons. Perhaps by sundown. FP

It was still early Friday morning when Cordelia awoke. She smelled coffee and realized Franklin was not in the tent beside her. No telling what he'd cook for breakfast if she didn't get up and see to the meal herself. Samuel Abercrombie and Daniel had brought back meat, lording it over the other families—or Samuel had, it wasn't in Daniel's nature to behave arrogantly toward anyone. Nevertheless, Cordelia gratefully accepted the shoulder of antelope Mr. Abercrombie gave her.

She felt more rested than she had since before they reached Ash Hollow. Seeing Joel revived her spirits, and staying in the same site for two days helped also. Though she wanted to nestle in her blankets longer, she eased from under the covers and dressed, careful not to wake her children.

When she exited the tent, she saw Franklin sipping a cup of coffee and smoking his pipe. "Want some?" he asked, pointing to an empty cup beside him.

"Please." She took the cup he filled and handed her, then drank. "Thank you." Getting out her frying pan, she asked, "Steak and johnny cakes all right? We're about out of flour, but I have cornmeal."

Franklin squinted at her. "What else are we out of? We'll need to replenish supplies at Fort Laramie."

221

"Need more sugar. Or we can do without. And any potatoes or vegetables we can find. We've had enough meat, so I still have salt pork."

"Make a list." Franklin sighed. "I hope Zeke and Joel get here by nightfall. Abercrombie won't wait another day."

"Thought you were waiting regardless."

"I am. But it would be easier if I didn't have to fight with Abercrombie." Franklin stared at his cup. "I made a mistake. Splitting up the company, leaving a third of the wagons behind."

Cordelia eyed him, but stayed silent. To tell him she'd believed all along it had been a mistake wouldn't help.

"But you knew that, didn't you?" he said, grimacing at her.

She nodded.

"You doing all right now? You don't look so pale today."

She smiled. "Much better. We'll have our boys back soon."

"And the new babe?" He gestured toward her belly.

"Quiet at the moment. Resting up afore he comes to greet us, I think." Her arm cradled her stomach. She loved this one already, almost as much as the ones already born.

"Still another month, ain't it?"

"About six weeks, I reckon."

"You'll tell me if you feel poorly?" Franklin's words were a command, but he asked it like a question.

"All right," she said, wondering what he'd do if her confinement proved inconvenient. How would he deal with Samuel Abercrombie?

Franklin puttered around his campsite, checking on leather harnesses and wooden yokes, kicking the wheels to be sure the iron tires were tight. He was mostly making up work while he waited for the other wagons to arrive.

After the noon meal, still antsy, he saddled his horse. "I'm riding out to meet 'em," he told Cordelia.

She nodded.

He'd only ridden a half hour out of camp when he saw a few wagons coming toward him. He galloped forward, then shouted when he recognized Zeke at the head of the small company.

"Pa!" Zeke cried, and cantered toward Franklin.

The two men stopped their horses when they reached each other, and Franklin beamed foolishly at his oldest son. "Ain't never been so glad to see anyone, son."

"Me, too, Pa." Zeke wiped his forehead with a dirty kerchief. "It's been a hard time."

"Joel said you lost a few folks."

Zeke nodded. "Four." And he recounted much of what Joel had already told Franklin.

"Let's get these wagons to Scott's Bluff," Franklin said, and he waved his hat for the travelers to follow him.

As the wagons rolled along the North Platte's riverbank, Franklin rode beside them, greeting everyone he saw. McDougall coughed from the back of his wagon, and when Franklin peeked in to say hello, the lawyer looked puny and weak. Clarence and Hatty Tanner were healthy, but seemed to have aged a decade in the ten days since their little boy's death. Mercer showed off his crutch—"I get around, but I ain't fast," he said.

Franklin rode alongside Doc Tuller's wagon awhile to discuss the ailments both groups had suffered.

"Cholera almost done a lot of folks in," Doc said. "We were lucky to just lose four."

"I had to amputate Bramwell's arm," Franklin said. "I'll want you to take a look at him as soon as you arrive."

"Joel told me. What happened?" Doc's bushy eyebrows came together in a frown.

"Cut himself with a hatchet. Got gangrene. Didn't see no other way to save him. Still ain't sure he'll make it."

But after Doc examined Bramwell, he told Franklin, "Couldn't have handled it much better myself. The stitches are a little sloppy."

Franklin grinned. "Blame the sewing on Cordelia. You don't see any signs of gangrene now?"

Doc shook his head. "Not yet. We'll have to watch him. But I think he'll live."

Franklin's grin widened in relief. "Thank you, Doc." Then he continued, "Go check on the others who're sick. I need to call the men together for a meeting tonight."

"Fool Pershing says he's gonna reorganize the platoons," Daniel's father grumbled to his family that evening over supper. "Guess we need to go to his meeting, boys. See why he thinks we need to change."

Daniel followed his father and Douglass to Captain Pershing's campsite. After two days at Scott's Bluff, the emigrants had unloaded most of their belongings from their wagons. It was hard to find a place to sit or stand near the Pershing family's camp where the captain could be heard.

Men jostled for position and grabbed for the whiskey bottle as it passed. Daniel took a swig and felt the warmth settle in his gut, then handed the bottle to his father.

Pa waved the bottle as he objected to Captain Pershing's explanation for reorganizing the company.

"Some platoons have lost two men. Others at full strength," the captain said. "We can come down a platoon. Put a wagon without a man in each group. Assign each a single man to help out."

"Who'll want to switch platoons this far in?" Abercrombie argued. "I ain't giving up mine."

"No one asked you to," Pershing said.

"I don't mind," Mercer said, leaning on his crutch. He could barely hobble about the camp. Daniel wondered if Mercer could even mount a horse and how he climbed into his wagon. "Divvy up my group. I'll go with McDougall, if no one cares," Mercer continued.

Nodding his assent, Captain Pershing assigned the families in Mercer's platoon to other sergeants. Then he called for the men to name a younger man to assist each platoon.

Daniel stepped forward, about to volunteer to go with McDougall's platoon. The Pershing wagons were still with Mac, and Daniel could spend more time with Esther if he were helping her family's wagons.

But Zeke said, "I'll stay with McDougall. I been helping him already."

It did make more sense for Zeke to stay with the platoon with the Pershing wagons, but Daniel was disappointed.

"Son, you're with me," Pa announced, and Daniel shrugged.

Then the men's conversation turned to provisions. Many families were low on food. Daniel had heard Ma say this morning they were out of cornmeal and the sugar was low.

Pa muttered, "We're moving too slow." He wasn't the only man saying so, Daniel noted.

"We're a week out from Laramie," Pershing said. "Maybe a day less if we push hard. Can we make it on what we got? Alternative is to go to Robidoux's trading post, but it's out of the way."

"I'm heading to Laramie," Pa said. "I got enough for a week. Don't want no detours."

Doc argued they'd have to travel slow so the sick and injured could mend. Pa bellowed they could always split up again.

"We ain't splitting up again on my watch," Captain Pershing said, frowning at Pa. "We didn't move any faster. Caused worry we didn't need. My mistake. I won't make it again."

Daniel had thought the same thing, and it made him think more highly of the captain that he would admit his error. Pa rarely admitted he'd done anything wrong, and now Pa mumbled under his breath as he stalked toward their wagons.

"Dad-gum Pershing is still tiptoeing toward Oregon," Samuel told Harriet when he returned to his campsite. "Won't push the lollygaggers. We oughta leave half the company at Laramie, those that ain't fit to move on."

"The captain's right," Harriet said. "We didn't move any faster after leaving the others at Ash Hollow."

"Only because we waited here for 'em. We would've moved faster under my watch."

"At least we ain't going out of our way, Pa," Douglass said.

"Make the best of it, Samuel," Harriet said.

Daniel sat quietly, but Samuel knew the boy admired Pershing, no matter what the damn fool did.

"Be ready to go at first light," he said, and shut himself up in the tent.

Come morning, Samuel made sure his family was the first to be ready after breakfast. He'd set the example for the rest of the company, by George.

The wagons headed northwest between the North Platte River and the bluffs to the south. The horizon beyond the river stretched into the distance as far as Samuel could see. By contrast, the bluffs towered grey above them, though by the time they stopped for the night, the cliffs had petered out and grassland opened in its place. Blue sky cheered him—if the weather continued clear, they could make good time.

He looked forward to seeing Fort Laramie. He planned to talk to men at the fort about the land they would traverse to the west. There were sure to be scouts more knowledgeable than Pershing.

The next morning after the wagons set out, Esther asked Jenny McDougall to walk with her. "Mac is still weak," Jenny said.

"We won't go far, and we can look for berries," Esther said. "See? The young'uns and I brought baskets." She gestured at Rachel, Ruth, and Noah.

Jenny agreed.

When the younger Pershings wandered off with their baskets, Esther clutched Jenny's arm and whispered, "He proposed!"

"Daniel?" Jenny sounded incredulous.

"Yes, silly. Who else?" Esther laughed, remembering the ride with Daniel. "Near Chimney Rock. I said how splendid it was. He said it looked like a church spire. Like the one back home, where he always thought he'd get married. And he asked me!"

"What'd you say?"

"I said yes, of course."

"How do your parents feel?"

"Daniel hasn't talked to Pa yet. Pa's been too busy. You're the first person I've told, so don't let on till Daniel talks to Pa." Esther decided not to tell Jenny Daniel had told his parents already—he might have betrayed her confidence, but she wouldn't betray his.

"I wish you both joy, Esther," Jenny said, smiling.

Maybe this was her opportunity to learn more about marriage. "What's it like?" Esther asked. "Being with a man."

Jenny shook her head. "Ask your mama."

Esther had been asking Ma ever since she was thirteen. "She just says to do my duty. Won't you tell me the truth?"

"It might not be the same for you as for me."

"Well, at least tell me what it's like to have a baby inside. Is it scary?" Esther worried about going through childbirth someday, though Ma never seemed to have any problem. Still, Daniel's mother had died, and Esther knew other women who had also.

"Sometimes. Nothing I can do about it." Jenny gave a little shudder. Jenny must be afraid, Esther realized. She supposed every woman feared childbirth, at least a little bit—even Ma.

Harriet walked on the south side of the wagons near the cliffs, admiring their tall beauty. She'd seen enough of rivers—no need to watch the Platte any more than she had to. Annabelle and Rose skipped beside her. Their mother Louisa was still weak and rode in a wagon, though her fever seemed to have passed. Daniel and Douglass tended the teams, and Samuel rode horseback ahead.

She was glad to be alone—the girls were no trouble—after three days in camp beneath Scott's Bluff. They'd had more than enough of one another in the closeness of camp. And she'd been tending so many people—from Louisa to those who were sicker than her daughter-in-law to Mr. Bramwell with his painful stump. While they'd waited, Harriet worried whether Samuel would confront Captain Pershing over the delay, but he only blustered as usual.

She wondered about Daniel and Esther. Would they make a good marriage? She thought so—Esther was a strong girl, and Daniel needed strength. He was a good lad, but his peaceable nature meant he fretted over disagreements as much as most girls.

It seemed Samuel had come to terms with the marriage. That was most of the battle. But Daniel hadn't talked to Captain Pershing yet—at least he hadn't told her he had. Would the captain and Cordelia be willing to let their daughter marry Daniel? Harriet believed they liked Daniel, but the conflicts between Captain Pershing and Samuel might taint their feelings about Daniel.

"Grandmother!" Annabelle shouted, "Look!" The girl pointed at a herd of antelope bounding across the grass to the south.

Even as Harriet spotted the animals, a shot rang out, and Samuel's horse galloped toward a downed beast. They would have fresh meat again tonight.

They'd had plenty of meat along the journey. But what she wouldn't give for fresh carrots and peas! And fruit for pies. Meat and beans and bread made for a wearisome diet. Perhaps Fort Laramie would allow them to replenish their provisions. She should ask Samuel how much they could spend at the fort. Then she'd dicker for the things she wanted most.

Chapter 33:   Requesting Her Hand

Saturday, 5 June 1847. Made 11 miles. Camped on a creek. FP

That evening, camped on a small rivulet not far upstream from where it fed into the North Platte, Esther helped her mother make supper. Their meal was happy and relaxed—Ma content to have Zeke and Joel back with them, Pa glad to be underway with the company reunited. The younger children seemed to sense the lighter mood, and none of them cried or disobeyed.

When the dishes were washed, Esther crept into the shadows away from the fire, hoping to slip away and find Daniel. They hadn't had a moment alone since he'd told her he'd talked to his parents. She wanted to urge him to talk to her pa soon—she couldn't live without her folks knowing.

"Where you going, Esther?" Ma asked sharply.

"Just thought I'd take a walk."

"It's nearly dark. Too late for you to be alone."

"Maybe Rachel would like to come with me," Esther said. "Would you, Rachel?"

In the flickering firelight, Esther saw Rachel raise an eyebrow. "All right," her sister said.

The girls walked away from their wagons. "You trying to meet Daniel?" Rachel asked. "I don't have a mind to be left alone in the dark."

"We'd walk you back to our wagons," Esther said. "Daniel's a gentleman."

"Is he as sweet on you as you are on him?" Rachel asked with a sniff.

"I'd say so! He asked me to marry him."

Rachel gasped and turned to Esther. "Marry him?"

"And I said yes."

"Do Ma and Pa know?"

"Not yet. And don't you tell. Daniel wants to ask Pa proper. That's why I need to see him—to ask him to hurry."

Rachel grasped Esther's arm and pointed. "There he is. Guarding the horses. He must be on duty."

Esther started toward him.

"Wait," Rachel said. "Don't leave me."

Esther stopped, hands on her hips. "Well, I can't talk to him with you around."

Rachel pointed to a tree nearby along the creek bank. "I'll wait there. Don't take long, or I'm heading back to Ma."

Esther rushed over to Daniel and took his hand. "I've wanted to talk to you all day."

He grinned down at her. "You alone?"

She shook her head. "Rachel's over yonder. I can't stay. Can you walk us back?"

"No," he said, rubbing her fingers. "I'm on watch. Till midnight."

"You've got to talk to Pa soon," Esther pleaded. "Your ma almost let it slip to my ma on Thursday. I thought I'd have to drown myself in the washtub."

"Don't be silly," Daniel said. But he stroked her cheek.

She turned her face into his hand. "It ain't silly. I can't keep the secret for long. I've already told Rachel and Jenny."

Daniel nodded. "All right. I'll talk to him tomorrow. I'll find a way." He leaned over and kissed her quickly. "Go on back with Rachel now."

A hard rain fell Sunday morning. Daniel yoked the oxen while rainwater spilled from his hat brim onto his hands. Over breakfast, Pa had grumbled Captain Pershing was likely to want to lay by for the Sabbath, but neither the captain nor anyone else suggested stopping. Everyone seemed eager to reach Fort Laramie.

Daniel wondered if he'd be able to catch a moment with the captain to ask for Esther's hand. Or would it be better to ask both Captain and Mrs. Pershing together in the evening? But wasn't he supposed to talk to Esther's father first? His fingers shook as he pinned the yokes around the oxen's necks—he wasn't sure if he fumbled because of the cold or his fretting.

"You asked Pershing yet, son?" Pa asked him.

Daniel looked up, startled. "No, sir."

"Best get it done."

"Yes, sir." Daniel finished the yoking. "May I ride ahead today, Pa? See if I can catch the captain alone?"

Pa frowned. "You think that's the right approach?"

"How'd you ask for my mother's hand?"

"Abigail? I don't rightly remember. And with Harriet, I asked her directly. She were already living in our house, away from her folks. We just up and got married, so you'd have a ma." Pa shrugged. "Go on, I'll tend the wagons today."

Daniel saddled his mare and rode out to find Captain Pershing. The captain welcomed him, but Zeke and Joel were there also.

"Just talking with my boys about scouting out a camp for tonight," Captain Pershing said to Daniel. "You want to go ahead with them?"

"I'd best s-s-stay near the wagons," Daniel stammered. "Pa might want to s-s-swap places with me."

"Suit yourself," the captain said, and continued his discussion with Zeke and Joel. The two young Pershing men rode off, leaving Daniel alone with Esther's father.

"Sir," Daniel began.

Captain Pershing frowned at him.

"Sir, I want to marry Esther. I've asked her, and she's willing. But I want your blessing, sir. Yours and Miz Pershing's." Daniel got the words out as quickly as he could.

The captain's frown deepened, and he didn't say anything.

Finally, "Marry Esther? She's only fifteen."

"I love her, sir. We'll wait till we get to Oregon. Till I stake my claim and build her a home."

Captain Pershing sighed. "I was afraid of this."

"Afraid, sir?"

"I seen the way you two look at each other. I seen you sneaking away from the wagons at night."

"I wouldn't do nothing to Esther, Captain. I love her."

The captain snorted, then sighed again. "Let me talk to her ma." Then he turned a stern eye on Daniel. "And don't you say nothing 'bout this till I've given you my answer."

"I've already told my parents, sir."

At that the captain raised an eyebrow. "Abercrombie knows you've asked my girl?"

"Yes, sir."

"What's he say?"

"He says when a man marries, he marries for keeps. And he says Esther's a good, strong woman." That might be stretching Pa's comment a bit, but Daniel believed his pa recognized Esther's courage and steadiness.

"He does, does he?" Captain Pershing seemed pleased. "I hope you'd think marriage to my daughter was for keeps. I don't want you trifling with her."

"No, sir. I never would."

"Hmm." The captain's face was stern again. "I been a young man, boy. Full of ginger. But Esther's been raised right."

"Yes, sir."

"You go on back to your wagon now. I need to think on how I feel 'bout this. And on what to say to Esther's ma."

Franklin watched young Daniel Abercrombie gallop to the south, then back toward the wagons in a big loop. He chuckled at the lad's exuberance, though he didn't think he'd given Daniel much encouragement. He hadn't rejected the boy's suit out of hand, but he hadn't agreed to the marriage either. Truth was, he didn't know how he felt.

Esther was so young. Younger than Cordelia had been when they married. He'd considered Cordelia barely out of the schoolroom, though before their wedding she'd kept house for her family since her mother died two years earlier.

Esther had matured quickly on this journey. In recent weeks, when Cordelia felt puny, his daughter took over most of the chores. Esther had seen death, she'd seen injury. She cared for her younger siblings, even when they riled her. She'd be a good wife, though Franklin had hoped she'd have more time with her parents and siblings before she wed.

And while he despised Abercrombie's bullying and cantankerousness, Daniel was a respectful and likable young man—the type of man he wanted Esther to marry someday. Still, the boy had no prospects yet, and wouldn't until they reached Oregon and he filed his claim.

An engagement now wouldn't hurt, would it? If Cordelia agreed, of course.

There was still plenty of time between here and Oregon.

When they stopped for the noon meal, Franklin pulled Cordelia aside. "You feel like a walk along the river?" he asked.

She glanced at him with a puzzled look. "All right. If it's brief." She turned to Esther. "You give the young'uns their bacon and biscuits."

"Yes, Ma," Esther said, with a worried glance at him.

Franklin winked at his daughter, then guided Cordelia down to the bank of the North Platte. They watched the water burble swiftly along.

"Daniel Abercrombie asked me today if he could marry Esther."

"No!" Cordelia's moan sounded from deep in her chest.

"Don't you like the lad?"

"She's too young."

"She's young, but she's old enough," Franklin said. "She's grown a lot since we left Independence."

"I don't want to lose her." Cordelia sniffed.

"Lose her?"

"You have Zeke and Joel. Esther's been my rock. I need her, with this babe coming."

"You'll still have her. They won't marry till we reach Oregon. Daniel don't have nothing to offer her afore then." He pulled Cordelia closer to his side. "Is it her marrying or Daniel you object to?"

"Both. The boy's too young also. And you don't want her marrying Samuel Abercrombie's son, do you?"

Franklin shook his head. "Not especially. But the lad's all right."

Cordelia sighed and leaned against him. "Yes, he is. Or will be when he gets established. And Harriet's a fine woman."

"What if we agreed to an engagement? Tell 'em they can't marry till we're all settled."

"That's still several months off," Cordelia said.

"Yes."

They stood silently. Cordelia stared toward the water. "All right," she said. She paused. "But no wedding till we're satisfied he can provide for her. And that Samuel Abercrombie won't make our daughter's life miserable once they're wed."

When the emigrants started on their way after the noon meal, Cordelia motioned to Esther. "Let's walk a spell," she said. "Rachel," she called to her second daughter, "take the young'uns off to search for greens. But don't let 'em fall in the river."

"Yes, Ma," Rachel said. The girl flashed a smile at Esther—had Rachel known about Daniel's proposal before Cordelia?

"I hear Daniel Abercrombie wants to marry you," Cordelia said stiffly when she and Esther were alone, walking alongside one of the wagons.

"Oh, Ma!" Esther said, grabbing her mother's arm. "What did Pa tell him?"

"He ain't said nothing to Daniel yet. I want to talk to you first," Cordelia said. "You're awful young to be settling down. How do you know he's the man you want to marry?"

Esther blushed.

So the boy had kissed her. "Just because you like his kisses ain't a reason to marry him." Cordelia knew she sounded harsh, but the girl knew so little!

"It ain't just that, Ma. He's made me feel so much better, comforted me—"

"Comforted you? How?" Just how far had the kissing gone? Cordelia wondered.

"He talked to me after Mr. Purcell died. And again after the baby died." Esther's face was solemn, her eyes wide. "He makes me want to be a better person."

Well, that was something. Cordelia sighed. "You've seen some dreadful things on this trek, haven't you?"

Esther nodded. "With Daniel around, I can bear them better. I feel so happy when he's with me."

"But are you ready for marriage, Esther? And is he ready to support you?"

"All I want, Ma, is someone to love me. Someone for me to love. Someone all my own. Like you have with Pa."

Like what she had with Franklin. Cordelia sometimes wondered just what she and Franklin had, they'd spent so much time apart. And now that they were together, they didn't always see eye to eye. Truth be told, it was troublesome to have to accommodate a husband all the time.

"Please, Ma? Won't you give us your blessing? If you agree, I know Pa will, too."

Franklin had consulted her, Cordelia remembered with a smile. Many husbands would have decided on their own what their children could do. "You always could wrap your pa around your little finger."

"Please, Ma?"

"It's only an engagement. We'll wait to see how your young man does in Oregon, what land he finds, what kind of house he builds you. I'm not convinced he's ready for marriage either. And what about his father Samuel? Does he approve, or will he interfere as he has with your pa?"

Esther threw her arms around her mother's neck and kissed her cheek. "Thank you, Ma. You are the best mother a girl could have."

Cordelia smiled. "Remember, Esther. Nothing has changed with respect to your conduct. You still are not to spend time with Daniel alone, not where your pa or I or Rachel can't see you."

"Yes, Ma." But Cordelia didn't think the girl was listening. Esther chattered on about weddings and houses and babies. My lands! Cordelia realized. Esther could have a child just a year or two younger than the babe she carried now.

That evening, as Cordelia finished the supper dishes, Daniel Abercrombie appeared in their campsite. "Ma'am?" he said.

With a sigh, Cordelia braced her back with a hand and stood from the washtub. Her mind had been in turmoil since she and Esther had talked. She'd told Franklin she'd accept the engagement, but she wasn't ready to declare her acceptance to Daniel. Yet here he stood, hat in hand, looking like he was the twins' age, instead of almost as old as Zeke. "Come sit by the fire, Daniel," she said.

Franklin stood and shook Daniel's hand, then the two men sat.

"Zeke," Cordelia said, "take your brothers and sisters for a walk. Esther, you stay here."

Zeke raised an eyebrow and grinned, first at Daniel, then at Esther. Then he called the young'uns away.

"Cordelia and I are willing for you two to announce your engagement," Franklin said. "But there will be no wedding till we're in Oregon and Daniel can provide for a family."

"Thank you, sir," Daniel said, rising to pump Franklin's hand again. He beamed at Esther, bowed to Cordelia, then took Esther's hand. "I'll take good care of her, I promise," he told Franklin, repeating the words to Cordelia. Then the boy made puppy eyes at Esther, who flashed her dimples back at him.

Cordelia sighed, "Go on, you two. You can join the others at the river. But no dallying."

Chapter 34:   Happy News Spreads

Sunday, 7 June 1847. Made 11 miles today. FP

Monday morning shone bright as the emigrants began another day of travel. Harriet plodded alongside her wagon. Louisa had finally recovered from her illness, and she and her two daughters walked ahead of Harriet, the girls frolicking beside their mother.

The Abercrombies had celebrated when Daniel returned from talking to Captain and Cordelia Pershing Sunday night. Even Samuel smiled when Daniel reported the Pershings had agreed to the engagement. Harriet pulled out the cherry cordial she'd been saving, along with her best glasses. The adults each had a small taste, and Louisa permitted her daughters to sip from her glass.

As they walked now, Harriet spied Esther arm in arm with Jenny McDougall a short distance away from the wagons. Cordelia Pershing, trudging ahead of Harriet, looked toward Esther and Jenny also, then wiped the back of her hand across her cheek. Was the woman crying?

Harriet hurried forward. "Cordelia," she called. "May I walk with you?"

Cordelia stopped and waited. When Harriet caught up, the two women walked on.

"I understand Daniel spoke with you yesterday," Harriet said. "Samuel and I wish Esther and our son much happiness."

"Yes," Cordelia said. "Franklin and I do also. But we've told Esther she cannot marry until Daniel can provide for her."

Harriet nodded. "Of course. We agree. But with free land in Oregon—"

237

"I want to know my daughter will have a good home." Cordelia sighed. "Daniel's a fine lad, but they're so young."

"Esther is younger than I was when I wed," Harriet said. "Though I came into a family already formed, with Daniel and Douglass to raise. That wasn't an easy task."

"She's younger than I was also. I was about Daniel's age. Franklin was older, of course—he'd spent a few years in the Army already." Cordelia stared ahead. "I was alone so much. With a new babe after each of his visits home. But I had my father and brothers nearby."

"Our children will have family also," Harriet soothed. "You and I will both be close. We'll surely all claim land near each other. Then we can help them. Just think—more grandchildren soon!"

Cordelia harrumphed. "I'm still raising my own. I'm not ready for grandchildren."

"You will be when you have 'em," Harriet said. "They are truly God's blessing in life."

"Mmm," Cordelia said. They walked on, and after a while Cordelia said, "I hope Franklin and your husband can mend their differences. And I hope Mr. Abercrombie lets Daniel farm without interference. Or it will be hard on us all."

Harriet couldn't think of how to respond. Anything she said would cast aspersions on Franklin or Samuel or both men. But—like Cordelia—she prayed fervently that their husbands would get along for the sake of their children. And that Daniel could find his place in the world apart from Samuel.

"Yes," she said. Then she took Cordelia's arm, and they continued in silence.

Esther had gone to find Jenny as soon as the wagons were underway on Monday. "I must talk to you," she said, linking arms with her friend. "Daniel spoke to Pa yesterday. Pa came around, but Ma don't like it." Even though Ma had agreed, Esther knew she wasn't happy.

"Why not? Daniel's a nice young man."

"She says he's too young." Esther sighed. "Pa likes Daniel, though he don't like Mr. Abercrombie. Pa usually lets me have what I want, and he said yes. There's land enough for everyone in Oregon. Once Daniel stakes his claim, he'll be able to provide for me." Esther knew Daniel would build a fine home. Once they were married and she was in her own house, they would be blissfully happy—she would have everything she had dreamed of.

"Your mama doesn't agree?"

Esther shook her head. "Says Daniel'll be stuck working for his pa. Says it'll be years afore Daniel can afford a family."

"What now?" Jenny asked.

Esther twirled around with a dreamy smile. "We're engaged. But no wedding date set." She prayed they could marry as soon as they reached Oregon.

"Then at least you and Daniel can spend time together now. In the open."

"Yes." Esther nodded. "But Ma'll watch me twice as close, don't I know it. She said as much." Ma worried too much, Esther thought. She cherished Daniel's kisses, but she knew better than to let him do anything more. Though that embrace when he'd pressed her to him—and there'd been another one like it last night in the dark—those kisses made her want to let him do anything he desired.

Should she ask Jenny again what loving a man was like? "Jenny—"

"I need to check on Mac, Esther," Jenny said. "He's still poorly, though he tries not to show it." She squeezed Esther's hand. "I wish you and Daniel every happiness." And she ran back to the wagons.

Monday evening Daniel stopped by the Pershing wagons. "Esther, would you like to walk awhile?"

Mrs. Pershing looked up from the bread dough she kneaded. "Not too long, mind you. And take the twins. They need to walk off some foolishness."

"Ah, Ma," one of the lads complained.

"You boys have any marbles?" Daniel asked. He'd gladly give them each an agate if they didn't pester Esther and him.

Their eyes lit up. "Yes, sir!" one said. "Do you play?"

"I do indeed," Daniel replied. "Let's stop by my wagon and I'll get my bag."

Esther frowned at him. "I thought you wanted to walk with me."

"We'll watch the boys play," he said. "It'll be fine," he whispered in her ear as he took her arm.

He led the three Pershings back to his family's campfire. While Esther talked to his parents, he found his marble sack. He returned to the boys and took out a large milk-white shooter. "Whichever one of you wins your game gets this shooter. No need to play for keeps with yours, just play for mine."

The twins found a flat spot of dirt and placed a lantern on the ground to light it, then drew a circle and started their game. Soon other children gathered to watch.

Daniel dragged a crate just outside the well-lit ground, motioned for Esther to sit, and sat beside her. If the crate was so small he had to sit close, his arm around her, he couldn't be blamed for that, could he?

She smiled. "Very clever, Daniel. No one's paying us any mind at all."

"As I'd hoped," he whispered in her ear, while putting his arm around her waist and pressing her to his side.

She snuggled nearer, leaning back against his chest.

Mrs. Tuller, the doctor's wife, bustled over. "I heard your good news, Esther. My best wishes to you. And congratulations to you also, Daniel."

Esther pulled away from him. "Thank you, Mrs. Tuller."

"Are those two rapscallions supposed to be your chaperons?" the older woman asked.

Daniel shrugged. "I guess so, Miz Tuller."

"Might be best if I helped 'em out," she said. "They're distracted by their game."

Daniel stood and pulled Esther to her feet. "Take our seat, ma'am," he said gesturing from Mrs. Tuller to the crate.

More adults assembled to watch the marble game. No one noticed when he and Esther crept behind a wagon into the dark. Esther leaned against the wheel, and Daniel kissed her thoroughly.

"It's more trouble being engaged than I reckoned it would be," he said against her lips.

"Don't waste time talking," she murmured.

He kissed her again, one hand creeping up her side to cup her breast. He wished he could see what he touched.

Chapter 35:   Toward Fort Laramie

Monday, 8 June 1847. Made 10 miles. Reckon we'll reach Fort Laramie in two days. FP

Tuesday morning the emigrants continued their trek toward Fort Laramie. Cordelia wheezed with the effort to breathe as she trudged along the trail. She couldn't see any rise in the route they traveled along the North Platte, but perhaps they were high enough for the air to have thinned. Or else she was short-winded because the child pressed on her lungs from within. Indeed, sometimes the baby's kicking caused her to grunt, as if someone had hit her in the stomach.

Esther walked beside her, chatting merrily about weddings and farmhouses. "Queen Victoria wore a white dress, you know, Ma," Esther said. She sighed. "Wouldn't it be lovely to be married in white?"

"But quite impractical," Cordelia said. "When would you ever wear a white dress again? Think of sweeping floors or going to market in white. Why, even going to church would get it filthy. Your hem would be black in no time."

"Yes, but so romantic. Like Juliet." Esther sighed again and hummed a silly tune.

Harriet and Louisa Abercrombie joined them. "Don't you think a white wedding dress would be beautiful, Louisa?" Esther asked her future sister-in-law.

Louisa shook her head. "Once my girls started crawling, my days in white were over. Except for pinafores. A crisp, starched pinafore in white is fine, but only if you're willing to bleach the cotton every time you wash it. Browns don't show the dirt nearly as much."

Cordelia's lip twitched, but she held back her chuckle. Esther might take advice from Louisa better than from her. "It's too soon to be worrying about dresses, anyway. You and Daniel don't have a date set. And won't, till we reach Oregon. It could be a year or more afore he has a house built."

"Oh, surely not, Ma!" Esther said. "I don't want to wait so long. How long were you and Douglass engaged, Louisa?"

"Two years."

"Oh." Esther was silent a moment, then asked, "What was your wedding dress like?"

"Plain blue wool. I still wear it to church on Sunday. Or did in Tennessee. I imagine I will again in Oregon." Louisa smiled and touched Esther's arm. "But it was new for my wedding. And I had a new bonnet, too."

Cordelia paid no mind to the conversation when it turned to bonnets. She worried about what to fix for the noon meal instead. They were running short of most foods.

"How exuberant the young are," Harriet said, interrupting Cordelia's planning.

Cordelia turned her attention to Daniel's mother. "Yes," she smiled. "It seems so long ago I worried about a wedding dress."

Harriet laughed. "You ain't even forty yet, are you?"

Cordelia shook her head. "Still thirty-nine. But I feel every year."

"Raising a family does wear a woman out, don't it?" Harriet said.

"I hate to spoil Esther's dreams." Cordelia took a deep breath, trying to fill her lungs. "She'll find out soon enough."

Esther gave up talking to her mother and the Abercrombie women about wedding plans. They weren't interested at all in making her ceremony a beautiful event. They only cared about keeping dresses clean.

After the noon meal, she went to find Jenny McDougall. Jenny was still young—younger even than Esther. Surely she had worn beautiful clothes when she was wed. Mr. McDougall was such a handsome man, more handsome than Daniel even, though Esther would never say such a thing out loud.

She shouldn't even think about other men, not after letting Daniel's hands roam over her body the way they had last night. She quivered and smiled remembering his touch. She hadn't known she could feel such lust. It was lust, wasn't it? It felt heavenly, and yet sinful as well.

"Jenny," she called when she saw her friend. "Come walk with me?"

Jenny smiled. "If you'll go slowly. I get tuckered out by afternoon, and I have months more to go."

"You ain't as bad as Ma."

"No, but her confinement will be over soon, and I'll be carrying until mid-September."

"Ma and Mrs. Abercrombie don't want to talk about weddings with me. Tell me about yours."

Jenny stammered, "It-it was v-very small. Only Mac and me and the witnesses. There isn't much to tell."

"Did you have a new dress?"

Jenny shook her head. "Just wore the best one I had."

Esther frowned. "You, too? Ain't you a romantic? Why'd you bother to get married if you didn't get a new dress?"

Jenny raised an eyebrow. "There's more to marriage than new dresses." She gestured toward her belly.

"But babies come later—" Esther stopped. Sometimes, she knew, babies started before the wedding, though only if a girl was wicked. Wicked, like she felt last night—was she the only woman who felt so wanton? "Yours came after, didn't it?"

Jenny blushed. "Of course." And that was all Esther could get Jenny to say about weddings or marriage.

Tuesday evening Daniel took Esther walking. They strolled along the creek bank near the wagons toward the North Platte a few hundred yards away. Captain Pershing and Zeke plodded behind them, talking about the next day's travel. There'd be no chance for spooning tonight, Daniel thought, other than a quick peck on her cheek when they returned to camp.

Esther glanced over her shoulder, back toward her father and brother.

"How long do you think it'll be till you're settled and we can marry?" she asked.

He nestled her arm close to his side. "I don't know. Maybe next spring? Pa's talking about building barns and houses through the winter, then we'll need to get the first crops sowed. We'll have three farms to manage—his, Douglass's, and mine. That's a lot of work."

Esther sighed. "So long."

"What did you think?"

"I'd hoped before Christmas. It's just—"

"Just what?" He stared at her.

She didn't meet his eyes. "I don't know if I can wait."

"Wait? Why not?" They'd reached the North Platte, and he stopped.

"You know," Esther said, looking at her feet.

It dawned on him—she liked the kissing and caressing just as much as he did. And wanted more. He grinned. Marriage might be more fun than he'd thought—a quick wedding as soon as they reached Oregon might be a fine idea. "I don't know if I can either, sweetheart. But we have all our lives to make up for the waiting."

"I do want a new dress. To go with my new home." She smiled at him happily. "It don't take long to make a dress. You hurry and build that house."

He peeked back at the men behind him. The captain and Zeke had stopped and were gesturing at the river. Daniel leaned over and kissed Esther's lips quickly. "Can't do any more'n that with your pa and brother back there. But I'd like to," he whispered, his heart beating rapidly.

Samuel Abercrombie sat by the fire cleaning his rifle and shotgun. He and Douglass had hunted south of the wagons all day, only returning at dusk. No more buffalo grazed in the area they traveled now, but antelope were still plentiful. They'd each shot one, plus some ducks. Their horses couldn't carry any more game, and what they'd killed would last their family until they reached Laramie.

Harriet had asked Samuel about provisions. He couldn't tell her what to buy until he saw prices at the fort. Most likely, the trading post would gouge the emigrants, wanting profits twice as high as in the States. "I'll go with you when we get to Laramie," he'd told her. "Won't have them trappers and roughnecks taking advantage of you."

"Won't the Army make sure the prices are fair?" she asked.

He snorted. "Army ain't in charge. Laramie's run by the American Fur Company. All they want is profit."

By gum, it was all a man could do to keep the wolves from the door—whether the wolves be human or beast. A clean gun would help with both, he thought, with a final polish of his Mississippi rifle barrel before he set it aside.

He watched Daniel and Esther return to camp, arm in arm. The girl leaned into his son as if she belonged beside him. Samuel felt a pang, remembering long walks with Abigail on summer evenings so many years ago. That lass had perished far too young. He'd never had to court Harriet—she'd always been there, ever since Abigail died. Maybe he owed Harriet more. She was a good woman.

Samuel resolved to let his wife spend what she wanted at Laramie—within reason, of course. Maybe there'd be some furbelow he could find for her also. And for the granddaughters, so it wouldn't look like he was singling out Harriet. She wouldn't want any special treatment.

Chapter 36: Arriving at Laramie

Tuesday, 8 June 1847. Should reach the fort by tomorrow evening. FP

Franklin pushed the emigrants hard all day Wednesday trying to reach Fort Laramie by nightfall. He was glad the sick members of the company were much improved, their illness and injury left behind. And McDougall was back to scouting, which was a help.

Mercer's leg, injured on the descent of Windlass Hill, still caused him to limp. With the aid of a crutch made from a cedar branch, he managed. He rode in his wagon each day, but did his chores around camp. Bramwell had come out of his delirium, and while he complained of pain in his missing left arm, he coped as best he could with only his right.

"He'll live," Doc Tuller told Franklin. "And no doubt prosper once his stump heals."

Franklin rode ahead of the caravan as they trekked toward Laramie, his son Zeke riding beside him. He hoped to stay a couple of days at their first outpost of civilization since leaving Independence and looked forward to the respite. Abercrombie would raise Cain about any delay, but the company needed a rest. They'd all seen the elephant now, and it had about shattered them.

The air was cool after several warm days, and a breeze wafted softly against Franklin's face. The massive sandstone formations like Courthouse Rock were behind them. Now they traveled through meadows of wild grass. More open land covered hills to the south, and the Platte continued to guide them on their right side.

"Ma says we're out of supplies," Zeke said.

Franklin nodded. "Most families are. We need to re-provision at Laramie. I hope the post shelves are well stocked." He remembered coming through Fort Laramie in 1842, before many wagons had traveled the route. There hadn't been much in the way of supplies then.

"Shouldn't they be?" Zeke asked.

"I think we're early enough. Later in the season, goods could run low. The American Fur Company only gets resupplied with foodstuffs a couple of times through the summer. Farmers 'round the post sell their produce to the fort, but there ain't many farms nearby. It's almost as hard for the fort to get provisioned as for us to carry what we need."

"Don't tell Ma," Zeke said with a chuckle. "She's counting on flour and sugar."

"And doing laundry." Franklin grinned back at his son. "All the comforts of home."

Cordelia walked with Esther all Wednesday morning, but by midday she was worn out. She climbed onto the wagon bench after the noon halt, while Esther strolled alongside. The girl was supposed to be minding the team, but Esther prattled to her mother about the house Daniel would build for her—"he says it'll be small at first, but we'll add rooms. As . . . as the babies come, he says."

Cordelia thought her daughter's cheeks pinkened, but it was hard to tell behind the sunbonnet. "Babies do come," Cordelia said mildly.

"Oh, Ma, will I like it?"

Cordelia raised an eyebrow. "Like what, child?"

"Being married. Having a husband. Having babies."

Cordelia sighed. "I imagine you'll like it as well as most women."

"Ma-aa." Esther dragged the word into a whine. The child hadn't grown up quite as much as Cordelia had hoped. "What does that mean?"

"Most women get accustomed to marriage soon enough. As for babies, the birthing is hard, as is the raising of them. But cuddling a little one," Cordelia's hand touched her belly, "well, that's a joy."

Esther walked beside the wagon silently for a minute. "That's what I thought," she said. She smiled up at her mother. "I'd best go let the lead pair know I'm watching 'em." And she ran ahead.

Not long after, Esther scampered back to the wagon, asking, "If there's pretty fabric at Fort Laramie, may I have a new dress?"

"What did your pa tell you in Independence? There's time enough for new clothes when we reach Oregon."

"But what if there ain't any cloth there? I need a new dress to be married in."

"Child, your wedding is months away. Next spring, your young man told you."

"Maybe sooner, he said. I'll only buy if there's a pretty print, Ma. I don't want to chance not finding anything in Oregon."

The girl was as bad as Ruthie at wheedling. "What if you find something in Oregon you like better?" Cordelia asked.

Esther shook her head. "I won't ask again. Not once I've chosen the fabric. And if there ain't anything nice at Fort Laramie, I'll wait to see what's in Oregon."

"I can't make any promises till I talk to your pa."

At that, Esther smiled, and Cordelia sighed. Her daughter most likely knew Franklin would give her whatever she wanted.

Sure enough, when Franklin stopped by the wagon later and Cordelia talked to him, he shrugged. "Let the girl look. If she finds something she likes for a wedding dress, we'll talk about it then. But not till you've bought your flour and sugar—that comes first." He flashed his most charming grin at Cordelia.

At Captain Pershing's holler late in the afternoon, Daniel raced ahead on his mare. When Daniel caught up, the older man pointed out a wooden stockade fence with a log guard tower rising above it. "Fort Laramie," the captain said. The fort was the first large structure they'd seen since they'd entered Indian Territory almost eight weeks earlier.

The wagon company wasn't on high enough ground for Daniel to see anything inside the fort, only the stockade walls. He wanted to gallop forward, but when he moved to knee his horse into a faster gait, Captain

Pershing stopped him. "We need to stay together. See the tepees outside the fort?"

The fort was positioned near the juncture of the North Platte and the Laramie rivers. Just upstream on the Laramie from the fort was a cluster of Indian dwellings. "Will they bother us?" Daniel asked.

Captain Pershing shook his head. "Doubtful. They're here to trade, just like us. We'll camp close to the fort. But unless the Army has troops on patrol here, we'll have to defend ourselves. American Fur Company don't take responsibility for the wagon companies passing through."

They made camp on the near bank of the Laramie, across the river from the fort and the Indians. After the wagons were in place, Zeke and Joel Pershing sauntered over to the Abercrombie campfire. "Want to go have a look?" Zeke asked Daniel. "We'll be back afore supper, but I've a mind to see what's inside the gates."

Daniel grabbed his hat and pistol, then saddled his horse. He and the young Pershing men splashed their mounts across the willow-lined Laramie to the fort. They arrived at dusk, but men still flowed in and out of gates in the thick adobe walls. Inside, more adobe buildings stood around an open court. The young men looked in the trading post and in a couple of merchant stalls, watched a ring of Indians playing a gambling game, and inspected the ponies an older Indian man had for sale.

"Prices seem high," Daniel said.

Zeke shrugged. "We'll see what Ma says. She's bound and determined to re-provision."

"We ain't seen this many folks since crossing the Kaw," Joel said, gazing around.

"More like Independence," Daniel said. "Everyone from whites to Indians to Mexicans."

A man in buckskin passing by turned to them with a toothless grin. "This ain't crowded. Wait till morning when all the vendors is here. Won't hardly be able to walk through the fort."

Samuel considered going with Daniel and the Pershing lads to the fort on Wednesday, but Harriet pursed her lips at Daniel's leaving. "What is it?" he asked her.

"Is it safe for him to be there after dark?"

Samuel spat. "Ain't dark yet. He's a young man, he'll be safe enough." But he decided not to worry her further—he could wait until morning to leave camp.

The next morning he pushed Harriet and Louisa to cook quickly. Right after breakfast he and Douglass headed to the fort. "I'll be back for you later," he called to the women. "I'll seek out the best prices now. Make your shopping easier."

Harriet sniffed and turned to the dishes. Samuel heard her tell Louisa as he saddled his gelding, "I think we could determine the best prices on our own, don't you? Somehow we managed not to bankrupt the family in Tennessee."

Samuel whistled to Bruiser and headed for the fort. Once inside the gate, he tied the horse to a railing, told the dog to stay, and entered the trading post. He found Franklin Pershing and Mac McDougall already inside talking to the storekeeper behind the counter. McDougall wandered off, and Samuel stood beside Pershing.

"What's the word on the Army taking over?" Pershing asked. "Heard tell back in St. Louis Washington is considering it."

"Ain't heard nothing," the man said. "I work for the fur company. As long as I get paid, I don't listen to no talk."

"Prices are steep," Samuel said, glancing at the shelves.

"Everything comes from Santa Fe or Missouri," the man said. "Ain't easy to get it here from either place. You know that after traveling this far."

"What you got?"

The man gestured around the store. "What you see."

Samuel moved to the shelves and barrels. Plenty of flour and cornmeal. Also sugar and salt pork. Some bolts of fabric in a corner. Deerskins and a bear skin hanging on one wall. Buckshot and lead.

While Samuel wandered the store, Pershing and the storekeeper continued to talk. "Indian pow-wow tonight," the local man said. "Lots of dancing. Some of your men might want to see it. But keep your ladies away. Can get purty wild."

"What's a pow-wow?" Samuel asked, returning to the counter.

"Just what I said. Dancing and singing. Some games. Good food."

It'd be almost like a circus, Samuel thought, to watch the savages perform. "Is it open to anyone?"

"It's considered mannerly to bring a gift," the man said. "Beads and trinkets. A blanket. Or food."

"You been to one?" Samuel asked Pershing.

Pershing shook his head.

"Think I'll take a group tonight," Samuel said. "Ain't nothing else to do."

Chapter 37:   Fort Laramie Pow-Wow

Thursday, 10 June 1847. At Laramie. Re-provisioning and resting. FP

Esther hitched a pair of oxen to one of the Pershing wagons, which they'd emptied out. Her mother gathered the family—everyone but Pa—and they headed into the fort. Pa had left earlier, saying he'd meet them at the trading post.

"What'd you see last night?" Esther asked her older brothers.

Joel shrugged. "Some stores. Lots of people." Zeke didn't have any more to add.

Esther could hardly sit still as they drove across the swift but shallow Laramie current and through the fort gates. It wasn't as busy as St. Charles on market day, nor St. Louis, which Esther had seen when they visited Pa at the arsenal. But there were more people here than she'd seen since leaving Missouri.

"Esther and Rachel, keep the young'uns close to hand," Ma said. "Zeke and Joel, come help me with the flour sacks." Ma bustled around the store, pointing at things for her sons to move to the counter.

Esther spied some bolts of fabric in the corner. "Let's go look," she whispered to Rachel. "Bring Ruthie and Noah." The twins had already escaped their sisters' grasps and were fingering a bearskin hung on the wall.

Most of the cloth was drab homespun or muted cottons, only suited for prairie life and housework. Nothing pretty. Nothing a girl would want to wear on her wedding day. But buried under two bolts of gray twill for men's trousers was a bright blue calico with yellow flowers.

"It's like what I saw in Independence!" Esther exclaimed. She pulled the calico out.

"Cotton ain't very fancy," Rachel said.

"But it's so cheerful. So pretty." Esther held it up to her face. "Don't it bring out the yellow in my hair?"

Rachel nodded and smiled. "It looks nice on you."

Ruthie gaped. "Like a princess."

Esther took the bolt over to her mother. "Look, Ma. May I buy a length of this?"

Ma frowned. "For your wedding dress?"

Esther nodded.

"Calico?"

"Please, Ma."

Ma fingered the fabric. "It ain't very heavy. Won't wear well. Color won't hold."

"I don't plan to wear it till my wedding day. And afterward, I'll have it for church. When it starts to fade, I can still wear it for everyday." Esther was pleading now, but she didn't care. She wanted the bright print. "I'll get lots of good out of it."

Cordelia didn't want to buy Esther the cloth. Such an extravagance—they might need the money later, and it'd be extra weight to carry something Esther wouldn't wear until they reached Oregon. But her daughter's eyes shone, and Cordelia remembered the joy of being in love, the anticipation of wedded bliss. The girl was so changeable—grown one minute and as childlike as eight-year-old Ruth the next.

She looked around the store, hoping to see Franklin, but he wasn't there. Zeke and Joel had added lead and gunpowder to the pile on the counter.

She sighed. "Put it with the rest of the goods. We'll see what the foodstuffs come to and how much I have left over."

Esther practically skipped to the counter carrying the bolt of fabric.

Flour and cornmeal prices were steep, but the lead wasn't too dear.

Cordelia wanted another bag of sugar, but decided against it—she'd buy the calico instead.

"Wrap it all up," she told the storekeeper and gave him the coins.

"Oh, Ma," Esther said, throwing her arms around Cordelia's neck. Behind her, Rachel and Ruth giggled.

Then Cordelia spied the twins climbing on top of a barrel and reaching for the bear's head high on the wall. "Boys," she called, "get down from there."

After breakfast, Harriet and Louisa started their washing. Samuel had already left for the fort, but said he would return for them. When he arrived and announced he wanted to get the shopping done quickly, the women left the clothes soaking in a tub while Samuel hitched one of their wagons to drive to the fort.

"What's the hurry?" Harriet asked her husband.

"Want our provisions stowed in camp by midafternoon," he said. "There's an Indian pow-wow tonight. I'll take Douglass and Daniel."

"May we all go?"

Samuel shook his head. "Man said not to bring women and children."

"Then how safe is it for you?" Harriet asked. "And for our sons?"

Samuel shrugged. "Won't have many opportunities to see the natives sing and dance. See just how human they are."

"I'm sure they're no different than slaves back home. All they need is bathing and Christianity to be the same as we are. Don't matter how they dance." Harriet didn't know if her abolitionist beliefs extended to the heathens in the West, but she didn't think they should be show-pieces like animals, which seemed to be Samuel's attitude.

"Well, me'n the boys will tell you all about it in the morning."

Harriet did her shopping in the trading post. Samuel seemed in a magnanimous mood. "Don't you want more sugar?" he asked. "And a candy stick for each of the girls?"

Annabelle and Rose bounced and skipped at the prospect of a sweet.

"Here's a fox skin," he said. "Wouldn't it make a fine muff?"

What had gotten into the man? Harriet wondered, running her fingers through the thick rust-colored fur. "It's lovely," she said. "But when would

I need such a thing?"

Samuel took the fur from her and added it to their pile. "The red would go well with your brown coat."

Franklin worried all afternoon about the Indian pow-wow. He wasn't sure it was a good idea to mix whites and natives beyond occasional bartering. Someone was likely to cause a misunderstanding. Even on the Frémont trek, the wily French trappers who traded with the tribes regularly got baited into arguments. And the emigrants in his company had no experience dealing with Indians. He'd seen that when they encountered the horse thieves.

But Abercrombie was determined and had gingered up the other men. Now fifteen or so men from their company were clamoring to attend the pow-wow.

Franklin pulled his sons aside. "You boys stay near me at the Indian camp tonight," he told them. "Don't get into any arguments with the tribesmen. I don't want no trouble."

"Yes, Pa," Zeke said.

"Abercrombie'll be there. He's likely to take offense sooner or later at something. Or cause a slight that'll anger the Indians, particularly the Cheyenne braves. Especially if they're liquored up."

Before they set out that evening, Franklin told his men. "Stay out of trouble," he said. "Oglalas ain't a problem, but watch out for the Cheyenne. What you got to trade?"

The emigrants showed him beads and trinkets they'd brought from home or bought at the fort. As they rode across the Laramie to the Indian tepees, the smell of meat roasting on spits grew stronger.

"What are they cooking?" McDougall asked Franklin.

Franklin sniffed. "Dog, most likely." He'd eaten some on the Frémont expedition. If a man got over the notion of eating dog, it tasted mighty fine.

Indian men danced and chanted, drums pounding, and whiskey flowed between travelers and natives. "Go easy," Franklin told his men quietly. "Indians get mean when they're drinking." As do plenty of white men, though he kept that notion to himself.

Samuel gazed around the primitive Indian encampment, listening to the throbbing beat of drums. Tepees of wood poles and dirty hide coverings were pitched haphazardly around a large open field that seemed to be an arena of some sort. Natives and whites alike sat around the performance area, in which masked men hopped and chanted in cadence with the drums. The chaotic scene reminded him of a circus he'd attended as a young man, where brown-skinned foreigners ate fire and danced with snakes. These heathens didn't use snakes, but their animal masks and bearskin costumes were just as strange. Just as barbaric.

Outside the circle of men watching the dancers, a few others gambled—mostly Indians, but a couple of emigrants also participated in the game. The players squatted near one young brave who rolled a pair of dice. Samuel wondered where the man had found the ivory cubes—they looked like ones he'd gambled with in Tennessee. And the game resembled craps—the bettors using a show of fingers to indicate what the total of the throw might be.

He ambled over to watch more closely. When he thought he had the hang of the game, he motioned he'd like to play. He took a sack of beads from his pocket to bet with. Playing with such trinkets didn't cost hardly a thing. The natives bet with their own beads, as well as with furs and tools. Maybe he'd win another fur for Harriet.

The brave with the dice nodded for Samuel to join in.

Douglass followed Samuel, and the two Abercrombies crowded into the circle of players and crouched. As the game went on, its pace intensified. The rounds of betting created a rhythm as compelling as the drumbeat behind them. Items changed hands as rapidly as two-bit coins in saloons in the States. After many rolls, Samuel won a knife from a Cheyenne brave, who then motioned he wanted Samuel to bet it on the next roll so he could try to win it back.

Samuel tested the blade. A fine Bowie knife—he could use it. He shook his head at the Indian's request.

The Cheyenne reached out his palm, slapped the hilt out of Samuel's hand, then kicked the knife into the pile with other items wagered.

The damn Indian wasn't playing fair. Samuel thrust his face into the brave's. "You bet. You lost. It's mine," he snarled.

Another Cheyenne flashed his own knife and pointed it at Samuel's gut.

Douglass drew his pistol and stood slowly. "Let it go, Pa," he said, keeping the flintlock pointed at one of the braves. The gun was a single-shot, but Samuel knew Douglass wouldn't miss at this range.

This was a matter of principle, of honor. "I ain't leaving till I get what I'm owed," Samuel said. He seized the Bowie knife he'd won from where the Cheyenne had thrown it on the ground.

Indians lined up behind the brave who'd lost the knife. Emigrants, including Pershing, circled behind Samuel and Douglass.

"Damn it. I said no trouble," Pershing muttered. Then he turned to the Cheyenne, holding his empty hands open in front of him. "We'll go now," he said. "No fight."

A gun fired, the stingy brave who'd denied Samuel his prize clutched his shoulder, and bedlam erupted. In the brawl that followed, a tribesman slashed Samuel across the forearm.

"Christ!" Samuel shouted as pain seared through him. He continued cursing as Douglass and McDougall dragged him out of the Indian camp toward their horses. They helped him on his gelding, and the emigrants rode back to their wagon circle.

"God damn it, Abercrombie, why'd you let this happen?" Pershing yelled when they had settled by a fire to inspect Samuel's wound.

More than principle now, Samuel wanted justice. "I ain't letting no savage cut me. He'll hang."

"Nobody's going to hang," Pershing said, as Doc Tuller cleansed the wound. "No one died."

"Gash ain't bad," the doctor said. "I can sew it up."

Samuel cursed again as the needle went through his skin.

When the doctor finished and the other men returned to their wagons, Harriet stared at him, tears in her eyes. "What would have happened to me if you'd been killed?"

"Now, Harriet—"

"No, Samuel. Listen to me. I'm only on this wretched journey because you wanted to go. I don't want to end up widowed. Not like Amanda Purcell. Not like Amos Jackson's wife. No amount of free land is worth it. No fox skin muff." She sobbed. "I don't want you trying to be sweet to me one minute, then later risking your life to best a savage." She'd forgotten all her platitudes about equality of the races now, Samuel noticed. "I need you alive," she ended.

"I'm sorry," he said.

Daniel had been watching the dancers and hadn't seen the confrontation between his father and the Cheyenne brave. He'd only noticed the danger when the Pershings and McDougall had risen to stand behind Pa. At that point, Zeke pulled Daniel's arm and Daniel followed him toward Pa and into the melee. Daniel landed a fist on one brave's jaw and narrowly avoided a club to his head—the heavy blow glanced off his shoulder and would surely bruise. They were lucky to escape with only Pa getting wounded. The Cheyenne Douglass had shot was still standing when they left, though he was screaming what Daniel guessed must be Indian-language curses.

Back at the wagons, he'd heard both the argument between Pershing and Pa and Ma's chastisement of Pa afterward. Why did Pa have to argue with everyone he encountered? Most men learned to live with folks in relative peace, but Pa had never mastered the art.

Daniel left his family's campsite and wandered outside the wagon circle. It was too dark to go for a ride, but he was restless.

"Daniel," Esther called softly from nearby.

He turned.

She ran over and took his hand. "How's your father?"

Daniel shrugged. "He'll be all right. Pride's hurt more'n his arm."

"Where are you going?"

He sighed. "I don't know. Just need to get away."

"I'll walk with you."

"No brothers or your pa with you tonight?" He smiled lazily, then took her arm and led her into the shadows.

She leaned against him, almost causing him to stumble. Daniel grabbed her shoulders and gathered her to him, taking his fill in a kiss. Her soft, wet mouth drew him deeper, and he braced her more closely against his body, pulling her hips to his, kneading her buttocks to mold her to him.

"More," she moaned.

Daniel sank to his knees, drawing Esther down with him. Then he laid her on the grass and covered her body with his.

As his fingers fondled her breast, she gasped, then groaned, "Daniel! We mustn't!" She tried to pull away.

He wasn't sure if she really meant it, but he lessened his grip and rolled off her, panting.

She sat up. "Oh, Daniel, how can we wait?" She rose and hurried back toward the wagons.

Chapter 38:   Aftermath

Friday, 11 June 1847. We must move on quickly. Abercrombie riled the natives last night. FP

There was no escaping it, Franklin decided the morning after the pow-wow. He needed to have it out with Abercrombie. The man had endangered the entire company. Franklin had no idea whether Abercrombie had been in the right or not, but he shouldn't have argued with the Cheyenne. After Franklin's earlier warning, it was insubordination, pure and simple.

Franklin talked himself into a rage so he wouldn't back down, then headed to Abercrombie's wagons. "Do you want to do this in front of your family, Abercrombie, or step away from camp?"

Harriet Abercrombie looked up from the spider pan she tended and gasped.

Samuel put his tin mug of coffee on a rock. "Say what you think I need to hear, Pershing." The big man stood and stepped closer, looming over Franklin.

Franklin swallowed, then found his ire again. "You could've been killed last night. Lots of us could've been. 'Tweren't smart to fight with the Cheyenne. Not in their own camp."

"I'm the only one what's paid for it," Abercrombie said, waving his bandaged arm.

"That ain't the point," Franklin argued. "Lots of us might've been hurt.

Even died. All because you wanted a knife."

"I won that knife fair and square. That brave lost, then demanded I let him try to get it back."

"It can't happen again, Abercrombie."

"What can't?"

"You disobeyed my orders—"

Abercrombie spat on the ground and shuffled his feet.

"I told you not to make trouble. Not to fight. And what'd you do? Started a brawl soon as you could—"

"Sorry."

"Your own two sons had to pull you off the brave. And was it Douglass that shot the Indian? Whole company'll have to pay for that—"

"I said I was sorry." Abercrombie sounded surly, but he said the right words.

Franklin stopped his tirade. He hadn't expected Abercrombie to apologize. He paused and rubbed a hand over the back of his neck, wondering whether to end the argument there. But he needed to say the rest of what he'd come to tell the man. "If you argue with anyone or get in any more fights—with others in the company or outsiders—I'll throw you out."

"Now listen here, Pershing." Abercrombie moved toward him. "I won't have you threatening me or my family."

"Your family can stay with us, but not you. Not if you won't obey my orders."

Abercrombie sneered. "Your orders." He spat again. "Your orders ain't worth my horse's piss. We'd be through the mountains already, if I had my way."

Franklin stepped back and pointed his finger at Abercrombie's chest. "I've said my piece. We'll move when I say and at the pace I say. If you can't abide by my rules, then you can leave. With or without your family." He took a deep breath and added his last point. "Have one of your boys bring me that knife. I'm taking it back to the tribe. To make up for Douglass shooting the brave."

Franklin turned away and strode off, his legs shaking. He hoped it didn't show.

Harriet frowned at Samuel after Captain Pershing left. She bit her lip, not knowing how to react to the captain's admonishments or her husband's anger.

Samuel cursed, then sat and kicked his tin mug off the rock where he'd placed it.

"He's right, you know," she said.

"The hell he is!"

"Samuel." Harriet glanced around to see if her granddaughters were nearby. "You apologized, as you needed to. You should have left it there."

Samuel cursed again.

"We have months more till we get to Oregon. Your son wants to marry his daughter."

"That ain't gonna happen now," Samuel shouted. "I won't have no ties to that sorry excuse for a man. Not any longer'n I can help it. As soon as we get to Oregon, I'll have no more to do with him."

Harriet braced her hands on her hips. "And I won't have you damaging Daniel's chance at happiness. You need to calm down and let us all be. And until you can—" She inhaled deeply, not knowing how to continue, then finally huffed, "Go . . . Go . . . Oh, go shoot something! I don't want you around camp today."

Cordelia stood from her laundry tub when Franklin returned to their wagons. She'd heard shouting from the Abercrombie camp, but she hadn't made out what the men said.

Franklin plunked down heavily on a crate and sighed. "I told him."

"Samuel Abercrombie?" Cordelia asked.

Franklin nodded.

"Told him what?"

"That he'd have to follow my orders or leave."

"Leave? Where would he go?"

"I don't care." Franklin stoked his pipe. "Not at this point."

"But Esther and Daniel will—"

Franklin stared at her. "How can Esther marry that man's son? Samuel Abercrombie is a scoundrel. He don't care a hoot for anyone but himself."

"Daniel's a good young man—" Cordelia began, then stopped when she saw Franklin's jaw clench as he bit his pipe. She swallowed and continued. "There's months yet till Oregon."

"Will you talk to Esther or shall I?"

"And tell her what?"

"I'm withdrawing my consent to her marriage."

"Oh, Franklin—can't we just let it ride?"

He stood. "I'll find her. In the meantime, get your washing done. We're leaving Laramie first thing in the morning."

After the argument with Harriet, Samuel found the Bowie knife, gave it to Douglass, then strode away from his campsite. What did the woman want, anyway? He didn't want to be tied to the Pershings through Daniel's marriage, not when Pershing insisted on his orders being followed—orders that were usually poppycock.

Samuel knew he shouldn't have confronted the Cheyenne. But what was a man supposed to do when he was being cheated? Let it pass? His arm throbbed. It wasn't a deep cut—he'd heal soon enough, not like Bramwell. But in the meantime, the pain was a constant reminder of the tension between him and Pershing. Between him and Daniel. And now between him and Harriet.

He took his wife at her word and decided to go hunting. He culled his gelding from the horses grazing in the wagon circle, then winced as he threw his saddle over the horse's back. He wanted to get away from camp, but wondered if he'd be able to shoot with a steady arm. So what if he didn't bring back game? He could ride for the pleasure of it.

Samuel trotted away from camp, away from the fort, south toward the hills. He followed a narrow valley with a creek running through the middle. A mile or two from camp he startled a herd of deer near the creek. He pulled his rifle from its scabbard, cursing at a stab of pain in his arm, aimed, and shot. A deer fell. He rode over to it. The doe thrashed on the ground, so he took out his pistol and shot it in the head. It lay still, eyes open. Dead.

The kill hadn't made him feel any better.

He dismounted, gutted the deer, then heaved the carcass over his saddle, grimacing again at the pain. Now that his horse was laden, there was nothing to do but ride back to camp.

He rode to his wagons and dropped the carcass beside Harriet. "Got a deer," he said.

Esther sat in the wagon mending clothes while her parents argued outside. She heard Pa say he was ready to throw the Abercrombies out of the company. Then he said he wouldn't let her marry Daniel! She gasped. She needed to find Daniel. She'd avoid Pa until she'd talked to Daniel—she had to know how he felt about their fathers' latest clash. Surely he could do something to make their parents continue to support their betrothal.

She dropped her mending and slipped out the back of the wagon, first peering around the cover to be sure Ma wasn't watching. Ma knelt on the ground beside the washtub, elbows propped on its edge and head in her hands. Was she sick? Or just upset? Esther couldn't worry about her mother now—she needed Daniel.

She hurried toward the Abercrombie campsite, but stopped when she heard Mr. and Mrs. Abercrombie arguing. Esther barely hid behind another wagon before Mr. Abercrombie stormed off. She didn't want to see anyone until she talked to Daniel.

But Esther couldn't find Daniel anywhere near his family's camp. She finally walked toward the Laramie River, and found him sitting on the bank upstream from the fort with his fishing pole dangling in the water. It wasn't a private setting for them to talk—people came and went from the fort on the nearby path. But it would have to do.

"Daniel," she said as she approached.

He turned to look at her, his face grim.

She stood beside him. "I need to talk to you."

He patted the ground beside him and she sat.

"Pa's upset with your pa," she said. "Threatened to throw him out of the wagon company."

Daniel shrugged. "Well, my pa's upset with yours, too."

"Why?" Esther asked. "Your pa had no call to fight with that Indian."

"You weren't there, Esther. I was."

"Are you saying your pa was in the right? To fight with the Cheyenne after Pa told the men not to?"

Daniel heaved a deep sigh. "It ain't that simple."

"Why not?"

"Pa won the knife fair and square. Indian tried to get it back after he'd lost."

"Did you see it?"

"Not really. But that's what Pa said."

Esther snorted. "And you believe him?"

Daniel turned to her. "What am I supposed to believe? That my pa deliberately provoked a fight? That he tried to get us all killed? All he wants is to get us to Oregon."

"That's all my pa wants, too. And he's the captain. Folks need to do as he says. If he says not to fight with Indians, then your pa shouldn't have started anything. You need to stand up to your pa."

"He didn't start it," Daniel said.

"Don't matter who started it. Now Pa says he don't want us to get married." Esther sniffed and swallowed. She didn't want to argue with Daniel—they needed to stand together against their parents. But he was making it hard not to take sides, and her father was the captain. His word was law.

"My father ain't too happy about it at the moment either." Daniel cast his line into the stream. They sat in silence for what seemed like ages. Then Daniel said, "Do you want to call off our engagement?"

Esther stared at him, stunned. "Do you?"

"It's up to you, Esther." He cast his line again. "A man can't break an engagement. Not without it looking bad. But a girl . . ." His voice trailed off, and he didn't look at her.

"You do want to end it. Because of your pa." Her words came out as a statement, though she'd meant to ask the question again.

"Our families—"

"I ain't marrying your pa, Daniel. I want to marry you." But Esther didn't want to marry a man who didn't love her. "But if you don't want me, then I don't want you." She stood and ran back to camp.

Where could she hide while she cried?

Daniel cast his line angrily into the water, not caring if he scared the fish away. He and Esther had fought, and he didn't know how to feel about it. He wasn't sure he should have defended his father's actions at the fort, but his father had only been trying to keep what he'd won. Perhaps he'd made a foolish blunder, but it hadn't been intentional.

And now Captain Pershing—whom Daniel respected—was mad at Pa. So mad he threatened to keep Esther and Daniel from marrying. Not only that, Esther thought her father was right and that he should confront his father. Daniel didn't see how he could satisfy Pa, Captain Pershing, and Esther, nor did he know how to raise the issue with his father.

He wasn't sure he'd even have the chance to try—Esther had stormed away, obviously near tears. Should he go after her or not?

As he pondered the situation, a fish bit. He took his time pulling it in. It was easier to deal with a trout than with Esther. Or their parents.

Chapter 39:　Overcoming Objections

Friday, 11 June 1847. Took the knife back to the Cheyenne. Leaving Laramie tomorrow. FP

Even after Franklin returned the Bowie knife to the Cheyenne brave, he heard the tribes continued to mutter about the melee Abercrombie had caused. The traders in the fort advised him to get his company away quickly. Though Franklin had hoped to spend another day or two at Laramie so animals and people could rest, he told everyone to finish their re-provisioning on Friday.

Early Saturday morning Franklin ordered the wagons into line, and they resumed their travel along the North Platte fork. Soon they'd cross this branch of the river and leave the Platte behind for good.

Jenny McDougall now rode a small mare—her husband had bought it for her at the fort from one of the Indian traders. Franklin wondered if McDougall had meant to appease his little wife or the Indians with the purchase. Maybe both.

Cordelia didn't ride well, or Franklin might have considered a pony for her. He watched his wife now, trudging with several of their children off to the side of the wagons. Beyond them in the distance to the south a mountain range rose, some of the peaks covered in snow from last winter. The sun above was warm, but the remaining snow wouldn't melt until August, if it ever did before the next autumn's storms began.

An hour or two beyond Laramie, the valley narrowed between

sandstone cliffs. Franklin slowed the wagons to permit walkers to go ahead, then ordered the wagons into single file between the red bluffs.

Abercrombie had stayed out of Franklin's path this morning. He hadn't talked to the man since their confrontation the day before. Franklin also hadn't talked to Esther about Daniel. Cordelia had convinced him to keep quiet—for now.

He thought something troubled his daughter. She seemed subdued. Maybe she and Daniel had quarreled. Maybe Franklin's fears about permanent ties to the Abercrombies were premature.

Cordelia wished they could have rested longer at the fort. She'd enjoyed seeing people not from their company, and she'd been glad to replenish food supplies, even if the post's goods weren't plentiful and prices too steep. But she wouldn't disagree with Franklin, not about his decisions as wagon captain.

She *had* disagreed with him about Esther and Daniel. After he announced he would no longer give his consent to their marriage, she pleaded with him to wait a few days before he spoke to Esther. Even though Cordelia had misgivings about the betrothal, it wasn't fair to their daughter if her parents vacillated in their approval. "You said Samuel apologized," she reasoned. "Give him a chance to show he's changed."

Franklin snorted. "That man won't change. I seen enough like him in the Army. And he told me what he thought of my orders."

"Please, Franklin. What can it hurt to wait a day or two?" They argued further, and he left after finally agreeing not to say anything to Esther for the moment.

A short while later, Esther rushed into their campsite in tears.

"What's wrong?" Cordelia asked.

Esther waved her hand as if to tell her mother to let her alone and climbed into the wagon.

Cordelia trundled to the wagon and peered in the rear. "Tell me, child."

"It's Daniel!" Esther wailed. "He doesn't want to marry me."

"Did he say so?" Cordelia didn't know what to think—was this the solution Franklin wanted or was it a simple misunderstanding between the young couple? And what should she tell her daughter—to drop the engagement or to pursue the young man she loved?

"We f-f-fought," Esther said, drying her eyes with a corner of a towel. "About Pa and Mr. Abercrombie. Daniel asked if I wanted to call it off. I could tell *he* wanted to, but he's too n-n-nice to say so." And she sobbed again.

Cordelia stepped on a wheel spoke and heaved herself into the wagon. She put an arm around Esther and let her daughter cry. When Esther's weeping subsided to sniffles, Cordelia said what was in her heart, "You need to talk to your young man again. Ask him point blank what he wants. But be prepared to tell him what you want first. If you love him—do you?"

Esther nodded.

"Then tell him so." She put a finger under her daughter's chin and turned the girl's face to look at her. "It won't be easy, Esther. It's likely Samuel Abercrombie will be a thorn in your side forever if you marry his son. But if you and Daniel love each other, you can weather many a storm. If you don't, then you're in for a hard time. So be sure of what you want." Then she told Esther to start packing the wagons for their departure from Laramie.

Walking along the trail with her children now, the morning after her conversation with Esther, Cordelia's breath came shorter as they headed into the mountains, and the infant inside her grew heavier with each hour. Cordelia leaned on Esther's arm as they plodded along. "Did you talk to Daniel?"

"Yes, Ma." Esther beamed. "He loves me. He wants to marry me."

Cordelia sighed. She still didn't feel happy about the marriage, but the joy on Esther's face was hard to resist. Franklin was still an obstacle, but she smiled at Esther. "Why don't we cut out your wedding dress tonight, if we stop early enough?"

Esther felt like dancing as she walked the sandy high plains after the noon meal on Saturday, remembering her conversations with Daniel and with her mother. She'd lain awake for half the night, worrying about what to say to Daniel after their argument on the Laramie riverbank. It had still been dark that morning when she'd dressed quietly and stolen from the tent to creep over to the Abercrombie campsite. She heard his father snoring so she figured Daniel must be on the opposite side of the tent. She whispered, "Daniel? It's me. Esther."

"Huh?" he said sleepily.

"Come out," she said. "I want to talk to you."

After some scrabbling inside the tent, he emerged, dressed in pants and an untucked shirt. His feet were shoved into boots he hadn't bothered to lace. Esther grabbed his arm. "Come with me."

She pulled him outside the wagon circle and toward the river. "I'm sorry for what I said yesterday," she said. "I love you. I want to marry you." She tightened her hold on his arm, eager to tell him how she felt. "But only if you love me. I won't tie you down if you've changed your mind."

His response was to lean over and kiss her. "I'm sorry, too," he said when his lips left hers. Holding her close, he whispered, "And, yes, I want to marry you. As soon as I can."

She nestled her head against his chest, feeling his heart pound. "I wish we were in Oregon now," she murmured.

As Esther remembered the sound of his heart thumping against her ear, she smiled and whispered again to herself, "I wish we were in Oregon now."

And Ma had said they would cut out her wedding dress tonight! Esther couldn't help twirling in a circle on the prairie. "You got a bee up your skirt, Esther?" Jonathan shouted. "You're looking mighty silly."

Esther ignored her brother. She called out to Jenny McDougall, who now rode a small Indian pony, "I don't suppose you'll walk with me, now you have a horse to ride."

"Don't be silly," Jenny said, bringing the mare to a stop beside Esther. "Poulette can carry both of us for a while." She helped Esther up behind her.

As they trotted along on the pony, Esther told Jenny, "I bought cloth in Laramie. For a wedding dress. Light blue with pale yellow flowers. Ma says I can cut it out tonight." And she and Jenny talked through the afternoon about trousseaux and weddings. She decided not to say anything about her squabble with Daniel, nor about Pa's reluctance to let them marry.

"I want all new things," she said. "Quilts and blankets and dishes. Won't happen, I know. I'll mostly get Ma's castoffs. I still dream about it.

My own home." She sighed, imagining a cozy house shaded by tall trees, children running on a lawn outside. "My own family."

Daniel watched Esther all day Saturday, whenever he could look away from the tasks his father assigned him. He didn't quite know what to make of her waking him that morning—they were lucky none of their parents had seen them. He'd been elated to patch up their quarrel, and he remembered again how she'd felt snugged up against his chest when he kissed her and told her he wanted to marry her. He'd yearned to do more than kiss her, more than hug her.

If he hadn't feared some other early riser in the company seeing them, he would have laid her on the ground and seen how far she would let him go. He respected her—she was the woman he would marry—but he wanted her now. How could he wait to marry her until they reached Oregon? Even then, he'd have to build her a house, clear some land, be ready to provide for her. He wanted to have everything in place that a husband should give his bride before he brought Esther into his home, but the delays seemed interminable.

When they halted for the evening, Daniel went to the Pershing camp. "Esther, would you walk with me?" he asked. "The spring nearby is warm water. Folks are wading in it."

Mrs. Pershing looked up sharply from her Dutch oven. "You may go, Esther," she said. "But take Rachel and Ruthie with you."

The three Pershing daughters jumped up. Esther took Daniel's arm, and her younger sisters raced ahead. At the water, all four of them took off their shoes and splashed about.

"The water is almost too hot to bear," Esther said, leaning on Daniel and wriggling one bare foot above the spring. "Ruthie, you be careful now."

The little girl giggled and jumped from foot to foot, holding Rachel's hand.

When he thought Rachel was watching Ruth, Daniel leaned over and kissed Esther.

"Daniel!" she said, "There's people about."

"They know we're engaged," he said.

She grinned. "Don't let Ma or Pa see you. Or Zeke."

Indeed, Daniel looked over Esther's head and saw Zeke glowering at them.

Ruth slipped on a rock and fell. She came up crying.

"Are you burned?" Esther asked.

Ruth shook her head. "My foot hurts. I want Ma!" she whimpered.

Daniel shrugged and picked her up. "Then let's go find her." He carried the little girl back to camp, with Esther and Rachel trailing behind. There hadn't been much opportunity for spooning, but he had Ruth laughing by the time they reached her mother.

The next morning, a Sunday, Cordelia stood quietly while Franklin conducted a prayer service before the company left the campsite at Warm Springs. Franklin had told her they wouldn't lay by for the Sabbath. The day was sunny and warm, and he didn't want to waste the fine weather.

When her daughters and Daniel had returned from the spring last evening and she saw Ruth in Daniel's arms, she'd jumped up from her cooking. The movement caused a catch in her side, more than a shortness of breath, a stabbing pain. Whether from worry about Ruth or due to the babe in her belly, she didn't know.

That baby never let her forget his presence these days. She'd been thinking of the child as a boy recently, though she wanted another daughter—she already had five sons and three daughters, a girl would help even things out. Besides, she would lose Esther soon to Daniel. She already mourned Esther's future absence, the separation from the offspring she felt closest to.

Zeke told her he'd seen Esther and Daniel kissing at the spring the night before. Her lips twitched at his account, but she turned to Esther sternly. "Is that true, young lady?"

Esther nodded.

"Don't you become a scandal for the rest of the company," Cordelia said.

"But, Ma—"

"And don't you 'but Ma' me. You may be engaged, and that allows you to spend more time in Daniel's company. But it don't allow him to take liberties, especially not where the whole camp can see." Cordelia sighed. It would be a long trip to Oregon, and she'd have to watch Esther every minute, no doubt. She wasn't sure whether Esther or Daniel was the more moonstruck youngster. She might love Esther dearly, but she knew full well her daughter was featherbrained at times and too eager for love to comport herself as she ought.

Now that they were underway, Cordelia fretted. Her pace was slow and her breath came in wheezes whenever they encountered a hill. Walking became more difficult every week as her bulk increased.

She and Jenny McDougall lagged behind the other women and children, though they managed to keep ahead of the wagons. She stopped and panted at the top of a ravine.

"Are you anxious about your confinement?" Jenny asked.

Cordelia's laugh turned into a gasp. "Anxious? That don't help none. Baby comes whether I worry or not." Then she realized—the girl was probably afraid for herself. "Are you scared, girl?"

Jenny nodded.

"Birthing's just part of being a woman. Not a thing you can do once it's planted." She patted Jenny's arm. "Don't you fret. I'll be there when your time comes. Mrs. Tuller, too. Lots of us to help." Then she changed the subject. "What you think about my Esther and young Abercrombie?"

"Esther seems to love him very much."

Cordelia snorted. She'd hoped Jenny would have a more sensible outlook. "Love ain't important. It's whether a man and woman can work together. Daniel's a good boy, but I don't know if he's ready for a family, if he's strong enough to manage Esther. She ain't one who'll push a man to better himself. Some women do. Others just want a man to dote on 'em. I'm afraid Esther's in that last batch."

Jenny raised an eyebrow. "She might surprise you, Mrs. Pershing. Maybe she thinks about dresses and such because she doesn't have much else to think about."

Cordelia nodded. Perhaps young Jenny did perceive character accurately. Esther had depth to her—her care of the little boy who'd died had shown so—even though she seemed flighty. They'd spent the last evening piecing together the pretty calico for her daughter's wedding dress. Esther chatted the whole time about the wedding she wanted, the home she'd have in Oregon. Not a word about hard work and making do.

Chapter 40:   Wanting More

Saturday, 12 June 1847. Made 10 miles from Laramie today.
The Platte crossing should be a few days ahead. FP

Samuel smiled to himself as the wagons set out on Sunday. Pershing hadn't even suggested they lay by that day. He and Daniel both rode horseback, while Douglass tended the wagons. Along the North Platte the route was straight enough—and the oxen were well-settled to the trail—so one man could mind both wagons. He called Daniel to him.

"Yes, Pa? I was planning to scout with Zeke and Joel." Daniel talked more independently than he used to. Was it Pershing's doing or Esther's?

"You was seen with Esther at the spring last night. Had her in a clinch, I hear tell."

"Pa!"

"Well, did you or didn't you? I thought you was taking it slow till we're in Oregon. Thought maybe you'd even call off your engagement."

"I can't do that to Esther. And I won't. I love her."

"Didn't seem so sure 'bout that a couple days ago."

"We quarreled," Daniel said. "But we patched it up."

Samuel spat, squinting in the distance. Esther and her mother walked with the passel of younger Pershings, or some of them at least. "Well, don't let yourself get forced into marriage," he said. "Best keep your hands off her. Otherwise, we'll have a shotgun wedding afore we reach South Pass."

Daniel shrugged. "Wouldn't be so awful. I'm going to marry her at some point, Pa."

Samuel shook his finger at his son's insolence. "You let me decide what's good and what's bad," he snapped.

They rode in silence a few minutes. Daniel wasn't a disobedient boy, Samuel reflected. Just a young man sniffing after a sashaying skirt. "How's your mare faring?" he asked.

"She's fine. Lost some weight."

"All our horses have. Grass is too thin. You best coddle her some. No galloping across the prairie."

"Yes, Pa."

"And no extra weight. Don't give the Pershing girl any long rides. You want to spend time with her, you walk where everyone can see you."

Harriet struggled to pull herself out of her bedroll Monday morning. The chill air felt more like March than mid-June. After she dressed and exited the tent to cook breakfast, she noticed fresh snow on the Laramie Range to their south. The peaks had been white-capped since they were first visible, but she was certain the snow now covered more of the mountains than yesterday. A storm must have passed during the night.

The evening before, Samuel had complained about the sparse grass, saying the horses and oxen were suffering. He'd shot an antelope on Sunday, so their family was well fed—though Harriet would dearly love some greens or carrots to relieve their monotonous diet.

"I wish we'd seen vegetables at Fort Laramie," she said to Louisa as they fried antelope steaks and flapjacks. "Wouldn't stewed tomatoes taste fine about now?"

"What's a tomato?" little Rose asked—her younger granddaughter had already forgotten many of the foods she'd eaten in Tennessee.

Once they were underway, Harriet, Louisa, and the girls walked with other women through parched stubbly grass. In June the ground should still be green, she thought, but here she saw only sand and thigh-high dried out bushes.

"Sagebrush," Captain Pershing told them when he paused to chat at the Abercrombie wagons. "We'll see more'n more of it as we go west. Other side of the pass is nothing but sage."

"Can we eat it?" Harriet asked.

The captain shrugged. "Might season the food a bit, but it ain't very tasty by itself. Best stick to the greens along the creek beds."

But Harriet didn't know what was edible. Maybe Hatty Tanner could help. The Negroes back home were used to finding wild things to eat.

During the noon meal, Daniel seemed silent. "What is it, son?" Harriet asked him when they were alone for a minute. "Something worrying you?"

"Pa don't want me spending time with Esther. How are we going to get to know each other better if we can't ride together during the day and we can't walk together at night?"

"You can talk when there's other folks around, Daniel. But it ain't wise to be alone with her. Not if you want her reputation to remain unblemished."

"She's going to be my wife as soon as I can make her so."

Harriet looked at him sharply. "You haven't taken liberties, have you, son?"

"No, ma'am!" But his face turned red. It would be hard to get the two young folks to Oregon without a scandal, Harriet feared. She decided not to speak to Samuel, but to keep an eye on Daniel herself.

Perhaps it would be better to let the couple marry before they reached Oregon. She would raise the notion with Cordelia Pershing.

Monday afternoon Daniel scouted with Zeke and Joel Pershing and Mac McDougall. Captain Pershing had ordered the young men to look for grass for the teams. Most of the emigrants' animals now showed their ribs from lack of feed. Daniel hated to see the beasts suffer. And if the oxen and mules weakened and slowed their pace, the emigrants would endure hardship as well.

He'd spent the morning with his father and the noon meal with his mother. Now he relished getting away from family. Both parents cautioned him not to spend much time with Esther. In fact, his father had done more than caution him. But Daniel itched to be with her.

If he couldn't talk to her, maybe he could learn more about her from her brothers. Daniel asked Zeke about growing up on the farm in Missouri, what kind of crops they'd raised, what animals they'd had. Zeke droned on and on about corn and wheat and tobacco, about cattle and hogs, but when Daniel turned the conversation to Esther, Zeke had nothing to say. "She's my little sister. She and Rachel stuck close to Ma. Joel and I sneaked away as soon after breakfast as we could, so Ma wouldn't order us about. Just like Jonathan and David do now."

"But—"

"You ain't got a little sister, Daniel. If you did, you'd understand." Zeke called to McDougall. "Do you have a sister, Mac? Did you let her follow you about?"

Mac grinned. "I'm the youngest. Like Daniel. And no sisters, only two older brothers. I'm the one who tagged along."

They searched all afternoon but found only scanty grass. Their horses and draft animals would go hungry another day. The company made camp that night beside a narrow creek with only a few scrubby cottonwoods, which they chopped for fuel. They went to bed early, not wanting to sit in the smoke of greenwood fires.

Daniel was one of the guards on first watch. When his duty ended, he crept to the Pershing camp. "Esther," he whispered, but only once so as not to rouse her parents.

After a minute she appeared, barefoot and in her nightdress, a shawl wrapped around her shoulders. "It's cold," she said, smiling at him.

He picked her up and carried her outside the wagons away from the guards, then set her on her feet. "Stand on my boots, if your feet are cold," he said, holding her close.

"Mmm," she moaned as she pressed herself to him. "You're so warm."

He opened his jacket and folded it around her, then lowered his lips to hers. He'd never kissed her with so few layers between them—just his shirt and her thin nightdress. One hand cupped her breast, while his other arm held her against him, pressing them tightly together from shoulders to thighs. Warm thighs. Reluctantly, his hand left her breast and trailed down her side to feel one of those thighs, then up to her center where he'd never touched a girl before. It was his turn to moan, and he lowered her to the ground under him, wanting all of her.

She let his hands roam, and her hands moved as well, from his chest to his waist, then she clasped his buttocks. She arched against his palm and gasped, "Daniel, we mustn't."

"I want you, Esther."

"I know," she said. "But we can't. What if I have a baby?"

"What if you do?" he whispered, still caressing her.

But he knew the moment had passed when she sighed and pulled away. "I can't. I can't disappoint Ma. And Pa would kill us both."

Daniel rolled off her, breathing deeply. "Next time I may not be able to stop."

She touched his lips with hers. "I may not be able to either." With another sigh, she stood and slipped away in the dark, leaving him alone.

Esther thrashed in her bedroll through most of the night, reliving every one of Daniel's touches. She wanted him to make love to her—that's how she thought of it now—but she knew what happened when a girl let a man take her before marriage. If anyone found out, her reputation would be ruined, even if they were engaged. If she got with child, she'd be the talk of the wagon train. She wanted to wait until she was married, but she yearned for Daniel now.

They would have to marry soon, she decided. Should she tell her mother what she and Daniel had almost done? Ma had already cautioned her to be careful. Esther didn't think she was brave enough to talk to Ma again.

In the morning she sought Daniel out as he saddled his horse. "I want to wed as soon as we can. I don't want to wait till we get to Oregon."

He stared at her. "Esther—"

"You said you wanted me."

"I do."

"Then will you marry me now? Why wait?" She took his hand.

He tucked a stray blond curl behind her ear. "I have to be able to provide for you afore we wed."

"I just want *you*, Daniel. We'll make do. You'll file your claim, and we'll be fine. And we'll be together months earlier."

He stared into her eyes. She gazed back, waiting, holding her breath.

Finally he nodded. "You talk to your parents. I'll talk to mine. If they agree, we'll marry now."

"And if they don't?" she whispered. "How can we wait?"

His Adam's apple rose and fell as he swallowed. Then he smiled,

"We'll just have to persuade them. I'll go hunting with Pa today. Pray for us to find some game to put him in a congenial mood."

Cordelia could tell something bothered Esther when they headed out Wednesday morning. The girl was bad-tempered with the young'uns—even little Noah couldn't get a smile out of her.

Cordelia felt irritable herself. Whenever she sat to rest, the babe kicked her in the lungs or bladder, sometimes hard enough to make her grunt.

"What is it?" Franklin had asked her during the night.

"Can't sleep," she whispered back. "Can't get comfortable."

"Are you all right?"

"Yes. Just tired."

She was thankful their conversation hadn't awakened the children in the tent with them, though she'd noticed Esther tossing in her sleep. Now she wondered what had made her daughter so restless.

Cordelia pulled Esther to her when they started the day's trek. "Walk with me a ways, daughter—until I tire."

Esther complied, but didn't seem happy to have her mother leaning on her arm.

"What is it, girl?" Cordelia asked. "Why the downturned mouth?"

"Daniel and I need to marry afore we get to Oregon," Esther blurted.

Cordelia stopped, shocked. Goosebumps rose on her arms despite the warm morning. "Are you with child?"

"No, Ma." Esther shook her head vigorously. "And I don't want to be."

"Then why?"

"Oh, Ma." Esther's eyes filled with tears. "I want him so bad. And he wants me, he says."

"Esther—" Cordelia couldn't say any more. Her own eyes brimmed. She wanted to feel again the way her daughter felt, that fierce passion, that urgency to be with her lover every instant. She used to feel it for Franklin, but now—now all she felt was tired.

"What is it, Ma?" Esther's voice was suddenly full of concern for her. "I don't want to disappoint you. I'm sorry. But I want—"

"I know, child," Cordelia said, leaning more heavily on her daughter. "I know." She paused. "Let me think on it this morning. You mind the young'uns and let me ride awhile." She gestured to Joel to stop the wagon, and she climbed in.

She worried as the wagon rolled along. About Esther. About herself. She didn't know if it was the child, the travel, her age, or something else. But the thought came to her almost daily that she might not survive this birth.

She had to live, she prayed—she wasn't done mothering her children. Zeke and Joel would be all right, but the rest of them, from Esther on down, they still needed her. If Esther married now, could Cordelia feel that at least one child was settled? That would still leave so many of them fledglings—Rachel, the twins, Ruth, Noah, and the one still to come. Yes, they needed her.

Was it better for Esther to marry now, while still on the trail, or wait until Oregon? Look at Amanda Purcell and Amos Jackson's wife—both widowed with children. The same could happen to Esther—she could be left with child. But if her daughter got with child and *wasn't* married, her life would be worse than if widowed.

Cordelia had no confidence in her ability to keep Esther and Daniel apart. Nor did she think Franklin, Samuel, or Harriet held any more sway over their offspring than she did.

Franklin would do whatever Cordelia said—she could convince him. She continued to fret through the noon halt. She didn't want to lose her daughter to marriage so soon. But what was best for Esther?

Daniel found his father in camp. "You hunting today, Pa?" he asked. "I could go along."

Pa squinted at him. "Why the interest today, son? I reckoned you'd be nosing after that girl of yours."

Daniel shrugged. "Just wanted to see some country away from the river."

"Don't Pershing need you as a scout?"

"Zeke and Joel can handle that. Or McDougall. Besides, if we find grass, we'll let the others know."

Pa nodded. "All right, then. We'll leave Douglass in charge of the wagons."

Daniel and his father left after breakfast, heading south into the hills. They traversed one ravine after another searching for game. After the coolness of the day before, the warm sun felt soothing on Daniel's back. His mare wanted to stop whenever a blade of green poked up from the dry ground, and often he let her.

About noon, Pa led them down a dry gully. At the bottom, a small pool sat in the middle of a few succulent bushes. "We'll rest here. Eat, let the horses graze."

They dismounted, and Daniel led his mare to the water. He thrashed through the bushes to the other side of the pool to fill his canteen and bent over the water. A rattle sounded. He jumped back just as the snake struck, then it slithered away under the brush.

"Did it get you, son?" Pa rushed over and grabbed Daniel's arm.

"My glove, I think." There were two puncture marks in the glove. He pulled it off. His hand looked fine. No wounds. He took a deep gulp of air.

Pa got his rifle and threw a rock into the brush. When a snake slipped out, he shot it. "Hope that's the one," Pa said. "And that it's alone."

Daniel's legs shook and he sat.

"You sure he didn't get you?" Pa asked. "You look a bit green."

"Scared me, that's all. I'm fine."

"Let me see your hand again." Pa turned Daniel's hand over to inspect both palm and back. He checked up to Daniel's elbow. "Don't see nothing. You're damn lucky." Pa gave Daniel his canteen.

Daniel drank deeply, then felt better.

Pa scuffed about in the dirt. "Best make sure there ain't any other varmints around." He got food out of their saddlebags, and they ate.

As Pa chewed his meat, he said, "Would hate to lose you, son."

Daniel stared at his father, surprised. Pa wasn't one to speak of affection. This was about as much tenderness as he'd ever heard from his father. "I wouldn't have wanted the snake bite either, Pa."

His father chuckled. "I suppose I'd rather see you married to the Pershing lass than in a coffin."

Daniel swallowed. This would be his best opportunity to talk to Pa, he decided. "Well, Pa, Esther'n me, we been talking. We'd rather get married now, on the trail, than wait till Oregon."

Pa took off his hat and frowned at Daniel. "What brought that on?"

"There doesn't seem any reason to wait. And we're all together here—"

Daniel didn't want to tell his father how close he and Esther had come to anticipating their vows.

"Can't keep your hands off her, huh?"

"Pa—"

Pa shrugged. "Wouldn't be a man if you could. It's why I married. Both times."

They sat in silence awhile. Daniel wanted approval from his father, but maybe he already had it. He opened his mouth to speak, but before he could, his father said, "I ain't fond of Pershing. Probably never will be. But his wife is a good sort, and so is his girl. You could do worse." Pa stood. "You find a preacher, I won't stand in your way."

Daniel grinned. Now he had it—Pa's blessing. His mother wouldn't be a problem, he was sure.

After the noon meal on Wednesday, Franklin was surprised when Cordelia asked him to stay with her awhile. "Are you all right?" he asked. She'd been moving slowly ever since they left Laramie.

"I'm fine," she said, though her voice didn't hold much conviction.

He sent Zeke ahead to lead the company, then walked his horse alongside the wagon where his wife sat. She instructed Esther and Rachel to mind the young'uns, leaving the couple as alone as they could be on the trail.

"Esther and Daniel want to marry soon," she said once the wagons were rolling at a steady pace. "Afore we reach Oregon."

"I thought we wanted them settled," Franklin said, his eyes widening as he stared at her. "Get young Abercrombie to build her a house on his claim first."

"I know." Cordelia sighed. "I don't know what to do."

"You think they should marry now?" Franklin's horse bobbed and shied at his harsh tone. He pulled the reins tighter. "I'm not even sure I approve of this marriage."

"I don't know what we should do. I suppose they could honeymoon as we travel. Be ready to buckle down when we arrive."

Franklin snorted. "Honeymoon? With the whole company nearby? 'Tain't much of a wedding trip."

"But they won't have any responsibilities, not like once they have their own place."

Franklin looked at his wife sharply. "Won't you need Esther when the baby comes? To mind the others?"

Cordelia sighed. "Yes. But we need to think of what's best for her. And she'll be close by."

"What's changed your mind about waiting for a wedding in Oregon?" She had been so adamant ever since they agreed to the engagement.

Cordelia shrugged. "I'm not sure I *have* changed my mind. But we should consider what Esther wants." She didn't speak for a moment, then said, "Have you seen them eyeing each other?"

He didn't understand. "What do you mean?"

"They're in love, Franklin. Need I say more?"

It dawned on him—the lad was pawing his daughter! "Has he hurt her?"

Cordelia laughed, a throaty sound like she made when he bedded her. "No. She's fine."

"I'll put the fear of God in him." The idea of any man touching Esther riled him, but it would come at some point. Daniel was as good a son-in-law as he was likely to get. Even if Samuel was a malcontent. Franklin sighed. "Let me think on it."

Through the heat of the afternoon, Franklin busied himself with minding the wagons. Late in the day, Zeke reported a creek ahead. "Not much grass there," he told his father. "But we ain't seen any all day."

"Pull the wagons into a circle. We'll stop."

Shortly after they were settled, Samuel Abercrombie and Daniel rode into camp, an antelope carcass behind each man.

Franklin watched the two men suspiciously—Samuel out of general principle, and Daniel because of what Cordelia had said. The Abercrombie father and son seemed more at ease with each other than usual, and Franklin relaxed.

Daniel looked up and caught Franklin's eye. The young man waved, then walked over. He held out his hand, and Franklin shook it reflexively.

"Evening, Captain Pershing," Daniel said. "I'd like to have a word with you."

Franklin waited.

"I'm hoping you'll see your way to letting Esther and me marry as soon as we can, sir. I promise I'll care for her. I'll build her a home as soon as we arrive in Oregon. But I love her, sir, and I want—"

"We're thinking on it, boy. I won't give you an answer now. But if you cause her any harm—now or after you're married—you'll answer to me." With that Franklin stalked away to tend his oxen. Not that they needed tending, but he wasn't going to listen to the young man's blathering any more.

As he checked the team's hooves, Esther came over. "Did Daniel talk to you, Pa?"

"He did." Franklin frowned at her. "You sure you know what you're after?"

"Yes, Pa." She smiled and hugged him.

"Careful of the beasts now," he said. "Stand back." He scratched his head as he looked at his daughter. "Your ma and I need to get used to the idea."

Chapter 41:   Young Folks' Outing

Wednesday, 16 June 1847. We need grass soon or the teams will die. FP

Samuel wasn't sure why he agreed so easily to Daniel's desire to marry soon. He awoke on Thursday morning wondering if he should change his mind, take back his approval. But then he remembered the fear he'd felt when the snake struck at Daniel—he'd been willing to grant the boy anything.

Samuel had always felt partial to Douglass—the son who could shoot, the son who followed his father's bidding. Daniel was like his mother Abigail and like Harriet—a dreamer, a boy who'd rather play with the chickens than slaughter them for supper.

Why did the lad have to fall in love with the Pershing girl?

But he'd given his word. He wouldn't go back on it now.

"I told Daniel he could marry Esther afore we get to Oregon," he told Harriet.

She tried to hide a smile. "That's nice."

He frowned. "Why are you smiling?"

She laughed. "I told Cordelia Pershing we wouldn't stand in their way."

"But you and I hadn't talked."

"No. But it was the right thing to do. Esther and Daniel want the wedding soon."

Samuel snorted. "Can't keep their hands off each other, is what you mean."

"Samuel!" Harriet looked around. "Keep your voice down. Do you want to scandalize the entire company?"

"Not me scandalizing folks, it's my son." He hoped he kept the pride out of his voice. "But I sure don't like the idea of him getting in bed with Pershing's daughter."

At Samuel's ribald comment about Daniel and Esther, Harriet turned suddenly furious. Arms akimbo, she glared at her husband. "If you're going to consent to this wedding, you need to act like you mean it."

"What do you mean?" He sounded aggrieved. "I said they could marry."

"Then treat the girl like she's your daughter. Not like a slattern." Harriet worried about how Esther would fit into their family. Samuel hadn't accepted Louisa until Annabelle was born.

"I never had no daughter. Don't know how to deal with a girl."

Harriet sighed in exasperation. "Then treat her like you do Annabelle and Rose." She turned to her frying pan. "You need to behave better toward her than you do me, or she'll go running back to Missouri."

"Harriet," he protested, "I treat you fine. Bought you a fox fur muff at Laramie."

"I'd rather have some courtesy and appreciation."

When the wagons set out again, Harriet walked with Cordelia Pershing. Esther started with them, but soon raced ahead to talk with Jenny McDougall.

"I ain't agreeing to nothing till we find a preacher," Cordelia said, breathing heavily though they were less than an hour out of camp.

"That would be best," Harriet agreed. Still, she feared for both families' sanity if the delay lasted long. "But when will that happen? We've only seen the Catholic priests, and I don't think Samuel would go so far as to let Daniel be married by a Papist."

"If only Franklin had seen fit to bring a minister along in our company." Cordelia sighed.

"That would have been a blessing," Harriet said. "We'll just have to keep our eye on our children till we find someone to conduct the service."

Cordelia walked with Harriet Abercrombie as long as she could. She liked the woman, and if Esther and Daniel were going to begin their married life happily, it would be up to their mothers to keep the families on amiable terms. Franklin and Samuel had an uneasy truce at best, and Cordelia didn't think it would last.

By midmorning she was wheezing and needed to rest. The baby didn't kick when she walked, but as soon as she sat on the wagon bench, he poked and rolled so she couldn't breathe any better than when she walked.

"Think I'll lay down in back," she called to Joel, who walked alongside the wagon she occupied.

He waved in acknowledgment.

She lay on her side on a pallet, supporting her belly with a pillow. The heat under the canvas cover wasn't yet stifling, though the sun shone brightly. She braced herself against the jolting motion of the wheels, but as time passed she relaxed.

Had she committed to this wedding? Only if they found a minister, she told herself. A part of her hoped a preacher would come along. She felt the need for someone to pray over her as well as to bless her daughter's wedding. She needed the Lord's hand on her to survive her coming labor. Ever since they left Missouri, this child had been different than her earlier pregnancies.

She feared for the babe, and she feared for herself.

She would survive because her children needed mothering, she told herself again. The Lord wouldn't take her from them. Even Zeke and Joel needed guidance. And Esther—Esther needed her mother with her as she married and established a household in Oregon . . . and likely the girl's own childbearing wouldn't be far off after the wedding.

"Please, God," Cordelia whispered. "Let me live. Let me see this babe soon, and then my grandchildren."

Thursday afternoon Daniel saw Zeke and Joel race back from scouting to talk to Captain Pershing. Daniel rode over to hear their report.

"Grass," Zeke said. "A large field near a creek just ahead. Looks like a good campsite."

Word spread quickly, and the mood of the company improved at the prospect of feeding their livestock. Even Pa seemed happy. "Animals can eat well tonight," he said. "They ain't had a good feed since we left Laramie five days ago."

But when they arrived at the creek, Captain Pershing cautioned the travelers. "It's all horsetails—see them reedy plants. Oxen can eat 'em but not the horses. Stuff poisons horses. Still, we'll lay by tomorrow and let the oxen feed."

"How'm I going to keep my horses away from it?" Pa bellowed. "All they's had is sage since Laramie."

The captain shrugged. "If you value your mounts, you'll make sure they stay out of the reeds. We'll set double guards tonight to watch 'em."

After supper Daniel was glad to see the fiddles come out. Singing and dancing followed. He found Esther and danced with her. He held her as close as was proper, but it wasn't close enough.

When the music stopped, he guided Esther away from the crowd. "Don't stay out long, Esther," Mrs. Pershing called after them. Esther waved at her mother.

Once he and Esther were hidden from the company behind a wagon, Daniel took her in his arms. She pressed herself against him and met his lips. When he stopped the kiss to take a breath, she whispered, "Daniel, how can we wait to find a minister?"

He muttered something in response then stooped for another kiss. He needed her. Soon. Now. One hand held her buttocks as he rubbed against her, the other hand fondled her nipple through her dress. He lowered his mouth to her breast and sucked her through the cloth.

"Daniel!" she gasped. "We can't!"

He unbuttoned her dress and bared the breast, tasting it for the first time. A moan was the only protest she made.

Voices approached, and he shielded Esther with his body while she righted her garment.

"Come on," she urged, and pulled him away from the wagons, deeper into the shadows.

Esther slept poorly that night and woke up still fatigued. All she'd been able to think about—dream about—was Daniel's hands on her body, roaming while her hands wandered over him. She hadn't let him pull up her skirts, though he'd tried. She'd wanted to let him do whatever he pleased as his lips worked magic on her breasts. But she couldn't. She couldn't get with child before she married. It would be sinful.

When Ma arose in the morning, Esther followed and silently helped her mother fix breakfast.

"Be nice to lay by today, won't it?" Ma asked.

Esther nodded, scheming about how she and Daniel could get away from the wagons by themselves.

Pa returned to the campsite from wherever he'd been, and said. "Hear tell there's a rock bridge nearby. Zeke ran across it scouting yesterday. A natural wonder, he says."

"Oh, Ma," Esther said, turning to her mother. "May Daniel and I ride to see it?"

Cordelia frowned. "Not without a chaperon. And what about a horse?"

"May I borrow your mount, Pa?"

Pa grinned. "I suppose it wouldn't hurt."

"You still need a chaperon, miss," Ma said. "Take Zeke or Joel."

"What if Mac and Jenny go?" Esther pleaded. "They're married. They can chaperon us."

Ma pursed her lips as if about to argue.

"The McDougalls are good folk," Pa said. "That would be fine."

Ma stayed silent, and Esther rushed off to find Daniel. He agreed to the excursion at once, so Esther went to find Jenny.

When she found her friend cooking breakfast, Esther said, "Pa says there's a rock bridge nearby. Daniel and I want to see it, but Ma says we need a chaperon. Would you and Mr. McDougall please come?"

Jenny and Mac were willing. As soon as the dishes were washed, Esther and Jenny packed food, then the two couples saddled their horses and rode up Horsetail Creek through a narrow gorge.

About a mile from camp, a bridge of red rock arched over the stream. "Let's climb down," Esther said, swinging off Pa's horse.

"It's too steep for me," Jenny said, staring at the rushing water. "I'll stay here." Mac said he'd stay with Jenny.

Esther clasped Daniel's hand, and they half-ran, half-fell down the slope to the water flowing beneath the natural span. It was a glorious day, bright and warm. "Let's wade," she urged Daniel. They took off their shoes and stockings, and splashed into the creek.

Esther slipped on the moss-covered rocks and shrieked. Daniel caught her against him, and they both laughed as they kissed. By the time they were chilled, her skirt was wet to her knees, and they climbed the hill back to the McDougalls.

"The water's cold," Esther said, giggling. "I don't know what Ma will say when she sees how wet I am."

"Then we'll wait till you're dry," Daniel said with a slow smile.

They ate their noon meal under the warm sun. Esther lay on the ground under the cloudless blue sky, her head pillowed in Daniel's lap.

"We'd best be going," Mac said, all too soon. "I need to check on my oxen."

Esther sighed. Would she and Daniel ever be as unromantic as Mac was? He and Jenny never flirted the way she and Daniel did. It was hard to imagine how her friend had ever gotten with child, as formal as the two of them were with each other.

Esther mounted Pa's horse, then followed Daniel back to camp, calling ahead to him whenever she saw something she wanted him to notice. And he grinned whenever he looked back at her.

Chapter 42: Family Discussions

Friday, 17 June 1847. Tomorrow we seek the North Platte branch crossing. FP

The travelers got underway again Saturday morning. Their route meandered along a plateau above the North Platte River beneath a hot, beating sun and mild breezes.

Cordelia spent most of the morning riding in the wagon. Esther joined her, wanting to describe the beauty of the rock bridge she'd seen the day before. "It was taller than any bridge back home, Ma," she said. "And the water was so cold. Must come straight from the snow fields."

Cordelia half-listened to her daughter. Her mind wandered to the thoughts she'd had of death, of leaving her family behind in this stark wilderness.

"Ma? Ma?" Esther grabbed her arm, pulling her into the present. "Did you hear me?"

Cordelia hadn't heard. "What is it, Esther?"

"When do you think we'll find a preacher?"

"I have no idea. Soon, maybe." Cordelia still wanted a blessing before her child came.

"Then you don't mind Daniel and me marrying now?"

Cordelia frowned. "I don't know, Esther. Let's wait to see if we find a minister."

"I want to be with Daniel so much." Esther sighed. "It's all I think about."

"Well, you'd better think about the work involved in setting up a house and farm." Cordelia spoke more sharply than she intended. Her daughter's prattle annoyed her—the girl only considered the romance of marriage, not the tedium of daily life. Not the drudgery and sickness and worry and grief.

As if Cordelia's thoughts had sprung into reality, the wagon passed by three graves with board crosses rising from the ground. She and her daughter stared at them in silence. When they had passed, Esther whispered, "I wonder who those people were."

"Could be anyone," Cordelia said. "No names on the crosses." Could be me, she reflected. And she shivered.

She vowed to see Esther settled before this baby came, whether the girl was ready or not. She would have to let the marriage take place. She must trust Daniel to care for her daughter, in case Cordelia was not there when they reached Oregon.

By Saturday evening, Franklin thought they were approaching Mormon Ferry, which the traders at Fort Laramie had told him about. The Mormons were hoping to establish a city in the desert, and their early settlers ran a ferry over the North Platte to accommodate later travelers. Though the crossing was intended for Mormons, they sold their services to any emigrants with coin to pay. Franklin decided to scout ahead for the ferry, then he would determine whether their company should use it or ford the river on their own.

He asked Mac McDougall whether he wanted to accompany him. Franklin had grown to trust the lawyer's sharp mind and level head. "Let me talk with Jenny," McDougall replied. "I'll need Zeke to help her with the wagon, if we're gone overnight."

Next Franklin asked Daniel Abercrombie. The young man was a good scout, and before the lad and Esther married, Franklin would like to see how Daniel acted away from his father for a day or two. "Let me check with Pa," Daniel said. At that, Franklin clenched his teeth—not a good sign for a man wanting to marry to ask his father about every action. But apparently, Samuel consented, because Daniel reported he would accompany Franklin the next day.

The scouts started out Sunday at dawn. The company would take a Sabbath rest, then bring the wagons to follow the scouts on Monday. By that time, Franklin hoped to have found the ferry, made a decision, and returned to intercept the wagons along the way.

As they rode, Franklin queried Daniel about the Abercrombie farm in Tennessee. He was impressed with Daniel's knowledge of crops and animals. The lad knew more about farming than Franklin did.

And it seemed Franklin's guess was correct—the Abercrombies had had a fine life in the States, they'd made a good living on fertile land raising tobacco and grains and horses. "Why'd your pa want to leave?" he asked Daniel.

Daniel shrugged. "He's always wanting more. And he worried about dividing what he had between Douglass and me. Weren't much land to buy for a reasonable price in the county."

"How'd you feel about leaving Tennessee?" The last thing Franklin wanted was for Daniel to decide to take Esther back East, away from her family.

Daniel looked up at the sky. "I didn't think much of it at first," he said. "Didn't want to leave home." He turned to Franklin. "But then I met Esther. And seeing all this"—his hand swept widely to encompass the hills and river and sky around them—"makes me realize how grand a nation we live in. I'm looking forward to taming a piece of it for myself in Oregon."

Satisfied, Franklin nodded. "It's hard to beat the wilderness for beauty. But settling it is a toilsome life."

Daniel smiled confidently. "Esther'n me can handle it."

McDougall had ridden ahead, apparently uninterested in the discussion of farming. Franklin squinted at the lawyer now, wondering why he'd made the journey. He didn't seem the pioneering type. More of an adventurer. Daniel would probably provide Esther with a more stable life than young Jenny McDougall would have.

They didn't reach the Mormon Ferry until almost sunset on Sunday. From a bluff above the river, Daniel watched the activity, flanked by the captain and Mac. The last rafts of the day were heading across the North Platte, while two empty rafts had been pulled out of the current on the near side.

"We'll camp here," Pershing announced. "Talk to the Mormons in the morning."

"I hear Mormons believe in angels and new Bibles," Daniel said.

Pershing nodded. "Mighty strange. But what matters to us is whether they got good boats and a fair price."

Daniel led the horses to the river to drink while the captain and Mac lit a fire and made supper. Then he took the animals back to their camp on the bluff and hobbled them to graze on the sparse grass—whatever vegetation had grown along the river had been beaten down by wagons and hooves, leaving the banks muddy and nearly bare.

After supper Captain Pershing pulled out a small flask of whiskey and passed it around. Daniel took a swig, wondering where the captain kept his bottles. So he asked.

The captain grinned. "Can't give away all my secrets. Need to retain my authority, now don't I?"

Mac chuckled. "You wouldn't have false bottoms in your wagons, would you?"

Captain Pershing's face fell. "How'd you know?"

"Maybe I got one of my own." Mac's teeth flashed in the darkness. "But I won't let on what I have in mine."

"Don't you worry about the extra weight?" Daniel asked. "And what if the wagons break?"

"That's a risk I'll take, son." The captain took a swallow from his flask and tucked it under the saddle he'd laid out for a pillow. "We'll be up at first light tomorrow. Good night."

Daniel lay down and thought of Captain Pershing's questions that day. He'd known the man was interrogating him, testing him as a son-in-law. He didn't mind. He wanted Esther, and he'd put up with a lot more to prove himself to her pa. He just hoped his answers had reassured the man.

He fell asleep dreaming of Esther in his arms.

After the Sabbath service concluded, Esther fretted as she neatened their campsite. If only she could ride through the hills with Daniel! But Pa had taken him to scout the trail. Why couldn't he have taken Zeke or Joel?

She must have asked that question aloud, because Ma said, "Your brothers are tired. They deserve a day of rest once in a while. Go get your embroidery. You want your trousseau ready when we find a preacher, don't you?"

Her trousseau—it was only two pillowcases and a set of sheets. The sheets were hemmed, and the embroidery on one case was finished—a pair of birds holding ribbons wrapped around the letter "E". Now that she knew her groom's name, she could embroider the "D" on the other case. She hated needlework, but she might as well get it done.

"May I join you?" Jenny asked, once Esther had settled herself on a crate in the shade.

Esther smiled. "What are you working on?"

"Baby shirts." Jenny held one up. "Your mama and Mrs. Tuller tell me to make them big, but it looks so tiny to me. I tried it on Mrs. Dempsey's baby girl, and it swims on her. I suppose it'll be all right." She frowned at the little shirt in her hands.

"Well, babies grow awful fast," Esther said. She'd watched her younger siblings long enough to know that. "Are you missing Mr. McDougall today?"

Jenny shrugged. "I suppose. But he'll be back." She smiled at Esther. "You're asking because you miss Daniel, don't you?"

Esther sighed. "I can't stand to be away from him. I want to be married so bad. I want it to be just Daniel and me." She sighed again, thinking how wonderful it would be when Ma and Pa and Zeke wouldn't interrupt, when she and Daniel could go into their own home and shut the door on the world.

"You'll have your family close by, at least," Jenny said. "First on the trail, and then wherever you settle in Oregon. I miss my mama. She should have had her baby by now."

"She was expecting? Just like my ma?"

Jenny nodded. "After my papa died, she remarried." Jenny bit her lip. "It was different at home then. I didn't seem to belong. But I still miss her."

Other women joined the girls—Ma, Mrs. Tuller, Harriet Abercrombie, and Hatty Tanner. Esther enjoyed the conversation but longed to be with Daniel. Sooner than she expected, her pillowcase was done. She blushed when the other women exclaimed over it.

Monday morning Cordelia ordered her younger children to pack up the wagons. Zeke and Joel worked with the other men to get the company moving. Once they were on the trail again, Cordelia went to find Harriet Abercrombie.

"We should talk about Esther and Daniel," Cordelia said. "Franklin and I are willing to give our blessing for a quick wedding. If you and Mr. Abercrombie agree."

Harriet sighed. "Yes. We've talked. He's come around."

"Then he didn't approve at first?"

"Well, neither of us did. You and the captain were reluctant also."

"But now . . ." Cordelia's voice trailed off. She didn't want to confess she didn't think her daughter could control Daniel's ardor—or the girl's own desires either. Nor did she want to speak of her fears for her own health.

Harriet smiled. "They're young and in love. They should marry. Samuel and I think Esther is a fine girl."

Cordelia heaved a deep breath. She was glad the Abercrombies would support a quick marriage, should they find a minister. "Maybe there'll be a Mormon preacher at the ferry."

"A Mormon!" Harriet gasped. "We'll agree to a wedding, but not one conducted by a heathen. Nor a Papist priest. We want a good Christian minister to bless their vows. So we know they're married before God and man."

"Well, then," Cordelia said. "Let's hope we find a good Protestant soon." When he returned, she'd have to ask Franklin when he thought they might find someone.

There was another delicate subject she wanted to raise with Harriet. "When we reach Oregon, what do you and Mr. Abercrombie expect from Daniel?"

"What do you mean?" Harriet looked puzzled.

"Will he be able to build on his own claim right away, or do you expect him to help with your house first?"

"Oh." Harriet bit her lip. "Samuel and I haven't talked about that. I mean, we assumed . . . . But now Daniel's marrying, . . ." She shrugged.

"Well, won't we all be helping each other? You have two strong sons to help with your house, and surely they'll be able to help other families as well."

"Zeke will have his own land also. And Joel can file a claim next year."

"I'm certain we'll all sort it out." Harriet stared straight ahead, her lips a thin line.

Cordelia persisted. "I just want Esther settled soon. In her own home. Particularly once she's with child. Women in my family carry easily."

"Yes, I suppose they do." Harriet's face saddened.

"I'm sorry," Cordelia said, realizing Harriet must be thinking of her own barrenness. "I seem to be putting my foot in it with everything I say. It must be because it's so close to my time. I worry. I want everything put in its place. Happens near the birth every time. I want to know Esther's cared for."

Chapter 43:   Crossing at Red Buttes

Monday, 21 June 1847. Waiting at Mormon Ferry for the wagons. FP

Samuel talked with Mac McDougall when the lawyer returned to the wagons Monday afternoon. McDougall didn't say much, only that Pershing would talk with the men when they joined him on Tuesday about whether to use the ferry.

Samuel questioned McDougall about the Mormon's rafts and the cost.

The lawyer shrugged. "They seem to know what they're doing, but you can judge for yourself when you get there. It's five dollars a wagon."

"Five dollars!" Samuel shouted. "Highway robbery."

"They're men trying to make a living," McDougall said. "Just like you."

Samuel spat a long stream of tobacco. "We'll see whether I let them earn their living off me and my kin."

The emigrant company reached the ferry Tuesday evening and made camp in an area Pershing and Daniel had held for them. Pershing convened a meeting of the men while the women cooked supper. "We can pay five dollars a wagon for the ferry," Pershing said, "or it's another day's travel to Red Buttes. Ford there is deep. Won't be easy. We may have to build rafts ourselves. But we won't have to pay the Mormons."

The men argued about their options, though Samuel agreed with Pershing this time—no need to enrich the pagan Mormons.

After the men voted to take the ford, Pershing told them, "Met some

Oregonians this afternoon. They're going east to bring their families west. Oregon City'll be a boom town soon."

"Good thing we're ahead of the crowd," Samuel said. "Claim our land this fall. Have our first crop harvested afore next year's wagons git there."

When they returned to their campfire, Samuel asked Daniel, "How'd Pershing treat you whilst you were scouting?"

Daniel pushed his hat back on his forehead. "He's a good man, Pa."

"Then you're still set on saddling yourself with his daughter?"

Daniel frowned at him. "Of course. I'm committed to marrying Esther. No use trying to talk me out of it."

"Hold on, son," Samuel said. "I ain't trying to talk you out of anything. Just testing your resolve."

"I'm resolved, Pa."

During supper Tuesday, Harriet decided it was time to talk with Samuel and Daniel about their homesteading plans in Oregon.

As they'd walked that day, Cordelia asked, "Will you talk to Mr. Abercrombie? I want to know Daniel will work on a house straightaway. Otherwise, I'll worry about Esther."

"There's plenty of time for that," Harriet said. "They aren't even married. And we're months from Oregon."

Cordelia sighed. "Then I'll talk to your husband."

"I'll do it," Harriet said. The last thing she wanted was for Cordelia to rile Samuel. For the moment he seemed reconciled to the marriage. Harriet didn't want that to change.

Harriet asked Daniel now, "Have you thought about the house you'll build on your claim?"

Daniel looked up from his plate of stew, eyes wide. "A little bit, Ma. Esther and I have talked."

She turned to her husband. "What are you thinking for us, Samuel? We won't need anything big, with just the two of us living there."

Samuel frowned. "I ain't rightly considered it. First step is to get the horses into a barn and the fields cleared and fenced from the deer. Might have to live in tents for a while. That's one reason to get there quick as we can—more time afore the ground freezes."

"When does it freeze in Oregon?" Douglass asked. "Likely earlier than in Tennessee."

"I want a home for our girls," Louisa said. "Father Abercrombie, they can't winter outside."

"How fast can we build the barns and three houses?" Harriet asked. "Maybe the barns can wait. I don't want my granddaughters—nor a young bride—to be in tents through the winter."

"None of my kin'll winter outdoors," Samuel said. "We'll hole up in one house together, if need be."

Harriet swallowed hard at that statement—Cordelia would never accept her daughter and Daniel living in the same house as Harriet and Samuel. "Our sons and their families need their privacy. Surely we can build three houses quickly. At least rough them in."

"Not at the expense of the crops. Nor the horses." Samuel was adamant.

Finally, Daniel spoke up. "I'll work on my own house, Pa. As a husband, I'll need to provide for Esther. Just as you do for Ma."

Well, Harriet thought in satisfaction, Daniel was ready to marry.

The wagons reached Red Buttes midafternoon on Wednesday. The emigrant company set up camp beneath the high brick-colored cliffs. It was a pretty spot, Esther thought, the ground shaded by trees and tall green grass. "We'll cross tomorrow," her pa told the company. "Let the teams feed today. Not much grass north of the Platte."

Esther went to find Jenny. Her friend wandered the ground right near the cliffs. "Look," Jenny said to Esther. "See what others have left behind."

Esther joined Jenny in poking through furniture and trunks abandoned by earlier emigrants. There was even a small armoire that Esther imagined standing in a fine parlor back in St. Charles. It looked sad as it lay on its back in the dirt, doors opened to reveal its emptiness. She sat in a chair with a broken back while Jenny and other women pawed through strangers' belongings.

"A quilt," Jenny said, holding up a bed-sized rag of faded blues and browns. "It's ripped, but I can mend it."

"Nothing here I want," Esther said. "Unless you find something new."

But there was nothing new in the cast-offs, nothing Esther thought worth dragging back to the wagons to persuade Pa to add to their load.

Later Esther walked with Daniel to the shore of the Platte. They found Pa pacing the bank with some other men. He frowned and gestured as he talked with them.

"What is it, Captain?" Daniel asked.

"Won't be an easy crossing," Pa said, then he glanced at Esther and seemed to stop whatever he'd planned to say next.

"You can speak in front of me, Pa," Esther said. "I ain't scared."

"Maybe you should be, daughter. River's mighty deep. Current's fast, too, even though we ain't had rain in ages."

"What's that mean?" she asked.

"Let us men decide." Pa didn't quite pat her on the head, but he might as well have. "We'll walk it in the morning. Hope it's come down. Don't you worry till then."

"I ain't worried," Esther insisted. She wished Pa would treat her as he did Daniel. "I been through enough rivers now. What'll we do?"

Samuel Abercrombie spoke up. "We'll either drive across or unload and build rafts."

Pa nodded. "That's about the right of it. Won't know till morning."

After supper Cordelia heard fiddles tuning, then a simple melody from one of them. The lowering sun behind the bluff sent sharp shadows across the glade where the wagons circled. She walked to a large fire built in the middle of the encampment. It was a pleasant evening, the warm air softened by the burbling river. Hard to think the current could be dangerous when they crossed it tomorrow.

"High water," Franklin had told her. "River's still full of snowmelt. We crossed with Frémont in July. Platte was a lot lower then."

"Is it safe?" Cordelia shivered and hugged her belly as she asked the question. She hadn't feared most of the crossings, but everything seemed harder as the birthing approached—no more than a month now until the baby came.

As she joined the music and dancers near the fire, Cordelia shivered again. The gentle breeze felt like a ghost's breath across her cheek. Esther and Daniel danced with other revelers, laughing as if they hadn't a care in the world. Cordelia sighed—the young lovers would face their own hardships soon enough. She'd let them enjoy themselves this evening, even if Daniel was holding her daughter a mite too close.

Cordelia found a place on a log to sit then hummed along with the fiddles. Rachel sat beside her clapping to the music. The younger children frolicked in the grass, and Zeke and Joel stood across the fire talking with Franklin and other men. What a lovely evening—she would remember this as one of the good days along the trail, ghost or no ghost.

When the young'uns started yawning, Rachel took Ruth and Noah to the tent for bed. Franklin took Rachel's place on the log. "Care to dance?" he asked Cordelia.

She shook her head. "I don't think you could swing me far these days."

Franklin put his arm around her in the dark. "I could try."

"I'm happy just sitting here," she said, leaning into his shoulder.

Thursday morning after the wagons were loaded and the teams hitched, Samuel sat astride his gelding near the riverbank, watching McDougall and Zeke Pershing ride across the Platte.

"Teams'll need to swim," McDougall said to Pershing when the young men returned. "Too deep to walk."

"Let's try pulling a wagon. Lot of work to unload 'em if we don't have to." Pershing pointed to one of Samuel's wagons. "Take that one."

"I'll drive it," Samuel said. "Won't let no one else near it."

He handed his reins to Douglass, dismounted, and climbed on the wagon bench. Daniel rode up to the lead pair and turned the oxen into the current. Pershing and others watched as the wagon sank into the swirling current. The wagon swayed as its wheels pitched over large rocks on the river bottom.

"Stop!" Pershing shouted. "Wagon box is flooding."

"Well, I sure as hell can't back up," Samuel yelled. "Confound it, what now, Pershing?"

"Take anything perishable out of the wagon," Pershing ordered. Men carried crates and sacks of flour to shore, while Samuel sat bellowing at them from the bench.

When Pershing gave the word, Samuel cracked his whip and Daniel pulled on the near ox's yoke. The wagon surged forward. Now lighter, it lifted off the river bottom, and they reached the far shore without any more trouble.

"Goddamn it, Pershing," Samuel said. "Why'd you make me go first?"

"You was closest to shore. Don't bellyache now, Abercrombie. We got more wagons to get across."

"I lost a barrel of flour, I reckon," Samuel seethed. "Ain't no reason for it, if'n you'd done your job."

"River's deeper'n I thought. But now we know." Pershing turned away and rode back across the river, leaving Samuel cursing.

Wasn't anything Samuel could do now but clean up the mess Pershing had caused. He checked his belongings in the wagon and moved some wet blankets. When his other wagon ferried the rest of their possessions across, Harriet spread the sodden things out to dry while the rest of the company crossed.

The crossing took all morning. Most wagons had to make two trips across the Platte to transport everything, because of the need to lighten the loads. The Abercrombies weren't the only emigrants to lose some food, Samuel noticed smugly, but soaked provisions were the only damage.

They ate their noon meal on the north bank of the river. Harriet made biscuits to salvage as much damp flour as possible. Before they left again, Pershing told them all, "Fill up your barrels. Not much water this side of the Platte. And keep your animals out of the alkali water. We got three hard days to the Sweetwater."

Franklin hadn't wanted to send Abercrombie's wagon across the Platte first, but it had sat closest to the bank. To ignore him and ask someone else to try the ford would have seemed odd. With a sinking heart, he'd ordered Abercrombie into the river.

Then the wagon had flooded, enraging Abercrombie. But the damage would have happened to whichever wagon went first. Until they'd tested the depth of the water, there'd been no way to tell if they needed to lighten the load, nor how much they needed to take out of the wagons.

Now they had three days of desert land to cross to reach the Sweetwater, assuming Frémont's map had marked the route correctly. The map had been accurate thus far, and Franklin had no cause to doubt the next stage of the journey. Not to the Sweetwater. Farther on there was a stretch that wasn't easy. But ultimately they would reach South Pass, then continue to the Snake River—another waterway to follow, though much rougher than the Platte.

Just after they found the Sweetwater, they'd be at Independence Rock. Mountain lore said if a man reached Independence Rock by Independence Day, he'd make Oregon before the snows. Franklin reckoned their company would reach Independence Rock about the first of July. That ought to make Abercrombie happy.

The man was right to worry about their pace. But he didn't have to be so unpleasant in voicing his demands.

Franklin rode at the front of the wagons, Zeke and Joel with him. They climbed away from the Platte until the ribbon of water they'd had followed for weeks was no longer visible. Ahead was an expanse of sagebrush and sparse grass, and in the distance the jagged peaks of the Rocky Mountains.

Franklin and his sons spoke little. They'd reached the stage of the journey where they were comfortable communicating with a pointing finger or a grunt. He hoped he'd reach that level of ease with Daniel Abercrombie. Assuming Esther married the young man, Franklin planned to treat the lad like another son. If Samuel would let him usurp any of a father's privilege.

"You all right with Daniel as a brother-in-law?" he asked Zeke. Joel had ridden on ahead, looking for Devil's Backbone, a ridge of stone that would be their next landmark.

Zeke shrugged. "Don't matter. It's what Esther thinks that counts."

"But do you?"

Zeke nodded once slowly. "I do, Pa. I'd ride with him anywhere. Let him tend my horse or plant my fields." From Zeke, that was praise indeed.

"Me, too," Franklin said. "Just wish I liked his father more."

Chapter 44:   Across the Desert

Thursday, 24 June 1847. Crossed the North Platte today. FP

Leaving Red Buttes behind, the company traveled into the high desert. Cordelia trudged ahead of the wagons with Esther. The girl still pestered her about approving a quick wedding.

"We've seen the priests as we've traveled, Ma. We're sure to find another man of God."

"Let's wait till it happens." Cordelia didn't want an argument. They'd only been walking an hour, and she was already fatigued. She needed to save her breath, not waste it in chatter. Every step was a chore. She'd have to sit in the wagon before long, though she worried the jostling would bring on early labor.

"Don't you want me and Daniel to marry?" Esther asked.

"I've said you can wed. But there's no need to hurry it."

"But, Ma—"

"I don't want you to end up like me," Cordelia said without thinking, then pursed her lips shut. She hadn't intended to share her fears with Esther.

"Not like you? What do you mean?"

"I don't mean nothing, child. Just trying to get a bit of quiet." Cordelia halted at the bottom of a hill and stared toward the top. Another climb. She had to catch her breath first.

"You tired, Ma?" Esther sounded concerned.

Cordelia sniffed. "I been tired ever since we left Independence. It ain't

305

easy making this journey carrying a child."

Esther took her arm, and they started up the hill. Cordelia leaned on her daughter more heavily than she liked.

"That's why I don't want you rushing into marriage," she said. "Be best if you don't start breeding till we're settled."

"You always made having babies seem easy," Esther said, hugging Cordelia's arm close to her body. "I watched you ever since I was little. I don't remember Rachel's birth, but I remember when the twins came. Then Ruthie, then Noah. Even the twins, you had no trouble. You never yelled. Not like Mrs. Dempsey did a month ago."

Cordelia chuckled. "Oh, I yelled. I told the midwife to keep you away."

"But I sneaked back." Esther grinned. "I wanted to be close to you. After all, I'm your oldest girl."

"And the first of my children ready to marry." Cordelia swallowed the sudden lump in her throat—she wouldn't cry. "Oh, Esther, I want everything good for you. I want to see you and your husband—Daniel, if that's who you marry—"

"I *am* going to marry him, Ma—"

"You and Daniel and your children. I want to see all my children grown and happy. But you're the first to leave the nest."

"You will, Ma—" Esther stopped suddenly. "Don't you think you will?"

Cordelia sighed and shrugged, feeling Esther's slight recoil from the shrug.

"You're afraid this time, ain't you, Ma?" Cordelia heard her fear echoed in Esther's voice.

"I'm afraid with every birth, girl. But yes, this time . . . given the wilderness we face . . . this time I'm more fearful."

"Oh, Ma! Pa won't let anything happen to you."

"It ain't your pa's to control. It ain't mine, and it ain't yours. It's up to the Lord."

"But the Lord knows I need you. We *all* need you." Without knowing it, Esther echoed Cordelia's prayer. Then Esther squeezed her mother's arm in emphasis. "You won't die, Ma. Nothing bad'll happen."

"I pray it won't, child. I pray every night it won't."

Esther stayed with her mother until Ma was ready to rest in the wagon. Then she ran ahead, trying to find someone to talk to—Rachel or Jenny or Daniel—anyone she could cry with after what Ma had said. Ma couldn't die, not when Esther needed her so badly.

But Rachel walked with Ruth, helping their younger sister recite times tables. Noah wandered near the girls, hunting for ant hills. It wouldn't do to interrupt the young'uns, Esther decided. And by the time she found Jenny, Esther realized she couldn't talk to her friend about childbirth, not when Jenny was already worried about her own confinement.

Daniel was nowhere to be seen, so Esther sought Mrs. Abercrombie to ask where Daniel was.

"Scouting, I expect," his mother said. "I don't think he's with the wagons." Mrs. Abercrombie frowned. "Is something wrong? You look distressed."

Esther shook her head, but when she tried to say something, a sob escaped.

Mrs. Abercrombie put an arm around her shoulders. "What is it, Esther?"

"Ma—"

"Is she in labor?" Mrs. Abercrombie looked worried. "Ain't it too soon?"

"No, ma'am, that ain't it." Esther swallowed, then said in a rush, "But she thinks she's going to die when her time comes." The wind whipped Esther's hair around her head, and she pulled the strands out of her face. She'd forgotten her sunbonnet again today.

"Oh, Esther." Mrs. Abercrombie sighed and patted Esther's arm. "We both know childbearing ain't easy. My own sister died at Daniel's birth. But your mother is strong. She's borne many children. If anyone will survive, she will."

"That's what I tell myself. But I can't live without her, Mrs. Abercrombie, I just can't!"

"You have your father. And Daniel. We'd all help you, girl."

"But I need my mother!" Esther felt her hysteria rise. She didn't want to break down in front of Daniel's mother. She wanted to seem capable and grown, ready to be his wife. But without Ma, how could she be happy? How could she marry Daniel? A horrible notion struck her—was this her punishment for letting Daniel take liberties?

307

"Calm down, Esther. You're full grown now, wanting to wed. You'll get through whatever sorrows God sends your way. You're as strong as your mother."

Esther nodded and said no more.

Daniel scouted with Joel Pershing through the day Friday. Wind scoured his face, and blowing tumbleweeds caused his mare to dance instead of holding to a steady pace. They searched for water but found only a few drying puddles.

In midafternoon they spotted a stagnant, swampy pool in a low spot in the hills. They rode back to tell Captain Pershing, who came to inspect the site. The captain tasted the water, then spat it out. "Alkaline. Poisonous spring, most likely. Can't let the horses at it. Did yours drink?" He squinted at Joel and Daniel.

"No, sir," Daniel said. "We came to get you."

"We need to warn the company not to stop here. I'll go back. You two find another campsite. Map says there's a stream maybe five miles farther."

Captain Pershing was right—they found a sluggish creek around dusk. When the company caught up, Daniel learned one man's horse had drunk from the alkaline pool as the wagons passed and now suffered from colic.

After supper Daniel went to find Esther. She was washing dishes while Rachel dried. "Want to take a walk?" he asked. "Though there ain't much to see."

She shook her head. "When I'm done here, I need to get Noah to bed."

"Ma and I can handle him," Rachel said with a grin. "You go spooning."

"Ma shouldn't be working," Esther said. "I'll—"

"It's all right, Esther," Mrs. Pershing said. "I'll finish with Rachel. You walk with Daniel. Just stay within sight of the wagons."

Esther frowned at her mother, but dried her hands and turned to Daniel.

When they'd moved out of earshot from the Pershing wagons, Daniel asked, "Is something wrong with your mother?"

Esther shrugged. "Maybe we shouldn't get married till we get to Oregon after all. She might need me."

Daniel turned her to face him. "What is it? Is she ill?"

"I don't know." Her voice trembled.

"Esther, what aren't you telling me?" He tried to pull her closer, but she resisted.

"I'm scared for her."

"That's why you want to wait on getting married?" It didn't seem like much of a reason to Daniel.

"I don't want to leave her. Not before the baby comes."

Daniel snorted. "That don't make no sense. You'll be near your folks all the way to Oregon."

"It makes sense to me, Daniel." She poked his chest as she said his name, as if annoyed.

"But we should have plans. Be ready, in case we find a preacher." He wanted to spend the evening dreaming with her, as they had on prior evenings. Dreaming and kissing. He bent toward her face.

"We don't even know if we'll find a preacher." She pulled away. "There's no reason to plan. No reason not to wait awhile."

"But—"

"Don't push me, Daniel. Not tonight." She turned and rushed back toward her family's wagons.

Daniel threw his hat on the ground with a curse. No dreams or kisses tonight.

Harriet watched Daniel trudge toward their campfire in the shadowy dusk. When he and Esther walked after supper, they rarely came back until full dark. This evening he was early and alone, and as he approached, his face looked grim.

"Something wrong?" she asked.

"Esther says she wants to wait on getting married." Daniel sat on an overturned bucket putting his head in his hands, elbows propped on his knees. He looked about ten years old. Harriet stifled her smile.

"Why?" she asked, forcing herself to look at him solemnly.

He shook his head. "All she says is she's worried about her mother."

Harriet sighed. "I talked to her earlier. She has this notion her mother's going to die. Seems Cordelia's afraid and let Esther know it."

Daniel looked up, his face brighter. "Is that all?"

"Son, it's no small matter. Women sometimes do die in childbirth, as you well know."

"But Miz Pershing has had lots of children. I mean—" He seemed uncomfortable talking about his future mother-in-law's confinements. "Why won't Esther even talk to me about getting married?"

Harriet decided to move to the heart of the issue. "Daniel, whether and when you wed is mostly between you and Esther. But you both have families that'll be a part of your life for many years to come, God willing. Your pa and I have given our blessing. You should be sure Captain and Mrs. Pershing approve as well."

Daniel nodded. "I'll talk to Captain Pershing."

Chapter 45: Cordelia's Blessing

Friday, 25 June 1847. Camped tonight on a brackish creek. Need more water and grass soon. FP

After a rough camp Friday night by the small stream, Franklin got the company underway early Saturday morning. He hoped to reach better water at Willow Springs by nightfall. The horses and mules were nervous from needing more to drink. The stolid oxen seemed fine, but even they would benefit from improved food and water.

Something wasn't right between Cordelia and Esther, but he didn't know what. His wife and daughter weren't angry with each other—he could tell that much, but something bothered them. He sent Zeke and Joel to scout, deciding he'd best stay near his family.

As he rode alongside his wagons, Daniel rode over. "Captain, might I have a word?" The young man seemed nervous. "In private." Daniel gestured at the wagons.

Franklin nodded and urged his gelding several yards away. Daniel followed.

"What is it, son?"

Daniel hesitated, then said in a rush, "It's Esther, sir. You know I want to marry her as soon as we can. Do we have your blessing on that? And Miz Pershing's? Because Esther seems uncertain."

Franklin pulled his horse to a stop. "Did Esther say she didn't want to marry you?"

Daniel halted beside him. "She says her mother might need her."

Franklin exhaled deeply. As he'd suspected, there *was* something going on with Cordelia. He needed to find out what. "Let me talk with Mrs. Pershing," he told Daniel. "But see here—I won't let you wed Esther if you and she ain't both ready and willing. You're a good lad, and you'll make a good son-in-law. If'—he stressed the word—"you and Esther are both of a mind to marry. Marriage is hard work. I won't have my daughter going into it if she don't want to."

"Yes, sir." Daniel looked troubled as he rode off.

Franklin returned to his family's wagons. Cordelia sat on one of the seats with Noah beside her. Esther walked alongside that wagon, while the twins minded the other. He didn't see Rachel and Ruth. "Noah, you go walk with Jonathan and David awhile. Esther, stop the oxen."

His daughter obeyed. After Noah scampered off, Franklin tied his gelding to the wagon and hoisted himself to sit by Cordelia. "Let's go," he ordered Esther, and she started the team again. "You stay where you can hear, Esther."

Both Cordelia and Esther stared at him.

"Daniel told me Esther ain't sure she wants to marry—" he began.

"Pa—"

"—Because her mother might need her," he continued, taking Cordelia's hand. "What's wrong?"

Cordelia shook her head. "Just fretting, that's all. Happens with every baby."

"I don't remember it happening before," Franklin said with a frown.

She snorted, her back rigid beside him. "You only been with me when Rachel was born. Missed all the other times."

"That one went smooth enough."

"I was twenty-six. A lot younger."

"Pa, Daniel and I can wait." Esther looked up at him with a wide-eyed stare.

"Hush," Franklin said. "Let your mother and me talk." He kept his eyes on Cordelia. "Did you tell Esther she shouldn't marry till we reached Oregon?"

"I only said she shouldn't rush into marriage. Do you want her to begin her new life weighed down like I am?"

"Cordelia—"

312

"I'm afraid for her." Cordelia started to cry. Franklin put his arm around her.

"Ma—" Esther looked ready to vault onto the bench with them.

"Let me get this straight," Franklin said. "Cordelia, you're afraid for Esther?"

His wife nodded.

"And Esther, you're afraid for your mother?"

Esther nodded.

"And neither of you is talking to me about it." He took off his hat and ran his hand through his hair, taking a moment to think on what to say to these women he loved but often didn't understand.

"Do you like Daniel?" he asked Cordelia gently, putting his arm back around her shoulders.

"It ain't Daniel I'm worried about. It's this country, this"—she waved a hand, seeming to struggle for the right word—"this wilderness, this beastly wilderness."

Franklin turned to Esther. "Do you love Daniel?"

"Oh, yes, Pa!" He could see she spoke the truth because her smile glowed.

"And do you want to marry him?"

"Yes."

"Do you want to wait?"

His daughter's smile turned to a grimace. "I don't know. We can wait, if Ma needs me."

He looked at his wife. "Cordelia?"

"I can't stop her, can I?"

Franklin sighed. "Yes, you can, Cordelia. She just said so. But do you want to? Look at her—she's in love, and she wants her young man. Seems to me I remember another girl, looked a lot like Esther, who also wanted a quick wedding."

Cordelia smiled and looked him in the eye for the first time since he'd joined her on the wagon. "Yes."

"Can she tell Daniel they'll marry if they find a preacher?" He squeezed her shoulders a little tighter and gave a shake, trying to get her to buck up, to show the backbone he knew she had.

But Cordelia didn't give him that satisfaction. She stared into the distance. "Let me think on it."

After the conversation with her parents, Esther returned to tending the oxen. She glanced back at Ma and Pa, who still sat on the wagon bench talking seriously.

Ma hadn't given her blessing for a quick wedding yet. Esther wanted to obey her parents, but Daniel was more and more important to her every day. She loved him. She yearned to build a life and a family with him. Yet she feared losing him. Why couldn't she have everything she wanted—her parents' approval and Daniel both? She could still care for her mother. The emigrants would all be on the trail together for months yet.

At the noon halt Daniel pulled her away from where she sat with her younger siblings. "I spoke to your pa. Then I seen your folks talking," he said. "What'd they say?"

"Ma ain't said yes yet." She gulped. "And I won't marry without her blessing." She knew that was the right thing to do, no matter how it hurt.

"Esther—"

"I can't, Daniel. I just can't." She had to remain loyal to her parents.

He took her hand and pressed her fingers as he talked, as if to emphasize the importance of what he said. "You told me I need to stand up to Pa. Well, you got to stand up for what you want, too."

"It ain't the same," she said, barely able to talk around the lump in her throat. "Your pa's a bully. I need to help my ma."

"This is about us, Esther." He continued to press her fingers. "Not our parents. It's time for us to make our own path."

She tried to pull away. "I have to go help with the noon meal."

Daniel kept hold of one of her hands and cupped her face with his other hand. She leaned her cheek into his callused palm and felt his touch deep in her core. "I want us to wed," he said. "Soon. I'll wait." He sighed. "But I hope I don't have to wait too long."

"If it weren't broad daylight and my little brothers watching," she said, "I'd kiss you. To show you I love you."

"And I love you," he said roughly. He leaned over to give her a quick peck on the lips. "I hope we find a preacher fast. And your mother agrees."

"I just want Ma to be safe," she whispered.

314

Daniel strode away from Esther. She said she loved him, but she wouldn't marry him until her mother agreed. She was still tied to her mother's apron strings. He didn't know whether to be mad at her or at her mother—or maybe he shouldn't be mad at anyone and simply accept the situation.

During the noon meal, he picked at his food in silence. Ma tried to get him to eat, offering honey for his johnny cakes. He shook his head.

"Don't mollycoddle him, Harriet. He's just love-struck," Pa said. "Better grow up, son—no woman's worth losing food nor sleep over."

Still lost in his thoughts after the meal, Daniel wanted to distance himself from the company. But Esther showed up as he mounted his mare when the wagons began to roll. "May I ride with you?" she asked.

What could he do but offer his hand to help her up?

She clasped his waist and pressed against him. Her breasts shifted against his back as she found her balance on the mare's rump.

"What color curtains should our cabin have?" she asked, as he kneed his horse to a walk.

"Curtains?" He hadn't imagined curtains, though he had considered putting in a window or two. "We'll have to be sure we can afford the glass afore we worry about curtains."

"Oh, we have to have windows," she said. "I'm thinking red curtains, to make our home cheery."

"It'll be a small place at first," Daniel said. "Maybe only one room."

She shrugged against him. "That's all right till we have a baby. Then we'll need more space." She nattered on about the cabin, while his mind stayed on the child she mentioned. He could be a father within a year, if they married along the trail.

He thought about making love to her, about filling her belly with his child. He wanted the pleasure of bedding her, but it began to dawn on him why Mrs. Pershing feared childbirth. The idea of Esther in pain from their loving terrified him. How would she bear it? How would he? And people had been doing this since Adam and Eve. He shook his head.

"Daniel?" Her voice broke through his reverie. "I asked you about making a rocking chair. One like Mrs. Tuller has in their wagon. Can

315

you?"

A rocking chair? The image of her rocking as she nursed their babe came to mind.

"Daniel?" she said again. "Aren't you listening?"

"I'm thinking of you rocking our child," he said, his voice husky. "You're both so beautiful."

She pressed a kiss against the back of his neck. "I want that," she whispered. "More than anything."

He shifted in the saddle. "But I worry about you. Like you worry about your ma."

"I'll be fine. And so will Ma." She leaned her cheek against his back and tightened her grip on his waist. "I hope."

"I want to hold you in my arms each night," he said. He held her hand and told her what he'd do to her in their cabin at night. He wanted far more touching than he could manage on horseback.

Chapter 46: Willow Springs

Saturday, 26 June 1847. Reached Willow Springs. Good campsite. Will lay by tomorrow. FP

Samuel rose early Sunday morning, ready to hunt. They'd reached Willow Springs midafternoon on Saturday, and Pershing had organized a group of men to leave at daybreak. Douglass went with Samuel, but Daniel refused. Samuel set out with Pershing, Douglass, McDougall, and a few others as soon as light appeared in the east.

Pershing led the hunters west into the dry hills beyond the springs. "Might as well scout whilst we look for game," he announced. When they reached the crest of one hill, he pointed out a valley in the distance. "Sweetwater's over there. We'll follow it to South Pass."

The land was treeless and rocky, sandstone cliffs climbing above deep ravines. After they traveled an hour or so, a deer bounded cross their path, followed by several more.

Samuel shouted, and the men split up to drive the deer into a narrow gully with no cover where the animals could hide. They shot five, then dismounted to dress the carcasses. When the meat was strapped on their mounts, they ranged farther, but found only a few birds to kill.

"Enough," Pershing said around noon. "This'll feed us for a few days. We best get back to camp."

Samuel wanted to argue, but decided against it. There'd be better hunting when they reached the Sweetwater, which was only a couple days

317

travel at most.

"Next stop is Independence Rock," Pershing said when they were almost back to the wagons. "I aim to rest there a day or two."

"Rest again?" Samuel said. Pershing would never change—slow and deliberate, no matter the situation.

"Saying is, if we reach Independence Rock by Independence Day, we'll make it to Oregon afore the snows." Pershing sounded confident. "We'll be at Independence Rock tomorrow or the next day—not even July."

"Can't hurt to get there ahead of the crowd, though, can it?" Samuel muttered.

Pershing either didn't hear or ignored him.

Cordelia was glad of a day in camp at Willow Springs. It was a pretty site, nestled in a green valley between rugged hills. After a Sabbath prayer, she and her daughters spent the morning baking with a white powder Doc Tuller had found around the spring—he said it was saleratus. Esther had gathered the soda, and now they had an ample supply for baking. It gave the dough a greenish tinge, but it rose fine. Cordelia hoped the loaves would taste all right.

She felt the tension in Esther as she watched her daughter stir the mixture in subdued silence. The girl spoke only when spoken to. But she hadn't asked again for her mother's approval of her marriage.

When they had the loaves baking near the fire, Cordelia said, "You know, there might not be a preacher for weeks yet. Maybe not till Oregon. Probably won't matter what I agree to."

"I know."

"You and young Abercrombie had better not behave like you're already married."

Esther glanced at Cordelia. Was it guilt or irritation flashing across her daughter's face?

"I seen you two riding yesterday. The trail was smooth. No need for you to hold on to him so tight."

"Yes, Ma." Her daughter paused. "You feeling all right today?"

Cordelia nodded. "Don't you worry about me." She turned toward the wagons to gather up the laundry. "I might as well get some washing done."

"Shall I bring water?" Esther asked.

"Go find your young man to help tote," Cordelia suggested. "Let him do something useful while he's mooning after you."

Esther blushed, and left with the wash buckets.

Cordelia remembered the conversation she'd had with Franklin and Esther the day before. Later in the evening when they were alone, Franklin had raised the topic again. "Are you so afraid, love, of this birth?"

Cordelia hesitated, then said, "It's being out here in the wild. I don't know what to expect."

"I'll take care of you, Cordelia. You know I will."

She sighed. "I know you'll try, Franklin. But you have the whole company to watch over."

"No one's more important to me than you are. We'll stop when it's your time."

"And if Samuel Abercrombie argues about the pace? What then?"

"We'll stop anyway. He don't scare me. He knows it was a mistake to part company at Ash Hollow. And he knows he erred in baiting the Cherokee at Fort Laramie. He's been chastened since then."

Cordelia shook her head. Mr. Abercrombie had argued about laying by at Willow Springs—she'd heard him. She had no confidence he would stay chastened for long. Still, Franklin's caring words warmed her.

Franklin was right—Esther shouldn't be made to delay her happiness for her mother's sake. Maybe Cordelia should agree to the wedding. For family harmony, if nothing else. Maybe she should simply hope they didn't find a preacher until after this baby came—better yet, until they reached Oregon.

But, Cordelia thought, if Esther's blushes were any indication, the wedding should happen sooner rather than later.

She sighed, as uncertain as ever—did she want Esther to marry soon or not?

For now, as she waited for Esther and Daniel to return with her water, Cordelia looked up at the bright blue sky and felt the sun on her face. Maybe this birth would go well. Maybe she shouldn't worry. After all, she was surrounded by her family's love.

Daniel had decided not to accompany the hunters because he wanted to talk to Esther again, maybe find a way to get her alone. He went looking for her after the Sabbath service, but she told him she needed to help with the baking. He was glad when she later came to ask his help in toting water for laundry.

After they'd brought the tubs to the Pershing wagons, he asked, "Walk with me, Esther?"

She shook her head. "I have to help Ma with the washing."

"And then?"

She smiled, her dimples showing. "Then I'll walk with you."

Daniel roamed aimlessly about the camp and headed to the springs, where he watched Tanner and his son catching frogs. He found a glade of willow trees not far from the water. One was large enough to form a room-sized space under its branches. He would bring Esther here, he decided, as soon as she was done with her chores. A private haven away from everyone.

He went to find a blanket and took it back to the willow tree. He spread it out on the ground and lay down to take a nap, imagining Esther beside him. Their home in Oregon wouldn't be much bigger than the space under the tree, he guessed. He pictured where the furniture would be, the hearth, the window and curtains Esther wanted.

And soon he slept.

In midafternoon Esther saw Daniel approaching the Pershing wagons again. He looked groggy and had a crease along one cheek, as if he'd just awakened from a nap. He was as handsome as ever, even when drowsy, she thought.

"Are you ready?" he asked. His grin told her he was more awake than he seemed.

Ma frowned at him. "You take care of her, Daniel Abercrombie."

"Yes, ma'am." Daniel tipped his hat at Ma, then took Esther's arm to guide her toward the spring. "I have a surprise for you. Just beyond the water." They reached the grove of trees, and he parted the hanging boughs of one large willow.

A green bower awaited her. "Like our own fairy castle," she whispered.

"Just what I was thinking," Daniel said as he leaned over to kiss her. He led her to a blanket on the ground and lay her down on it.

"Daniel—"

"Shhh. Don't talk," he whispered against her lips.

They groped each other hungrily, Esther's hands wandering as freely as Daniel's while she lay cradled in his arms.

"We'd best stop," Esther said, though she wasn't sure she could make him halt what he was doing. "I told Ma we wouldn't."

"Is your ma going to be in our marriage bed with us?" Daniel asked, nuzzling her neck.

"No. But this ain't our marriage bed." Esther pushed at him.

"You don't really want to stop, do you?" Daniel's hands continued to move over her breasts and hips, and she quit pushing. He unbuttoned her bodice and bared her breast, then suckled a nipple.

Esther gasped. "Daniel!" She'd never felt anything so glorious, though she knew it was wrong. She held his head in place and arched her hips into him, her body moving of its own accord.

He pressed against her and moaned, sucking harder and thrusting his hips. She felt him hard against her thigh and knew she had to stop him. Before she couldn't.

She waited another blissful minute, then pushed at his chest. "Daniel," she whispered. "We mustn't."

"Well, then, marry me soon," he said through gritted teeth as he rolled away. "I can't keep being with you like this. Or I'll ruin you, for sure."

Would it be ruin? Esther wondered. A part of her wished he would just take her. Surely it wasn't sinful to feel so heavenly. How could she wait until they married?

But Ma trusted her—how could she not wait?

Daniel was right—they couldn't go on like this much longer. How could she get Ma's approval?

Chapter 47: Toward Independence Rock

Sunday, 27 June 1847. Leaving Willow Springs in the morning. Next stop Independence Rock. FP

As the company rolled away from Willow Springs, Franklin rode ahead of the wagons, leading them into the desert hills. A drizzly gray sky hung low over the caravan, but he was glad for the damp as they crossed the otherwise arid land.

He mulled over his recent conversations with Cordelia and Esther. His daughter had caught him Sunday evening when he returned from hunting, asking again if her mother had changed her mind. Franklin thought Cordelia was softening, but he shook his head at Esther. "Leave it be," he said. "Let your ma stew on it for a few days."

His daughter swallowed hard and nodded, hugging her arms across her chest. What was eating at the girl? he wondered.

The wagons creaked slowly through ravines and rocky ridges. They switchbacked up steep hills, and after they'd been underway about two hours, they encountered loose scree.

Franklin sat on his gelding above the lumbering wagons watching their slow progress. From his vantage, he saw one wagon teeter on the brink of the narrow trail. "Watch out!" he shouted. "Rear wheel's on the edge."

As he spoke, the wheel slipped off the path. The driver cracked his whip to speed up his oxen, and the wagon lurched forward to firm ground.

By the time they stopped for the noon meal, the entire company was unnerved by the difficulty of travel. Abercrombie sauntered over to the Pershing wagons where Franklin sat chewing his dinner. "Taking us twice as long as it should," Abercrombie complained, thrusting his thumbs in his suspenders. "Meandering through these hills. You know where you're going?"

"You want to scout?" Franklin asked.

Abercrombie spat. "That's young men's work."

"Then let the boys do it," Franklin snapped. "Zeke and Joel are doing fine. Soon as we hit the Sweetwater, we'll have another river to follow." He shouted at his sons to move ahead of the wagons, then got the company underway quickly after they repacked their dishes.

All afternoon he worried about Abercrombie's bullheadedness. At first the man had seemed remorseful after the debacle at Laramie. But now? He'd resumed his belligerence.

Franklin shook his head—poor Esther. He hoped his daughter loved young Daniel enough to put up with an obstinate father-in-law. He didn't see any hope of Abercrombie improving.

That night they made a miserable camp on a rocky hill. Squeezing the wagons and tents on flat ground was difficult. But a small creek offered water and a little grass for the teams, making it one of the few possible sites they'd encountered during the hard day of travel.

Through the day and evening Monday, Esther watched her mother, waiting for Ma to say something. But as Pa had suggested, she didn't wheedle or plead about her wedding. The next day's travel brought more of the same country—rocky and hilly, hard on the teams pulling wagons and hard on the travelers who trudged on foot.

In addition to eyeing her mother, Esther tried to stay away from Daniel, unless members of her family were nearby. Monday night they'd fished in the little creek with the younger Pershings, but she hadn't wandered off with Daniel as he'd urged. She wanted no more trysts under willow trees.

Well, she *wanted* to be with him, but she knew she shouldn't.

She could tell her reluctance irritated him. Last night he'd pointed to a large boulder upstream from where they fished and whispered in her ear, "Come with me. Behind the rock."

She shook her head and said, "I should stay with the young'uns."

"Are you going to turn me away after we're married?" he asked.

"We're not married. That's the problem."

"What are you doing to bring your ma around?"

"Pa says to leave her be. Besides, without a minister, we can't wed anyway."

Daniel sighed and rubbed her fingers. "Your father said there'd be other companies at Independence Rock. Folks stop there to rest and reconnoiter. We might come upon a preacher there."

"If we do, I'll get a yes or no from Ma."

When they stopped at midday Tuesday, Esther found her father. "Is it true there'll be other emigrants at Independence Rock?" she asked.

"Won't know till we get there. But I wouldn't be surprised. Most companies want a rest afore they head for the summit at South Pass."

That afternoon Esther walked beside her mother, who seemed to breathe harder with every day of travel. "Ma," she asked, "what if there's a preacher at Independence Rock?"

"Why do you think there might be?" Ma sounded annoyed by the question, but Esther pressed on.

"Pa says so. One of the companies might have a minister."

Ma sighed. "I told you I'd think on it. I'm not holding back because of my plight. I'm thinking of what's best for you, daughter."

"Daniel's getting anxious, Ma."

Ma stopped. "What do you mean?"

"He's done more than kiss me."

Ma stared at her, frowning. "Could you be with child?"

"No!" Esther shook her head. "Not yet." She wasn't sure what put those last words in her mouth—was she simply being truthful or trying to coerce her mother into giving her blessing?

"Honestly, Esther, after the work I put into raising you. Don't do anything that could cause you harm."

"It don't feel like harm, Ma."

"Well, it would embarrass me and your pa. I'll tie you to the wagon if I must to make you behave." Ma sighed. "What am I going to do with you?"

"Maybe you could let us marry soon."

"Don't you talk back to me, young lady."

"Ma—"

"I'll do what I think best for you. And that's that."

Esther opened her mouth, then closed it. She couldn't persuade her mother by herself. She ran off to find Jenny McDougall—her mother seemed taken with the young bride.

"You've got to talk to my ma," she pleaded with Jenny. "Tell her I should marry Daniel as soon as I can. We can't wait."

"Of course, you can," Jenny said.

"No, Jenny, I don't think I can. And I don't want to." No one seemed to understand how much she loved Daniel.

"I don't want to get between you and your mama," Jenny said, shaking her head. "She's a good woman, Esther. She only wants what's best for you."

"What's best for me is marrying Daniel—soon. Please." Esther grabbed her friend's arm. "Please talk to her."

Jenny sighed. "If I find a chance. But I won't seek her out. It isn't right for me to interfere."

The conversation with Esther shook Cordelia. She hadn't realized her daughter and Daniel had progressed to greater intimacies than kissing. How had that happened with an entire company of travelers in close proximity? She never felt any sense of privacy with all the people about.

Esther seemed determined to wed the boy, even to the point of sassing her mother. Cordelia couldn't put her decision off much longer—and if she didn't agree to the marriage, she might cause a rift with Esther that would be difficult to repair.

Tuesday evening after the wagons had circled and supper simmered on the fire, Cordelia went to find Jenny McDougall. She'd seen the girl talking with Esther after her daughter ran off.

Cordelia sat on a large stone near the McDougall wagon. She was still short of breath from walking in the thin mountain air all day. After a few minutes of chitchat, she said abruptly, "Esther wants to marry the Abercrombie boy soon. You put that idea in her head?" She knew it wasn't fair to blame Esther's fast ways on Jenny, but Jenny had been promiscuous before marriage also—even more wanton than Esther, if her daughter told the truth about how far her lovemaking with Daniel had progressed.

"No, ma'am."

Cordelia sighed. She decided to confide in Esther's friend. Maybe Jenny could help her understand her daughter. "She has some romantic notion life'll be better after she's married. You tell her that?"

"No, ma'am."

She squinted at Jenny. "Well, what do you think?"

"Daniel's a nice man, Mrs. Pershing."

"You reckon they oughta marry now?"

"It's not for me to say, ma'am." Jenny was such a polite little thing, no matter what trouble she'd gotten herself into. The kind of trouble Cordelia wanted to keep Esther from finding.

She stared out into the hills beyond the wagons. What would spare Esther the most heartbreak—marrying or waiting? "Soon as she's married, she's going to find herself like us. Swelling up with a baby. No idea what's in store for the child." She turned back to Jenny. "You want that for her?"

"Like I said, ma'am, it isn't mine to say."

"She always could wheedle the captain into anything. So I'm the one standing in her way." Cordelia sighed again. She didn't want to keep Esther from happiness. "I just want what's best for her. Don't know if Daniel's the one for her."

"You'll never persuade her otherwise. At least not unless there's another man she thinks better suited."

Jenny knew Esther well, Cordelia decided, despite their short friendship. "That's the truth. She'll always want some man around." She took a deep breath. "Captain says Oregon men are rough. I suppose Daniel's better than some she might find."

Cordelia heaved herself to her feet and nodded good-bye to Jenny. She would lose this battle with Esther in the end. And if she didn't capitulate, her daughter might be breeding before marriage. She might as well bless her daughter's union.

Back at her own campfire, she nodded at Esther, who stirred the evening stew. "When we find a preacher, you can marry Daniel. But don't be alone with him afore then. I'll be watching."

Despite Ma's caution, Esther rushed to find Daniel right after supper and told him the good news. "Ma says yes!" He picked her up in his arms and whirled her about, then planted a long kiss on her lips. The kiss wasn't disobeying her mother, Esther told herself—they weren't alone, they were in full sight of his family.

Wednesday morning, once the wagons were underway, Esther went in search of Jenny to share her joy. Jenny rode her little Indian mare beside her husband on his black stallion. Esther ran over to them, blond curls streaming behind, sunbonnet hanging from its ties down her back. "May I ride with you?" she asked.

Jenny and Mac exchanged a glance, he nodded, then Jenny reached down a hand to help Esther scramble behind her. "Ride off a ways. I want to talk," Esther said.

After they trotted a short distance from the wagons, Esther clutched Jenny's arm. "Thank you for speaking with Ma."

"I didn't do anything," Jenny said.

"Well, she's agreed. Next preacher we see, I'm getting married."

Jenny reached to touch Esther's hand. "I wish you and Daniel every happiness."

Esther couldn't stop chattering about the wedding she hoped to have. "I've finished my wedding dress. So I'm ready. And Ma says she'll spare me some bedding."

"Which family will you ride with?" Jenny asked. "Yours or the Abercrombies?"

Esther hadn't considered that. "Oh, it don't matter," she said. "We'll work it out." She felt sure she and Daniel would stay with her family—Ma needed her.

They camped Wednesday night beside a large pool Captain Pershing called Saleratus Lake. More of the white powder for baking lay about its shore. As soon as the wagons were in place, Daniel went to see the Pershings. "Thank you, ma'am," he said to Mrs. Pershing, holding his hat in his hand and bowing slightly. "You won't regret letting us marry. I'll take good care of Esther."

Mrs. Pershing sniffed. "Mind you take care of her afore you marry, too. Ain't no telling when we'll find a preacher to make your union right afore

God."

"Yes, ma'am," Daniel said, thinking he was making a promise that would be hard to keep. He turned to Esther. "Shall we walk around the lake?" She smiled, took his arm, and they set off.

Once they were away from the wagons, Esther asked. "If we marry afore we reach Oregon, will we camp with your family or mine?"

Daniel shrugged. "Does it matter?" He pulled her closer. "As long as we have a tent or wagon to sleep in by ourselves."

She blushed. "It's just that Ma—"

"I won't take you away from your family, Esther. I hope to start our own soon enough, but I'll make sure you can help your ma during her confinement."

"Thank you, Daniel." She reached up and kissed his cheek. On the far side of the lake, behind a clump of reeds, he returned the kiss more passionately.

"Ma says we mustn't," Esther said once she was breathless, and she pulled him toward camp.

Thursday morning Daniel scouted with Zeke and Joel. They hadn't traveled more than an hour when Daniel saw a huge treeless rock on the horizon—shaped like a loaf of bread half buried in dirt. He pointed it out.

"Must be Independence Rock," Zeke said. "I'll go tell Pa." He turned back toward the wagons.

Daniel and Joel continued riding. The gigantic mound loomed ever larger, with a river meandering to the south of their path. "Think that's the Sweetwater?" Daniel asked.

Joel shrugged. "Probably. Pa'll know for sure. See them dots?" He pointed at groups of white spots beneath the rock. "Must be wagons. And over yonder—teams grazing by the river."

Sure enough, Daniel made out smaller dark spots near the water that could be oxen or mules.

When Captain Pershing and Zeke reached them, the captain confirmed they were approaching the Sweetwater. "Should get to the rock by noon," he said, squinting. "Think you boys can lead the wagons there? I aim to ride ahead and see who else is in camp."

Chapter 48: Finding a Preacher

Wednesday, 30 June 1847. Should reach Independence Rock tomorrow. FP

Franklin left the young men behind and trotted toward Independence Rock, reaching the granite mound in about an hour. He found the leader of one wagon company and asked about the travelers already camped at the base of the landmark.

"Folks from Illinois by the Sweetwater," the man replied. "Mormons from Missouri just east of 'em. My party come from Tennessee. Some soldiers on patrol camped nearby, too. Where y'all from?"

"We organized in Missouri, but got families from all over," Franklin said. "Boston to Tennessee."

"There's also a small group of missionaries from New York, aiming to convert the heathen." The man pointed to a few wagons near the rock, away from the river.

"Missionaries?" Franklin asked. "Are there ministers in the group?"

The other captain nodded. "Two or three preachers, as well as two doctors. Plus their families and guides."

Franklin's heart sank, fearing Esther and Daniel would insist on marrying here. Was he ready for his oldest daughter to leave his care? But he'd promised, and Cordelia had now agreed—she'd told him so, saying she might lose Esther if she didn't.

Esther would find out about the preachers soon enough. Franklin needed to be ready to talk to her. With a deep sigh, he headed for the missionary camp. After exchanging greetings, he asked, "How long you folks staying?" Maybe they would depart before a wedding could be arranged.

"Until the Fourth, I think," a man in buckskins said as he sat cleaning a rifle. He didn't look like any preacher Franklin had ever seen—perhaps this one had some gumption. "That's when we're meeting guides from Oregon here. Unless they arrive sooner."

"My daughter and her fiancé want to wed. Would you marry them?"

The missionary smiled. "I'll talk to the couple first, but if they're as willing as most young folks are, I'd be happy to."

Franklin sighed. "Then I'd better prepare our family for a wedding." And he rode off to stake a camp beside the Sweetwater.

Once their wagons had circled, Esther walked around the large camp at the base of Independence Rock, which looked like the back of a tortoise raised above the sandy ground. She was surprised to find so many people thronged beneath the stone landmark. The crowd wasn't as big as at Laramie, but tents and campfires and wagons lined the ground along the Sweetwater.

"You might be getting married sooner'n you think," Jonathan came running to tell her. "There's a company of missionaries here."

"Where?" Esther said, looking around, her heart racing at the news.

"Over yonder," his twin David said, pointing.

"It's rude to point at folks," she said automatically, but she was already heading toward the missionary wagons.

As she approached their camp, her steps slowed. Did she really mean to ask if one of these preachers would marry Daniel and her? Without talking to her parents or to Daniel? But she'd wanted to be married and to have a family ever since she'd known what marriage was. And she loved Daniel. That thought gave her strength, and she strode forward.

A man in buckskins sat beside a fire. "Sir," she said, wishing she could keep the quaver out of her voice. "I hear there are preachers in this company."

The man grinned. "We have two, miss. Both Methodists, I fear. I'm one of them. Do you have need of salvation?"

Esther shook her head. "No, sir. I aim to get married."

The man chuckled. "You have a husband in mind?"

"Yes, sir. Daniel Abercrombie. He's in our company."

"Are you by chance the daughter of Franklin Pershing?"

"Yes, sir." Esther was confused. How did the man know Pa?

"That fine captain was by here earlier. Said his family might have need of a minister. I make it a practice to talk to couples I marry before I join them in matrimony." He nodded. "You bring your young man here, and we'll have a word. Tomorrow morning."

Esther beamed. "Yes, sir. I'll bring Daniel to meet you right after breakfast."

She raced back to the wagons. Would it really be this easy? She and Daniel could be married by nightfall tomorrow.

"It's too soon, Franklin!" Cordelia paced in front of her husband when he told her there were ministers in the neighboring missionary company.

"Esther's bound to hear. We gave her our word."

"But that was only a few days ago! How can I part with her so soon?" She'd thought she would have weeks more before she lost her daughter. Maybe not until they reached Oregon.

"How can you hold her back, Cordelia? You've promised her." Franklin led her to sit on a crate next to one of their wagons. "We like Daniel. It's best to get her settled afore they cause a scandal."

Cordelia dropped her face to her hands, distraught. "I didn't raise her right, Franklin."

"You did fine, love. She's young, and so is Daniel. You remember what it was like, don't you?"

Cordelia raised her head. She smiled weakly at him. "You couldn't keep your hands off me."

"I thought the feeling was mutual." Franklin grinned. "Wasn't it?"

"Ma! Pa!" Esther ran into their campsite. "There's a preacher. He wants to talk to Daniel and me. Then he'll marry us! Oh, Ma, I'm so happy." Esther twirled in a dance around the fire.

"Not so fast, young lady." Cordelia stood.

"Ma! You promised."

"I want to meet this preacher afore I say for sure." It was the only reason Cordelia could think of to delay giving her consent.

"I said I'd bring Daniel to him in the morning. You can come, too."

Cordelia nodded, seeing no way out of it. "All right, then. We need to get supper on now. Your pa and I'll talk with the Abercrombies tonight, then I'll meet this man in the morning."

Instead of helping with supper, Esther ran off.

The force of Esther's hug nearly toppled Daniel when she bolted into the Abercrombie campsite and into his arms. "What is it?" he asked in alarm. "Are you all right?"

"Did you hear?" she said. "There's a minister. A real one—a Methodist. He'll marry us after we talk to him. First thing in the morning."

Married? Daniel stood silent, in shock. So soon?

"Now hold on, girl," Pa said, standing.

"Samuel—" Ma said in a soft voice.

"Ain't no son of mine getting married till I've said so."

"But Mr. Abercrombie—" Esther wailed.

"Girl, you want to wed my son, you best learn your manners."

"Samuel," Ma said. "I think we should let Daniel and Esther talk. Let them decide they're ready for this marriage. Daniel, why don't you and Esther take a walk around camp?"

"Thank you, Ma." Daniel said, reaching for Esther's arm.

When they were out of earshot of his parents, Esther described her conversations with the minister and with her parents, hardly pausing for a breath, and ending with, "So Ma says we can meet with the preacher in the morning. Then I'm sure she'll give us her blessing."

Daniel inhaled deeply. "And this is what you want, Esther?"

She halted her steps. "Of course, don't you?"

It was what he wanted, and yet— "It's a big step. We can't undo it, once we're married."

"Don't you want me?" Tears glistened in her eyes.

"Yes. Yes, I do." That he was sure of. "I want my whole life with you. But should we move so fast?"

"I swear, Daniel Abercrombie"—her hands were on her hips now, and her eyes flashed—"if I'm going to have to make all the decisions in our household, then I'm not sure I want to—"

He stopped her with a quick kiss. She was adorable when she was mad, but he didn't want to be the cause of her ire. "That's all I need," he said. "Just to know you want our wedding as much as I do." It was going to happen—she wouldn't let anything get in her way. He should put his worries behind him, his fears of inadequacy. "Let's go talk to Pa and Ma."

Chapter 49:   Wedding Plans

Thursday, 1 July 1847. At Independence Rock. Met with preacher headed for Oregon. My daughter and Daniel Abercrombie plan to marry here. FP

Esther woke before dawn Friday—she might be getting married this day! She just had to convince the preacher and Ma.

As soon as the camp began to stir, she rose, dressed, and left the tent to cook breakfast. Pa and Mr. Abercrombie were going hunting, and Zeke and Joel planned to accompany them. She'd made sure Daniel was staying in camp to meet with the minister.

Esther served the men, then cooked more food before Ma and her younger siblings arose. Breakfast was flapjacks and fried meat, like so many mornings along the trail. But everything felt fresh and new.

She served her family cheerfully, and said to Ma, "What time shall we meet with the preacher?"

"Midmorning, I think. Whenever Harriet and Daniel are ready."

Esther and Rachel washed the dishes. "Ma," Esther asked, "may I take my bedding when Daniel and I wed." She blushed as she spoke, but she wanted to get Ma talking.

Ma frowned. "I suppose. Will he at least be providing you with a tent, since he ain't got a house to offer a bride?"

"I don't know. We ain't talked about it."

"Seems there's a lot you two ain't talked about." Ma sighed. "I wish—"

But she didn't finish her thought.

Daniel and his mother arrived at the Pershing camp just before nine.

"Your pa won't raise an issue, if he don't meet the preacher, will he?" Esther asked Daniel. She didn't want anything or anyone to interfere or cause a further delay.

Daniel shook his head. "Said he don't need to meet with no parson."

Mrs. Abercrombie said, "Don't worry. I won't let him hold you up."

Ma rose and tightened her shawl around her shoulders, with only a bare nod at Daniel's mother. The four of them walked in silence to the minister's camp.

"Greetings, Reverend," Esther said. She was the only one who had previously met the man. She introduced Ma, Mrs. Abercrombie, and Daniel. Ma's lips tightened as she scrutinized the preacher's rough clothes.

The minister asked Esther if she was convinced she wanted to wed Daniel. She smiled and nodded. When asked about marrying Esther, Daniel answered a strong, "Yes, sir."

"Are there any concerns from the parents?"

Ma sniffed. "She's my first to marry, Reverend. But I want what's best for her."

The man said gently, "Ma'am, do you believe this marriage is right for your daughter."

Ma's hands were twisted together, but she nodded.

The preacher looked at Esther. "You will become an Abercrombie, but you remain your parents' daughter and will continue to owe them your devotion."

"Yes, sir. I will, sir." This was as solemn as the marriage vows themselves, Esther realized. "I know my ma needs me. And Pa and the young'uns, too."

"And you," the minister turned to Daniel. "Your family will welcome your bride, I'm sure." Mrs. Abercrombie smiled. "But you, too, have a duty to Esther's family. A marriage is a uniting of two families before God. Are you prepared to accommodate your wife's kin when needed?"

"Yes, sir." Daniel gave another firm response.

"Well, then, when shall we conduct the ceremony?"

"Oh, thank you!" It was all Esther could do not to throw her arms around the man's neck and kiss his cheek.

"We need to prepare a wedding feast," Ma said. "Such as we can in the wilderness."

"Oh, Ma, must we wait?" Esther groaned.

"Tomorrow afternoon?" Mrs. Abercrombie suggested.

Ma nodded, though her face remained grim. "'Spect that's the best we can do."

The missionary bowed. "Tomorrow afternoon it is. Our party cannot leave until our guide arrives."

"Well, then, Cordelia," Mrs. Abercrombie said, "shall we plan a wedding?"

When they left the missionary camp, Daniel offered Esther his arm. Their mothers walked ahead. Esther bounced along beside him with her deep dimples flashing. "Tomorrow!" she said. "We'll be married tomorrow."

"And then?" he asked. He didn't want to dampen her enthusiasm— indeed, imagining the wedding night sent a surge of lust through him.

"What do you mean?" She slowed her pace, and they dropped farther behind their mothers, who walked with their heads close together, gesticulating as they talked.

"Are you willing to camp with my folks each night? Or do we stay with yours? Or split our time?"

"Well, the wagons ain't that far apart. I reckon we'll manage. Ma needs me—"

"And me, Esther? I want you with me, if you're to be my wife."

"Of course, I'll be with you, Daniel. That's why we're marrying. I'm not worried about where we'll pitch our tent."

"It's customary for a wife to join her husband's family."

"Then I'll camp with you, unless Ma needs me. But then I'll have to be with her." Which seemed to settle the matter for Esther—she really didn't seem concerned. She prattled on about pots and pans and bedding for their cabin in Oregon, and she was still chattering when they reached their wagons. Then her mother pulled her aside and they began talking.

"Go on, Daniel," Esther said. "Ma and I have to plan for tomorrow."

Daniel went off to his family's campsite, feeling lost, but not knowing what else to do.

Cordelia put her fears for herself and for Esther behind her. They had work to do to be ready for the morrow. She rummaged through their food stores. "Do we have enough sugar left for a cake?"

"Ma," Esther said, "don't worry about a wedding cake."

Cordelia turned to Esther. "You're my first child married. You won't start with much, but you'll have a cake if I can manage it." This wasn't how she'd imagined Esther's wedding—not in the wilderness with a stone mountain for a backdrop. Where was the church? Where were the cousins and friends—the girls like Amy Boone, whom Esther had grown up with? "Oh, Esther," she said. "I want you to be happy."

"I know, Ma," Esther said, hugging Cordelia. "I will be. *We* will be." Cordelia didn't know whether Esther's "we" meant her and Daniel or the Pershing family.

"I pray to God you're right."

Harriet Abercrombie joined them. "Word is getting around," she said. "Everyone in the company is ready to pitch in for a meal after the wedding."

"I'll make a cake. Won't have fine flour, but it'll rise enough." Cordelia sighed. "Maybe even enough sugar for icing."

"I have sugar, if you need more," Harriet said. "And we'll supply meat. I'm sure Samuel and Douglass will bring back enough to share."

"Ma, may I pack up my clothes and blankets? I want to be ready to put them with Daniel's belongings after the wedding."

Cordelia's heart fell at her daughter's words. She was losing Esther. "Yes, dear. Do what you like." The baby kicked her lungs and she couldn't breathe. Poor child would scarcely know his older sister. And here she'd thought Esther would be like a second mother to him.

"All packed, Ma," Esther said, coming out of the wagon after a short while. "I'm going to find Jenny. Tell her my wonderful news."

Samuel had rousted Douglass out of bed at first light, and they rode out of camp along with Mac McDougall and the Pershing men. Harriet had asked Samuel to go with her to meet the preacher, but he had no interest in doing so. His contribution would be fresh meat for the wedding feast, whenever it was set. He'd heard there were goats in the mountains nearby. Goat meat would be a tasty change from venison.

He hoped the vows would be spoken that evening, so they could get underway. But as they rode, Pershing said he planned to keep the company at Independence Rock another day or two.

"Two more days!" Pershing's horse shied at Samuel's bellow.

"Trappers from Oregon coming any day now. I want to hear what they say about the route. And talk with the Army platoon that's here also."

"What'll they tell us we don't already know?" Samuel muttered. "Mountains to cross, rivers to ford. And snows can come as early as October." Pershing stopped to palaver every chance he got, and he never learned a thing new.

They hunted all morning, but all they found were sage hens and jackrabbits. "Too damn many wagons and people," Samuel complained.

They ranged farther, and around midday they found sheep with large curling horns in the hills beyond Independence Rock. "Bighorns," Pershing said. "Didn't see 'em this far east with Frémont."

They'd lose the beasts if they didn't stop gabbing and start shooting. Samuel pulled his rifle and yelled, "Fire!" He shot, as did other men. Five of the strange animals dropped.

Mac and Zeke went back to camp for a wagon to help haul the meat, leaving Samuel and Douglass with Franklin and Joel Pershing to field dress the sheep.

"Be enough for a feast now," Samuel said as he gutted one carcass.

"Wonder when the women set the ceremony," Pershing said.

"Guess there ain't no hurry if you're keeping us here all week."

"Not all week," Pershing said. "Just till we get the lay of the land beyond here. I want as much information as we can get afore we reach the high mountains."

Samuel spat.

"You all right with your son marrying my Esther?" Pershing asked. "If you ain't, you tell me now. I don't want her bearing your ill will when it's too late to change matters."

Samuel stood up from his task. "It ain't Esther I got a problem with, Pershing. She's a fine lass. If she tends to my son, I'll have her in my family."

"Well, that's good then."

Samuel squatted beside the carcass again. "But that don't mean I aim to stop telling you what I think. I ain't cottoned much to your running of this company, and that ain't likely to change."

Pershing stood and glared at him. "I can take your cantankerousness, Abercrombie. But if you take your displeasure with me out on my daughter, I'll make sure you pay."

Samuel shrugged. "Then we understand each other."

Franklin and the other hunters returned to Independence Rock about supper time, the mutton they'd butchered filling a wagon. As soon as Franklin arrived at his campsite, Esther told him all about the conversation with the minister.

"Well, Cordelia," Franklin said when he heard the news. "Looks like our daughter is getting married tomorrow." He moved behind his wife to hug her, large belly and all, as she stood mixing a batter of some type.

"No time for foolishness, Franklin," she said, swatting him away. "I'm making a cake. Along with supper for your family and bread for the morrow."

"Esther just climbed in the wagon," he said. "Shouldn't she be helping you? And where's the rest of our brood?"

Cordelia sighed. "I don't have the heart to make her work on her last night with us. Noah's in the wagon with her, napping. Rachel and Ruth went for water." She shrugged. "Don't know about the other boys. . . . Oh, there's Zeke."

"Zeke," Franklin said, turning to his eldest, "go find Rachel. Help her tote water for your ma."

"Yes, Pa." His son loped toward the river.

Franklin put his arm around his wife's shoulder again. "You all right?"

"I'll manage." Her voice sounded strained.

"You're tired."

"Same as always. I'm fine."

"Go sit a spell."

"I have to get this cake ready to bake. Can't frost it till it's cool."

"Cordelia, you need to rest. Won't do Esther no good if you're plumb worn out tomorrow."

She sighed. "Franklin—"

"I can beat a cake. Give me the bowl."

She thrust the bowl and spoon at him and sat on a log. "Go ahead then."

"You ain't regretting giving your word about the marriage, are you?"

"No." But she dragged the word out into three syllables. "I just wish she were starting off with more."

He shrugged as he stirred the batter vigorously. "We had the farm your pa gave us when we were wed, but not much to go with it. Couldn't afford much on a soldier's pay. We made do. Esther and Daniel'll manage all right also, once they have their own land in Oregon."

"I suppose."

"That mixed enough?" He held the bowl toward her. "And we'll be there to help them if they need anything. Just like your pa helped us."

When Pa and Douglass returned from hunting, Daniel was certain Pa would question him about the wedding. Sure enough, Pa began as soon as he and Douglass distributed the meat from the hunt.

"When's the wedding to be?" Pa asked. "Though don't look like there's any need to rush. Pershing plans to take it easy from here on." He spat tobacco juice in what Daniel took as a show of disgust.

Ma described the meeting with the preacher. When she finished, Pa said, "You ready for this, son?"

"Yes, sir."

"Well, then, I guess you'll be a husband by tomorrow night," Pa said, sitting on a log to pull off his boots.

"Yes, sir, I guess I will."

"Guess you'd better find your brother," Pa said. "Tell him he's standing up with you." He chewed on his plug awhile, then said, "Thought you might as well have your mare. As a wedding present."

A lump caught in Daniel's throat. He hadn't received a gift from Pa since he got a rifle for his thirteenth birthday. "Thank you," he said, when he felt he could speak without choking. He loved that mare.

"Breed her to McDougall's stallion, and you'll get some fine colts. Add to your farm income."

Ma stood behind his father with a hand over her mouth. Had she known about the gift, or was she just as surprised as Daniel?

When Harriet finally went to bed in the tent after a long day of cooking and baking, she whispered to Samuel, "That was a fine thing you did, giving Daniel his mare."

"Boy's got to have his own horse. He raised that one. Did a crack job of it, too."

"They'll be fine, Samuel, him and Esther."

"Better be. Won't be no way to undo it, once they're hitched." With that, Samuel rolled over and began to snore.

Harriet smiled in the dark. And prayed Daniel and Esther would be happy together. If they muddled along as well as she and Samuel had, their lives would be better than most folks got.

Chapter 50:   Married

Friday, 2 July 1847. Esther Pershing and Daniel Abercrombie will wed tomorrow. FP

Finally, the day of her wedding dawned. Esther had spent a sleepless night, worried yet excited. By nightfall she and Daniel would be married! And then would come the wedding night, when she and Daniel would be alone to love as they wanted. At last.

As soon as Ma rose and left the tent, Esther got out of her blankets and laid out her wedding dress. She put her friend Amy's lace handkerchief with it to carry while she said her vows—a symbol of her old life merging with the new.

Then she donned an old frock—she wouldn't put on her wedding dress until the last minute—and followed her mother. A fine mist fell, and Esther wondered if it would burn off or turn to rain. "Morning," she said to her mother.

Ma turned to her and smiled. "Well, daughter, it's your wedding day."

Esther beamed. "It is." Then she sobered. "Do you really approve of my marrying, Ma, or are you just allowing it?"

Ma turned to fry meat from yesterday's hunt. "You're not going far. Won't be but a few wagons away."

They'd be eating mutton for days, Esther thought. Or rather, the rest of her family would be—she might be eating with the Abercrombies, and she didn't know what food stores they had. The changes marriage would bring

342

to her life now seemed imminent and solid. "I worry about you, Ma."

Her mother turned to her, her expression that of one grown woman talking to another. "I won't lie, Esther. I still fret about this child." Her hand touched her belly. "But you need to live your life, not stay tied to me. If Daniel is the husband you want—and he's a fine man—then you will be blessed."

"I do love him, Ma."

"Then marry him and have your own babies, like you've always wanted." Ma turned back to the skillet. "Rachel's older than you were when you started helping me. She'll step into your chores. She's grown up on this journey, just as you have. Now, go rouse her and Ruthie. We have a wedding feast to finish."

All morning Cordelia ordered Esther and Rachel about, trying to get most of the cooking done before the heat of the day. Clouds gathered overhead, and the drizzly air felt warm and humid. She dragooned Zeke and Joel and even the twins into rigging up tents as a canopy in the middle of the emigrant camp. "Looks like rain," she told them. "Don't want folks getting soaked during the wedding."

When that task was done, she told her sons to drag barrels and crates under the makeshift pavilion. "And find some boards to put on top those boxes. So we have a table for the food."

By late morning Cordelia could scarcely breathe, panting from fatigue. Franklin told her firmly, "Sit down, Cordelia. It don't do no good to tire yourself out."

"My mutton pie ain't done yet," she said, but she dropped heavily on the crate he led her to.

"Rachel," he shouted, "take care of the pie." Then he squeezed to sit beside her and put an arm around her shoulders. "The only thing you need to do is get yourself and Esther dressed. I'll handle the rest."

Elizabeth Tuller, the doctor's wife, bustled over, a quilt draped over one arm and a blue ribbon dangling from her other hand. "I brought Esther something," she said. "Her dress is blue, ain't it? Well, I've been saving this ribbon, and I want her to have it." She held out her hand.

"Esther," Franklin called, "you have a visitor."

343

Esther climbed out of the wagon and stroked the silk streamer Elizabeth handed her. "Oh, Mrs. Tuller, how pretty!" she said. "I didn't have anything for my hair—we can't find any flowers around here, the ground's so beat up from the wagons. The color is lovely."

"This quilt is for you also." Elizabeth held it out. "I been working on it since we left Illinois, made from scraps of my boys' old clothes. Decided you might as well have it. Probably won't have much else to call your own till we reach Oregon."

At that Cordelia stood and embraced the doctor's wife. "This is truly a gift from the heart, Elizabeth. Something to be treasured. But don't you want to keep the memories of your sons?"

"I have the memories, Cordelia. Don't need the quilt to remember." Elizabeth turned to Esther. "May you and Daniel know great happiness in the years ahead."

"Thank you, Mrs. Tuller."

When Elizabeth left, Cordelia said, "Well, daughter, it's time we dressed."

Hefting herself into the wagon, Cordelia put on her better skirt and a clean blouse. Not many clothes fit her at this point in her pregnancy. Then she told Esther to climb in and put on her wedding dress. Esther's blond locks glowed as brightly as the yellow flowers in the cotton fabric. "Let me see what I can do with your hair," Cordelia said. She tied up Esther's curls with the blue ribbon from Elizabeth Tuller and wove the ends through her daughter's tresses.

"That's your something new and something blue," she said when she had finished. "Now what about something old and something borrowed?"

Rachel stood behind the wagon peering in. "My locket," she said. "You can borrow my locket, Esther."

Cordelia snapped her fingers. "The lace my mother tatted—that's old. I've saved a long strip to put on a dress, next time I make myself a new one. I'll let you wear it to hold the locket." She dug into a box in the wagon and found the treasured keepsake. She strung Rachel's locket on the lace and tied it behind Esther's neck.

When the locket was in place, Cordelia turned Esther to face her. "You look beautiful, dear." Cordelia choked the words out as she kissed her daughter's cheek, overcome by love and loss. Her first child married.

344

Franklin wondered if every wedding celebration led to as much anxious activity as this day. Or did it just seem frantic because this was his family and he fretted about both Cordelia and Esther? Cordelia was doing too much, or trying to. It wasn't good for her or the child she carried. And Esther alternated between giggles and tears all morning. Was she really ready to marry Daniel? Or any man? Franklin still saw her as a wide-eyed toddler staring up at him in awe.

Finally, it was time. Esther stood dressed in her finery, and the rest of the family was ready to move to the tent. "You all go on," Franklin said. "Esther and I will be right behind you."

"I'll let you know when everyone is gathered," Zeke said. "Then you can escort our blushing bride." He grinned and winked at Esther, who reddened as if on cue.

"Don't tease her, Zeke," Cordelia said. "Joel, give me your arm." And they left Franklin alone with the bride.

"Esther," he said, "last chance to back out." He didn't think she would, but he wanted her to know he'd support her in anything she chose.

"Oh, Pa—"

"I'm not telling you to. I'm just saying, you still can change your mind."

"I don't want to, Pa."

He leaned over and kissed her cheek. "Then may God give you and Daniel a long and joyful life together." He swallowed the lump in his throat—he was losing his little girl, but he wanted her happy and prosperous with the husband she loved.

Zeke sauntered back. "It's time," he said, then returned toward the crowd.

Franklin gave his daughter his arm, and she clung to it, a huge smile on her face, as they walked through the lingering mist to the wedding pavilion.

Samuel watched as Esther and her father walked under the canopy. Nothing good would come of allying with the Pershings. He'd never agree with Franklin Pershing on how to get their company to Oregon, nor on how to treat the natives they encountered. Strength was the only currency that lasted, and Pershing was weak.

Unfortunately, his son Daniel—though he loved the boy—was more like Pershing than like him. Soft. Almost womanly at times, in his care for animals and his dislike of shooting. Yet he'd watched Daniel with Esther, and knew Daniel was a man where it counted. He'd father fine sons, and Samuel would be there to watch his grandsons grow.

He turned to see Daniel now. Daniel and Douglass both stood beside the preacher, who still wore buckskins. Samuel snorted—he had trimmed his beard and wore his frock coat out of respect for the occasion. The minister's lack of proper dress made him think less of the man.

Daniel looked dazed as he faced Esther and her father walking toward him. He should be dazed, Samuel thought—no groom knew on his wedding day what marriage brought. Over his lifetime Samuel had learned marriage brought lust and satisfaction, joy and weariness, tragedy, and—if a man was lucky—affection.

He thought of the two women he'd married. First Abigail, who'd loved him and given him two sons before she died. Then Harriet, who stood beside him now. She'd helped him through his worst days until his grief passed. He hadn't been smitten with her like he had with Abigail in his youth, but Harriet was a steady woman who treated him well and told him when he needed to toe the mark. He'd been smart to marry her before some other man realized her value. He took her arm and tucked it in his as the minister began to speak.

Daniel saw only Esther, her bright face smiling, her hair like a cloud of sunshine around her head, with something blue woven in her curls. Her dress was a blue and yellow print, and she carried a lace handkerchief in her hand. As she neared him, he saw a locket tied around her neck beating in time with her heart. He marveled at how he could notice such details when his blood pulsed so hard his head throbbed.

Captain Pershing placed Esther's hand in his, and all rational thought fled. Daniel squeezed her fingers gently, wanting to show her he cherished her as he was about to promise until death did them part.

He scarcely heard the minister's opening words, "Dearly beloved, . . ." Then it was time for him to speak, and he said with all the resolve in his heart, "I do."

Esther's voice sounded sure as she, too, repeated the vows.

And then he could kiss her. He stooped to touch her cheek, but she turned her head. Her lips met his, and he was lost, forgetting the crowd for a moment.

A fiddle played as they broke the kiss, a man shouted, and another man began to call the dancing.

Mrs. Pershing—his mother-in-law now—tried to get people to line up to eat, and her voice rose above the music. Their companions along the trail broke into groups to feast and dance and congratulate the newly married couple.

As soon as he could after greeting the well-wishers, Daniel turned to his wife. "Dance with me?"

Chapter 51:   After the Wedding

Harriet stood near the edge of the canopy watching Daniel and Esther spin in a reel. It had been a lovely wedding, and the party now underway promised to be festive and merry. The emigrants were taking every advantage of the occasion to let off steam, to relax after almost three months of arduous travel.

Mr. Mercer sat not far off, matching the beat of the music with thumps of the crutch he still used for his healing ankle. Mr. Bramwell held his hat under the stump of his left arm, while he forked food with his remaining hand. Amanda Purcell and Amos Jackson's widow stood in a corner chatting quietly. So much loss, and the journey only half over.

But today was a day for celebration, for joy. Esther looked radiant as she smiled up at Daniel. Daniel caught Harriet's eye and whirled his bride over to stop beside her. "Ma," he said, "may I have the next dance with you?"

Harriet laughed. "Oh, go on with Esther. You don't need to spend time with an old woman like me."

"No, Mrs. Abercrombie, please," Esther said, taking her hand. "You've helped make our day simply perfect. Let Daniel thank you properly."

Harriet allowed her son to sweep her into the dance.

"Esther's right, Ma. The day is perfect."

"Despite the weather?" she said.

"The weather?" Daniel peered under the canvas roof. "Oh, you mean the rain? It ain't bad. I think it's letting up."

She smiled. "I'm glad you're happy, son. That's all I've ever wanted for you."

His broad smile let her know her hopes for him had been fulfilled—her favorite son was happy.

Franklin watched the revelers sing and dance, wishing every day on the trail could be so lighthearted. They'd traveled almost a thousand miles from Independence, Missouri, and still had more than a thousand miles to go before they reached Oregon. They'd faced hardship and grief, and would likely encounter more during the remainder of the journey.

But today was a joyous occasion. Bittersweet for him, perhaps, as he watched Esther laughing in Daniel's arms. He'd rejoice with her more, if he didn't fear additional trouble from Samuel Abercrombie before this trip was over.

Cordelia sat on a barrel near the food table. She'd done well today, managing Esther and the wedding feast. Franklin went to stand in front of her and bowed. "You won't turn me down for a dance at our daughter's wedding, will you?"

She smiled. "Perhaps a short one."

He pulled her to her feet. "Do you think it's proper for an old married couple like us to dance?" he whispered in her ear.

She laughed, low and husky. "Proper enough. You can't hold me very close with my belly between us."

"I'm waiting for this babe to make his exit, so I can get closer," he murmured.

"I'm waiting, too." Cordelia smiled at him. "But it might be awhile after the birth afore I'm feeling friendly toward you."

"I'll still be here." He led her in a long, slow turn.

After he ate his fill and talked with the men in his platoon, Samuel decided he'd had enough festivities. Pershing had confirmed the company would stay at Independence Rock through a Fourth of July celebration the next day, so he didn't need to pack up in preparation for moving on. Still, jawing all night—whether with friends or strangers—did not appeal to him.

He found Harriet. "Going back to our wagons," he said. "You coming?"

She shook her head. "Think I'll stay awhile."

"Suit yourself." He clapped his hat on his head and turned to leave the gathering.

"Congratulate Daniel and Esther afore you leave," she called after him.

He shrugged and peered at the dancers. How would he find his son in the crowd? Then he saw the bride and groom sitting and eating across the tent. He sighed, took his hat off, and walked toward them.

When Samuel reached the newlywed couple, Daniel stood. "Thank you, Pa," the boy said, sticking out his hand. "It's been a wonderful day."

Samuel took his son's hand. He didn't know what to say as they shook. "All the best," he finally managed. "To you and your bride."

Esther rose and hugged him. "Thank you, Mr. Abercrombie."

Samuel leaned over and pecked her cheek. The lass wasn't a bad sort. Too bad she was Pershing's daughter. But if she made Daniel happy, he'd try to choke back his harsher comments about the man.

After dancing with Franklin, Cordelia sat on a crate in the corner of the tent, congratulating herself on the day's success. Esther and Daniel looked happy, everyone was well fed, and the revelry continued hours after the marriage.

It was done. Her daughter wed. Cordelia felt the loss again, no matter how many times she chastised herself for her selfishness. Of all her children, Esther was the one closest to her, she acknowledged. Or had been. That bond would weaken, now Esther was married.

Rachel would step into the role of Cordelia's primary helper, and the twelve-year-old would do well. But Rachel didn't have Esther's sunny outlook on life, she was more bookish and quiet. She wasn't a rebellious flibbertigibbet like Esther—and like Cordelia had been.

The babe in her womb kicked hard, and she gasped. Maybe this coming child would fill the hole she now felt in her heart.

Then Cordelia shook her head. She should crush such sorrowful notions. Esther was still her daughter. Their relationship would change, but they would still be linked—two women each making a home in the wilderness. She had plenty yet to teach her daughter. Esther would probably give Cordelia a grandchild to love within the next year. Cordelia's child and her grandchild would likely play together as they grew—wouldn't that be a blessing?

Change came to every family. She had managed with Franklin and without him for over two decades. She would make the best of whatever changes came in the years ahead.

Cordelia rose and returned to her campsite, where she listened to the music play until she drifted off to sleep.

Esther had danced all afternoon and evening—with Daniel, her father and brothers, Mac McDougall, and most of the other men in the company. By the time the late midsummer dusk fell, her dress had wilted, and the blue ribbon straggled from her knot of hair. She could not remember ever being this happy, though as the sky darkened she realized how tired she was. The light afternoon rain had ended, and a brilliant sunset now deepened in the west.

Zeke and Joel and other young men began banging on pots and pans. "Shivaree!" someone called.

"Oh, no," she said to Daniel, hiding her face in his shoulder. "I didn't think they'd do it."

"Your brothers?" he asked, chuckling. "Is this a family tradition?"

"It wasn't afore now. I'm the first to marry. But they've been threatening me."

Daniel laughed again. "Well, let's make the best of it." And he led her over to where Zeke and Joel, the McDougalls, and other young folks from their company waited.

Their friends hooted and hollered and sang as they escorted Esther and Daniel to a wagon that had been moved a short distance from camp. Someone shot a rifle into the air, and travelers from their company and others watched as Daniel lifted Esther into the wagon. The quilt Mrs. Tuller had given her was spread on the wagon floor over blankets to cushion the hard oak surface.

"You'll be safe enough here, even though it's outside the wagon circle," Zeke said. "Joel and I'll come around through the night to check on you."

At that Daniel frowned. "I think not, Zeke. Esther and I will manage fine on our own."

Zeke laughed. "We'll see."

After several more minutes of banging on the pots and singing, the young folks left.

Esther turned to Daniel and reached for him. They were alone. And married.

Daniel took Esther into his arms in the suddenly quiet wagon. Alone at last. Though he had enjoyed the day, he had waited impatiently for this moment. First, when he gazed at Esther while they said their vows, and later as he spun her while they danced. He'd wanted her alone, so he could love her as he wished and make her his own.

He laid her down on the soft quilt and kissed her. They had all night, yet it didn't seem like enough time. He wanted to move slowly but found his fingers trembling with urgency as he reached around her and tried to undo her buttons.

She laughed lightly at his efforts and turned her back to him. "Will this make it easier?" she asked.

He kissed her neck and his fingers became more sure. Soon the dress was off, then her chemise, then she was bare to him entirely, just as he had dreamed.

She faced him again, saying, "My turn." While he kissed and fondled her, she stripped him of his shirt, and her hand reached surely for the buttons on his pants.

"I'll do it," he murmured, afraid he wouldn't last if she touched him. When his clothes too were gone, he pulled her naked body against him. She fit as perfectly as he had hoped.

"Forever mine," he murmured. And they were one.

Chapter 52:　　American Falls

Saturday, 7 August 1847. Left Fort Hall this morning. Now camped near American Falls on the Snake. FP

Holding her two-week-old brother Jonah, Esther stood on the cliffs above the Snake River staring at the great cascades of the American Falls. Men had died trying to navigate these falls some years earlier, she'd been told.

The current tumbled, beautiful and yet forbidding—obsidian buttes above churning cauldrons, water plummeting over house-sized boulders toward the sea. Like life, she mused, bountiful and treacherous, bringing love and sorrow in equal measure.

She pressed a hand to her stomach, where she suspected a child already grew, only a month after she and Daniel had wed. Just as Ma predicted, Esther and Daniel would begin their family quickly. Daniel's response when she'd whispered the good news to him was everything she'd hoped for—a huge grin, plans to make a cradle, dreams of the home they would build together in Oregon.

Esther smiled at the memory, then her throat closed on a sob. She yearned to tell her mother of this blessing, but Ma was gone—dead just two days after birthing Jonah. They'd buried her in a desert grave, wrapped in the quilt Elizabeth Tuller gave Esther for her wedding. Despite her joy over her new brother and her own potential motherhood, Esther ached with grief like she'd never known before, distraught over Ma's passing.

"Oh, Ma," she whispered as she felt a cool breath of wind waft against her cheek from the waters below. "How can we keep going without you?"

As an eagle soared overhead, Esther heard her mother's voice say clearly, "You're mine forever, Esther. Wherever my young'uns are, I'm with them. But you *can* go on without me—you're stronger than you think. You have Daniel. And soon you'll have the family you always wanted."

Esther sighed, knowing her mother was right. She *was* strong, far stronger than she'd been before this journey. She'd done what needed doing ever since they left Independence, and she continued to care for her family without her mother. With Jenny's help, she'd bought a milk cow, and Jonah thrived. She coped daily with the ongoing difficulties between Pa and Mr. Abercrombie. And after each day's hardships ended, she and Daniel found comfort in their love.

She'd get them all to Oregon, and she and Daniel would start their family. Ma would be with her every step.

Esther sniffed the sweet-sour scent of her newborn brother nestled against her shoulder, then she touched her belly again. "If I have a daughter, Ma, I'll name her 'Cordelia,'" she vowed.

Low in the west, the sun peeked out from behind a white cloud and turned the mist above the falls to sparkling diamonds. And above the mist, a rainbow shone.

THE END

Author's Note and Research Methods

This book is a work of fiction. Although its events are imaginary, I have tried to stay true to the geography and customs of the Oregon Trail as it existed in 1847. For those of you who have read *Lead Me Home*, which I published in 2015 about this same fictional wagon train, you'll notice many of the same events told from different characters' points of view.

A few historical personalities pass through these pages, including the ferry operators (Joseph Papin and his wife Josette, and Louis Vieux). I have put these historical characters in scenes of my own imagination.

Fort Laramie was named Fort John in 1847. However, I have called it Fort Laramie in this book to orient today's readers.

John Frémont journeyed west for the Army in 1842 and 1843, but the character of Franklin Pershing is imaginary. Frémont's cartographer, Charles Preuss, published seven maps of the Oregon Trail route in 1846, under the title *Topographical Map of the Road from Missouri to Oregon*. I have the fictional Captain Pershing using these maps, which showed the major rivers and many tributaries and landmarks along the trail. However, the maps were far from a daily guide. Frémont's lengthy report to Congress, published in 1845, provided much more detail. I followed Frémont's route in 1842, though there is a better record of Army men accompanying him in 1843. (In the first published version of *Lead Me Home*, I had Pershing travel with Frémont in 1843; the second printing of *Lead Me Home* changes this to 1842, to be more historically accurate and to be consistent with *Forever Mine*.)

My characters ride in their wagons more than most real emigrants did. Even bedridden people made the arduous trip, traveling in the wagons the entire time. But able-bodied travelers walked most of the way, rather than ride in the jostling wagons. Also, people guided oxen by walking alongside the teams, not with reins as horses and mules were. My characters sometimes drive from the wagon bench, which makes their conversations easier.

I tried to be accurate in depicting the life of emigrants and their travel along the Oregon Trail. I relied as much as possible on the Frémont maps, pioneer diaries, and other first-hand accounts in describing landmarks as they appeared in 1847, as well as in determining distances traveled, locations of campsites, and the weather each day along the route.

I also used Google Maps to trace the route the emigrants took, making allowances for natural and manmade changes to the topography over the last 170 years. It's amazing how many places through the West still bear names like "Emigrant Road." The Oregon Trail remains traceable along much of its route.

There are numerous books and online resources available on the Oregon Trail. I recommend the following books in particular:

- *The Oregon Trail*, by Francis Parkman (1846) (the classic first-hand account of travel along the trail)
- *The Oregon Trail: A New American Journey*, by Rinker Buck (2015) (a first-hand account of traveling the trail by covered wagon in the 21st century)
- *Oregon Trail*, by Ingvard H. Eide (1972) (excerpts from pioneer diaries describing points along the trail, accompanied by beautiful photographs)
- *Traveling the Oregon Trail*, by Julie Fanselow (2nd ed. 2001) (a guide for travelers seeking to follow the trail by road today)

I take responsibility for any historical errors in *Forever Mine*.

Discussion Guide

These questions are intended to help book clubs and other reading groups discuss *Forever Mine*. Students might also use them as essay topics.

1. What did you learn about travel along the Oregon Trail? What more would you like to know?

2. Would you have seen the dangers of the journey to Oregon as an adventure, a hardship, or something else?

3. How did roles of men and women differ in the wagon trains? How did their roles overlap?

4. How did the relationship between Franklin and Cordelia Pershing differ from the relationship between Samuel and Harriet Abercrombie? How were these marriages similar?

5. How did courtship and romance differ in the 1840s from today? What similarities did you notice?

6. Do you think Esther and Daniel married too quickly? Why? Do you think their marriage will be more like Esther's parents or Daniel's?

7. How did getting the story from the perspectives of so many different characters—Esther, Daniel, Cordelia, Franklin, Samuel, and Harriet—help you experience the journey? What did each one teach you about the trip?

8. What were the different attitudes toward Native Americans, African Americans, and other ethnic and religious minorities expressed in this book? Do you think these opinions were realistic for the 1840s?

9. Have you been involved in conflicts like that between Franklin Pershing and Samuel Abercrombie? How did you handle the situation?

10. Which character was your favorite in *Forever Mine*? How did this person change and develop during the journey?

11. For those of you who have also read *Lead Me Home*, what secrets were Jenny and Esther keeping from each other? How did this impact their friendship?

12. How did you feel about the ending of *Forever Mine*? Did you want to know what happened to Cordelia?

If you enjoyed **Forever Mine***, you might also enjoy* **Lead Me Home***, which describes Mac's and Jenny's experiences on this wagon train, or* **Now I'm Found***, following Mac and Jenny through the California Gold Rush. Both books are available on Amazon and Barnes & Noble.*

Acknowledgments

I continue to appreciate the many contributions of my writing friends in the Sedulous Writers Group, Homer's Orphans, and Write Brain Trust.

My thanks as well to early readers and editors of this book, specifically Ellen, Joyce, Juliet, Mike, Patty, and Vickie.

As authors everywhere know, no book is created solely by one person. *Forever Mine* is richer because of these partners' input.

About the Author

Theresa Hupp grew up in Eastern Washington State, except for two years in the Willamette Valley in Oregon. Her ancestors include 19th century emigrants to Oregon and California, and she now lives in Kansas City, Missouri, near the beginning of the Oregon Trail.

Theresa is the award-winning author of novels, short stories, essays, and poetry, and has worked as an attorney, mediator, and human resources executive.

Lead Me Home, Theresa's first novel published in 2015, follows Mac McDougall and Jenny Calhoun on the same wagon train as *Forever Mine*. It has been a #1 bestselling novel about the Oregon Trail in Amazon's Kindle Store. *Now I'm Found*, published in 2016, follows Mac and Jenny through the California Gold Rush. It, too, was a bestselling novel about the Gold Rush.

Theresa has also published another novel—a bestselling financial thriller—under a pseudonym, as well as an anthology under her own name, *Family Recipe: Sweet and saucy stories, essays, and poems about family life*. In addition, Theresa has written short works for *Chicken Soup for the Soul*, *Mozark Press*, and *Kansas City Voices*. She is a member of the Kansas City Writers Group, Missouri Writers Guild, Oklahoma Writers Federation, Inc., and Write Brain Trust.

Please follow Theresa on her website and blog, http://TheresaHuppAuthor.com, where she often posts about the topics in her novels. You can also follow her Facebook Author page, http://facebook.com/TheresaHuppAuthor, and her Amazon page at http://www.amazon.com/Theresa-Hupp/e/B009H8QIT8. Theresa writes a monthly newsletter—you can subscribe to that through her website.

Readers' Praise for *Lead Me Home* and *Now I'm Found*

Lead Me Home:

> . . . on the challenging Oregon Trail of 1847 . . . the going is slow and scary and dusty behind a team of oxen. With well-researched attention to detail, [Hupp] takes us on this journey and shows how her characters cope and grow under these difficult circumstances.

> . . . so realistic that the reader might believe the diary entries . . . came from a real traveler.

> . . . an incredible story, amazingly and beautifully written.

Now I'm Found:

> Hupp has done extensive research on . . . traveling the Oregon Trail and prospecting for gold in the California mountains. The descriptions of those closely related periods of history are exciting backgrounds for a tender love story.

> . . . Great character development and story line. As in Hupp's previous book, it is well researched and written. Well worth your time.

> Engaging drama, strung along by the slow communications of the day. . . A love story served well by the pioneer notions of courtship, loyalty and marriage. Hupp does history and fiction well!

All Theresa Hupp's books are available online at Amazon or Barnes & Noble, in paperback or ebook formats.